D1524926

Tales of the ENCHANTED WILDWOOD

ANGELA J. FORD

SECRETS OF THE LORE KEEPERS

BRIDE OF THE KING

LORD OF THE CASTLE

HEART OF THE RAVEN

CONTENTS

QUEEN OF THE WILDWOOD

CURSE OF THE HEALER

QUEEN OF THE
WILDWOOD

MAGIC TWITCHED in my fingers as I scattered the last of the sage and salt over my sister's grave. I was alone, kneeling in the thin mist that always hovered over the village cemetery at this time of day.

A prickling sensation crept down my spine, the tell-tale sign someone was watching me. I whipped my head around, scanning for the voyeur. Out of the corner of my eye, crimson flashed behind an ash tree. My heart beat a pitter-patter while my fingers finished their hasty work.

Three months ago, my storm of magic had killed my sister, and I was sentenced to serve the Sisters of the Light. Each month I snuck out of the temple to draw a rune of protection over my sister's grave. The Feast of Mabon was coming, and during the winter months, the barrier between my village and the forest grew thin. The wood was alive with demon-kind, controlled by the Queen of the Wildwood. I feared my sister's soul would join the wild creatures of the wood when winter blanketed the land with frost.

The bone-rattling caw of a coal-black raven made me flinch, and I lifted my head, watching the unusually large bird that perched on a nearby tombstone. It eyed me with contempt, as though it knew my secret and warned me of my impending doom. It was already high noon, much later than I'd realized.

A lump swelled in my throat. I couldn't be late for rune practice. With haste, I leapt up and ran through the trailing brambles.

When I reached the temple courtyard, a light breeze scattered ash-white cinders, the remains of Fires of Blessing, lit by frequent worshippers. A cloud of silver mist kicked up as I passed and the aroma of mint and lavender wafted through the air. Motes of magic shimmered beneath the layers of dust where runes had been carved deep into the stone floor of the atrium. I swept my pure-white robes past the crevices and quickened my pace as I headed for the stairs that led to the entrance.

High, gray arches loomed over my head like hawking eyes frowning down at my tardiness. The four-story temple had a domed top, and its height seemed to kiss the heavens. It served as both a home for the Sisters of the Light and a fortress should any trouble come to the village.

Broad stairs led to double doors, also carved with runes of protection. I slipped into the shadows of the columns, keeping my footsteps silent lest I disturb the worshippers, villagers who came to recite prayers and offer sacrifices as the Feast of Mabon neared.

Maids in white habits walked silently up and down the atrium, offering candles to the worshippers. One of them made eye contact with me, ducked her head, and then spoke in a tentative quaver. "Mistress Yula?"

I jerked to a stop, eyes narrowed, for the maids rarely spoke to me. In fact, the Sisters of the Light went out of their way to avoid me, except to give orders and make sure I knew my place in the sacred ritual. They needed me, although they feared the strength of my magic. Even the worshippers who visited the temple avoided eye contact when they saw me. I knew they blamed me for my sister's untimely death.

Because of my unpredictable magic, I was not allowed to leave the temple. It was my prison and the use of my magic for the ritual during the Feast of Mabon what they deemed a fitting atonement. Swinging from the hanging tree by my neck would have been better, for magic raged within me like the wild waves of a sea battered by endless storms. Often, I could not sleep, for guilt weighed heavily upon me. I'd torn my family apart.

My jaw clenched. "Aye?"

"Head Mistress asked me to tell you practice has begun, and you are to take part once you enter."

Forcing the scowl off my face, I gave her a quick nod. "Thank you."

The Head Mistress knew I'd left the temple and this was her backhanded way of threatening me. After the whispers I'd overheard from my fellow sisters—whispers of murder, betrayal and contriving to take down the Head Mistress—I was not surprised.

Each time I entered the musky hall of the temple the

5

smell of herbs made my shoulders relax. Massive stones surrounded me, and the air was cool. The walls of the passageway had been painted with bright symbols and scenes of former Sisters of the Light, performing their rituals which drove back the evil that occasionally threatened the land. Even now painters were at work, mixing rich colors and completing a scene of the Feast of Mabon. I tugged my white robes straight as I crept to the gathering.

The ritual chamber was a circular room in the heart of the temple. Above the chamber perched the dome, sending a cascade of graceful light to bless each ceremony. The room was empty aside from a slab of rock by the door, the altar. I'd heard rumors that in the heathen days it was used for human sacrifice, but the Sisters of the Light claimed it was pure myth. A bowl of salt and sage perched on the altar, waiting, and nine of the ten sisters stood in line. There were twelve of us. Ten sisters, including me, the Head Mistress, and her second in command, the Priestess.

Head Mistress paced in front of the nine with her shoulders thrown back. She held her bony body tall and rigid. Because of her height, her white robes barely grazed the freshly scrubbed stone floor.

The nine stood like tender trees of the forest clothed in white robes. Eager faces flushed with innocence waited for their moment to practice the ritual. We were forced to wear similar attire, braid our long hair back and keep our bodies hidden within the folds of our rough robes. Plain and simple were the rules we lived by. Vanity was not tolerated.

"Sisters of the Light." Head Mistress lifted her hands, palms up. "Again, we join together to prepare for the Feast of Mabon which takes place in three days. North of us lies the enchanted forest, and in the heart of it lies the domain of the Queen of the Wildwood. The Dark Queen. She demands our magic in exchange for protection from the wildings, orc-kind, and the nightmares that dwell in the wood. We conduct this ritual every year at summer's end. The runes we create with salt and sage give the Dark Queen power to bind the evil of the forest which desires to escape and destroy our world. This ritual is of the utmost importance and a high honor for the Sisters of the Light to perform. You have been chosen because of your strength, your fortitude and, above all, your magic. For it is only with the union of twelve that we can appease the Dark Queen and keep our people, our home, safe for another year."

I lifted the bowl and went to stand in line with the nine chosen ones. The youngest, Greta, scowled at me when I fell in step beside her. Ignoring her, I stared at the bare wall, all too aware of the way the Head Mistress' hawkish eyes bored into my skull.

I glanced down at the condition of my robes. Dew-dense grass stained the frayed white hem. If the Head Mistress hadn't already known about my disobedience, the stains would have been a clear indication that I had betrayed my vows and snuck out of the temple again.

Worry plagued my thoughts, but when the low murmur of blessings filled the temple, calmness seeped through my soul. Practicing my magic was the only thing that made the storm within abate. I spoke the words of blessing and recited the prayer we would say at midnight on Mabon when the season turned to autumn and the wild winds of winter crept near.

The Sisters of the Light vowed to forsake all other duties and an opportunity at normal life. We would never marry, and our vows forced us to remain celibate, but I'd had few experiences with men that made me miss that sort of intimacy. There was only one man who still made me burn, a man who sometimes visited the village, but any chance I had of catching his eye had vanished three months ago when I became a Sister of the Light.

Usually, the sisters were chosen when they were still in their teens, for it was a momentous decision. A choice I had not been able to make. I was already in my twenties, which made me much older than the younger recruits who were still in their blossoming years. The marrying age had come and gone for me.

Given a choice, I would not have joined the Sisters of the Light. But my mother had passed a few years ago, my magic cost my sister her life, and my father was wrapped in grief. Being trapped here, far from all I loved, was my only chance at redemption, although secretly I longed for freedom. A future spent in the cold, lonely halls of the temple only tempted my desire to flee.

The Head Mistress waved her hand, and the practice ritual began. We each had a series of runes to draw. I scattered sage and salt in a circle, allowing the rhythmic movements to slow my frantic heartbeat. I leaned into my work, desperate to forget my sister's death and the whispers I'd overhead. My tongue suddenly felt swollen in my mouth, and I stumbled, sending a cascade of salt down my robes.

"Yula!" The sharp *tsk* of the Head Mistress hissed. A hand wrapped around my thick black braid and yanked. "Pay attention, girl. This is the third time you've almost ruined the rune during practice. Runes must be perfect on the night of the blessing, or how will the gifts of the harvest be given to us?"

I silently fumed and kept my eyes downcast. The Head Mistress was fond of humiliating me in front of the others. Despite how much I worked. I'd never be good enough for her.

The flow of the ritual imbued me. The sisters chanted softly under their breaths, expressing gratitude for the past season, the abundance of the harvest, and the balance nature brought to our lives.

Moving in a circular path, we each drew seven runes on the floor. I was on my second one when the shape warped under my hand, turning into a symbol of a slithering snake with a forked tongue.

The mark of the Dark Queen.

The sign of evil froze me as the rune seemed to come to life. The forked tongue flickered in and out, and a low hum of whispers penetrated my thoughts.

Before I could wipe away the evil rune, a crackle of pain riffed across my cheek. My head snapped back, and I dropped the bowl. Eyes wide, I stared as the bowl fell, my heart thudding so hard I thought I'd vomit.

The clay bowl smacked onto the stone floor with a sickening thud and shattered. Jagged shards, white salt, and green sage mingled together in a horrific display of desecration with the evil rune at its center.

With a twist of my fingers, I could undo what had been done, but before I could, a hand snatched at my elbow.

"Stupid girl," hissed the Head Mistress. "Will you never learn? I should have listened when they brought you to me. You're wrong. *All* wrong for this. Your blood will never sing with magic. You bring nothing but calamity on this house."

My nostrils flared, and a tightness came to my eyes. I did not mean to, but I yanked my arm out of the Head Mistresses' grasp in an overt display of disrespect in front of my elders.

"It was a mistake," I said through gritted teeth. But my voice was quite contrary, and my rigid stance would not halt the impending punishment.

"I have given you chance after chance." The Mistress swept her hand over the salt, extending the magic that put everything into place, just as if it never was.

And then she turned. Her tall, bony figure loomed over me, and her stern face twisted.

I cringed inside. Malice glimmered darkly in the Mistress's deep-set eyes, and she squared her shoulders. I knew what would come next.

"Sisters of the Light." Her hard voice cut through the tension in the temple. "Today's rune practice is dismissed due to the ineptitude of Mistress Yula." She turned her severe stare directly at me. "Ten lashes for daydreaming, desecrating a holy place with wicked symbols, and violating your vows by leaving the temple. Pain will remind you not to shirk your duties."

Dread froze my nerves. Ten lashes. With the heavy cane. A whip used to punish boys and yet somehow the Mistress found it useful to challenge the girls who learned the rituals of blessing from her. She taught the magic and extracted pain in exchange. Despite her, I lifted my chin and steeled myself against her power that hurled me against the altar until I was immobilized, bent in place, waiting for the torture to begin.

As the custom, my robe was removed, leaving only my thin shift. Shame. Another punishment. Shame and pain so I would never forget, never make another mistake.

My hands clenched into fists, and I gritted my teeth. I would not cry out. I would not let them see how much this hurt me, both physically and mentally.

The first blow cracked against my thighs and sent a burning wave of heat up my back. The second came just as quickly, setting a blaze on my skin. I worried my lip between my teeth to keep a yelp from escaping as another blow fell. Waves of fire consumed me, and the beating went on as the Head Mistress tried to elicit a sound. It felt as though she used her magic to make the whipping more intense than it should have been.

When at last she finished, I slumped to the ground. Pain laced down my back, bottom, and thighs. Sweat soaked the armpits of my shift and trickled down my forehead. The Head Mistress walked away, putting the cane down on the dais. Then she strode back toward me.

My head rang, but I heard sharp, unkind words pour from her lips, although I could not make sense of them in my confusion. Deep-seated anger rose, and a torrent of fury boiled in my belly. Instead of holding back, I curled my fingers, opened my mouth, and let loose the flood.

Screams were the last thing I heard as my rage exploded, and then I was lost in a violent wind storm.

2

I WOKE to the waning light of the afternoon sun, alone in the village glade, far outside the temple. Eerie silence lay all around. The enchanted forest loomed on one side, while the path back to the village rose on the other. Only…

Cold dread filled my heart. In the distance, where the temple usually rose above the town, was—nothing. Nothing but plumes of smoke.

Goddesses. What had I done?

Trembling, I struggled to stand, stifling a cry as pain shot down the left side of my body like a lightning bolt. Numbness stung my feet, and I staggered, flailing for purchase before collapsing in the grass.

I crouched, noticing for the first time I was covered in grime and as naked as the day I was born. My black hair hung in waves around my dark skin, offering some semblance of modesty.

Wind filled my ringing ears as storm clouds gathered overhead, but I still caught the snap of twigs cracking and the rustle of woodland animals in the wood.

A hooded figure stepped out of the forest into the meadow and moved swiftly toward me. The sunlight did not penetrate his dark shroud, and the frightful tales I'd heard of what dwelled in the forest danced on the edges of reason.

A frightened shriek tore from my lips. Bending to hide my nakedness, I scuttled backward.

"I will not hurt you," declared the shadow, lifting the hood from his head.

My uninjured hand trembled and my fingers curled, ready to hurl magic, ignoring the effects that ravaged my body.

He stopped a few paces away, a question in his dark eyes as he stared at me. I was surprised to find his gaze did not linger on my nakedness. Instead, he seemed to wait for me to allow him closer. With a sharp intake of breath, I realized I knew who he was. It was him, the man who made me burn.

Aelbrin.

On the eve of every full moon, he came to my village to trade. He always stopped by my booth to finger the sheepskin my family used to trade in—although it had been months since I'd seen him. He was a loner, tall, bronze-skinned. His dark hair was disheveled, unruly, almost standing straight up on his head, but he was handsome in a woodsy way. Almond-shaped eyes— deep set in his face below tousled hair—gazed at me with calculated measure. He was shrouded in a forest green cloak, and his stance made me think of the ash trees of the forest, deeply rooted yet growing tall and strong, offering shade and shelter. My eyes fell to a glitter of crimson I'd never seen before. On his hand was a rune which shone blood-red in the sunlight.

At first, heat crept to my face at my state of undress, but at the sight of the rune on his hand, the blood drained from my face. I'd assumed Aelbrin was a friend, for he often shared kind words with me, and brought me a bright red rose during each of his trips. He always wore gloves when he visited, which is why I'd never seen the rune. He'd told me tales about a Mother Tree who protected a tribe of people. They drew magic from her roots and thrived in her shade until a legendary firedrake came down from the mountains and burned the Mother Tree.

The enchanting stories he'd told me fled, and our brief flirtation seemed a trick of the past. My fingers curled once more, readying the magic that flowed within. "Do not come any closer," I hissed.

Pain laced up my side when I spoke.

Aelbrin's hazel eyes remained calm until his gaze followed my stare to his hand. A flush rose to his cheeks, and he hid the rune within the folds of his cloak.

I was both surprised and intrigued at his embarrassment. The mark on his hand—the symbol of a snake with a forked tongue—clearly indicated he was a knight of the Dark Queen. Had she sensed a change in magic and sent a knight to deliver me? Even though I liked him, I should end him where he stood. If I had the courage.

My jaw tightened, and I waited for the magic to well up inside me like hot flames licking through my innards. My magic often felt like a storm, using threads of the wind to rip everything apart, but if I focused, I could also use it to bring things together.

Nothing happened.

Angry tears pricked my eyes. I was naked, exhausted, and worst of all, I had destroyed the temple and killed the Sisters of the Light. I was too weary to perform magic in my time of need. The enchantments had never failed me before. Why now?

"I know what you think," Aelbrin acknowledged.

His voice whispered like the leaves of autumn falling from the trees to grace the forest floor. That voice that sent shivers up my spine and a longing in my heart.

"I serve the Queen of the Wildwood," he said, "but she didn't send me here. I was patrolling the southern end of the forest and saw a wave of magic. The queen will send someone to investigate. If you wish to escape her notice, you should leave."

I stared. Did Aelbrin intend to help me? Or simply warn me away?

"I cannot leave," I choked out. "Not until I know what happened here. It's my fault the sisters are gone, and I need them to complete the ritual!"

Aelbrin had already turned to leave, but when I spoke, he glanced over his shoulder.

His eyebrows lifted. "Did you do this?"

Averting my gaze, I nodded woodenly. Magic was a curse.

Aelbrin glanced at my hand and the curve of my fingers. "Will you burn me too?"

My head ached as I shook it.

He slipped the cloak from around his shoulders—revealing a pattern of swirling runes on his arms—and approached me. The silky material slid across my body, cool and warm all at the same time. My numb side throbbed and warmed as blood flowed again. His cloak smelled like the wood on a moonless night, warm and intoxicating with a heady compulsion.

"Mistress Yula, you must come with me, for they will be here soon and they will be ruthless."

I tilted my head back and met his piercing stare. There was something about him that made me feel calm even though my magic was simply an empty husk.

"They?" I asked. "Who are they?"

His hazel eyes flickered to the wood, and his lips thinned. "The teeth of the forest. Orc-kind. They will seek out any survivors and take them to her."

My hand went to my throat, my gaze tearing across the meadow, searching for the invisible enemy. "What about the village? The people?"

His eyes dimmed. "The temple is gone. The Queen will kill them."

"It is my fault," I whispered.

He said nothing, only slipped his hand under my elbow, helping me to my feet. Tears blurred my vision, but I set my jaw and forced myself to stand. A wave of pain washed over me as my numb side awoke, sending pinpricks down my fevered skin.

"Mabon is coming," I lamented as the full weight of what I'd done settled on my shoulders.

Again, I raised my eyes to the Aelbrin's strong face. There was something compelling about him. Something within me called out to him, and I dropped my gaze.

I could not trust him. He belonged to Her, a knight of the Dark Queen whose power protected my village from the devilish creatures of the forest that sought human blood. But only if she received the blood and sacrifice she demanded, something I could no longer offer, not without the Sisters of the Light to perform the ritual.

Would the Dark Queen allow evil to roam free? She would. I knew it in my bones.

I turned toward the village, guilt heavy in my heart. "I must do something. The people cannot suffer because of me. I need to make the Queen see reason."

"There's no reason with her," Aelbrin said.

I faced him, determination steeling my spine. "Then I will make a bargain with her."

His gaze drifted to the wood where thick trees rose, gray and green, shutting out all light. The thick smell of musk wafted from the forest, and I followed his gaze, noting the intricate webbing that wrapped around the dark trees like a blanket. Plump vines curled around oak and ash trees which grew so close together, it seemed impossible to walk between them. Dry leaves covered the forest floor along with scattered nuts and bramble. Despite the warmth of the cloak, I shivered. It was not wise to enter the domain of the Dark Queen.

My heart quailed at what I would ask of Aelbrin, but I lifted my chin and squared my shoulders, determined to accept responsibility for my actions. I would do this one last act to wipe my slate clean of the trail of misery I left behind. Magic brought nothing but grief, but perhaps if I traded years of service, my magic, or even my soul to save the village, I could forgive myself for my past. Loss enveloped my heart with grief, and the forest blurred before my eyes.

A muscle in Aelbrin's jaw ticked, and a sigh escaped his lips. "Time is short. If you wish to make a bargain with the Dark Queen, I will take you to her court. I warn you; her woods are not for the faint of heart."

My lip curled at his words. Did he underestimate my strength? "Take me there. What do you require as payment?"

His eyebrows arched. "Payment? I serve the will of the Dark Queen. You should know that she will be very glad I have brought you to her court, but only because you possess such powerful magic." He leaned close. "Know this. She will see you as a tool. You will need to bargain well."

I stepped forward and cringed as the numbness faded from the left side of my body.

His eyes went soft. "Are you hurt?"

"No." I put out a hand to keep him at a distance.

"Stay close, then," he said with a glance at the wood. "If you want to live."

The evil creatures of the forest would be close. Surely they wouldn't harm Aelbrin, however. Not the knight of the Dark Queen.

Still, the very thought of what lurked in the shadows sent a chill down my spine. But I took a deep breath, fighting against a squeeze of panic, and followed him into Wildwood.

3

THE SMELL of sulfur came to my nostrils and faded as we traipsed into the dense wood. I clutched a hand around the cloak to keep it from billowing out. My bare feet tip-toed across the uneven ground. Although my soles were tough, broken twigs bit into them, and unexpected rocks forced me to fumble for balance. After a time, I found myself panting.

As I walked, my thoughts returned to the Sisters of the Light. I understand why they kept themselves apart from the world. Magic was a great power, and it also made me a target. Often, families of those with magic were held hostage or blackmailed in exchange for the use of that magic. I had fallen to that fate and put those I loved in danger. It was only because of my power-gone-rouge that the Sisters of the Light had vanished, leaving no one to protect the village.

No one except me.

Aelbrin moved ahead, quickly and silently like a forest cat prowling after delicious prey. The sunlight shone dimmer here beneath the canopy, rendering his bronze skin a shade dark as night and from time to time I saw the mark on his hand glistening in the dim light. I bit back words to concentrate on walking, but curious thoughts whispered impatiently in my mind. Where did Aelbrin come from? Why did he serve the queen?

"Mistress Yula," Aelbrin's voice floated back to me on a stale breeze.

I itched a scratch on my arm. "Please. Just call me Yula."

"Yula," he repeated.

My name sounded like music on his tongue.

"I recall you traded in wool, not magic. The villagers must hold you in high esteem for your abilities," he assumed.

The last thing I wanted to talk about was myself. My tone came out hard and clipped. "Yes. And no. When the villagers discovered I have abilities, they forced me to train with the Sisters of the Light. My magic is supposed to protect the people from the forest."

He ducked under a low-hanging branch and glanced back at me, his eyes alight with curiosity. "You have great magic. I've sensed it before, and I sense it now. Are you sure you will not change your mind and return home?"

Filtered sunbeams blinked through the forest, and for a titillating moment, Aelbrin's profile lit up in the delicate light.

A fluttering sensation passed through my chest, and a sudden urge to trail my fingers over the swirling runes on his skin came over me. Before today, I'd allowed myself to dream about the man who brought me roses. But now the truth of our circumstance and the truth of who he really was pressed up raw and realistic. I was a mage. He was Her knight. Any dreams I'd once held of stolen kisses and star-crossed love suddenly seemed a lifetime away.

My voice turned rough to hide my attraction to him. "You do not understand. I do not have a home to return to."

Aelbrin gave a brief nod, his face returning to a mask of indifference. Then his focus drifted down my body to my bare feet. He gestured impatiently toward them. "Why didn't you say something? Your feet will be torn up walking through the woods."

"I did not notice," I mumbled in bewilderment.

"Will your magic conjure shoes for you?" he teased, reaching up to snatch a strip of bark off a tree. Setting his teeth, he tore it quickly and held out the mutilated strips.

Surprised at the gaiety in his tone, I bit back a laugh. "Magic is not used for creation, only to bring energy together. I can push away objects and pull them back together. I can change the shape of matter, especially herbs, salt, and blood. I can call on the wind to bring forth a storm, but I cannot create shoes with a snap of my fingers. Although that would be convenient."

Aelbrin flashed a lopsided grin at me, and the transformation lit up his stoic features. I swallowed hard as he rested his bulk against a fallen log and tip-toed his fingers down its side. His fingers stroked and searched in such an intimate way that heat rose to my cheeks.

Blushing, I looked away, furious at myself for the weakness I felt.

Aelbrin pulled moss out of the crevices and packed it into the shallow boats of wood he'd created from bark. "Here," he held them out to me. "These will keep your feet from experiencing too much discomfort. I keep extra supplies in a cave nearby and will likely find something fitting for you there."

First a cloak and now shoes.

"Thank you." Our eyes locked, and I gave him a genuine smile.

To distract myself, I reached out to take the shoes and unwittingly brushed his sun-kissed hands. A tingling sensation went through me, and suddenly I saw visions.

Aelbrin dragging people out of a fiery structure.

Aelbrin fighting a scaled creature that breathed fire and tried to consume the people he'd saved.

Throwing his arms around a woman who looked like him, the same sharp nose and deep-set eyes, possibility his mother? Or sister?

The Dark Queen riding out of the forest and banishing the firedrake but requiring souls in exchange for her actions.

Aelbrin yanked away, nostrils flaring, his voice rough. "What did you do?"

My cry died in my throat. Aelbrin's tales hadn't been tales at all. They'd been stories about his life.

My voice softened with sadness for him, but curiosity bloomed. "Was that your past? Your people?"

Aelbrin's face closed, and his eyes went dark. Lips set in a grim line, he dropped the shoes and marched away.

I tugged on the wooden slippers but still had to run to catch up with his long gait.

His hands were balled into fists, and when I caught a

glimpse of his face, his jaw was set and his eyes steely with resolve.

Words tumbled out of my mouth with urgency. I had to know.

"What did I see? That was your past, wasn't it? You offered your service in exchange for those people's lives. Didn't you? That's what I want, to make a bargain with the Dark Queen, to offer myself to save the villagers."

"You shouldn't want it," Aelbrin growled, tossing his words over his shoulder. "Committing your life to the service of the Dark Queen will cost more than you know."

"I have nothing left to lose," I protested. He could not tell me how to live my life.

He paused and spun around so quickly I almost ran into his chest. Rough hands came up and gripped my shoulders, and his eyes were dangerous, disapproving as he glared at me. He angled his tousled head closer to mine, making sure each word sank in. "You have your soul, untarnished, unblemished. You should keep it that way."

I stared at him, gaze roaming over the lines of his face. I moistened my lips with my tongue. "I have no other choice."

He shook his head, eyes haunted yet unrelenting. "We always have a choice, and yours should be to find another way."

I trembled under his gaze, under his touch. When he lifted a hand and brushed my black hair out of my eyes, my heart pounded so hard I thought he might hear it. His finger lingered on my cheek, trailing a line down to my neck. His gaze flickered from my eyes to my mouth, as though asking permission to kiss me. I opened my mouth to respond and felt something bite down on my foot.

Panic seized me, and I slammed my palms into Aelbrin's chest, shoving him away from danger. Waves of magic poured out of my fingers, blasting into the creature whose jaws clamped down on my ankle. Hot pain rippled through me as the creature let go with a hiss, but it was too late.

I growled when I saw the snake, thick as my arm with a diamond-shaped head as big as my hand. A chant rose in my mind, and my lips moved soundlessly. My fingers curled, twisting the snake into knots.

"No," I faintly heard Aelbrin's strangled cry.

My ankle throbbed as I lifted a rock and smashed it on the adder's head. When I faced Aelbrin he stared, slack-jawed.

He scraped his fingers through his disheveled hair, making the ends stand up even more. "What have you done?" he whispered.

I glared from him to the dead snake. "Don't tell me this was your pet."

I'd heard of such oddities; the wild creatures of the wood would tame poisonous and dangerous beasts to do their bidding.

Aelbrin shook his head. "Not mine, the Dark Queen's. She will demand payment in exchange for his death." His eyes went cold, lost in a fated horror.

"I am aware, but it is still my choice," I protested.

"We will worry about that when the time comes." His gaze trailed down to my bare leg. "For now, we need to worry about you.

Weariness overcame me, and I suddenly felt faint. I reached for the nearest tree because the explosion of magic had exhausted my already spent body.

Aelbrin pressed his hand to my waist to steady me. "Listen. Night falls quickly in the woods. We should seek shelter before the orc-kind take over. My watch post is not far from here, and the Dark Queen does not expect my report for a few more days. Let's rest there and get rid of the venom."

I wanted to disagree. We should press on so I could save the villagers as soon as possible. But another wave of tiredness passed over me, and my vision went fuzzy.

The poison. I needed to draw it out of the wound before it spread through my entire body.

I lifted two fingers. "Do you have a knife?"

His grip on my waist tightened, and his lips turned down into a frown. "Are you mad? If we cut open the wound here, we are done for. The creatures of the night hide in the shade. Once they smell your blood, you will be finished. We need to make for shelter."

"But the venom will set in," I protested. I attempted to push him away, but my limbs shook with weakness.

"Your magic is spent," he said gently.

Before I could object, his powerful hands swept me up into his arms, and he set off through the forest.

The poison affected my vision. I knew we traveled uphill and at one point, Aelbrin began to climb, his breath coming hard and fast as he worked. The corded muscles in his back moved under my hand, and sent a surge of emotion though me. I wanted down. It was inappropriate to travel in a man's arms and went against everything I'd learned from the Sisters of the Light.

My willpower faded when we reached a hidden cave and ducked behind the branches of a willow tree to enter. Somewhere, I thought I heard the music of water, perhaps a nearby creek.

Aelbrin placed me on a pallet and set to work. He opened my wound, bled out the venom, and closed it with an herbal paste. I lay still, eyes too heavy to open even a sliver, lulled by rough fingers softly caressing my face.

"Sleep, my beauty," Aelbrin whispered, his voice so close I felt the heat of it on my lips.

Without a fight, I surrendered to his command.

4

THE WHISPERING sound of music woke me. I jerked, struggling to sit up. My gaze tore around the room, and then I recognized it, the gentle, aching lullaby.

I pushed heavy blankets away, noting the cool air, and pulled the cloak more securely around me. When my eyes adjusted to the darkness, I saw Aelbrin. He sat at the edge of the cave at an angle that allowed him to watch both me and the outside. His eyes glowed faintly in the dark, like those of a wild cat. He held something long in his hands, and when he put it to his mouth, that low tune came out again, a mournful melody. A prayer. A wish.

An ache began in my heart as I watched him play his flute. Memories took me back to my father, a happy time when he would come in from the fields and sit in front of the fire, playing a tune for my sister and I. We giggled and danced while Mother, finding her helpers gone, first scolded and then joined us, feet tapping, skirts flying.

Moisture gathered in the corners of my eyes, and I swallowed hard.

"Can't sleep?" Aelbrin's hollow tone scattered my pensive thoughts. He sat staring out at the forest where the wind wailed and monsters roamed, hunting in the thickets. Every now and again I heard a hair-raising howl or a low moan.

I left the pallet and limp toward him. He ran his fingers through his hair but never turned his face toward mine.

"That was beautiful," I said. "Where did you learn how to play like that?"

"My people are known for their songs." His hazel eyes met mine. "But I didn't mean to wake you."

My voice went wistful, and I felt my wall of solitude crumble. "It reminds me of my family."

"I'm sorry," he said. "I saw you this morning at the graveyard."

I stiffened, recalling the flash of crimson and the noisy raven.

"Were you close to the deceased?" he went on.

"It was my sister," I offered. There was something cathartic about speaking about what happened, and I let my jumbled thoughts out. "Occasionally a band of mercenaries would come to the village, seeking those with magic for their personal gain. They had heard about me and trapped my sister and me at the river during wash day." My chest went tight as I recalled that fateful day, the smell of bog water, the soft mud, and my sister's laughs as she scrubbed clothes. She was to be betrothed after Mabon, and the thought of a husband

and babies filled her spirit with gaiety. "The mercenaries grabbed my sister. They planned to sell her for profit and take me as their mage. I used my magic to create a windstorm as a distraction. When they realized the strength of my power, they cut her throat before I could stop them. If I had gone peacefully, she would still be alive, and I could have escaped. Later. The villagers decided I had to join the Sisters of the Light, and my father was too devastated to stop them. . ." I trailed off as tears stung my eyes.

"I'm sorry," he said again.

A silence hung, sweetened by the whispered hush of the nearby creek. Sharing my story felt good; it brought a sort of closure and lessened the burden of grief and guilt I carried.

Aelbrin touched my hand, and warmth went up my spine. "Mistress Yula," he mused. "Do you know what your name means?"

A bitter laugh escaped my throat. "I don't believe my parents named me Yula because of the meaning. I suppose they liked the way it sounded."

"Ah." Aelbrin said. "It means 'sacrifice.' That's what you do, isn't it? Sacrifice your happiness for others?"

I stiffened, torn by the words that raked my soul. "What I want is not important," I said bitterly, for sacrifice was the price of magic.

"It *is* important," Aelbrin insisted. He touched my bare arm, his fingers tracing a line from elbow to wrist. "If you always sacrifice your happiness, you will only be left a hull, a shell of your inner self and your potential."

I scowled, in part at his words but also because his

touch awoke a hunger deep within. Shifting on the cool ground, I changed the conversation. "What makes you say such things? Will you tell me how you came to serve the Dark Queen?"

At the mention of Her, his hand dropped away, and I felt a loss at the connection between us. The silence stretched. A cricket chirped in the darkness, and slowly other creatures took up the nocturnal melody.

Aelbrin sighed. "The tales I shared with you moons ago are true. I grew up in a grove with my tribe, far north of here. My mother died during the birth of my sister. I knew her briefly, and I supposed I should have missed her. But my tribe was a tight-knit community and more than made up for her loss. My father was a warrior, one of the highest honors of my tribe. I trained to become like him. A protector. We had something others did not: a source of wisdom and magic called Mother Tree. Her deep roots and thick branches covered the entire glade. She protected my people and gave us magic. Until the fire came. One fateful day a firedrake flew down from the mountains and attacked my village. It almost destroyed the Mother Tree, killed my father, left my sister badly burned, and my people in terror and chaos. Many claimed that more firedrakes would come and our line would end. I decided to take the risk upon my shoulders, for I thought I had nothing left to lose. I'd heard of the Queen of the Wildwood— many stories tell of her deeds—and became determined to strike a deal with her. She took the remains of the Mother Tree and promised me, as long as I serve her, my people are protected."

Regret, mixed with pain and sorrow, filled the air. I

wanted to offer him a token of peace, but words seemed inadequate. To protect his tribe, he served the Dark Queen, for it was the only choice he had.

I sensed the undercurrent of revulsion each time her name was mentioned, and how he glared at the mark seared into his skin. It was not a fate he would wish on anyone.

"Tell me about your people," I encouraged gently, steering the conversation in a safer direction.

His voice was distant when he spoke, and I could tell he thought of past times. Happy times. "My people are ash trees. The spirit of the forest incarnate in the flesh. When we die, we return to our trees and rest until we are awakened and asked to live anew. Our purpose is to bring balance to nature and humankind. But the people respect us no longer. They cut us down and burn our wood. They create pastures for grazing their animals. They build homes on the land they took from us, and no one remembers the sacred forests. In part, that is why I thought to give my service over to the Dark Queen, for she understands the sacredness of the enchanted wood. But it is not as I thought it would be. She only thinks of what will benefit herself and her kingdom. I regret that I did not seek to understand before I let her take my soul."

His pain made me ache.

"Is there no way you can escape?" I begged, forcing myself to breathe. My mind told me I should stand up and walk away now. I could not be drawn to him because of his sad story. I had to make my own decisions, stand firm, and find my own way, as I always did.

He shook his head. "Once you give the Dark Queen your soul, damnation is the only escape."

I closed my mouth, and a tense silence filled the air. Instead of returning to the pallet, I did the one thing I knew better than to do. I reached out to him. My smooth fingers brushed his rough hands and gave a comforting squeeze. My breath went shallow as he turned his face toward mine, a hunger in his hazel eyes.

"Yula," he said. "If you go to the Dark Queen, I will never see you again. Will you not reconsider?"

"I cannot," I choked out.

He stroked my cheek, the contact making my pulse quicken.

Foolishly, I leaned into his touch, starved for connection. Starved for *him*. He was the dream I'd thought I'd never have. The dream that would probably never come so close to my grasp again.

There was a strange note in his voice when he spoke again. "I have wanted you for a very long time, my rose girl, and now you're here, determined to sacrifice yourself away. I cannot say I don't understand, but I also cannot say I don't wish you'd change your mind. With you here, I find myself suddenly selfish. I would damn worlds to keep you at my side."

I stared at him, unable to do anything more than nod.

His breath tickled my face, and his mouth hovered just above mine. "May I kiss you?"

I pressed against his solid body, suddenly alive with need and craving his touch.

When he ran his thumb over my bottom lip, a

breathless sigh escaped my throat. His other hand parted the cloak and rode up my bare back. His lips met mine—warm, rough, and intoxicating. Better than the sweetest wines served during Mabon.

Instinctively, I responded to his kiss and caress, my passion mounting. From deep inside his chest, a groan rumbled and rose, escaping his throat like a low growl. His hand slid lower, moving over and then clenching my warm bottom.

The cloak fell open as his fingers undid the clasp, displaying my flesh. The sudden coolness made my nipples flare and his fingers trailed down my throat to stroke and cup those tender buds.

Wild with need, I spread my legs, pressing harder into him. A moan rolled out of my throat, and my hips moved as my fingers fumbled against his breeches, searching for flesh. His hardness, firm and pulsing in my hand sent a delicate shiver through my body.

"Aelbrin," I whispered, unable to explain what I wanted.

Shifting his weight, he allowed me to straddle him. When his warm mouth closed over my nipple I panted, inviting his touch. Rolling my erect buds between his teeth, he sucked and pulled, biting gently and then not so gently at all. Setting my loins on fire. I threw back my head, clutching at him desperately as he twisted a hand through the waves of my hair, pulling me closer to him.

When he lifted his head, both of us breathing as though we'd raced through the forest, his eyes glazed over with an intense longing.

He met my gaze and studied me, naked in the moonlight. "Yula," he whispered, his voice husky. "Are you sure?"

My thoughts flickered back to our first meeting, and I recalled the connection I had felt even then. This only seemed right, an inevitable conquest before the brutality of life ripped us apart.

I nodded, chewing my lower lip, almost ashamed of my nakedness. But the look in his eyes reassured me. His arms wrapped around my waist and pulled me tight against his chest, holding on as though for dear life. The longing in that embrace seeped through me and heat flared between my thighs.

"I need you," I whispered, my lips close to his ear.

In one smooth motion, he carried me to the pallet where he lay me down, kissing my forehead, cheeks, and lips again and again. Shaking off the last of his clothes, he opened me to him, his fingers sending a ripple down my spine as though my skin were on fire.

He pressed hot, open-mouthed kisses to my neck, shoulders, and breasts as he worked his way down, making me hiss, desperate. I'd never felt such intense desire, such need before.

When he touched the delta between my legs, I dug my fingernails into his shoulders as though to anchor myself in the moment.

His fingers stroking, teasing. And then I felt his hardness. He hesitated, and I squirmed, arching my back, frantic. Gently, he slipped inside me, filling me to my core. I opened my legs further, and a delicious shiver went up my spine. He thrust, slowly at first and then harder, faster, his breath coming ragged as he made love to me.

I held on to him as my pleasure mounted. We were together, one soul, as he drove into me again and again. I felt as though I were careening, falling headlong.

And I never wanted it to end.

5

SILVER MIST GREETED us in the morning. Vague shapes appeared in the fog—fingers, the face of a lady, the form of a hulking orc, an overgrown wolf. The atmosphere was thick with animosity, and a darkness hovered over us. Something in the air reached out, seeking to take hold.

Aelbrin led the way, saying nothing about our intimate night of pleasure. He'd taken me again and again, as though that alone could stop time and our inevitable separation. Even now I sensed a deep sadness emitting from him.

My hair stuck to my back and my feet hummed with discomfort at each step, for the boots he'd given me were too large. The shirt I'd borrowed billowed out, adding to my discomfort. The pants slipped off my lean hips, forcing me to continually hoist them up. My limbs trembled as I stumbled uphill, slipping on moss, broken branches, and pine needles.

Aelbrin turned back often to assist me. When his

hand touched mine, my skin went hot, and I willed myself to follow through with my decision. Once he led me to the Dark Queen, I hoped he'd flee, even though he believed he led me to my doom.

I pushed those dreadful thoughts away and flexed my fingers, forcing clarity into my mind. Practicing magic was dangerous when I was confused or distracted. I needed to concentrate. An unclear mind led to emotions overriding my control. I couldn't let my rage balloon into devastation again.

When we reached the hilltop, a gust of wind rushed across the knoll. It lifted my hair, blew out my clothes, and examined me from every angle. I heard a cruel laugh before the wind fizzled out. Violation made me cross my arms over my chest for protection.

"What was that?" I demanded.

Aelbrin glanced back at me, and the look he gave me almost swayed my resolve. The wind had blown his wild hair straight back, giving him a rather severe look. His haunted eyes had gone dark. "That was the gate-keeper, checking to ensure you carry no weapons. She will report her findings to the queen."

A bead of sweat trickled down my forehead.

"Yula. My dear rose girl. This is your last chance," Aelbrin urged. "I've brought you this far, but if you wish to flee and seek another way to save your people, I will help you."

A memory of his warm, insistent kisses plagued my thoughts. We were good together, and he was wise, but try as I might, I could see no other way. Besides, if we failed, people would die, and I was tired of people dying because of me and my magic.

Only one path was clear, and I had no choice but to take it.

My stomach twisted but I lifted my chin. "I can do this."

Aelbrin held my gaze as he came to stand before me. His fingers grazed my wrist and sent a tingling sensation down my spine. He scanned my face as though searching for something.

My heart kicked against my chest. Was he going to kiss me again?

The moment snapped as he let go of me. "I warn you, beware of the raven who will bind your magic." He pointed to a thick grove of trees just ahead. "Ascend into the domain of the Dark Queen. She is expecting you."

My gaze followed his. The trees opened up, displaying a wide set of stairs which led to an obsidian castle. The fortification sprawled across the hill, the horrifying might of it both an intimidation and a curse. Wicked towers glared back at me as though warning me away.

I gawked, a horror of entrapment growing in my mind. I wanted to flee, turn and beg Aelbrin to take me back to the village. But then what? I'd be right back where I started. A night in the enchanted forest all for naught.

I squared my shoulders and forced fear to the back of my mind, and as I stood there, the teachings of the Sisters of the Light came to me:

Fear is your ally, not your enemy. When you feel fear, it is only a sensation, a reminder that you must think before proceeding. Fear is an indicator of what could go wrong if you do not have a plan, but remember, fear is not always correct, it is only a thought, a path, like the roots of a tree branching to different dimensions. You are in control of the path you follow, so let fear guide you to the right choice. In the face of fear remember to use your mind, not your emotions.

Magic made me strong. I would use my mind in this, not my gut reaction to flee. Turning, I extended my hand to say goodbye to Aelbrin, but the spot where he'd stood was empty. I spun around, searching for him. But he'd silently vanished, as though he were nothing but a figment of my imagination.

Irritation rose and, blinking back tears, I left the forest behind and walked toward the black castle.

6

THE STAIRS LEADING to the monolithic fortress zigzagged back and forth across a cliff with sharp drop-offs at each side. It was a defensive position with one way in and one way out. The castle itself rose like a frowning monster casting a nightmarish shadow over the forest. Columns of gray smoke rose from the surrounding bluffs. At first, I thought they were clouds, but as I passed through the mists, low moans wailed from them.

I shivered in the clammy air. All of my instincts told me to turn and run away.

Once more I glanced back, missing the comfort of Aelbrin. I cursed myself for longing for something that was impossible to have. I'd allowed myself to forget, last night, that he still belonged to Her.

A wailing scream came from the castle, and my hands went to my ears to hold back the blood-twisting sound. My heart thudded in my throat, but I forced my feet to take one brave step after another. I climbed into the mountain of mist and the wicked castle steadily grew closer.

Black feathers glistening with a shiny gloss flittered through the air. A sharp caw made me jump, and then a man materialized in front of me. On his head he wore the skull of an overgrown raven, with the beak intact. Across his body flowed black feathers, covering him from head to toe. Ghastly eyes stared at me.

I paused and closed my fingers into fists, preparing my magic to toss him over the cliff if necessary. He cocked his head, and his beady eyes examined me from head to toe.

Offended, I crooked a finger. A rock from the path dropped onto his booted toe. The man glanced from his foot to my hand. His eyes gleamed with mischief. He shook back the feathers, and they transformed into a cloak, offering a glimpse of a lean, hard body underneath the curtain of black.

"Aelbrin sends a gift to the queen?" the man quipped, grinning rather suddenly.

I glanced over my shoulder, still sore at the way Aelbrin had vanished without a word. Or instructions. "I am no gift; I have come to make a bargain with the Dark Queen."

The man's coal-black eyes drifted to my chest. "You can make a deal with me first. It shall be more entertaining."

Rage boiled in my belly at his indecency. With a flex of my fingers, the rocks and rubble scattered at our feet rose into the air, each stone a deadly weapon in the hands of a mage. "There's more magic where that came from," I warned him.

The man leered wolfishly. "No doubt." He extended his fingers and made a brushing motion.

My spell evaporated, leaving me furious at how effortlessly he rendered my magic useless. "Who are you?" I hissed. "A gatekeeper?"

"Forgive me," the man gave me a mock bow. A lock of his jet-black hair fell across his forehead. Scowling, he brushed it back. "I am Raven. Since Aelbrin left us, it is up to me to escort you to the queen."

I huffed. "Lead on then and stop boring me with your words."

The perfect sneer on Raven's face went tight. A hostile light came to his dangerous eyes. "When the queen is done with you, perhaps you'll think better of my hospitality. You have come to be disappointed."

I wished my magic could bring hail down on his head. My fingers twisted, but the spark of magic had vanished.

Raven gave me a cruel smile. "If the Dark Queen allowed everyone to perform magic, well, this would not be her domain. I have bound your magic until she says otherwise."

Raven turned, pivoting to give his coat of feathers the best view in the light. Despite Raven's warning, I tried my magic again. I imagined a pillar of rocks, piled one on top of the other, but when I moved my fingers, nothing happened. If Raven was the beginning of the nastiness waiting for me, what hope did I have to save the village?

I crept behind Raven. The iron balusters rose like teeth, wicked and sharp, ready to pry the magic out of my body. Surely that wasn't possible. I'd heard of Sisters of the Light who lost their magic by performing some dark deed or making an intentional choice to join the Shadow Sisters. A ritual could bind their magic, just as the Sisters of the Light bound the darkness of the forest. I hoped the Dark Queen would be merciful, but as we entered the castle, I doubted it.

A sour stench hung in the air. The slow trickle of water penetrated the silence. Ivy, black as night, hung down from unlit chandeliers, and a thick dust covered the floor. Raven led me up a curving staircase where light dared to enter the gloom of the castle. Gray mist twisted into various shapes, showing first monsters with curved teeth and wicked snouts, and then sensuous creatures that romped around them, unafraid of the monsters and the great evil of which they were capable.

Dread filled my heart, and when at last we came to a door with spikes around it, I wished I'd taken up Aelbrin on his word and fled when I had the chance.

Only there was no turning back now.

The black iron doors swung open with a resounding *boom*, revealing a mist-filled throne room. Raven strode across the threshold, shoulders thrown back and head held high, the gray fog curling around him in greeting. His coat of ebony feathers danced with every swaying step. When he reached the center of the room, he dropped to one knee and bowed his head, touching his fist to his forehead. He remained in position, waiting.

I froze just inside the doorway, staring into the eerie lair of the Dark Queen.

BOWLS OF INCENSE smoked on either side of the room, the coals turned by women with collars around their necks and irons on their hands and feet. Long hair hung wild around them, and their bodies were smeared with ash and soot. The red irises of their eyes stared vacantly across the room.

Tearing my eyes away, I looked up at the throne. Although roughly twenty paces away, it towered above me, casting a shadow of evil over the doors. It spanned the curved wall of the room and looked like an ash tree with roots—thick and twisted—growing through the stone.

A tree. Mother Tree?

Someone had taken flame to it. Leafless branches reached out of the scorched remains in every direction, as though seeking the light. White mold stood out on its decaying branches, and yet I sensed life. The tree struggled under the oppression of the wicked castle, begging to be set free and grow in health away from the dark and rot. The pain of the tree seeped into me, so real and full of sorrow that my eyes smarted from the strong sense of misery.

At last I understood the burden Aelbrin carried. If this tree knew torture just from existing in the Dark Queen's presence, what fate lay in store for his people who were cut down to stumps or burned to dust? I could imagine the spirit of the forest carried within the hearts of every one of his people, twisting in agony even as it continued to fight for life.

Perched in the center of the tree, in a seat forced out of twisted tree branches, sat the Dark Queen. She lifted a hand, and curved nails hung off her fingers like the fangs of a snake. "Rise."

Raven returned to his feet and marched back toward me. His eyes narrowed, and a wolfish grin came to his dry lips.

"Our guest has arrived." The queen pointed a razor-sharp finger at me.

Fear threatened to overrule my spirit. I struggled against it, biting my tongue fiercely. Clasping my hands behind my back, I dug my fingernails into my wrist. I would not fail.

I studied the milk-white face of the queen. Dark circles covered her eyes, the tell-tale sign of rot, and her raven black hair hung in waves down her back. She wore a corset that pushed her breasts high, the heavy swells moving up and down with every breath. Her lengthy gown was a combination of black-night and blood-red, and offered a glimpse of bare thigh. When she licked her scarlet lips, her tongue came out, forked like a viper.

Ah. Everything made sense. The rune I'd accidentally drawn at the gathering, the mark on Aelbrin's skin, and the snake that bit me in the forest were all reminders of the Dark Queen's power and constant presence. Had she been watching all the while?

A warning hummed through me. Was my meeting with the Dark Queen a coincidence? Or a trap?

"My queen," Raven placed his hand on the small of my back, and I tensed, fingers trembling, desperately longing for my magic. "Aelbrin brought this sweet for you and fled." He licked his lips. "He will have some explaining to do when he returns."

The queen pursed her lips and waved her hand at Raven. "He did not go far. Find him and bring him to me."

Raven left with a victorious smile on his grim face.

The *tap-tap* of the queen's fingernails on hollow wood drew my attention. I knew I should hold her gaze, show her I was bold, determined, and unafraid. But the white pallor of her face was so hideous I focused on the tree roots, until they began shrieking in agony, that is. It was as though they knew I alone could hear their mourning plea for help. It was an awful sound, the cries of a dying spirit.

"Tell me why you are here." The queen said. "I sensed your magic when you approached my kingdom, just as I sensed a disturbance outside of the forest, the night before last. You are brave to come here."

She gave a cruel laugh which rankled my nerves. How I wished I had my magic.

I squared my shoulders and addressed a spot just above her shoulder. "My name is Yula. I come from the

Sisters of the Light with a request. As we do every year, my people offer you gifts, and the Sisters of the Light perform a ritual to bind the evil of this forest. This year, the Sisters of the Light are not here for the blessed ritual, and since it is too late to train another sisterhood, I came to make a bargain. In exchange for mercy, and to keep the orc-kind and other creatures of the forest from destroying my people, I would like to make a deal with you."

The queen cocked her head. "You came to me. To make a deal? Oh, the irony of it." She cackled. "The Sisters of the Light taught you nothing. Haven't you been warned? I do not respect the wishes of mortals. I do not make bargains."

The tree hurt my heart, and its cry made me feel dizzy.

The queen stood tall and started down the stairs which were nothing more than contorted tree branches. As she neared, horns appeared on her head, gnarled and curved.

I swallowed hard; my tongue thick. "Have you not made bargains with others in the past? People who now serve you?" I dared ask.

Those voluptuous red lips curved upward, and I could not help but glance at the dark sockets of her evil eyes.

She sashayed toward me. My feet involuntarily backed away toward the doors.

"As you said," she replied. "In the past. I no longer make bargains, for they tend to be more work than they are worth. If you have something that is worthy of my time, come out with it now. I know you decimated the temple and the Sisters of the Light, and there will be reparations. You took power, magic, from me and think you can stroll into my kingdom and ask for a blessing. There shall be no deal with you. You have a penance to pay."

I licked my dry lips and took another step back. My fingers shook as they met the cold iron of the doors. I almost tripped over my own two feet as the queen strode toward me. She towered above me, much larger than she'd appeared on the throne. The strength in her arms looked devastating.

She knew what I'd done. She saw my guilt as though it were a rune, inked on my forehead. Quickly, I racked my brain for words, desperate to say something that would please her. "I have magic, and I know the rituals. I can convince others to make you happy. I can rebuild and train new sisters how to satisfy your demands for magic."

The queen smiled, and something dark glittered like a struggling light in her eyes. "Magic," she said, her voice soft as she trailed a sharp fingernail down my cheek. "You think I have no others to serve me in this way?"

A warm trickle of freshly drawn blood streaked down my face. The Dark Queen leaned forward, as if to kiss me, but instead that forked tongue lashed out, tasting the rivulet now staining my cheek.

She gripped my chin hard and stared into my eyes, a drop of my blood pearled on her lip. "The magic of your sisters fed me, and I offered my protection in return. But now, days before Mabon, *you* destroyed them, *you* failed me. Don't you realize that I exist off such magic?"

She leaned close again, her breath fetid. "I can feed off other things as well, though. The soul of a tree. The spirits of the elements." Her gaze darted to my cheek. "Even the blood of a mage."

I reared back in an attempt to move further away from her, but the doors were behind me, and the dark queen slithered closer. Her hands rested on my shoulders. Nails bit through the clean shirt I wore and there was nowhere for me to look but up into her fearsome face.

Vomit boiled in my belly. This had all been for naught. She would not let me save my village. I had sealed their doom by losing control of my magic. I saw it clearly now. I'd weakened her, and she was furious. Revenge burned in her dark eyes.

Sharp nails ripped through my shirt, and the hardness of the iron gate burned cold on my bare back. My hands came up, clutching the shirt over my chest, and my eyes went wide. I blinked hard to keep the tears at bay. How could this be happening again? Every time I tried to rise strong, I was taken and humiliated.

My thoughts drifted back to what had started this—the strike of the Head Mistress' rod on my back—and rage welled out of me. Memories went back further to the persecution I suffered when I was young, because I was odd. My skin was dark and my eyes wild, a strong indication I was not like the others. I recalled the screams and cries of the children when my anger came out, broken limbs and blood, so much blood. They had all lived although it took some time for them to mend, but my parents were shunned and forced away, because of my magic. Determined not to fall prey to the orcs, they moved to another village. I discovered it was because of the Sisters of the Light. Against my will, they forced me to bend to those who held magic, who were stronger than me, and could teach me to use it for good, instead of hurting others.

But the rage came up again and again, manifesting in a windstorm. I heard what they whispered about me when they thought I was out of hearing. I knew what they thought. I was a cursed one with magic stronger than even the Head Mistress. They believed one day a great evil would befall them, because my dark soul called out to it, like seeking like, darkness calling darkness.

And they were right. So why should I try to save the village? Every time I tried to change my ways, to save something, anything, it failed. Why should this time be any different?

My knees gave way as The Dark Queen's nails dug into me like knives and ripped the tender skin of my back. My body shook with spasms, and only when I cowered on the ground, in a pool of tattered rags, did she step away.

I shuddered and swallowed a sob, keeping my head bent while my hair curtained around me. Trails of blood flowered down my back, and when a finger touched one of my open wounds, I gave a sharp hiss.

The Dark Queen knelt in front of me and fisted a clump of my hair in her hand, forcing me to raise my head. Her forked tongue came out and licked the blood off her fingertip. Eyes flashing, she laughed. A deep, rough, evil sound that made my skin go cold. This was the end, wasn't it? She would kill me, for I did not have the strength or magic to fight her.

"I sense defiance in your nature," the queen said, malice dripping from her lips.

She jerked the roots of my hair harder, forcing a wince out of me. My shoulders came down and rage rose in my throat.

"Defiance will not save you, but your magic is dangerous, strong, something I can mold for myself. I shall truly enjoy draining it from you." She smirked. "It is fortuitous you came to me. I must thank you for giving me the opportunity to teach him a lesson."

Him? A heaviness came over me. Who was she punishing?

"He led you here, didn't he? Despite his conflicted heart. You wear his clothes which carry his scent which means you dared to tryst with one of my knights. It will not be forgiven. Ending your life will serve as a reminder for him of what it means to serve me."

My soul wilted in defeat. Despite everything, the consequences of my magic still followed me. I pressed my hand to my mouth to keep the sob from escaping my throat.

A grim look crossed the Dark Queen's face, and her eyes stared into the distance. "Or perhaps I shall kill him for his disloyalty."

"Please," I choked out.

I did not want to care what became of Aelbrin. I needed to save myself, save my village, but the vision I'd seen when I touched him came back to me. I saw the firedrake consume his people, the cry of Mother Tree in the throne room, the screams of the wounded, the pleas of the downcast, the broken, the downtrodden, those whom the world would always turn a blind eye to.

"Please," I whimpered; hands clasped at my chest. "I will do what you ask. I will give you my magic, my soul, anything. Only spare him. This is not his fault."

A cackle came from the Dark Queen's red lips. She stood tall, dragging me by the roots of my hair. Heat seared my scalp, and a scream tore out of my throat. I clawed at her hands and arms to fight her off, earning long scratches from her nails. She flipped me onto my back. The stone cut into my wounds, but when the sharp point of her foot slammed between my ribs, I curled up into a ball. A moan came from between my lips as she kicked me again. I felt a rib crack, and breathing turned difficult.

8

"YOUR MAJESTY," a male voice intoned, almost with a question.

The queen ceased kicking me, but I dared not look up.

Aelbrin. I knew it in a heartbeat. Did he know why he'd been called there? Did he know what the queen had in store for him? I wanted to warn him but couldn't, afraid if I looked at him everything I felt in my heart would be revealed on my face.

"Sir Aelbrin. My knight," the queen quipped. Her brutal grip suddenly let go, and she stalked toward him.

I whimpered. How futile it would be to hurl myself at the queen's feet and beg—again—for her to change her mind?

"My queen—" Aelbrin began.

A snap of her fingers effectively cut him off.

"Aelbrin. I am displeased," the queen said, shades of darkness in her tone. "I heard from Raven that you brought me a gift, a gift you tarnished by stamping your scent on her."

"My queen," his deep voice held no emotion. "She was naked when I found her. I gave her clothing." His eyes chanced a glance at me, quick as the flutter of a hummingbird's wings. "That is all."

"Naked. Clothed." The queen gave a mirthless laugh. "That's how you hope to escape your fate? Why didn't you deliver her yourself?"

"You and I both know you'd rather be left to deal with new subjects as you see fit," Aelbrin reminded her.

"Oh," the queen spat. "Then you will not care if I take her magic and do away with her useless life."

Aelbrin's breath whistled between his teeth.

"Aha," the queen snickered. "You do care. I thought as much. It has been long since you let your emotions overrule your decisions, Knight. This woman came here to save her village, a village she brought doom on by destroying the Sisters of the Light. But I see her as a lesson for you and a source of magic for myself. Now, I give you a choice. I can kill you, end our bargain, and let this woman walk free. Perhaps I will even grant her a boon since she seems desperate to save her village. Or. . ." The queen waited, giving a chance for her words to sink in. "I can kill *her* and let the people of her village die. It's up to you. *Knight.* You choose who lives and who dies. Mabon draws nigh, and my monsters need a chance to enjoy the spoils of being good all year long. Tell me. What do you choose?"

I dared to lift my head and saw the queen stood with her back to me. Aelbrin faced her, head down, eyes lost in thought as he considered the impossible request. I wanted to end this, to save him from this choice, but how? There was no fleeing. The Dark Queen would hunt us to the end of the earth. And there was no magic savior.

My gaze scanned the throne room and landed on the ash tree. Gnarled roots, scorched with fire, stood out. If I could reach one of those hollow branches, perhaps I could do something, anything, before dying.

I began to crawl, even though my back cried out against my movements. My elbows dug into the stone floor, and I eyed the chained slaves, but they continued their languorous movements, eyes on their work, chains clinking as they turned the coals over the fire. As I crawled, I heard Aelbrin speak up.

"You ask much of me. As always. I would request that you reconsider, for no matter my decision, innocent lives will be lost. If you wish to punish me, then do so. Only leave the innocent out of this."

"Bah," the queen snorted. "No one is innocent. This you know to be true. I gave you a choice, now end this once and for all, for if you don't choose, I will."

Aelbrin's voice sank lower, the edges of pain bleeding out. "Your Majesty, I would remind you. How long have I been your servant? How long have I served you without question? Have I ever broken my word or betrayed your trust?"

Her piercing laugh seemed as though it would shake the foundations of the castle.

In a movement so quick I barely caught it, she snatched a fistful of Aelbrin's tunic and yanked him near, as though he were not as solid as a rooted tree. "You think I don't know?" she said. "You've become bold. I saw the wolf you healed, the fox you saved from the orcs. I saw you grace the owls with your presence to learn the music of the night." She leaned close. "You took extra game to the village to feed the elders. You watched this woman and kept her safe from Raven whenever she snuck out to visit the graveyard. You think I don't know what you do when you're not here, in my presence, but you forget. I see your comings and goings. You have grown soft enough to believe you can cross me. Retribution was always coming, but this woman makes it all the sweeter."

Aelbrin said nothing, but I sensed his anger all the same.

"But," the queen continued. "If you would spare the innocent, so be it. Take up your sword, oh knight of mine. Step forward and slay the woman."

My arms scrapped the floor. I pressed my tongue firmly against the roof of my mouth to keep from crying out, and I tasted iron in the back of my throat. I had to make my last action count.

Again, I saw Aelbrin's hazel eyes hiding a deep well of thoughts, but every decision led him down the path of an impossible choice. He was damned. If he did not obey the Dark Queen, he would damn the last of his people.

But what about my people? Even now, the queen roused an army to destroy them, an army of nightmares and orcs to tear through the village. It was impossible to warn my people.

Ignoring the pain, I crawled closer to the tree. A smell emitted from it, the odor of a slow death. I reached out my hand, unsure why I felt the need to touch the tree. My fingers wrapped around wood, smooth instead of rough, and emotions flashed in front of me, heart-rending and terrifying.

A scream bolted out of my mouth, but the sensation was quickly replaced with a flood of warmth. My eyes closed, and a smile came to my face as a happy memory of my past rose in my thoughts.

I recalled sitting in front of the fire, wrapped in a blanket in my mother's arms. She hummed a tune under her breath and rocked back and forth, back and forth. I reached out my tiny hand to wrap it around one of her slender fingers, and she squeezed me tightly. I felt safe, sure, right. Nothing terrible could ever happen to me.

A plethora of feelings surged through me as though I were standing on a cliff. The spirit of the tree nudged me and a velvety voice whispered, so softly I almost did not hear it at first. "Will you take the burden? Will you take our pain? Will you save us?"

Tears brimmed over, striking my cheeks. "Yes." I whispered. "Yes. If I can."

"Hold tight," warned the tree. Mother Tree.

I closed my eyes and squeezed a knotty root. My senses took over, and the queen shouted in a murderous voice. "Let go of the tree, you fool! Let go. You know not what you do."

I held on tighter.

"Aelbrin, take up your sword and kill her," the queen shrieked. "If you do not do so this instant, I will send the firedrakes to slay your people."

"My queen, a blood oath cannot be forsaken so easily," came Aelbrin's horrified voice.

"Do you not know the heights of my power? Do it now!" she ordered.

I clung to the tree, even as I heard the ominous ring of a sword being drawn from a scabbard.

Would he do it? Even after our night of passion, would he really slay me to save his people?

A humming began in my head. The tree was pouring into me, its thoughts, hopes, and dreams. A thousand memories flooded in, moving in the blink of an eye. It churned within me like a windstorm blowing into a cyclone so powerful and intense none could stand in its way. Something vibrated in the pit of my being and my fingers went stiff. Magic pushed against the binding spell, undoing Raven's work and seeped out of my hands.

Overwhelming sensations convulsed through me. My teeth clattered, and my eyes came open, as though I were filled to the brim and could not contain my magic any longer. Still holding onto the tree, I opened my eyes, stood to my feet and turned around.

My mouth hung open at the sight I saw. The slaves were crouched on the ground in front of the braziers, cowering and weeping. Aelbrin stood in the center of the room, facing the queen. His sword was drawn. It was a wide blade, meant for cleaving heads from shoulders, its weight forcing him to hold on with both hands. Designs etched the hilt, many of them old runes I'd studied before, blessings and curses. He swung the sword, and I realized he intended to kill—not me—but the Dark Queen.

His bravery emboldened me. Why would he sacrifice himself, and his people? Surely not for me? For if she were gone, who would stand between the people and the dark forest? Who would hold back the tide of her demons, leaderless and ready to turn every village into a blood bath?

"Let go," whispered Mother Tree.

I obeyed and aimed my tingling palms at the Dark Queen.

She evaded Aelbrin's blade, laughing and swearing, telling him the many ways she would torture first me, forcing him to watch. She seemed to have forgotten I was behind her, and a grim smile came to my lips.

The power bubbling within me felt good and strong, and although I sensed a dark energy behind it, I liked it. It was like a forbidden fruit. Once tasted, the delectable pleasure became too heady and delicious to let go of ever again.

Energy surged through me, out of my fingers like lightning, and slammed into the back of the Dark Queen.

A stillness came over the air, and the queen's body went rigid. Her blood red mouth came open in a silent scream of shock. Her body doubled over. Bent at the waist. She held out her arms to keep her balance, staying on her swaying feet.

Pent up rage poured out of me, and the foundations of the castle shook with the current of power flooding through my veins. My ears popped, and I realized I was howling as every unfairness, humiliation, and shame in my life was dealt with, one after the other, making the queen the noose upon which I hung the evil that had befallen me.

Aelbrin's blade went up again. Before he brought it

down, he glanced at me. There was a question in his eyes. Although his jaw was tight, I understood he was asking permission, asking me to back down so he could finish what he started.

Power surged through me, and I reached out to hold it back, but it seemed like a broken dam, churning with strength, too strong to pull back. I managed to nod at him, even though magic leaked out of my eyes in a dazzling array of green and gold, casting its shimming luster across the throne room.

The sword came down, straight and fast, glinting in the firelight, and the Dark Queen's head rolled end over end. Her cold dead eyes glittered as they stared directly at me, as though she could see, even in death, what I'd done.

I lowered my hands as weariness consumed me. The sudden energy faded, and I leaned back, collapsing into the seemingly waiting arms of the tree. My vision swam but I still made out the figure rushing toward me. Aelbrin. He cupped my face.

"Yula? Yula!" he called.

And then I faded.

9

MY EYELIDS FLUTTERED, and a softness surrounded me. I heard my name, whispered through the wood. I opened my eyes and saw I sat on the throne, and below me, where the court of the Dark Queen had been, was the destruction of the castle. The smoking bowls of incense were gone, along with the chained dancers, lost souls who hopefully found their escape.

Fingers tip-toed across my arm, and I turned my face to meet Aelbrin's dark eyes. Blood splatter stained his shirt, and his cloak had been tossed over one shoulder. Unruly hair framed his gallant face, and my heart flip-flopped. I touched his shoulder, gratified by what he'd done. Whether it was for me or him did not matter. He was free.

And then I noticed something. I snatched up his hand, staring at the smooth skin. The rune of the Dark Queen had faded, melted away in the aftermath of her death.

"Is it over?" I whispered.

His hazel eyes were serene, and a calmness enveloped me as he squeezed my hand. "Not yet. You have taken the place of the Dark Queen, but Mabon still comes. If your magic is strong enough, you can bind the forest and keep the creatures of the night from escaping to terrorize the world outside our borders." He frowned, and his eyes shifted away.

"What is it?" I asked.

"The Queen of the Wildwood used the energy of the runes to help hold back the night terrors. If there are no rituals, no runes, your power might not be strong enough to hold back the creatures. Especially when the seasons change into the dark months."

Understanding overwhelmed me, and I swallowed hard but kept my eyes fixated on him. When he touched me, an undercurrent flowed from me to him and him to me. A power. I felt it strong and intense, like nothing I'd experienced before.

I squeezed his hand and I knew, with certainty, my power was far stronger than the Dark Queen's. The monster within had been awakened. Its presence tugged on my heartstrings, begging to be let loose. I'd survived the dam, and I could survive this. "I can hold them. But what of your people?"

A light came over his shadowed eyes, and his fingers grazed my knee, a reminder of our tryst in the cave. Despite myself, I shivered, and an ache for his touch filled me.

"My people are safe from the firedrakes. For now. They will continue to live in the grove and return to the trees they were birthed from. But you did something else, something greater. You healed Mother Tree," he looked up at it with reverence. "She will grow again and become a mighty tree of the forest."

I gazed at him with amazement. "And what about you?" Wonder thrummed through my voice. "You are free now, too. You can return to your people."

He blinked. "That life is gone. If you will have me, I will stay here with you, and help thwart the plans of the dark forest. It is still thick with the seeds of evil she planted long ago. If the forest realizes its mistress is dead, it will fight back. I'm afraid you have exchanged your soul in servitude to the wood. I've always been drawn to you, Mistress Yula. I didn't know why until now."

He tilted his head, bringing it closer to mine. Despite what we had been through, he still smelled like the wildwood. His warm breath lingered above my lips, and I angled my head, teasing him.

"I hope your attraction to me is not only because of my power," I said.

His hand squeezed my knee. "Nay, I know you have felt the connection too."

Without allowing me another word, his warm lips captured mine.

A moan escaped from my throat, and my arms went around his neck, pulling him closer until there was no space between us.

"Aelbrin," I whispered when he pulled back, a warm flush coming to his face. "Thank you."

He helped me to my feet and held me close. I relaxed against him, enjoying the calm after the storm.

"Thank *you*, Yula," Aelbrin said softly, kissing my

cheek. "You are Queen of the Wildwood now. And I'm your knight."

CURSE OF THE HEALER

1

SUNBEAMS DANCED across my wood table as I cleared away my breakfast dishes. A mug of warm tea and a bowl of gruel. It was midwinter and my food supply was growing low, but fear and embarrassment gripped me when I considered going to town to trade for more.

A flash of red drew my eyes to the back window of my one-room hut. I tip-toed over and glanced out of the frosted windowpane. Dark green vines and rich brown wood met my eyes—the entrance to the enchanted wildwood. Eyes stared back at me framed by black fur and then vanished into the thicket. My hand went to my neck and a shudder rippled down my spine. Once again I considered whether it was wise to live so close to the enchanted wildwood.

A knock at the door pulled me out of my thoughts. It was almost midday, and I wasn't expecting visitors. No one came to visit me anymore. Months ago, it was different. I was held in high esteem as the healer of the village of Moon Leaf and had been for fifteen years. When I was twelve, my grandma—who was the healer at that time—claimed I was old enough for the gift to awaken within me and ready to begin my training. We mended broken bones, calmed fevered children, and helped mothers give birth. Once, a babe was breached, and Grandma's hands were too shaky to turn the babe around in the womb. So I did it. The babe was born hale and happy.

From then on, a kind of luck shined down on me. Every child I helped birth was born fat, healthy, and never became sick. They recovered quickly from bumps and bruises, and when the baker's son fell out of a tree on his fifth birthday and broke his arm, it healed completely in a week.

But ever since the incident, I was seen as a disgrace. When I went to town I heard whispers of "witch" and "cursed one". The village wardens threatened to take my land because I was a burden. If they had come to pay me a visit, I did not know what to say or do.

My throat went dry and my fingers trembled as I unbolted the door. Cold daylight streamed in, and my shivers of fright turned to relief when I saw who it was. I chewed my lower lip, suddenly ashamed of my shoddy appearance. My white wool dress was quite plain, and my black hair tumbled in unbrushed waves down to my waist. I tucked one of my wild curls behind my ear and looked up at the handsome man standing on my doorstep.

He was much taller than myself with a thick torso, great arms and legs bulging with muscles. Sandy blond hair hung past his wide shoulders but was pulled back from his chiseled face and fastened at the nape of his neck. He wore a long-sleeved shirt, open at the front where golden hairs spilled out. His pants clung to the muscles of his legs and were tucked into his boots. In his arms, he carried a bundle of wood.

"Mistress Talia." His deep voice was low and melodious.

My skin tingled at the sound of my name on his lips. "Wilhelm, come in." I held the door open wider and moved back to give him room to enter.

His presence filled up the room, and a smile played around the corners of my mouth as I watched him. Wilhelm had been my one consistent companion throughout my trials. Aware that I was a young woman, living alone, he took it upon himself to check on me from time to time, coming around with fresh-cut wood or bringing me wares from town. He was handsome and gentle for a man whose body carried so much strength. I'd admired him from afar and rewarded his visits with a cup of tea, a home-baked slice of bread or a knitted hat for the winter, when I had time. But today I had nothing to give, and perhaps he knew that, for after setting down the wood, he moved toward the door, a furrow in his brow.

"Are you well, Talia?" He asked, twisting his fingers.

"I am," I lied, meeting his dark green gaze. "Thank you for bringing more wood."

"It is the least I can do," he said, his eyes holding mine. "Are you sure you want to stay here? Alone?"

I swallowed hard, desperately wishing my attraction

to him was not one-sided. The way his green eyes looked at me made me feel breathless, and yet he kept moving away as though my bad luck would rub off on him. Perhaps it would be best for him to leave, but I twisted my fingers, desperately thinking of something to say to make him stay. "I am, and I have work to complete before the festival of Yule begins."

Wilhelm nodded but took another step toward the door. "Aye, I'll leave you to your work then."

"Are the villagers still angry?" I blurted out. I had not wanted to ask the question and immediately regretted it when I saw the pity in Wilhelm's eyes.

"Some are," he admitted, his voice quiet. "They are used to looking to you for help, and they don't understand what happened. I think I know how to—"

"I understand," I cut him off, my voice ringing with bitterness.

His eyes clouded over, and he paused. "Talia. I came to warn you about the wildwood. The creatures within are always restless during a festival. If you feel frightened or uneasy you may stay at my home tonight. I have an extra room…" He trailed off.

I realized why he said what he did, for he was trying to be kind. Disappointment made me glance back at my knitting strewn across the table.

Wilhelm stepped outside, rubbing his hands together. "It is a cold day. I will return tomorrow, if you will have me."

I wanted him to stay, but he strode off, as though he could not bear to be around me anymore. "Until tomorrow," I whispered, and shut the door.

After putting another log on the fire, I sat down in my rocker and reached for my knitting. The jug of spiced wine sat on the table beside me and, knowing a drink would help ease my anxiety, I poured a cup and drained it dry.

2

A NOISE WOKE ME, and I bolted upright, sending the rocker I sat in into motion. My eyes squinted at the sudden confusion of being startled from deep slumber. A slight headache pinched between my eyes, and I listened.

It happened again, a gentle tap-tap on the door of my sparse one-room cottage accompanied by a faint scraping.

My arms trembled—still weak with sleep—as I forced myself out of the rocking chair. A ball of bright yellow yarn rolled off my lap and my knitting needles clattered to the floor. I failed to suppress a cry from escaping my lips. When had I become so jittery?

The sound at my door trailed off as I caught my breath and took in the room's state. The fire burned low and the air was tainted with a sour scent. I sighed and rubbed my hands over my arms. My shoulders slumped at the fading light in the window. Sundown. I'd slept through the afternoon. Again.

My gaze was drawn to the telltale reason: a flask of spiced wine. How many glasses had I drank?

My stomach rumbled as I reached for the fire poker. An iron rod with a pointed end. Although the scratching noise at the door might have been an animal, the makeshift weapon made me feel better. There was a stray cat I usually left a bowl of milk for, but I'd forgotten that afternoon. Perhaps it was hungry and wanted to get in.

I made my way to the door, heart pounding in my throat. My fingers closed around the doorknob, and I took a breath to steel my nerves. I yanked it open and brandished the poker, ready to stab any intruder who stood outside of my hut.

Crisp frosty air blew in, sending the last of my fire to embers, but there was no one there. I blinked in the frostiness. Gold stars shone pale in the velvet sky, and the silvery moon was almost full. Cool air eased the edges of my wine-induced headache.

The beauty of the night reprimanded me. I needed to stop drinking. The festival of Yule began tomorrow night, and I would miss it if I carried on this way. Especially because the blacksmith's wife was still kind to me, although suspicious. She offered to sell my wool blankets during the festival. Using that money I could buy all I needed for the rest of winter. Only, the blankets weren't finished because I kept getting drunk.

Yule was my favorite time of the year, when the villagers came together despite the cold to celebrate and welcome the sun back to our lives. We decorated the great tree that had stood in the center of the village for ages. The pond was frozen over, and it was funny to watch the children skating, laughing and shouting as they tried not to fall over, their faces pink and rosy. Best of all was the feasting and gift giving. During that time, we were one people, happy. All transgressions were forgotten, something I desperately needed. I had to redeem myself in the eyes of the villagers.

It had been months since the incident but I still remembered it like it were yesterday. The Lord of Moon Leaf called me to his manor for the birth of his firstborn. He and his wife hoped it would be a male heir to their land titles and wealth. Because of my reputation, they called me to be present for the birth, scorning the servants and the healer who had worked for their family line.

I recalled that day vividly. The eve of Mabon. A great celebration was to be held the next day, and the house was tense with excitement. It was the largest manor home I'd ever seen, with stone walls and rose bushes around the entrance. It would have been a beautiful place to raise a child with every comfort that could possibly be given. I'd walked inside, and my luck had turned. Nothing went as expected. The lady labored long and hard, losing far too much blood for my liking. The child was born without making a sound and died within the hour.

I'll never forget the smell of blood. The rage and disappointment in the lord's eyes. Or the wails of the mother as she beat her breast, crying out for her stolen child. I'd left, a foul mixture of sweat and blood staining my clothes, anxious that I'd find myself swinging from the noose. Although there was no punishment from the lord, word got out about my failure. The next child I delivered died as well. As did the third one, and then failure swallowed me. I gave up my post as healer, retreated to my one-room cottage to hide, knit and drink.

Whenever anxiety rose, beating like the wings of a trapped bird in my chest, I reached for the wine, drank one too many glasses, lost track of time, and fell asleep. The blanket I'd been hired to knit wasn't even half done, all my working hours lost to drunken stupor. Drinking myself to sleep each afternoon was pathetic – and if I lost my commission, the wardens would take my land - but I did not know how else to stop the madness from seeping in.

My fingers twitched as I looked out into the night, a dismal reminder that it was time for another drink. At times when I was deep into my cups of spiced wine, I'd stare out my back window at the enchanted wildwood. I saw things in the wood. Grotesque orcs crept through the vines, the dim light revealing their blue-gray skin and abnormal features. Trolls with long noses and fat, sagging bellies. My imagination ran wild at those times and I often shut the curtains, returned to my rocking chair and pretended I'd seen nothing. Despite my fear of those creatures—real or imagined—the winter air felt pleasant and cool against my skin. A walk after sundown was not a smart idea, but spending some time out in nature might help me heal.

I took a step, and my foot bumped against something. On my doorstep lay a shape, obscured by the gloom. I narrowed my eyes and cocked my head to examine it. A round object, shaped almost like an egg but roughly cut at the ends. The low light from the fire flickered in the background as I leaned over. Black hair fluttered around the edges, but then I saw two eyes, wide and unseeing. Human eyes. A severed head.

My hands flew to my mouth, and I screamed into the quietness of the night. I backed away in horror, my stomach queasy and fingers shaking.

Black shadows moved in the darkness. Heart pounding, I slammed the door shut and snatched up the block of wood I used to bolt it. No sooner had I'd lifted it than the door flew open and clocked me in the head. Pain exploded across my vision, and I fell, landing on my bottom with a jarring thud as masked figures bounded over my doorstep.

With my vision swimming in pain, I couldn't tell if there were two or three of them. I kicked one in the shin, but it didn't deter him. The block of wood was still in my hands, and I swung, determined to hit one. How dare they enter my home and try to rob me!

But my efforts were in vain. They ripped the wood from my hands, rolled me onto my belly and pulled my arms behind my back. Strong fingers squeezed my cheeks, forcing my jaws open. They crammed a hand-kerchief into my mouth even though I gagged and coughed and spit.

A hood went over my head, and a sharp blow set my ears ringing. My consciousness ebbed as arms lifted me and bore me away.

3

CONSCIOUSNESS CAME SLOWLY with the sluggishness of returning memory and awareness. I opened my eyes to darkness, my eyelashes scraping against the heavy blindfold tied around my eyes. I sat upright, my head lolling to the side against a rough board of wood. The cool winds of winter did not kiss my skin, so I must have been inside somewhere. Sitting up straighter, I strained my ears for sound, but the blindfold muffled any noise. A dull ache of discomfort ran from my skull all the way down my spine to the knotted ropes which tied my hands behind me. I twisted my fingers to determine how tight they were. They did not move. Next, I attempted to dislodge the gag in my mouth. The cloth was foul, and bile boiled in my belly at the taste of it. My mouth was dry and aside from the gag, the sour taste of wine still lingered in the back of my throat.

Where were my abductors who had the audacity to take me from my home and tie me up in the dark? I wanted to go home, eat a good dinner and go back to sleep. I squirmed in frustration, and fear pulsed a rhythm in my heart. I would not be missed until at least midday when Wilhelm returned to check on me. Usually, the village folk did not venture out to my land. I lived far too close to the enchanted wildwood where the dark queen reigned and demanded sacrifices from the village to protect it from the beasts within.

I shivered, not simply because of the thought of sacrifices, but also because of the head on my doorstep. I had not recognized it, and in my horror hadn't thought to examine it to see if it were a fresh kill. Nay, it must have been a diversion to frighten me because I was the cursed one. The disparaging thought made me cringe.

Grandma said the goddess had blessed me, and I'd accepted it with grace and humbleness, knowing I did not possess such magic nor did it run in my family blood. In fact, just the opposite. Papa had gone off to fight in the king's war, abandoning Mama and I. She passed away when I was ten from an ailment she'd been fighting most of my life. It left her sick and weak, and even Grandma's gift could not help her. I spent many days by her side, knitting to keep my hands busy, and telling stories of what I'd seen and heard in the village. Spiced wine eased her pain, and when she wasn't looking, I snuck sips of it. At first the bitter taste made me choke, but when the warmth swept through me, all my worries melted away. After Mama passed, Grandma kept me busy so I wouldn't feel too sorry for myself. I'd always been good with my hands, but I was better at being a healer. Until three months ago.

My fingers went still under the knowledge that I was

useless to my village. There was no longer a place for me. But I pressed on. Grandma would not want to see me that way. She'd passed seven years ago, when I was twenty, and made me promise I would make a name for my family. And what had I done? Failed.

I twisted my numb fingers, trying to work blood back into them as I considered my predicament. And then I heard voices, muffled but coming nearer. I sat up straight and listened. Footsteps grew louder, metal scraped—a key being thrust into a lock—and a creaking door swung open.

4

THERE WAS SILENCE, and then a man cleared his throat. His voice quavered as he spoke. "Well. There she is, just as you requested."

"And you paid the men who helped you?" The second male asked. There was a higher squeak to his voice like he'd never fully reached manhood and his voice was still going through a traumatic sequence of highs and lows, trying to find the perfect level of deep manliness.

"Just as you requested," the first man said.

I chewed my lower lip. They'd paid someone in the village to capture me?

"Did you have to truss her up so?" The second man groaned.

"I'm sorry, Teague. Will she do for the sacrifice?" His companion asked, sounding somewhat cowed.

"Aye, she'll do," Teague responded. "Get her up and let's go. The watchers have gone quiet, now's our moment to move before the Dark Queen notices us."

My kidnapper sniffed, weeping. "The Dark Queen is dead. The new Queen of the Wildwood is unpredictable--"

"All the more reason we should move. Go. Get her up."

My fingers moved frantically within my bonds as thoughts careened through my mind. The Dark Queen was dead? There was a new Queen of the Wildwood? I gasped against the gag, my breath suddenly coming short and fast. For as long as I'd been alive, stories of the Queen who ruled the enchanted wildwood circulated. Children were told stories as babes that the forest held horrors, monsters who would come eat us alive, and the Queen protected the surrounding villages from the monsters, provided we granted her an annual sacrifice, filled with magic to make her strong. Strong enough to protect us. But if she was so strong, how could she be dead?

Anxiety bloomed in my chest. Now I knew, my wine inspired visions were not dreams at all. The wildwood was alive with monsters, and this new Queen of the Wildwood wasn't holding them back. They'd watched me from my home, and it must be these same monsters who had captured me, luring me out and stealing me away in the dark of night. Rumor had it the forest came alive as festivals drew near, but each of villages that surrounded the wood had a responsibility to protect their people. I'd heard of the Sisters of the Light who were the strongest during Mabon—a pivotal festival when the year turned from light to darkness. What if they had failed and allowed this new queen to rise?

Goosebumps snaked up my arms as footsteps drew nearer. I tried to scream through my gag and thrashed, but it was useless. Meaty hands gripped my arms and hauled me to my feet, which were also bound. I almost fell over.

"Eh," grunted the man, or perhaps beast. "She's a lively one."

"The point is to capture her, not kill her yet," Teague replied. "Hurry. It will soon be midnight, and the feast of Yule will begin. Now's our time."

Time for what? I wiggled my shoulders and tried to kick my feet, but my bonds were secure. The man lifted me up and tossed me over his shoulder with no more ceremony than if I'd been a sack of wheat. We moved. The creaking door clanged shut, and the key once again turned in a lock. I had the nasty sensation that I hadn't been alone in that prison, and a shiver went up my spine. Who were these people? What did they want with me? Why was time of the essence? Oh why, oh why hadn't I taken up the woodcutter's suggestion and stayed with him? I belonged to no man, and yet the safety of his house would be preferable to this. At least he wouldn't have let anyone take me in the middle of the night. I assumed my home near the enchanted woods was safe. What a fool I was, to lock myself away in grief.

Blood rushed to my head as we moved at a fair gait. Cold air bit through my wool dress, the only detail that told me we'd moved outside, and then came a long trek. My captors did not try to stay quiet but huffed and puffed, rustling through the underbrush, and often sticks and branches poked at me. I knew I should save my strength, but I couldn't help but thrash and hiss through my gag, letting my abductors know I was very unhappy with their treatment of me.

It was useless.

Time passed as slowly as a stone being mined from a quarry, and I gave up my futile attempts. The blood in my head made me woozy, and the lack of food and water left me sick and achy. On top of all that, my bones were cold, my dress doing nothing to shield my body from the unforgiving cold of winter.

At last we came to a stop and with a hiss of "Careful" I was set down on my numb feet. My body leaned up against rough wood. A tree? But before I could regain my senses, there was a rustling and a length of rope was wound around my stomach and chest—restricting my breath even further. I was secured to what I assumed was the trunk of a tree. With my hands pinned behind my back and ankles tied together, I was useless to resist. Now they would do what they intended to do. Bile filled my throat, although with the gag it had nowhere to go. I trembled, but not simply from the cold.

Hands came up around my head and untied the blindfold. It fell off, settling around my neck, and I blinked against the low light of night. I was in a wood, that much I could tell among the shadows. The fresh scent of pine and fir along with fresh snow filled my nose. It took my eyes a moment to grow used to the darkness, for aside from the moon, there were no other lights. Trees surrounded me on all sides in a circle, leaving a small opening for moonlight to pour through.

I looked at my two captors and a bolt of fear shot through me. Panic rose up in my throat to choke me. Tears came to my eyes, and I wished they'd left me blindfolded.

5

"THERE, THERE, GIRLY," the smaller one—who seemed to be in charge—said. He was a small, squat man with a thick beard and shoes that curled up at the end. He only stood as high as my waist, and in the moonlight, it was difficult to tell whether he was a gnome or a dwarf. His head was rather large on his short body, but he was hideous to boot.

"See Dak," the dwarf scolded. "I told you we should have left the blindfold on."

Dak grunted, and my attention went to him. A cry died in my throat. He was an ogre, albeit a stunted one, for I'd heard rumor that they were big beasts, as tall as trees in the forest. Or perhaps those tales were lies. He was bald with skin the color of gray stones, covered in wrinkles and sunspots. He had an upturned nose, rather dull looking eyes and thick fingers. He stood a head taller than me and a foul scent emanated from him. I shuddered to think that I'd been on his back, being bumped along while he carried me with those thick hands. At least he hadn't tried to grope me, and yet still, fear made me sag in my bonds.

He scratched his head. "Eh, should we do it here?"

"Of course," the dwarf—Teague—grumbled. "Here is the best place. Get the stones, I need to sharpen my knife."

My eyes bulged as the ogre pulled a sack of stones off his belt and adjusted his loin cloth, inadvertently showing me an unwanted view of his hairy testicles.

I blanched and my throat constricted.

Teague walked closer. "Now girly, if we take out the gag you must promise not to scream. There are beasts in the wood who would like to eat you."

I nodded frantically as my spit threatened to choke me.

The dwarf held out his hand to the ogre. "I'll do the stones. Take off her gag."

Dak moved toward me, tilted my head back and yanked out the gag. Instantly I leaned over as far as my bonds would let me, choking and spiting as vomit poured out of my mouth and splashed around my feet. Now my throat was raw, and I was desperate for something, anything to drink. What I wouldn't give for more spiced wine to put me out of my misery.

"Stop," I begged, my words coming out hoarse. "You don't have to sacrifice me. Just...tell me what you want."

"She speaks," Teague giggled as he lay out stones in a circle around me.

My eyes went wide and hysteria rose. An old chant came to mind, a chant I wasn't supposed to know.

A circle of stones
A circle of bones

The blood of a maid
Without seed of her mate
Use the blood of one never wed
Make your wish, call forth the dead

Before I could say anything more, there came a howl, long and high. A wolf hunting at night, even though it was the eve of the first day of Yule, and the wolves should be gone. Yule heralded the rebirth of the sun and the last half of winter as we looked forward to spring. Ironically for me, the howl of the wolf suggested a darkness which did not exist on such a night.

The dwarf's fingers twitched, and a stone dropped out of his fist. Straightening, he glanced uneasily at the forest, scratched his neck and inched closer to the ogre.

"Dak," he whispered, "do you have the knife? We should hurry."

"It's just a wolf." Dak shrugged as he pulled a curved knife from his belt and held the ornament handle out to Teague. "I can rip a wolf apart with my bare hands."

"No, you fool," the dwarf snapped, "it means we were followed, and he might try to save her."

Save her. Save me? I straightened at the thought and tried to create enough moisture in my mouth for a scream, but my voice came out raspy. "Help!" I coughed out, no louder than a whisper. "Help me."

"I told you not to scream," Teague dropped the last stone and snatched the knife from Dak's oversized hand. "Now you'll be sorry."

I hadn't screamed, but there was no point in explaining. The dwarf was about to slit my throat, and I pressed my body against the tree trunk as though it would save me.

It didn't. Instead, the bushes split in half and a wolf leaped out, hair as black as night and eyes red as blood. It bounded toward the dwarf, teeth bared, and as it did an axe hurled out of the wood and sank into the ogre's skull. The beast fell, plopping on its back into the underbrush.

If my voice were not powerless and raw, I would have screamed at the sheer horror of it, and yet my heart beat faster as I wondered whether I was being saved or captured by another monster of the wildwood. I twisted in my bonds, and a man walked out of the wood into the moonlight.

He was a large man, taller than myself with a thick torso, great arms and legs bulging with muscles. I gasped in surprise even though it sent a surge of pain through my throat. The hulking man strode closer to me, pulling a knife from his belt. The moonlight shone over his face, displaying it clearly to me, the set jaw, the clean-shaven beard, and those eyes, dark green, just like the wildwood, that gazed at me with a smoldering ferocity. Despite my predicament, my body went warm, and I opened my mouth in astonishment.

"Wilhelm?" I rasped.

6

WILHELM THE WOODCUTTER'S green eyes drifted away from mine just long enough to survey the fallen ogre and dwarf.

"On guard," he called to the wolf, his deep voice low and melodious.

A shiver went up my spine, not of fear, but of relief and gratitude. I'd never suspected Wilhelm would come to my rescue in the middle of the night, nor did I know he had a pet wolf. My eyes studied his face, and a blush tinged my cheeks. I'd been sweet on the woodcutter for a while, but I assumed he had his own life. After Mabon, after I'd fallen from grace in the eyes of the village, I assumed he continued to help me only because he felt sorry for me. But now?

"Talia. Did they hurt you?" he asked, a growl in his tone as he bent to cut the rope from around my feet.

"No," I whispered, my eyes going to his rich blond hair and wide shoulders.

Standing, he side-stepped the pile of vomit—I

blushed again, this time with embarrassment and shame
—and he cut the rope from around the tree. I sagged
with relief at the freedom and tried to step away from
the tree, but my feet were numb and I staggered. Before
I could fall, Wilhelm's warm hand clamped around my
forearm.

"Here, let me help you," he said, putting one arm
around my waist to steady me. My head bumped up
against his shoulder and I leaned into his unintentional
embrace while he cut the rope from around my wrists.
The untended proximity was distracting, for he smelled
like spruce and fir, a clean scent that surrounded him
unlike whatever pungent odors—fears, sweat and wine
—which were emanating from my body.

I hissed as he freed my hands, distracting me from
my unbidden thoughts. The coarse rope had cut into my
skin. Numbness and fright ebbed away, leaving only
exhaustion, pain and a sharp relief that Wilhelm had
found me.

"Lean on me," Wilhelm instructed, one arm still
circling my waist while the other tucked away his knife.
"You might find it hard to walk for a while."

"How did you find me?" I asked, more than content
to lean into his strength.

A twig snapped, and the black wolf trotted toward
the sound, then sat on its haunches, turning its red eyes
on Wilhelm for instructions.

"I am sorry it took so long. It was Rex here," he
jerked his chin toward the wolf, "who alerted me that
something was wrong."

I glanced at the wolf, knowing I should be afraid of

the hulking beast, but I owed it my life. "Thank you," I said as a wave of exhaustion came over me.

As though he could read my mind, Wilhelm scooped me up in his arms, allowing me to rest my head against his broad chest. My cheeks went hot when I felt the hard, ridged muscles beneath his shirt.

"Come, I will take you to my home," Wilhelm said, "and guard you until sunrise. Your abductors might come again when they realized they failed."

I blinked against the sleep that threatened to consume me, despite my late afternoon nap. "There were only two of them and they are dead," I protested.

"I will explain in the morning, Talia," Wilhelm murmured. "I think I know what's happening to you. And I believe I can help."

I wanted to snort with laughter as Wilhelm carried me through the forest. How could he know? Even I didn't know why the babies died, while life evaporated from my fingertips instead of the hale and happiness that should have happened. Grandma said I had the gift, and yet on the night of Mabon, everything had changed. Death came out of me instead of life. And then the creatures of the forest choose to kidnap me. Why? Suddenly the loss of my magic and my kidnapping did not seem like a coincidence.

7

THE CRACKLE of flames licking up firewood woke me in the morning. I opened my eyes, taking in the unfamiliar room and the cool light that streamed in from the window. My mind was clear, sharp with clarity, and I realized for the first time in a long time, I hadn't drunk myself to sleep. I lay on my back, a blanket pulled up to my chin. My ankles throbbed, as did my wrists. When I glanced at the rope welts on them, last night came flooding back with hints of panic, embarrassment and then relief.

I was at Wilhelm's house, in his room, in his bed! The door to the room was ajar, and it was silent out there. I recalled that he'd taken some blankets and created a pallet on the floor in front of the fire, assuring me he was used to sleeping with only a bedroll. Still, knowing I'd stayed at his home sent shivers of desire up my spine. If only the villagers knew I'd spent the night at an unwed man's house, I would be further shamed for allowing myself to be taken advantage of. Rules. There were so many rules in the village. In a short space of time, I'd gone from a well-known healer to nothing more than a drunk. Perhaps they would add whore to the list.

What the villagers thought did not matter though. Not anymore. Shaking myself out of my thoughts, I stretched my sore limbs and rose. There was a cup of water by the bedside, and I took a long draught. After last night's events, it seemed I could not drink enough to quench my thirst. My black hair hung in wild curls past my shoulders, still tangled from the chaos of last night. Using my fingers, I detangled them as best I could then twisted my hair back.

Some women in the village wore hats on their heads, so as not to distract men with the shine of their hair. My wild curls were unmanageable, and I either left them to hang loose or wore a braid to be more demure. But at Wilhelm's house, I was unsure what my behavior should be. More like the women in the village? Although it was hopeless that he should want me as a lover. We were of a similar age, and a man who wanted a wife had one by now.

Perhaps—despite all his strength and muscle—he was in love with someone else. Someone unattainable. Frustrated at the thought, I crept out of the bedroom into the main room. It was dark when we'd returned, and I'd fallen asleep quickly, thankful to be safe and exhausted by the events of the evening. Now, I had a chance to study Wilhelm's home. Most cottages were one room—which helped keep the warmth during the winter—but his was larger.

The fireplace took up one wall, lined from floor to

ceiling with stones like a room out of an ancient castle. The opening for the fire was set a few feet off the ground and large enough for a child to crawl inside—if they could reach it. It was at the perfect height for cooking without bending over too far. Wilhelm's pallet lay before the fire—although he was not lying on it— and there was wood stacked up on either side, drying. A warm glow came from those stones and I marveled at the warmth and comfort of the woodcutter's home.

A round wood table sat in the middle of the room with a husk of bread, a jar of water or perhaps wine, a knife, a few plates and cups on it. But my eyes were drawn to the shelves beside the solid oak door, for on it were Wilhelm's weapons. A knife, his axe—that I hadn't recalled him retrieving the evening before—a quiver of black-feathered arrows and a bow. He was a hunter as well as a woodcutter as was apparent from the skins hanging from the rafters on one side of the room. On the other side of the room hung vegetables and dried meats, a collection of stores for the winter. Past the hanging food was a basin and a window.

Wilhelm stood before the window, washing his face and hands. His shirt was off, draped over one shoulder, and I paused, my eyes inexplicably drawn to the lines of muscle on his back and arms. The way his pants slung low on his hips. A sigh escaped my lips.

The noise made him turn. "Talia," Wilhelm wiped his hands and tugged on his shirt, his mouth open in a yawn as he did so. "Did you rest well?"

A smile touched my lips and my breath caught in my throat as I met his forest-green gaze. An unruly curl tumbled across my forehead, and I swept it back. "I did, although taking your bed is a poor thanks for what you did for me last night."

I meant my words to bring a smile, but instead his expression turned serious, as though he were working up the courage to tell me something awful. Suddenly fear beat a pitter-patter in my heart and my attempt at light-heartedness faded like the sun on a stormy day. I bit my lower lip and twisted my fingers together. Was he worried about his reputation?

"Is something wrong?"

Wilhelm sighed and opened the cupboard, taking out a slab of cheese and a knife. "I would speak openly with you, Mistress Talia," he moved toward the table, although his eyes held mine the entire time. He placed the cheese on the cutting board and sliced great slabs of bread, placing each on a plate which he set before the fire.

I twisted my wild curls through my fingers in discomfort as I watched the cheese melt in front of the flame. I was an inconvenience. I should leave before my situation grew even more uncomfortable.

When the cheese was melted, Wilhelm returned the plates to the table and took a seat. "Will you sit with me?" He gestured to the chair opposite him.

I bit my lip as I sat, my heart beating in my chest like a child in trouble. Concern rode me, even though the scent of cheese and bread made my stomach growl with hunger. This was much better food than the mushy gruel I served myself each morning.

Wilhelm poured two cups of water and sat one before me. "I hope my words will not frighten you."

I was relieved to see there was a gentleness in his

eyes, a kindness there, but no pity. Maybe I'd misread him.

I took a bite of bread and cheese, and warmth swept through me, restoring my courage. "I will listen, please, go on. Last night you claimed that you know what happened to me."

"I believe I do," he agreed, ducking his chin.

He rested his calloused hands on the table. Tempting. I wanted to reach over and grip those powerful hands with my own, full well knowing their warmth would make me feel safe and secure. Instead, I forced myself to keep eating.

"You know me as Wilhelm the Woodcutter," he began. "Which is true. I do live in the village, but I spend my time between here and the enchanted wildwood. You know as well as I do that the Dark Queen ruled the wildwood, requiring sacrifices to fuel her magic in exchange for protection. Until the night of Mabon."

Night of Mabon. A wail shot through my memory at his words, and once again I was back at the manor house, the scent of blood and bile thick in the air, and the child, slick with its mother's blood lying limp in my hands. Tears glistened at my eyes as I blinked away the memory. I tried to wipe my tears away without Wilhelm noticing, but his dark eyes were gazing at me, an unreadable expression on his face.

One of his big hands came up, as though he would wipe away my tears, and then he reddened and dropped his hand back down on the table. He cleared his throat, and a moment of uncomfortableness hung in the air, unsaid words as thick as grief. I wanted to tell him to continue his tale, but the words stuck in my throat. I dropped my eyes back down to the table.

"In one of the villages to the east of us," Wilhelm continued, "a storm of magic destroyed the temple of the Sister of the Light. There was one survivor with strong magic. She ventured into the enchanted wildwood and defeated the Dark Queen."

I gasped at his words. Defeated the Dark Queen? How was that possible? There was no one alive with magic stronger than the Dark Queen's, and if there was, what did that mean for us? As Wilhelm's words sank in, other thoughts rose. Whatever gift I had, whatever it was called, had fled the night of Mabon. Was it because. . .

"Everything has changed now that the new Queen of the Wildwood is in power."

Questions flitted through my head and burst out of my mouth. "How do you know these things? Will the new queen uphold the old ways and protect us from the forest, like the Dark Queen did? Is she to be trusted?"

Those dark green eyes studied me, and there was a sadness behind them. His shoulders slumped, slightly. "I used to walk the forest during the days when the Dark Queen ruled. I met one of her knights, Sir Aelbrin. He told me stories about the wildwood, including the downfall of the Dark Queen and the rise of the new Queen of the Wildwood. It's also where I found Rex, ensnared in a trap for disobeying the Dark Queen's demands. I set him free and now he follows me. But walking the wood isn't without its peril. Aelbrin told me that the new Queen of the Wildwood hopes to make amends for the Dark Queen, to make things better, easier for the village folk. She has a good heart, but she is young and unused to the wildwood. Her power is strong, but the dark creatures of the forest are vast and pit their power against hers. More than anything, the darkness wants to escape out of the wood into our world. The new queen hasn't been strong enough to hold all of them back, and magic has leaked out, changing things. I believe the change has affected you, the magic which flowed in your blood has gone, leaving only death. Perhaps if you speak with the Queen of the Wildwood, she can help you."

My heart dropped at his words. The Queen of the Wildwood was young and did not know what she was doing. If she couldn't keep the dark creatures from leaving the wildwood, how could she help me? Nothing but death flowed from my fingers.

I dropped his gaze and twisted my hands together in my lap, suddenly feeling sorry for myself again. My lower lip trembled as I considered my options. Being a healer was my life, my only role to play in the village. Without it, I was nothing but a drunk, but that wasn't who I wanted to be. I wanted, well, I'd been too afraid to consider what I wanted. No need to displease the goddesses. I was content; I had everything I needed. *Had.* It was ripped asunder now, and what was left? I studied my fingers, the broken nails, the threadbare garb I wore. I'd meant to buy a new winter dress, but after Mabon the money had run out and no one wanted to barter with me. I was cursed.

I lifted my chin as a flare of defiance went through me and glanced up at Wilhelm. He waited patiently, although his fingers lightly tapped the wood of the table, as though he were listening to the beat of a drum, somewhere far away.

Jealously spread like an open wound through my body, and my words rang with bitterness when they came out of my mouth. "Wilhelm, I thank you. Truly I do. I don't know what I would have done if you hadn't found me last night. But…it's the first day of Yule. You should celebrate with the village. It's cold outside, too cold for a journey into the wood. Besides, I can take care of myself."

The light in his eyes darkened a bit, and he opened his mouth to protest. I held up a finger to stop him. "Please," I whispered. "What happens to me is not your concern. I will return home and prepare for Yule."

8

WILHELM STOOD AS I ROSE. A pained expression crossed his handsome face. "Talia…" He faltered, his deep voice husky with…what? Remorse?

The way my name rolled off his tongue made my heartbeat quicken. I could listen to him whisper my name over and over again, shivering at the delightful sensation it created. Inwardly, I cursed at my folly.

"Your home," he stammered. "I was going to tell you. It's been…The creatures of the wood…They burned it down."

I stared, rigid with horror. My jaw dropped and my eyes went wide. The breath stole out of my body and then returned as a rising sense of panic came over me. My home. Burned? It could not be! Gathering my skirts in my hand, I bolted out the door.

Icy air kissed my face, but I ignored the wind that tugged at my dress like fingers determined to drag me back to warmth. Lazy snow twirled in the wind before landing on the barren ground. Snow on the first day of Yule was a good omen, but I couldn't breathe as I ran.

My grandfather had built the house for my Grandma. He'd worked for the king in the mountains, earned a fair wage, and traveled out to the village to start a new life. My Grandma captured his eye during the celebration of spring, and he built the house just for her. It was where they'd spent their happiest days. My mother had grown up there, and I'd inherited it after Grandma passed.

When I reached my home, the structure was still intact, but charred, leaving nothing but smoking remains. Everything was gone, destroyed in the fire, and anything I found would smell of smoke and ash. So many memories destroyed in one night.

My knees buckled, and I sank to the ground, tears blurring my vision. My life had turned into one stroke of bad luck after the other. In one cursed night, I'd become a beggar. I wouldn't survive through the rest of the cold winter. Dreams of warmth, a husband, and my own fat babies rose and dispersed like smoke in the wind. I clasped my hands to my lips, and a sob shook my shoulders.

I wept until I had no tears left to cry. Wiping my grubby face with the back of my hands, I stayed on my knees, gazing at my lost home. Grandma taught me never to give in, never give up when grief hit me the hardest. Her lessons were the reason I went on, long after both her and Mother had passed through the doors of death. Now it was time for me to stand up for myself and determine my fate, my future. Yet, it seemed so hard, sitting there, with nothing but the clothes on my back. I sniffed. My eyes drifted to the wildwood where gnarled branches shut out the light, leaving it looking more sinister than ever in the daylight.

Something rustled behind me and I whirled, surprised to see it was Wilhelm, standing a few paces away. His face turned red as he met my eyes, but he looked prepared for travel, with a bundle on his back, a cloak over his shoulders, and a hat—one I'd knitted for him—over his sandy blond hair. If anything, he looked even more handsome. Despite my grief, I wanted to lean into him and feel his strong arms around me, reassuring me.

"I'm sorry, Talia." His forest-green eyes were imploring. "I'm sorry I could not stop them."

Numbly, I shook my head. "It wasn't your fault," I offered, making no attempt to rise to my feet. My gaze was pulled back to the forest. "Why me?"

"If I had to guess, it's because the dark creatures sense your magic," Wilhelm suggested. "I'm not sure how it all works, but I believe magic can be released when someone passes, some kind of transference. I think the creatures of the wood seek to capture your magic and use it against the new Queen of the Wildwood."

I frowned, considering Wilhelm's words. Suppose I were to take him up on his offer and meet this queen? I had a few choice words to say to her for ruining my life, no matter how inadvertent it had been. Why couldn't she let the old ways stand? Why did she have to defeat the Dark Queen?

"Talia?" Wilhelm spoke my name like I was some rare treasure. "Will you let me help you?"

Grief gave way to frustration. My head hurt and I desperately wanted a sip of spiced wine to take me away from the painful moment. But I had nothing left to lose, so I stood and flattened down my wrinkled skirts, well aware I must look a frightful sight.

"Why?" I breathed. "Why do you want to help me?"

He stood a step forward, tentative at first, then growing bold he continued until he stood only a breath away from me. His proximity forced me to look up into his wide-set face where his eyes misted over. One of his hands reached out and his fingers brushed my arm. Even though I wore long sleeves, a shiver of desire went up my spine and resistance melted away like fog under the heat of the sun. My breath caught in my throat at the look he gave me, and for just a moment, his gaze flickered to my lips. His fingers closed around my arm, gentle, yet strong.

When he spoke, the heat of his breath warmed my lips. "Because I care, Talia. I've always cared, and it grieves me to see you so unhappy. I would see you smile again, hear you laugh and dance, carefree, with no worries."

My heart turned over in my chest and tears sprang to my eyes. His words touched my soul with something more powerful, more precious than the sensation spiced wine provided. It gave me hope. My hand closed around his arm, holding on to him so he would save me again. Save me from turning into a beggar, a drunk or worse. I held on, breathing in his masculine scent while the snowflakes drifted around us.

"I did not know you felt this way," I whispered, unable to make my voice any louder. "I..." my words drifted away, for I was unsure what to say or how to explain my own feelings. Instead I settled for this. "Wilhelm, I accept your help."

9

WEARING A BORROWED CLOAK, I followed Wilhelm into the enchanted wildwood. The light snow could not penetrate the thick tree boughs, and dead leaves and twigs crunched underfoot. Thoughtful as ever, Wilhelm had brought the rest of my breakfast, and I nibbled the slice of bread, leaving a trail of crumbs behind me. A green haze hung over the forest, filtering out daylight. I jumped at every creak of the trees and rustle in the underbrush. My imagination was vivid with thoughts of dark creatures, hiding in the foliage, watching us.

At first, Rex trotted along with us, before disappearing into the thick woods. Wilhelm followed an invisible trail and within an hour I was hopelessly lost. I glanced up at his broad shoulders now and again, when I wasn't watching the path, trying to keep my feet. Even though it was winter, there was much for me to slip, slide or trip over.

"How long will it take?" I asked, my words falling to the floor of the forest.

There was a sense of oppression in the air making me want to run. Run far away before I was devoured.

"The realm of the queen is three days from here," Wilhelm admitted. He paused, glancing over his shoulder, his eyes studying my face. "Will you be okay?"

I nodded, twisting my cold fingers into the folds of my cloak. My life was ruined. Even though I should feel devastated, walking through the frightful wood with a man I had feelings for did not seem so bad after all.

We walked in silence until my legs ached, and a dullness in my stomach told me I was hungry. Despite the cool air, a bead of sweat trickled down my forehead. With my head down, I almost walked into Wilhelm's back. He'd stopped and stiffened. Noticing me beside him, he wrapped an arm around my waist and drew me to his side.

"What is it?" I tilted my head to look up at him.

He moved his mouth closer to my ear, his breath warm as he whispered back. "I think we are being followed."

Dread thudded in my chest, and memories of the ogre flashed in front of me. As if sensing my fear, Wilhelm squeezed me tighter against him. "Don't worry Talia, I will protect you."

A smile came to my lips, yet fear squeezed my heart in its foul grip. "I just don't want any harm to come to you."

What would I do if he got hurt and left me in the forest alone, with a wounded man to care for? Especially when my healing power was gone. It was selfish of me, but the smoldering look in Wilhelm's eyes told me I'd said something right. He leaned closer, his lips hovering close to my neck, drinking in my scent. The moment broke as he let go of me, and his hand went to his belt.

Instead of taking off his pants and taking me right then and there like I'd secretly hoped, he handed me a knife, handle first. "I'd feel better though, if you had this. In case anything happens."

A blade instead of a kiss? I grasped the handle firmly in my hand. "Thank you," I said, trying to keep the edge of disappointment out of my voice. All the same, I trembled, aware of what the knife meant.

"Stay close," he whispered.

We crept forward again, my footsteps stirring up the sleeping leaves and dead underbrush in the wood. In the distance I heard a low moan. Was it the wind? Or a spirit? The undead spirits of the forest should be asleep after the festival of Samhain, but no, it came again. My hand trembled and then came a thrashing in the underbrush. Something big was headed toward us, running.

"Come Talia," Wilhelm ordered, his hand closing around mine, pulling me forward as he broke into a run.

The thrashing grew louder, and then a growl, a sharp cry, and a bark. We ran as though the devils were at our heels until I tripped over a root and went flying. My hand ripped out of Wilhelm's, and my body hit the ground with a thump, knocking the breath out of me. I lay on my belly, gasping for air even as I struggled for my footing.

A roar split the air, and a monstrous beast surged out of the underbrush. I rolled onto my back and sat up as it leaped over me, a blur of black fur and curved claws. Out of the corner of my eye, Wilhelm spun and hurled his axe at the creature.

The axe sank into flesh and bone with a resounding crack. With a whimper, the monstrous beast lay still. I staggered to my feet, frozen in shock as I stared at the thing. It was the size of Wilhelm, with two long legs like a human and what looked like arms, yet it had run on them like a four-legged creature. Thick clumps of mattered black hair covered its body, and I gasped. What I'd first assumed was a wolf was actually a grotesque mix of human and wolf. Eyes wide with horror I reached out for the tree trunk to steady myself, but Wilhelm was already on his feet. He snatched the axe out of the creature and leaped over the prone body to me.

"Talia," he murmured, "we have to go. Can you run?"

I nodded in shock, for words refused to escape my throat. Unsaid questions rose in my mind, but my feet gave in to panic. Wilhelm took my hand again and dragged me onward while his bloody axe dripped from his other hand.

The forest shook again and there came another combination of a bark, a growl and then a cry. Another monster leaped out of the road, this time in our path, and knocked us down. I sprawled on my hands and knees, a scream ripping out of my throat in terror for my life. But the beast wasn't on me, it was on top of Wilhelm, curved fangs snapping as it growled and golden eyes blazing. It would rip his throat out if I did not stop it.

Without thinking, I snatched up the dagger and drove it into the creature's throat. It gave a final growl, then rolled off Wilhelm. He buried his axe into its fur as he stood, ensuring the creature was dead.

When he faced me there was sweat on his forehead and blood on his shoulder. "Thank you." He reached for my hand. "I hear Rex out there fighting, but more will come if we don't keep going."

My lips trembled as I eyed him, surprised at his calm composure. "Where are we going?"

After all, we were in the enchanted wildwood, nowhere was safe for us. I was tempted to tell him we should give up this quest and return home. The wood was too perilous for us.

"There are safe places," Wilhelm assured me. "Bound by light magic throughout the wood. There's one not far from us, come on."

I grasped his hand as if my life depended on it, and we fled through the forest while the creatures howled around us. Two more dashed into our path, but Wilhelm was ready with his axe. Though they knocked us down each time, we escaped with only minor scratches and bruises.

It wasn't until darkness threatened to envelop us that Wilhelm pointed at an odd structure.

1 O

THERE WAS A HOLLOWED opening in the middle of two trees which grew together, as though they'd found their roots intertwined and they could not do without each other. Green ivy covered what looked like the tree trunk, but Wilhelm walked up to it and pulled it open. I lifted a grimy hand in surprise and stared. A hidden cottage inside the wildwood.

Wilhelm motioned for me to follow him, and we ducked inside, shutting out the forest behind us.

"What is this place?" I breathed as Wilhelm lit candles.

It was surprisingly warm inside, and my shivers from fright and the winter air melted away.

"When the Dark Queen ruled the wildwood, she had knights who did her bidding. They ensured that the villages surrounding the wildwood performed the rituals that gave the queen her magic. As the knights traveled through the forest, they needed places to stay with food, blankets, weapons and spare clothes, if needed. They are called safe houses, some are trees, others are caves, but they exist throughout the wood."

"It's comforting," I admitted. "I did not expect a place like this in the hostile wood."

The candles lit up the inside of the tree. Green moss curled up the sides of the trunks, shooting up toward the sky before tapering off into darkness. The room I stood in was just that, a room with a pile of furs in one corner and a stack of what looked like clothes and supplies in another. It was clear that one came here just to huddle down, eat and sleep. There wasn't much room for two people, and I blushed at the thought of being so close to Wilhelm for the night.

A lantern hung from a study branch near the ceiling. Standing on his toes, Wilhelm lit it, and the room instantly brightened enough to allow me to see his face clearly. His face was drawn and pale from our dash through the forest. In an attempt to be helpful, I made for the supplies, pulling out a fresh shirt and searching for water.

"Sit, Wilhelm." Now it was my turn to take care of him. "You look tried. We can rest here tonight."

Wilhelm staggered as he made his way to the pile of furs.

I drew in a sharp breath, my eyes suddenly noticing the caked blood on his shoulder. "Wilhelm," I cried, fear gnawing at me.

He lifted a hand to his neck as he tugged at the shirt. "It bit me. . ."

"Why didn't you tell me sooner?" I reached for a waterskin and a bundle of bandages.

"I did not know," he gasped. "Talia, it's a Lycan bite. They are poisoned. I could turn."

"No," I whispered. "Lie still, let me help."

He lay on his back as I pulled away his shirt, cleaned the blood and discovered the wound. Sure enough, there was a three-inch-long bite on his neck. It was a wonder it had pierced only soft skin. All the same, a faint odor came from it as I washed it and bandaged it.

"Can you eat?" I asked when I was done.

He merely shook his head and held out his hand to me. "Sit with me, beautiful Talia. Talk to me."

His hand was warm in mine, almost clammy, and I realized he would find himself lost in a fever dream soon. There was nothing I could do to help him. Outside was the wood and through our flight I'd seen no herbs, nothing to starve off a fever. What would I do if he became too sick to go on? What would I do without Wilhelm? I blinked back tears as I realized the truth of what I felt. A surge of love burst out of me, except it had been there all along, blossoming silently while I went about my days, assuming I'd be alone for the rest of my life. Wilhelm had been in front of me the entire time.

"Wilhelm," I lifted his hand and kissed it gently. "You walk the wood, and you are brave enough to risk your life for me. But it's just you and I. If this is indeed poison, we need the Queen of the Wildwood to help us."

"When the bite takes over, I have one, maybe two days," he murmured, his eyes closing. "Talia, when morning comes you must go on. You have the gift, and the Queen of the Wildwood can still help you with your magic. I only wish that I'd been honest with you, that we had more time before I turn into a monster."

"No," I shook my head. "I won't let you turn into a monster, Wilhelm. You may walk this wood, but you're not one of them. You are good and kind and generous. You save lives, not destroy them."

He squeezed my hand. "Regardless, you must go before I turn mad. My mind will not be my own and I could not live with myself should I harm you."

Tears filled my eyes, and even though I wanted to sob, I simply nodded my head. "I will save you, Wilhelm," I vowed. "You saved me. Life would not be worth it without you."

"I've always loved the sound of your voice, Talia. You used to sing, will you sing for me?"

"Of course, my love," I replied even though grief sat heavy on my chest.

All this time wasted. All this time my love was right beside me, and I'd never had the courage to speak up, to let him know. I'd played along, waiting for him to make a move, to say something, when I could have admitted how besotted I was by him.

Tears brimmed and trailed down my cheeks, but I opened my mouth and sang him to sleep.

I DID NOT SLEEP that night. Instead, I tried to make Wilhelm as comfortable as possible. I changed out of my dress into a shirt and pants, then stacked food and water beside him. Leaving the lantern lit, I blew out the candles, one by one, packed a sack and squared my shoulders.

Although I did not know where I was going, I hoped the Queen of the Wildwood would find me. And Rex might lead me to her, if he knew the way. She was my only hope now, and not for myself. Nay, I did not care what happened to me. My fingers trembled as I opened the door. I had to find her in time to return with the remedy to heal Wilhelm.

At first light I left the hut, a naked blade held tightly in one of my fists. I kept a bundle slung over one shoulder and closed the door behind me, whispering prayers to the goddess that I would return in time.

Rex sat on his haunches, eyeing the door, red eyes gleaming at me. Swallowing my terror, I stood in front of him, reminding myself he had saved my life. "I don't know if you can understand me. But I'm desperate. I need to find the Queen of the Wildwood, she must know a remedy to heal Wilhelm from the Lycan's bite."

Rex cocked his large head, and for a moment all I saw was a flash of teeth which could rip my body to shreds. A shudder went down my spine, but I stood firm. My bravery wasn't for me, it was for Wilhelm.

As though he sensed my determination, Rex stood and set off through the forest, pausing shortly to glance over his shoulder. I moved after him, and we traveled quickly and silently through the winter-stricken forest.

As we walked, my thoughts were with Wilhelm. Was he breathing easier? Was he in pain? Did he find the food and water I left him? Oh, how could I leave him alone in his misery?

The wildwood lay silent that day, the second day of Yule. Celebration, not hunting and killing, should be the focus. Goddess forgive me, when this was over I would stop drinking, I would own up to my responsibilities as a healer and move past the death that plagued me.

When evening came, Rex led me to the mouth of a yawning cave and settled at the entrance of it. Once again I found a pallet with furs and a few other items, including a flute. Someone else had been here recently. I tried to sleep but nightmares plagued me. Wilhelm bleeding out. Fire burning down the village. A hideous ogre chasing me through the forest.

I woke before dawn. As if sensing my mood, Rex rose and padded up to me, his claws making a clinking sound against the cool stone floor of the cave.

"I'm worried about Wilhelm," I told Rex. "I know the

woods are dangerous at night, but I can't let him die. I must go on."

I dressed quickly while Rex waited by the cave entrance, and then we set off. It was pre-dawn and the trees were just undistinguishable shapes.

We walked until the wood turned silvery under the light of the sun, hidden somewhere far above those great shady boughs. It was warm yet still oddly silent. I suspected we must be in the domain of the Queen of the Wildwood.

Eventually we walked up a hill. Swelling at the very top in an open glade was a massive tree. It was larger than any of the trees I'd ever seen in the forest, its trunk as thick around as ten men standing side by side, while branches shot out from every direction, some crawling along the ground, others lifting up their branches to the sky. Its tree bark was covered in a patchwork of brown, white and black, as though at some point it had been burned, scorched, and new white wood grew from its ruins, turning brown as it healed, creating new life.

A strange magic ebbed from it, powerful and potent. I dropped to my knees, breathless. It shimmered all around me, in such a way it was almost visible. When I blinked, a filmy gloss, like fog, covered my eyes and then vanished before fully displaying itself.

I placed my bundle on the forest floor and the knife along with it like a sacrifice. I did not feel like I needed a weapon, and it seemed dishonorable to bring one into the circle of magic which emanated from the tree. With hands clasped in front of me, I studied the tree, wondering whether I should call out or recite a prayer.

Surely this was the court of the Queen of the Wildwood.

No sooner than the thought left my mind, a woman appeared as if brought by the wind, and stood near the trunk of the great tree, watching me. A red dress hugged her curves, and a green cloak was tied around her neck. Black hair tangled down her head, and her skin was a beautiful rich brown. But it was her dark eyes that held mine, studying me without a hint of emotion.

I squared my shoulders and forced words from my mouth. "Are you the Queen of the Wildwood?"

"I AM," she said. "And who are you? Why have you braved the wildwood to speak to me?"

There was an edge to her voice, a distinct unfriendliness. My heart sank. What if she declined to help me? Would she be more favorable if Wilhelm was with me?

"I am Talia, the healer of Moon Leaf." I tried to remain formal but then the words shattered from me. "I come to you on behalf of Wilhelm, the Woodcutter of Moon Leaf. He walks your woods. He has a kind heart, but he tried to help me and now he lies a day and a half's journey from here, dying from the bite of a Lycan. Please, I need a remedy to save him. Tell me what I must do!"

My words came out sharp and begging, but the Queen of the Wildwood did not change her stance. She only watched me with those odd eyes, listening yet not reacting. "Tell me, Talia. You are a healer, you know healing properties. I've heard of you and your village. Those you heal do not ail, and the babes whose birth you attend grow up hale and happy. Where is this gift now? Why come to me?"

Anger flared up at the mention of my gift. Forgetting formality, I rose from my knees and stood tall, chin jutting out and fingers curled into fists. Fye! She would not help me, would she? She was too high and mighty. She'd come here to defeat the Dark Queen and now she thought her magic was too precious to share. The words I'd originally wanted to say to her flew out of my mouth. "I *was* a healer," I stressed. "I did have the gift of health until the night of Mabon. Now only death flows from my fingers. Wilhelm thought I should come here to ask you to help find out where my magic went, why my gift is gone. Because you're the new Queen of the Wildwood, and things have changed since you became queen. But I don't care about my gift anymore, I just want to heal Wilhelm, before he turns into a monster!"

Something changed in the queen's eyes. Her gaze went to Rex who sat by my side, guarding me. My heart pounded in my throat as my anger evaporated. I was afraid of losing Wilhelm, afraid the queen wouldn't help me, and afraid of being left in the enchanted wildwood alone, where I might be captured again and sacrificed.

"And where does dear Wilhelm lie?" the Queen asked.

"A day and a half from here," I admitted, shoulders slumped. "He does not have enough time. Please..." I choked down a sob.

The Queen of the Wildwood walked closer to me, and this time concern was written across her face. "Talia, have no fear, I will help you."

The words sounded awkward coming from her

mouth, as though she were not used to being kind or having others look to her for help.

"I know what it is like to lose someone you love, and if you lose him in this forest, he will turn into a Lycan. I will help you, but you must know, magic is never fair. In exchange for life, there will be a cost."

My nostrils flared, and I wanted to ask more, and yet I grasped at the words she spoke. She would help me and I would accept, no matter the cost. "What must I do?" I breathed, my fists coming unclenched as relief seeped through my body.

But the Queen cocked her head and narrowed her eyes slightly. "As I said, I will help you, not Wilhelm," she repeated slowly. "Even from here I sense the curse that rests over you, a curse of death that I must lift. Once you are free, you may return and heal him."

My eyes widened. "I don't know how to heal him from the bite of a deadly creature." I held back the tears which pressed against my eyes. Was the Queen toying with me? Did she want to see me suffer?

"You do," the Queen said. "The magic has always been with you, that's why you have come to me, is it not? For I will reveal the hidden things. Now stay here while I gather my supplies."

She disappeared around the massive tree. I wiped my face with the back of my hand and took slow, steady breaths. She would help me, that's all I needed to know. But with each passing breath, Wilhelm could be turning. I needed to return to him. Quickly.

When she returned, the Queen held a small bag in her hands. She walked up to me, and close up, I saw her clearly. She could not have been much older than myself, but there was an intensity in her eyes, as if she had seen too much, had been through much. An apology rose to my lips. I'd judged her without knowing her tale. Perhaps there was a reason she had to defeat the Dark Queen.

I lifted a hand and touched her arm. "Thank you. I don't know you at all—we are but strangers—and yet you are willing to help me."

A light shone in her eyes, and the tension between us faded away. "It is rare that one thanks a queen," she admitted. "I did not intend to rule the wildwood, but the Dark Queen refused to honor my request. I discovered more about my magic than I could have imagined, and you remind me of myself." There was a bittersweet sadness behind her eyes. "I destroyed much before I discovered who I am, but I had help. So shall you."

The Queen of the Wildwood walked around me, tossing handfuls of salt and herbs in a circle around my feet. A light breeze carried the scent to my nostrils. My chest went tight for there was a weight on my shoulders, something dark and ugly binding the light and joy I used to carry. I closed my eyes and swayed against it while the Queen of the Wildwood chanted, words I did not understand. Her voice rose in a sing-song cadence.

The grip on my chest grew tighter while pain radiated out of my core. Pressure built in my head as though it was squeezed between two boards pressing harder and harder. I cried out, but the voice of the Queen rose higher, firmer, stronger, fighting against the darkness. I squeezed my eyes shut and planted my feet, but my knees buckled all the same and I went down, catching myself on my hands. I shook my head, in an attempt to wipe away the memories that rose like fingers to choke the breath out of my lungs.

Again I saw the dead babes, one with a cord wrapped around its neck, another covered in blood with eyes, dead and unseeing. The wailing of the mothers who were robbed of the precious gift of life cut through me like a freshly sharpened blade. I was there, back there in those dark rooms filled with piss and blood and death. So much death, when I was supposed to give life.

The pressure in my head intensified, and I choked as my breath whisked away. Agony streaked up and down my veins. Memories of grief and sorrow faded as pain took over until I could think of nothing else but ripping my soul to shreds. A scream ripped from my lips, and my hands clawed the air, fighting against the unseen. The voice of the Queen was my only beacon of hope in the violent storm within, and yet my hope faltered. What powers did she fight against? Would her magic be enough?

Without warning, the darkness snapped, the pain fled, the tightness in my chest vanished and the burden on my shoulders lifted. I sat back on my heels, wiping salty tears from my cheeks with the back of my hands. When I could see clearly again, the circle of salt and herbs around me was black and burnt. The Queen of the Wildwood knelt in front of me, her eyes anxious.

When I met her gaze, something dark flickered there, as though she'd taken the curse that haunted me and consumed it herself. Then she blinked, and the darkness faded.

"It's gone," I cried out, surprised both at the strength

of my voice and the clarity in my head. I hadn't noticed the dark cloud that hovered about me, but it was gone, taking with it the urge to sit in front of the fire, drinking and feeling sorry for myself.

I reached out to embrace the Queen as joy surged through me. She stepped back before I could touch her, but grateful words poured out of my mouth. "Thank you," I breathed, ensuring she heard those words. I would not be a thankless wretch.

She stood, a small smile playing around her lips. "The curse of death has been lifted, your magic should run pure. Return to the one you love and heal him. Now go, hurry, before daylight leaves."

I gathered my bundle and knife as I stood, but paused. "What is the cost? What do you ask of me?"

Her eyes went to the giant tree. "One day I might need help to drive back the darkness. The wood is wild, and creatures stir up trouble against me. If that day comes and I call, will you come?"

"Yes," I said, for there was nothing more to say. She'd given me more than I could repay.

"Then go. The wolf will keep you from harm on your journey back. May the blessings of Yule rest upon you."

Without another word, I turned and ran out of that magical place, back into the enchanted wildwood, determination surging in my chest.

13

WITH THE BEATING of a pure heart and the knowledge that the stain, that curse on my power had been wiped clean, I dashed through the forest with Rex at my side until I could run no longer. Then I walked, and for the first time, I saw the magic of the enchanted wildwood. No longer was it dark and frightening. Motes of light shone under flattened toadstools, and hope sparked beneath green moss. The domain of the Dark Queen had passed and something else was taking root in the forest, something new and pure, like what I had experienced in my heart. Hope.

Evil had fled, leaving freedom in its wake. Although the hard times might not be over, I had strength and determination to carry on, to go the distance, and with that knowledge I just needed the courage to heal again.

When I reached the tree with the hidden chamber, my footsteps slowed. My breath turned cold, and my fingers twitched on the latch. Wilhelm. Would he be himself? Or was I too late? A low moan met my ears as I pushed open the door.

The darkness of the hut sent a pitter-patter of fear down my spine. With shaking fingers, I left the door open to let in what little light it could and crept toward the pallet where the body of what was once Wilhelm the Woodcutter lay. A blanket was pulled over his form and he lay still, so still I wondered if he still drew breath.

And then it came, slowly at first, another long drawn-out moan. A shiver of fear shook my body. Or was it the howl of a wolf-creature?

Tears pricked my eyes. "Wilhelm." I knelt by his side, uncaring whether he had transformed into a monster. "Dear Wilhelm, I'm here now. I have the gift, I can heal you."

A slight chill went through me. What if... but no. I pushed doubtful thoughts away. The Queen of the Wildwood had taken the curse of death. When I touched Wilhelm, instead of dying he would live. Evil whispers tried to steal my confidence away, but I shut out those thoughts and reached for him.

Perhaps it was good I could not see him clearly in the darkness, for his head was clammy with sweat. He tried to move away from my touch, but he was too weak. He moaned again, a wretched sound that brought tears to my eyes. Placing my hands on either side of his face, I squeezed my eyes shut and searched within myself, within my very being for the light. The healer's touch I had inside me, the magic that made others healthy and hale.

A heat built in my core and with it came the light I had lost. At first it felt like the rushing of water and then like a basin overflowing, but it was pleasant. The magic tingled all the way down my body, flowing out of my hands into Wilhelm. As my magic surged, I had a vision of light filling a dark space, driving out all darkness and shadows which fled, shrieking to get away from the light. But the shadows were not fast enough. When the light touched them, they disappeared like a puff of smoke, leaving nothing but the light, blazing in all its glory.

Under me, Wilhelm shuddered and convulsed, first moaning, then growling until, finally, he lay still. My mouth went dry. Had I brought him back? I opened one eye and then both, my jaw dropping as I took in the room. Every candle was lit up as well as the lantern swinging from the branches above. Rex stood in the doorway, watching me. When our eyes met, he sat on his haunches, relieved he did not have to protect me from what might be within.

A hand squeezed mine, almost making me jump. When I turned, my eyes met Wilhelm's dark green ones. His hair was mattered and sweaty, but his eyes, although tired, were clear, grateful. He smiled at me. "I knew you'd return," he whispered. "I knew you'd find what was lost."

"Wilhelm," I whispered. Tears of relief rolled down my cheeks.

14

HE REACHED up to brush a tear off my cheek and I leaned into his touch, closing my eyes against the warmth of his hand.

"Talia," he breathed. "I feel your magic within, consuming me. The darkness has gone, the pain from the bite, the dreams of madness. I am bewitched, not by the wildwood, but by you."

My eyes came open at his words and a tingling sensation of desire began in my lower belly and then surged through me, sending goosebumps up my arms, although it was not cold. "Wilhelm." I trembled under his touch. "The words you say…"

He sat up, leaning closer until our foreheads almost touched. "Are not meant to frighten you, Talia. I've loved you for a long time but thought no one could bear my secret. Most are fearful of the wildwood but it calls to me. Perhaps it was meant to bring us together."

Love. There it was. The words I'd dreamed he'd say.

I melted under the intensity of his gaze. In response, I kissed his palm. "I always thought there was someone else."

"No one but you." Tossing away the sweaty blankets, he leaned back against the solid oak and pulled me onto his lap.

His shirt was open to the waist, and shivers of delight twisted through me. One of my hands went to his bare chest and the other around his neck. There was something magical in that moment. A power, stronger than the healer's touch, surged within me. Light and strength returned to Wilhelm's body, along with the need, the desire for me, and only me. An ache began between my legs, and a longing consumed my voice.

When Wilhelm unbuttoned my cloak and tossed it away, my body trembled with anticipation.

"I love you," I whispered, surprised at the surety of my words.

This was truth, pure and honest, almost too good to be true. Here I was, in his arms, after saving him. The fog between us had passed, leaving only strong clarity, a surety of love. Just as the festival of Yule symbolized rebirth, so had our love been reborn without secrets or strife or death.

"And I you," Wilhelm responded and then his lips were on mine.

Fire licked through my veins at the tantalizing passion of his kiss. His arm tightened around my waist, pulled me against his chest while fingers twisted through my hair. Something deep and carnal awoke within me, and I moaned. My lips parted as I leaned into the kiss, responding as his tongue thrust into my mouth. I pushed up against his body, desperate for more, aching for the skin on skin contact to bind us together.

He broke the kiss and pulled back, his voice both husky with need and breathless with passion. "Talia." Those eyes, those beautiful eyes were dark with desire. "I want you. All of you."

I nodded, unsure if I were capable of speech. The years of waiting fused into one urgent moment, and my fingers traced the hard muscle of his arms, down to his chest. I kissed his jaw, then his neck as I worked my way down. A strangled cry came from his throat. He touched my cheek, drawing my lips up to his again. This time he kissed me gently, while his fingers explored. His hands rubbed my arms while his lips kissed my neck and dipped lower, to the bare skin around the neck of my dress. Fingers tugged, pulling my dress until it came up, over my head. For one breathless moment my arms were pinned in place by the fabric.

Wilhelm paused. The flickering candlelight allowed him to see the shape of my body through my sheer shift. Slowly he let the dress fall free, pooling the floor while his eyes glazed over with need.

The look in his eyes was worshipful, and I took advantage of his pause to tug his shirt off his broad chest, gasping at the bulge in his pants. No sooner than I reached out to touch his chest, he grabbed me around the waist and spun me until I lay on my back on the pallet. Slowly he lowered himself between my legs, gazing at me all the while. My shift rode up to my waist, and heat tinged my cheeks as I realized the view he had of my naked body.

"You have nothing to be ashamed about, you are beautiful and perfect in every way," he murmured as he kissed my legs, moving slowly up my calf to my knee and then higher, holding my thighs achingly wide as he kissed and nibbled his way up.

I bucked underneath him, the heat in my body turning into an inferno under his caress. I wiggled under his touch, my back arched, shamelessly seeking more.

Fingers stroked my wetness, and a cry of pleasure burst from my lips. He spread my legs wider, and there a wicked glint in his eyes before he dipped his head. The flicker of his tongue caused a ragged cry to burst from my lips. My fingers dug into his shoulders as he teased me, licking gently, sucking, playing with me, bringing me so close to the height of my climax and then back down until I was practically screaming.

Finally he stopped, stepped out of his pants and lay by my side, so close I could hear his heart thudding. He buried his head in my neck and peppered me with kisses.

"Talia," he murmured. "Will you have me?"

"Always," I whispered back, rising to straddle him.

He tried to sit up, but I pressed one hand on his firm chest and kissed him hard. His manhood rubbed up against my bare bottom and, stripping off my shift, I hovered above him. He entered me in one swift thrust, his broad hands covering the bare skin of my hips.

"Closer," he gasped, pulling me down until we were face to face. He kissed me with a passion that stole my breath away as I rode him, over and over again.

One by one the candles went out. One for each sigh,

another for each kiss, and yet another for our love-making which lasted throughout the night. When at last, exhausted, we lay still. Wilhelm cradled me in his arms, and a buzz of contentment hummed through the enchanted wildwood.

15

MAGIC TWIRLED through the air as hand in hand, Wilhelm and I walked down the winding path to the town. Even before we arrived, I heard the merry shouts of children and the deeper laughs of adults. It was the fourth day of the festival of Yule, and there was nothing but merriment in the town, for young and old, rich and poor.

Wilhelm and I returned to his home, put on fresh clothes, and slept for one peaceful night without worrying about the monsters of the wildwood. The next morning before we crossed over into town, I dared glanced back at the enchanted wildwood one last time. I imagined the Queen of the Wildwood in her ongoing battle to drive back the darkness. I also understood the gift she'd given me, the curse she'd lifted, the life she'd returned to me. I could have been like her, doomed to wander the wildwood. But instead she let me return to my village, to redeem myself. When she called, it would not be hard to return and help her drive back the darkness.

A light squeeze made me look up at Wilhelm, and his forest green eyes gleamed at me, with hints of passion and lust dancing behind his eyes.

"Wilhelm," I scolded, "we are about to enter town."

He threw back his head and laughed. "I'm glad you are well, Talia."

Then he swept me into his arms and kissed me, and for the first time, I believed, truly believed, in the magic of Yule.

LORD OF THE CASTLE

The lord of darkness hides in his tower
Saving the land from dark monsters
Stay at a distance, he will protect you
Get too close, he will consume you

1

THE SOUND of a whip crackled through the air. Oxen bellowed in distress.

"Is that necessary?" I shouted at the man whipping the oxen. "They are stuck, perhaps gentler methods would help free them!"

I yanked my boot out of the mud, and it came loose with a soft sucking sound. I scowled. Marshy country and my unknown destination made me feel both grumpy and slightly ill. Everything I'd worked for in the kingdom had unraveled and now I was being escorted to the country town of Whispering Vine. A town rumored to be cursed to protect the exiled lord.

The tradesman scowled and his lip curled as he stared at me out of beady brown eyes. He'd been giving me lewd stares as soon as he realized I was a woman, dressed in the garb of a warrior. I was a shield-maiden stationed within the walls of the King's city. At least that had been my post until now. Banishment to Whispering Vine was my punishment. I jutted my chin out and returned his gaze. The man wouldn't give me trouble, and yet he still had underhanded ways of getting under my skin.

The air was dense and warm, and the wagon kept getting stuck in the soft layers of mud that covered the countryside. Clouds of thick white mist covered the landscape. Sweat trickled down my spine, but I refused to remove my mail, gauntlets and boots. My sword and knives hung heavy on my belt. I'd taken my helmet off and carried it tucked under my arm. My scant bundle of necessities was stowed in the wagon, but at this rate, I'd get to Whispering Vine faster if I left the tradesman by himself. Only, I didn't know the way.

The tradesman licked his lips and raised his whip again. Oxen sweat dripped off it, but the animals, used to his cruelty, bellowed again and strained. The wagon came loose with a creak, and we were off again.

"See, Mistress Mariel?" He pointed the whip at me. "My methods are effective. I don't tell you how to fight, and you don't tell me how to tame my beasts."

I lifted my chin and turned away. Fair enough.

My journey had begun with a handful of peasants following the tradesman as we wove our way from the King's city into the countryside. Some dropped off at the first town and more at the second. But it was I who continued onward, just the tradesman and I into the thick of the land toward the village that bordered the enchanted wildwood. I'd heard nightmarish tales about it, tales that turned a heart cold, but I assumed it was the way of countryfolk who were superstitious and kept unusual traditions. They believed the forest was alive, that animals could speak to them and magic was real.

The villagers were plain folk, peasants and simple-minded, and yet, their hard labor helped the kingdom flourish, therefore it was important to protect them. The exiled lord I'd been called upon to protect would live until the danger passed. I was good at following orders. Well. Except for my last diversion.

I recalled the hiss of the commander as he'd taken me by the arm, spittle flying as fury rolled out of his mouth. "How dare you take matters into your own hands and act directly against the orders of a superior. As punishment, you are hereby stripped of your rank and sentenced to serve a minor lord in a village to the north. He and his family have been exiled for they refuse to give the crown the respect it deserves. Each year a guard is sent to protect him from the terrors crawling out of the wood, for he is lame, and each year, the guard never returns. Your task is to kill the lord and make it look like an accident. Because you are a woman, you will not be suspected. Once he is dead, return here and you will be restored to your rank. Do you understand?"

"Understood. Captain." I spoke evenly, all the while rage boiled inside of me.

A message was sent via hawk, and two days later, I'd packed my belongings and joined the tradesman, headed north.

The wagon jolted to a stop, and the tradesman curled the whip under his sweaty arm and pointed to a rotting post which sagged beside a winding trail. "There you are, the road to Whispering Vine."

My fingers balled into fists of frustration. It was nothing more than a track leading uphill and then disappearing into a grove of trees. There was no sign of the village nor the castle I would stay at for my duration in the town. My predicament was hateful, and yet, I would do as asked to regain my position. I'd show the commander. He'd see that I could follow orders, and I'd return to the King's city.

The tradesman simpered at the tight expression I wore. "Ye din have to go down there if ye don't want to. You could come on with me. It will be a long night, but I'll make it to the next town and a comfortable inn." He winked suggestively.

"In your dreams," I muttered and snatched my bag from the wagon. "You're lucky I don't run you through with my sword."

"I could run you through with something else," he leered. "It would be more pleasant than that..." he pointed at the road.

Unfortunately, he was probably right. I had no qualms sharing a bed with a man and the tradesman wasn't bad looking, just arrogant and cruel. Poor oxen. I considered being rash, stealing the oxen from the tradesman and driving them to Whispering Vine. Nay, not even there, but onward, far into the world where no one commanded me.

But my resolve faded, and my training surged back. I would do what needed to be done without thought for myself. Slinging my bag over my shoulder, I turned to the road and marched uphill, as though I were back in the city with my regime, marching toward war. Although I'd never marched to war. Regardless, I did not know what to expect on the other side of the wood.

The tradesman's snigger echoed in my mind as I

followed the track uphill. The air was cooler, yet the stickiness remained, my clothing clinging to my damp skin. My chin-length, short black hair coiled around my face, and although I tucked loose strands behind one ear, it still stuck to my neck and made my skin itch.

Dark green trees arched overhead, tree trunks curved inward and branches stretched out to cover the track with shade. An odd welcome. I swallowed hard and eyed my surroundings. Did I walk through an enchanted glade? Was this the entrance to another realm? Stories whispered in my mind, impossible tales of those who'd found hidden portals and walked through them only to discover another land, another civilization, another species.

I had messed up. And given my commander a compelling reason to get rid of me. There weren't many shield-maidens, and after I completed my training with the Sisters of the Sword, I'd been stationed in the King's city with my ill-tempered commander. He was not pleased to have a woman join his ranks and soon grew weary of the jokes, the laughter, the bribes, the taunts - all things I also resented but had gotten used to. Aye, if he wanted to get rid of me, this far out country town was the place.

When I reached the top of the hill, the trees cleared, opening up to a green meadow with a thick wood on one side. The trail, instead of hugging the wood, descended into the meadow. Beyond it, up on a steep hill, perched an impressive black castle. My eyes went wide, and I paused to examine the thick trees on my left with vines and foliage so thick I could not see past them into what lay at the heart of the forest. Nor did I want to.

A rustling of bushes and snapping of twigs made me jump, and then the voice of a bird, chirping, whether in warning or greeting, made me shiver. Wildlife made me feel nervous. This was not the city. Would they have warm meals and hot beds? Was it too late to catch up with the tradesman?

But daylight was failing and the open meadow was reassuring, although the bulk of the castle was not. I'd assumed my commander was joking when he mentioned the castle and thought I'd be staying at a large home, much like the lords and ladies of the court. Not a fortress, strong and steady. There was no sign of a village where the rest of the people lived, and in the fading light, it was impossible to see whether the path continued down into open lands, for it was swallowed up by the wood again.

A sensation of entrapment made my pulse quicken. Doom hung over this place. I was sure I walked to my demise, where it would be impossible to slay a lord and return to the King's city. Failure surely awaited me.

The wind blew suddenly, rustling the wood. Reluctantly, I dragged my feet onward, but as I moved, the sound of a thousand hushed whispers came to my ears.

Oh, look. A newcomer.

It's been a long time since anyone new has come here.

Do you think he's lost?

It's a she. Don't you see? The petite angles of her face are too delicate for a man.

Oh. I assumed covered in mail and armor like that. She's an odd one then, isn't she? Few women want to fight.

Maybe she has magic? But judge not, we know nothing about her yet.

Not yet, but soon all shall be revealed.

I whirled around but saw no one. Eyes wide, I set off running toward the dark castle.

2

THE BLACK CASTLE loomed above me, its peaks and towers displayed like the jagged teeth of a wild bear. My bravery descended into trepidation. The wind twisted through the treetops, moaning like an old woman shivering in the cold. I glanced back at the track which was quickly fading from view as the sky darkened. There was no hope for me down there, so I turned my gaze to the door.

It was arched and high, a solid block of impenetrable wood. An ornate knocker carved into the shape of a lion, hung in the middle of the doorframe. I knocked. Three loud raps echoed into nothingness.

The castle was silent. Unease made the hair on my neck stand up straight. I considered whether this all was a joke. It was easy to envision myself eaten by wild creatures and left for dead. Just as my hysteria mounted, the door opened with a bang.

I jumped, and a squeak almost escaped my throat. Two figures stood before me. One was a man, tall and as thin as a pole, with a sharp nose and sallow cheeks. His mouth was turned down in a permanent frown, and he wore a black suit with a white shirt underneath. When he saw me, his frowned deepened, and he turned to the side, holding the door open as though he'd rather shut it.

The other figure was a woman, old enough to be my mother, but she was short and plump with rosy cheeks, an ample chest, and a wide bottom. Her white hair was pulled up in a bun, and her hand was over her heart, as though she were out of breath.

"Well, bless me," she wheezed, bright blue eyes staring at me in surprise. "What a bit of luck popped up on our doorstep this evening. Are you lost?"

Her accent was thick, but she was warm and friendly in a way that made me feel as though I had an ally. But I quickly chided myself. I wasn't allowed to have allies. The only person I could count on was myself.

"Not lost," I breathed, relieved to talk to someone who wasn't hostile. My fingers fumbled for the paper I'd been given with my orders. "Is this the castle of Lord Cedric?"

"Aye, tis his castle," the woman bumbled, her eyes widening as I handed her the letter. She didn't open it but gawked at the red seal as though it would bite her. "Blessed be. They sent *you*?" Now she stared at me, mouth flapping like a fish out of water, and then… "Well come in, come in. It's just that we were expecting a man. I did not even know there were woman warriors."

There it was. The stigma. I stiffened and tucked my helmet more securely under my arm. "Will it be a problem?"

My eyes went to the thin man, but he stared straight ahead, ignoring me.

"No. No problem." The plump woman's kindly voice returned. "In fact, you must be famished. I'll whip up a pot of tea and fetch the master. Julius, here will show you to the study."

The woman handed the letter to Julius who took it from her hands, holding it gingerly between his thumb and forefinger as though it were a snake that might bite him. I stuck my tongue in my cheek to keep a sarcastic remark from flying from my lips.

Even though I did not want to be here, in this grim castle, I needed to be on my best behavior. Now I knew there would be witnesses, others who lived in the castle who could gossip about my disappearance if I killed their Lord and ran. I needed to win them over, and when the time came, I would leave, none the worse for my unlucky adventure.

The castle was cold, and the scent of dank water hung in the air, damp and moist. My boots echoed on the stones as we walked, although Julius' shoes must have been made of skins, for they made no sound at all. I pricked my ears, listening for the whispering voices I'd heard on my way in, but there was none of that either.

The hall was not well lit, and I gazed at the arching stones, taking in what I could see in the poor light. The short hallway opened into a wide space, a gathering place of sorts that reminded me of the King's court. A grand staircase rose several feet in front of me, broad slabs of white marble and a golden balustrade leading up into the castle. Passageways branched off, winding into various halls, and I imagined more rooms and staircases beyond it. My eyes went wide. The castle must be immense, and I hadn't seen the half of it in the shadows of sunset.

Julius cleared his throat, and I realized I'd slowed to a halt, staring at the glory in front of me. Quickly, I ducked my head, squared my shoulders and fell in line behind him, a proper solider once again. He moved to the left and led me to a room where yellow flames cast shadows against the high walls.

It was a large yet homey room with rich rugs carpeting the floor. Two deep, comfortable chairs next to a roaring fireplace took up most of one wall. Gray stones created its elaborate design. Warmth flooded me, and the chill from my walk faded away. For the first time since entering the castle, I was embarrassed with my lack of poise and grace. I glanced down at the carpet. My boots were muddy, but if Julius had qualms, he said nothing.

He pointed to one of the chairs. There was a small table between them, the ideal setting for tea—as all rich lords and ladies had throughout the day. A thick book lay open on the table. Someone must've been reading then had abruptly left.

"Have a seat," the butler said coldly. "Your bags will be taken to your room." He glared down in disapproval at my one bag. "The lord of the castle will be with you shortly."

I opened my mouth, but words would not come out. Instead, I sat. My bag dropped to the carpeted floor where the butler snatched it up, held it between two fingers with disgust, and marched out of the room.

Left alone, I continued to study my surroundings,

but there wasn't much else to see. The room was simple with two enormous windows looking out on what might be a garden. I could not tell, for the sky had darkened completely, leaving the roaring fire the only light in the room. The scent of pine hung in the air, but it didn't overpower me. It reminded me I was in a home— a place I hadn't been fortunate enough to have.

Memories rose. The smell of booze, the coarse laughter and shrieking of ladies. My mother was a whore, and I was born in a brothel—one of the many accidental births there—and yet, they did not get rid of me. Although the memories of my mother were faint, they were happy. She always squeezed me tight and whispered lullabies, soothing me amid the noise and chaos of the guests coming and going.

A step roused me from my thoughts. The next moment, the rosy woman I'd met at the door bustled into the room, rolling a cart with tea and hot cakes.

3

THE FAINT SMELL of cinnamon made me sit up straight, stomach growling. I blushed, aware of how hungry and dirty I was. The woman's expression turned to one of compassion as she glanced at me. "Oh my dear, he won't be long. Here. You must be famished and exhausted. Have a spot of tea and a cake while you wait, it will take the edge off. I'll have the maid draw up a warm bath so you can soak before dinner, and we'll find you something to wear while we clean your armor. Don't worry about anything here."

I gave a heavy sigh and met her kind gaze. "Thank you. What is your name?"

"Bless me." The woman patted her generous bosom. "Here I go forgetting my manners, but here in the castle it's easy to lose touch with the pleasantries of court, not that we mind at all, but we are behind the times here. I'm sure it matters more to you than to us, but this is the countryside, you see. Life is different here without kings and courts and armies. I didn't know they let women be soldiers now. It was a bit of surprise to find you on our doorstep, but they send someone every year so we were expecting you at some point. We just... Bless me I've gone off rambling now. You may call me Betty. My family has served the lords of the castle for nigh on a hundred years, a proud tradition I am glad to keep up. We are a fiercely loyal family, and the lords saved my family from destitution and being sold to work the mines. I wouldn't be alive today if not for the lords father..."

As curious as I was to learn about where I was, the constant rambling wore me out. I wondered if she'd talk herself blue in the face, but while she spoke, she busied herself pouring tea and pushed the cart up next to me. I helped myself to a cake and had to admit, if she were the cook, she did a wonderful job. The lightness of the cake and the sweetness of it was much better than the rations soldiers were entitled to. The tea smelled like lavender, and I lifted the porcelain cup gently, noting the spray of pink and gold flowers painted on it. The smell relaxed me, and as soon as I tasted the tea, warmth spread throughout my body.

The anxiety of my trip and the complexities of my situation melted away as though I'd been put under a spell. Betty sat down in the chair opposite from me as though she—and not the lord of the castle—were entertaining me.

"There now, that's better, isn't it?" She leaned forward and her face went serious. "Tell me now, why did you truly come?"

I looked at her, but my eyes kept sliding off her face, and her voice sounded far, so far away. I drained the last of the tea and tried to sit up, to tell her why I was there, to confess. It would feel so good to confess, to tell someone else what I had done, to let my secrets be more than just my own.

"It is my fault I'm here. I've always been a trou-blemaker."

Betty sat back in the chair, and her voice was as gentle as velvet. "A troublemaker? Why?"

"I wasn't born a lady, or even a peasant. My mother was a harlot and worked a brothel outside the city gates. I was no more than five when the barbarians swooped down to steal the women. The Sisters of the Sword came to the aid of the brothel but many died, including my mother. After that, the Sisters of the Sword trained me to fight. I also had a benefactor within the King's city. A man who claimed to be my father. He was an inventor and a shy man." I fell silent at the memory. He used to take me to his workshop to show me his tools, and as I grew older his fingers used to wander and he'd tell me how much I reminded him of my mother. A dark beast stirred inside of me at the thought of him. "When my training with the Sister of the Sword was complete, I was given a position as shield-maiden in the King's army."

"Why the King's army? There are other roles for women in a kingdom."

I shrugged. "I wanted to do something honorable, to protect. I thought it would be better than the dullness of court and the petty drama between lords and ladies. But serving in the King's army was just as dull, and boring. When I heard about a conflict in a nearby village, I asked my commander to send us there to assist. He said no, and so I talked a small group of soldiers into striking down the raiders with me."

"Did you succeed?" Betty leaned forward.

The room blurred a bit, and I focused on the fire. "We did. But my commander was furious when we returned. He told me I should have stayed in the barracks. Disobeying orders endangered the status of the King. But I didn't understand. I saved lives, and yet those lives did not matter to them. This is my punishment, my banishment for not following orders. If I do well here, I will gain a second chance to serve in the King's city."

I trailed off, even though there was more I wanted to tell her. About the knife I'd been given and instructions to kill the lord of the castle and make it look like an accident. But I couldn't tell Betty. Those words were locked so far away, they wouldn't come out. Besides, there had to be a reason the commander had condemned this man. Although, if the kingdom truly wanted the lord dead, I was unsure why they sent one guard each year instead of a small battalion. I determined to wait until I met the lord of the castle and decide what to do later.

"Is there more?" Betty prompted.

The flames made me feel woozy. I closed my eyes and shook my head.

There was silence, and then a hand touched my shoulder. My eyes fluttered open as Betty pressed two leaves into my hands. "Chew these. The lord of the castle will join you shortly."

Then she was gone, whisking away her cart of tea and cakes.

I sat alone in front of the roaring fire, floating on a sea of warmth, and wondering if my limbs were still attached to my body. I opened my mouth, and it seemed the leaves drifted in on their own. I chewed them, and although they tasted bitter, my reason returned to me. The fog in my head cleared, and my muddled thoughts returned. But there was also a sensation of bile in my belly and a pain in my head.

She'd poisoned me! Tricked me somehow to discover my true intent!

I had to be careful in Whispering Vine with people I did not know and could not trust. I'd been warned before I left, and yet I already hadn't been careful enough.

As I considered my predicament, my eyes wondered down to the open book. The blur of words focused into a ditty, and as I read it, fear clenched my chest.

> *The lord of darkness hides in his tower*
> *Saving the land from dark monsters*
> *Stay at a distance, he will protect you*
> *Get too close, he will consume you*

I wondered if I should leave the room, search for the lord, put a knife through his throat, and flee while I could. Even though the very thought of killing in cold blood made my hands tremble. I'd killed before, but only people who deserved it, and I wasn't sure what the lord of the castle deserved.

I heard a sound. It was soft and yet still there, as though someone were dragging something against the stone floor. Thud. Drag. Thud. Drag. It came closer, and my heart climbed into my throat. My fingers slipped down to my sword hilt. Even though these people did not seem to fight the way I fought, they used clever words, herbs and food, not blades.

The step, and the drag, came closer. A hulking figure appeared in the doorway, ducked, and then limped into the room. A shadow crossed over the fire, and the flames leaned back, physically moving away from that darkness. I blinked. Perhaps it was the remnants of the potent herbs Betty had given me, for just as suddenly, the flames leaped higher, dancing among the stones and licking up the wood with a fury.

I turned to see who the shadow was and froze.

It was a barbarian of a man who stood well over six feet, so tall that if I were standing, my head would only reach his broad chest. His arms were thick with corded muscles; perhaps he had been solider in his prime. Now he was rugged with long black hair that swept past his shoulders and a neatly trimmed beard. He had a scar under one eye, giving him the appearance of a wildling, one of the barbarians who came down to raid the outer villages surrounding the kingdom from time to time. But he was a tamed barbarian, for even though his hair was long and his scar frightening, he was dressed in fine clothes like a lord, all in black, with flourishes of purple. Flourishes which matched his eyes. Startling, purple eyes, wide-set under dense eyebrows. Those eyes stared at mine with an intensity I could not read.

Breaking eye contact, I dropped my gaze, and saw the source of the thudding sound. He leaned on a staff made of two tree branches twisted together in an unending dance. The top of the staff tapered into a closed flower blossom, masking a faint glow that came from within. But I did not study the staff long as realization struck me and I breathed in sharply. My commander had told me the lord of the castle was lame, and indeed, one of his legs was twisted, forcing him to lean against the staff when he walked. Aside from his brute strength, it would be impossible for him to move quickly. Which made my secret task easier.

Those purple eyes studied me from head to toe, taking in my short-cropped, thick black hair, green eyes, the freckles that stood out on my dark skin, my lean, trim soldier's body, my dirty armor and muddy boots. His expression hardened as though he were displeased. Words rumbled out of his mouth like the sound of booming thunder at the brink of a storm. "I am Lord Cedric, but you may call me Cedric. Why are you here?"

The gruffness of his words gave me strength. My herb-induced haze faded, and I rose from the chair, even though the heat of the fire became uncomfortable under his smoldering gaze. My tongue stumbled over words for he quite literally stole my breath away with his outwardly presence. He did not belong in the castle at all but out in the wild, hunting in the vast forest outside his doorstep.

"I hail from the kingdom," I cleared my throat, my tongue thick. "I was sent to protect you. Rumor has it that during this season, your castle and village is most vulnerable."

He pressed his lips together and studied me again. "Is it. And do you believe this rumor?"

I squared my shoulders. "It does not matter what I believe. I am here to do my duty."

A faint smile crossed his lips. "But you realize that being sent here is not an honor, but a punishment. After all, a King's guard is sent every year, but I do not believe it is for protection. I believe you are a spy, just like the others."

I frowned. He was quite bold and unapologetic. His eyes bored into me like they'd unravel all the thoughts in my mind, picking them apart until he found what he wanted. If I were someone else, a highborn, a lady, I would give into his gruffness but resistance built in me. I was a solider, I had to be resilient.

"As I said, I am here to do my duty and—" the lie came easily— "I want to find out why the guards who came before me never returned."

An eyebrow lifted. "Ah. I see why they sent you. You are straightforward, aren't you? That is a question easily answered. They did not return because they did not want to."

"Where are they now?" I shifted my weight from one foot to the other, confused by his answer. It was not possible for everyone who had come before me to change their minds and decide not to return.

Lord Cedric shrugged. "I did not follow them after they left my castle nor ask them to write letters."

This time he smiled, the light of humor dancing in his eyes. Was he making a joke?

"It is my understanding that they were killed," I blurted out, trying—and failing—to turn the conversation serious again. His lightness unnerved me. Now was not the time for playful banter.

He waved his hand. "And this assumption is based on... Rumor?"

I scowled. "I intend to find out."

"Of course," he replied, a hardness returning to his features. "Since this is your first evening here, you are welcome to be skeptical, but there is much to learn. I assume we will spend the next few weeks in close quarters, given that you are here to *protect* me."

He turned the word into a sarcastic snarl. Another jest. But by the look of his upper body, he did not need much protection.

He opened his mouth to speak. "A warning, Mistress…"

"Mariel."

"Mariel." He said. "Too pretty of a name for a mere shield-maiden."

I could not tell whether his words were a joke or a compliment. The heat of the air suddenly seemed too warm, and beads of sweat trickled down my neck.

He moved closer until naught but a breath separated us.

"A warning. Mariel. Although you are here to protect me, the walls of this castle are fortified. No one goes in and out without my permission, especially after dark. I will leave you tonight, but I am curious to discover whether you are like the may flowers that come forth bringing light, or whether you have hidden thorns, which will leave us awry." He turned, his bulk causing shadows to weave across the room once more as he took his leave.

Dumbfounded, I collapsed on the edge of the chair, legs trembling and stared at the flames as I twirled his words over in my head. The smell of him and the cadence of his voice stayed with me. He was handsome, and his presence filled up the room. He was different from any man I'd ever met. And those purple eyes? No! I needed to get a grip. I could not be attracted to a man I was supposed to kill, even though sensations I thought I'd never feel fluttered through me.

His haunting words followed on their heels though. Mystery surrounded this place, and I needed all my wits to discover what was happening here. But there was already a sinking suspicion in my heart: this would be much harder than I initially assumed.

4

I WAITED while Lord Cedric's uneven footsteps echoed down the hall. Then I crept to the door and listened, my heart thudding unnecessarily in my chest. I was no spy. Sneaking and planning and scheming wasn't for me, but after staring into those dark purple eyes, I knew I should complete my task as soon as possible and run from this devilish place as fast as my legs would carry me. Despite Lord Cedric's warning. Surely the road would lead me to civilization. I'd find another trader and be on my way back to the kingdom, leaving this nightmare behind.

Low voices interrupted my thoughts. The deep gravel tones of Lord Cedric were first. "It will happen tonight. Let it."

"But my Lord," the next voice was higher, unhappy. Perhaps Julius the butler? "It is too risky, what if your foresight is not correct—"

"Let it happen," Lord Cedric growled again, and then his stumbling footsteps continued.

I scurried back to my seat. No sooner than my bottom met the fluffed velvet, a step came at the door and in sashed a young woman I had not met before. She was willowy with hair as light as sunlight piled up on top of her head. Her skin was a beautiful brown and her face was long with high cheekbones setting off nut brown eyes and ruby red lips. She had a body the ladies at court would kill for. Her simple blue gown was open at the top and showed off her perfect cleavage. She sighed heavily when she saw me, and there was a bit of a spoiled pout on her face.

"Come my lady, I will show you to your room," she gestured.

She turned her back on me and walked out of the room before I could move. I hurried after her. Her long legs moved quickly through the castle, but her velvet slippers were silent on the stones. I made a note of that even as my muddy boots rang out, loud and harsh in the silence.

Gentle candlelight lit our way, and the pouting woman led me back to the marble staircase I'd seen with Julius.

"My name is Mariel," I offered. "I'm not a lady."

The woman snorted. "And I'm not a maid."

I pressed my lips together tightly, taking the hint. I could tell when I was not wanted. The maid held herself rigid as she glided up the stairs, making no attempts to be friendly. The walk was long and silent as we went up another flight, down a corridor and a wide hall to a door she flung open.

"Betty wanted you to have a nice room, since you are a lady. Your bath is ready in the adjoining room. Night clothes and slippers have been provided. Leave your armor and muddy boots." The maid flared her nostrils at my clothing and gave another dramatic sigh. "Someone will collect them."

I knew that someone would not be herself. She might think she were a fine lady and needed to be waited on hand and foot. Although the staff at the castle seemed small, perhaps she had her way most of the time.

I entered the room, my eyes widening at the sight. A massive bed—large enough for four to sleep on—took up most of the space along with other furniture. There was a couch, a small table, a looking mirror and windows that stared out into the darkness of the night. Candles lit each corner of the room, and a crystal chandelier hung above my head. My jaw dropped at such magnificence, and I turned in small circles, taking it all in.

The hiss of the maid brought me back. "You are not welcome here. Go back to where you came from, before it is too late."

A retort rose on my lips as I glared at her. But instead of hostility in her eyes, I saw fear.

Before I could respond, she spun on her heel and shut the door firmly behind her. A lump settled in my throat. Why the warnings and what was she afraid of? The ditty I'd seen written in the book crossed my mind: *Stay at a distance, he will protect you. Get too close, he will consume you.* But no, I would not give in to speculation and doubt.

Left alone in my new and intimidating rooms, I stripped out of my clothes and made for the bath.

Steam rose from a tub so deep and wide I thought I might drown myself in it. I climbed in, and the scent of roses drifted to my nostrils. A memory of my time in the brothel came back to me. My mother humming as she bent over a tub, far smaller than this one, scrubbing my small back with rose-scented soap. There had been rose petals, red and white, strewn across the room.

"Flowers become you, my Mariel," she hummed. "If I had known you'd be so pretty, I would have named you Rose. I should have named you Rose, but when you laugh..." She tickled my underarms, and I giggled helplessly.

"My merry girl," she'd hummed again.

"Mama, sing the song," I begged, so small and happy.

She rubbed soap through my curly black hair and sang.

"Flowers for the children.

Flowers for the child.

Roses for the lord

In his tower wild.

Lord of the castle.

Lord of the moor.

Come to the house.

To bring us more."

I MUST HAVE DRIFTED off to sleep in the tub, for my dreams were filled with swirling roses, a lord in a dark castle, flashing blades and blood. So much blood.

When I woke, the water was lukewarm, and candle-light cast eerie shadows across the room. A cold shudder went through me, as though there were some-thing else in the room, a spirit of sorts, creating a coldness which chilled me to the bone. I hopped out of the tub and dried off with a fluffy white towel. A blue gown lay over the back of a chair along with slippers. I pulled the warmth over my head, appreciating the loose but cozy garment. It was more comfortable than my armor, which I noticed was gone. Someone had been in the room while I slept, and that thought was disconcerting. Immediately, I went to the door to see if it had a lock. It did. I turned it and leaned against the door, feeling secure for a moment before I studied my chambers.

On the table was a covered tray, and a delightful aroma rose from it. My stomach growled. But I stepped back. The food could be drugged just like the tea. Although sleep would be nice, I wasn't keen on being poisoned again. Instead, I pulled on the slippers, tucked my wet hair behind my ears and went to my weapons. My sword was too long to carry through the castle and awkward to use in close quarters. Nay, my knife would do. It was easy to slip in between ribs or slit a throat. I needed to kill the lord of the castle. After meeting him, I'd decided it was likely he'd killed the guards that came before me. He was too flippant with their whereabouts, and given my uncanny attraction to him, I had to act quickly before my emotions overruled my duty.

Swallowing hard, I unlocked the door and slipped out.

The castle was silent. I took a candle with me as I moved down the hall, recalling the route the maid had led me. I returned to the staircase shaped like an arrow. I stood on the east wing of the castle and looked to the west. I had a vague sensation, a feeling that I should enter and I would find what I was looking for.

When I saw the light, I almost hid, until I realized they were lanterns purposefully left to illuminate the castle. I walked among them, silently, watching the shadows dance as though they were watching me. I hurried past the stairs and entered the west wing. The faint scent of roses hung in the air as I moved up the staircase. There were vines along the balustrade and with each step I took, the more my heart called me to turn around and go back. I should not be here, treading in an unknown sanctuary.

The halls were darker, and I couldn't help but feel there were a sinister presence resting there. Forcing myself to go on, I crept through the passageways, with only a vague knowledge that the shapes were pictures on the wall and tapestries that moved when I passed. The further I went, the more I realized this was a fool's errand. Once I killed the lord of the castle, I'd have to make my way back to my room, and I was already lost. Then there was the matter of my missing armor and boots... It had been an ill-conceived plan, but I was too far gone to stop now.

Then a light glowed from under a door. I held my breath as I pressed my ear against the wood and listened. I heard the faint flicker of what might be a fire, but with the thickness of the door, it was hard to tell. My hands closed, one around the hilt of my knife and the other around the latch on the door.

It swung open gently and revealed a carpeted room with chests, blankets and books piled on shelves and chairs. There was a large bed in the middle of the room and a fire burning low, spreading little warmth but just enough to let the firelight flicker under the door. I almost held my breath as I tip-toed toward the bed.

Lord Cedric lay on his side, his back to me, his long hair trailing down his back. The bed was rumpled as though he was not sleeping well. If I could reach his side I could drive my knife into his back.

I moved slowly at first and then dashed up to the bed. I stood above his body with the knife raised.

My hand shook while the blade winked in the dying firelight. Fighting in the heat of battle differed greatly from sneaking into someone's room and slaughtering them. A memory rose, sharp and clear as I recalled my mother, the attack and the blades that ripped through skin. Bright red blood and screaming, so many screams. I'd wanted a blade, desired it, knowing that if I held a weapon, someone I loved would never have to die again. That's why I'd become a warrior; that's why I trained hard with the blade. But instead of protecting, I'd sat in the barracks, bored out of my mind. There were no heroics, no one to protect—only politics, leaving me a hollow shell with no meaning.

Even though it's what I thought I'd wanted, I knew now I did not want to be back in their good graces. I wanted freedom. I wanted a purpose. I wanted to belong. Killing a lord in cold blood was wrong. I would not, could not, follow through.

A tear snaked out of my eye and trickled down my cheek. My hand shook harder and then the shape on the bed moved. In a whirl, Lord Cedric spun, hair flying. A powerful hand curled around my hand, and my fingers loosened, dropping the knife. He hurled me onto the bed. I landed on my back in a whomp that knocked the breath out of me. My head bounced against the gentle give of the bed. Involuntarily, I squirmed in a half-hearted attempt to rise, but Lord Cedric landed on top of me. His broad hands curled around my wrists, pulling my hands above my head and pressing them against the bed while he straddled me.

He wore a white shirt, unbuttoned at the top, and I was suddenly aware of his chest hair curling out and the warmth of his body as he pressed against me. A desire awoke somewhere deep within, a longing for more of his warmth and weight. I shivered and lifted my chin, hoping defiance would obscure my lust. If Cedric noticed, he did not mention it. Instead his intense purple gaze traveled to where the knife lay, somewhere beyond my sight on the floor.

The pad of his thumb came up and wiped the wetness off the corner of my face. My nipples went hard at his touch, and my breath came short and fast as though we had been wrestling minutes before and he'd finally trapped me.

"You had the opportunity," his deep voice rumbled as he studied me.

I liked the sound of his voice, even though I didn't want to.

His eyes held mine, daring me to look away. "You could have killed me, yet you hesitated. Why?"

My stomach balled tight, and shame washed over me. I turned my head away from his penetrating gaze. "It's not who I am." The words came pouring out, words I needed to say out loud. "I am not a killer. Being a shield-maiden isn't what I thought it would be. We are supposed to protect, but there is no one to protect, only the endless training, standing around and following orders. Orders that make no sense."

I couldn't stop the tears from choking my voice even though no more trickled down my face. "This is my punishment for doing what I thought was right. For disobeying orders, for following my heart and saving a village. My commander forced me to come here and told me to kill you. But I'm not an assassin, a killer. Still I failed in my assignment. I have nowhere to go."

His hard face gentled, and the scar under his eye seemed less fierce. "It was brave of you to save others, you should follow your heart in that regard." He glanced at the fire, and a thoughtful look came over his face. "What do you want?"

"I don't know," I mumbled, studying the lines and angles of his face. Just looking at him made my heart ache, and it was easier to do so when he wasn't staring at me.

He shifted his weight. "Then you should stay, as my protector." A wry smile crossed his lips. "Until you decide what to do. I could use a bit of protection here, but understand, until we learn to trust each other, you will not have your weapons or your armor."

I stared at him and protested. "But I am not wanted here."

His lips thinned. "You are here, and there is no point in returning. It is too dangerous." He closed his eyes briefly and sighed. "If you want to know what happened to the others, you will stay."

I raised an eyebrow. "I thought…"

He angled his head toward mine, his eyes flickered

to my lips. "There is much for you to learn about our customs, our ways, and the ways of the forest."

The whispers I'd heard on my way to the castle came back to me. A chill shook my body. "What about the forest?"

He rolled off of me and sat up, his broad back to me. I studied the lines of his back as I attempted to steady my racing heartbeat and cursed myself for being distracted.

Finally, he spoke. "The forest is evil."

5

ALTHOUGH THE BED was soft and warm—the most comfortable bed I'd slept in—my mind kept me awake, restless, turning back and forth. After Cedric's ominous comment about the forest being evil, he refused to talk further and led me back to my room. Where he'd come inside and taken my sword. My insides quivered at the thought of being left without a blade—my protection from everything—and while the loss of my sword attributed to my lack of sleep, it was thoughts of Cedric himself who kept me awake.

I had to admit there was a connection between us. Memories of his weight pressing against me left me with a longing to rip off his shirt and run my fingers over the skin that lay beneath. I imagined it would be rippling with muscle and covered in scars. And his arms... What would it be like to be held by him? My lower body tingled with desire. Heat came to my face, even though there was no one to see. I tossed off the covers and turned on my side.

Those eyes, those vivid purple eyes had looked as though they'd like to possess me. Discover my thoughts, unravel my secrets, little by little, then devour me whole. I shivered because I wanted the same thing. But a shield-maiden and a lord would never mix.

When I finally slept, my dreams were punctured by blades, blood, and burned wood. I woke up, eyes heavy, both yearning for and dreading my next day in the castle. There was a tap at the door. Before I could decide what to do, it swung open and in bustled the round-faced Betty with a tray of food. My lips turned down. I'd forgotten to lock the door when I returned. How careless of me.

"Oh dear," Betty fretted as she straightened the bedding even though I hadn't gotten up yet. "You look as though you didn't sleep a wink, I have just the thing. A spot of tea and a cake or two would wake up anyone."

I frowned. I wasn't a noble lady meant for her fussing. Forcing myself not to glare, I met her eyes. I'd never backed away from a fight, and I wanted to clear the air between Betty and myself as soon as possible.

"I know you poisoned me yesterday," I challenged. "I am disinclined to try your tea and cakes again."

She had the decency to flush. Her cheeks went pink, but to her credit, she held my gaze. "My apologies. We are rather protective of Lord Cedric, and I cannot keep myself from meddling when strangers come around. Especially since we've never had a woman here before. I wasn't sure of your intentions."

This time it was I who dropped her gaze, knowing I couldn't lie. Another reason I could not be a noble-woman for they were experts at manipulation. A trick I should have learned from my mother, but honesty—instead of clever lies—dripped from my lips. "I came to kill him, if you must know."

Her hand went to her heart, her face white.

I swung my legs over the side of the bed. "You must understand though, that I couldn't, and I wouldn't." Quickly I told her the same thing I'd told Cedric last night, about becoming a warrior, how disappointing it had turned out to be, and my banishment to the castle.

She listened carefully, and when I was done, her shoulders relaxed. "So soon. You changed your mind so soon. Well then, that must be why Lord Cedric wants to see you in the garden this morning. Come, I've brought a fresh dress, and there are no herbs in your food. You must be starving after leaving your dinner."

I glanced at the tray, and my stomach growled as the tantalizing aromas drifted from the plates. "It is true," I admitted. Then I caught sight of a gown she'd placed on a chair. "But I prefer my own garb."

"Now, now," Betty said, brushing my words away as though I hadn't said them. "We haven't had a woman in the castle for a long time... Humor me, will you? I'd like to spoil you while you're here."

"What about the maid?" I asked.

"Bah. Sasha is Lord Cedric's cousin. She has a mind of her own and believes in her own natural beauty. She doesn't want me fussing over her."

My brow wrinkled, so she was a noblewoman, posing as a maid?

Uncovering the tray of food, I sat down to eat, practically inhaling the biscuits and sausage. There was fruit, berries and a cup of milk, more food for a meal than I'd seen in a long time. I ate with relish while Betty bustled about, straightening the room and chattering.

"She seemed upset with me," I remarked.

"Sasha? Ah, she can be unfriendly. You see, she likes it when the men come. Gives her something to do, someone to flirt with other than old Julius. I keep telling her she doesn't have to stay here, not forever at least. Spring is when she'll leave, since none of the men in the village have caught her eye."

"And what of the lord of the castle? He is not married?" I tried to feign indifference.

"Nay, he keeps to himself here and makes it difficult for others to see him as he truly is." She paused and folded her hands. "There, I've said too much. If you're all done now, I'll help you dress and take you to him."

The fall air was crisp as I walked out into the garden. All the same, it was a relief to breathe in fresh air, a floral scent twirling through my nostrils. My eyes widened as I took in the landscape. I stood on a paved path which led to a raised patio with two benches. In the center, a small water fountain flowed merrily, adding a lightness to the air. Rose bushes bloomed on either side of the walkway—red, white and yellow, although why flowers were blooming in fall was a mystery to me. The sight of them made me forget my surroundings and the mysterious castle. I reached out a hand to touch one perfect petal, and my worries drifted away.

"Ah, so you stayed."

I jerked at the low rumble of Lord Cedric's.

My hand went to my throat, and I gasped for I hadn't seen him, leaning up against a wooden post, his staff by his side as he watched me. Today he wore black with flourishes of light blue, and that color made him appear less fearsome. The sunlight softened his scar, but all the same, my heart fluttered at the sight of him.

"I did not see you there," I said, rather self-consciously, very aware of the way the peach colored dress I wore hugged my curves. "Of course I stayed."

He shrugged. "You could have fled in the night. It has happened before."

I crossed my arms over my chest, determined to ignore the way he made me tremble with need. I wanted to gain answers once and for all. "You told me no one leaves the castle without your permission. Where else would I go? Besides, you have my weapons."

Lord Cedric limped toward me, leaning on his staff. "Your weapons are that important to you?"

Was he joking? "I'm a shield-maiden," I countered. "The way of the blade is my life."

"Is that so?" He paused in front of a bush and plucked a white rose. "And what would you be willing to risk for the return of your blades?"

I raised an eyebrow. "What are you offering?"

Lifting the white rose to his nose, he sniffed it before tucking it into the pocket of his shirt. Catching my eye, he gestured to the benches. "Sit with me, Mistress Mariel. Perhaps we can come to an agreement."

The babbling fountain and the distant chirping of birds were the only sounds as I followed down the garden path. The path continued on the other side of the patio, and green vines twisted away, leading up into the mountainside which the castle sat against. And then there was the evil forest. I shivered as I sat and tried not to stare as Lord Cedric slowly limped up and sat down across from me.

"I was forward last night," he began, mischief stirring in those dark eyes. "I hope we can start over."

I bit my lower lip, for I'd been the rude one last night. I had tried to kill him, after all. I closed my fingers into fists and swallowed. "I would like that."

"Good. Now this is the part where I say I hope you enjoy your accommodations, but you and I both know that's not what you care about. I will be honest with you, since you would like your weapons back, and I need to protect my village."

"Village?" I interrupted. "What village? All I've seen is this castle."

His eyes laughed at me. "It is down the road, an hours' ride by horse. I have many in my stables should you choose to ride with me."

He leaned forward as he said the last few words, and I realized he was asking, daring me to go riding with him.

I twisted my fingers together in my lap. "Yes, I will ride with you," I said, unsure what else to say.

His eyes darkened. "Excellent, we shall go tomorrow. I shall enjoy showing you my small kingdom… If you will allow me the liberty of calling this small town a kingdom. But the festival of Samhain draws near, when the spirits of the forest come alive—"

"Are you teasing me?" I interrupted, stopping just short of rolling my eyes. The tales I'd heard of the forest and the superstitions of the villagers came back to my mind. This was pure nonsense, wasn't it?

The light in Cedric's eyes faded. When he spoke, his voice was low but deadly serious. "I can assure you, Mariel, this is no joke nor a tale meant to spread fear. The spirits of the forest are real. Very real. During the Festival of Samhain, the barrier between the enchanted wildwood and my village is thin. The dark creatures of the wood sneak out to cause chaos, and if it were just chaos, I would not mind, but they also prey on the living. Using their tricks, they tempt those who are weak minded to succumb to them. If they do not get enough blood, they attack. If you are willing, I'd ask your help to hold back the spirits of the wildwood before they overtake the castle and the village."

I gaped at him. He was mad! Stark raving mad. There were no such things as spirits. . .

No sooner than I thought those words, I heard whispers.

She doesn't believe him. Does she?

Bah. The fool. She'll be surprised.

And easy to take advantage of.

Hush, she looks ashen.

Think she can hear us?

No one has before. Other than...

Hush!

"You look frightened," Cedric observed.

"Yes!" I squeaked. "No. Not frightened of battle but. . ." Should I tell him about the whispers? Nay, I did not know him well, and he'd only think I was mad. "You have to understand, it is difficult to believe that there are spirits in the forest who will attack. Are you sure it isn't some enemy trying to trick you?"

Cedric's lips thinned, and he stared off into the colorful rose garden. "Mariel, it is understandable that you do not believe me, no one has before you. I do not expect that you will be any different. But I have lived here all of my life. I know what my duty is, and even if you do not believe me, will you stand with me as protector?"

6

I GLARED AT HIM, unsure whether I was still angry with him for trying to frighten me with stories of spirits or his polite request. After all, I was here under the guise of protection, and standing as shield-maiden was my first duty. "I will stand with you, but you don't have to frighten me with stories."

His shoulders slumped and he leaned back, as though relieved at my answer. "If I told you there were soldiers from the other side of the forest, would you believe me then?"

I scowled. "Yes."

"Then that's what we shall call them."

"Why?" I persisted. "Why the shadows and secrecy and mystery? And why does the kingdom only send one person to help you if you face these beasts alone?"

Cedric snorted and shook back his long dark hair. His scar practically glowed at me. "I think you know the answer."

Those devilish violet eyes appraised my body before he yanked his gaze away and spoke to the rose bushes. "The answer to that question is the very reason why you were sent here."

I recalled the hushed voices I'd heard after I'd first met him. *Let it happen.* "You knew the kingdom sent me to assassinate you?" I breathed, my voice thick with emotion. "And you were just going to let it happen?"

"What someone does or doesn't do under pressure reveals their true character. The fact that you couldn't kill me surprised me."

I swallowed a lump in my throat. "What happened to the others who were sent to guard you? Did they also try to kill you?"

"They did, after a time. None so quickly as you."

Those eyes returned to study me again, and a shiver went down my spine. "I thought if I got to know you, I would not want to kill you," I admitted, wanting to gain a reaction from him.

He stood, a smile playing around his lips, and when he spoke, his voice was gentle. "Is that what you thought? After we met for mere moments, and yet still, you came. You tried. That is something I cannot forget. The others were not honest, and even though I gave them their lives, perhaps I should not have." He sighed. "The first four guards died fighting by my side. The next three I was forced to sacrifice to the Dark Queen and the last one never attempted to take my life. He lost his way in the wildwood, chasing the whispers of the wood." His eyes misted over. "So much death, for no reason. Perhaps he is still out there, or perhaps he is lost, like many others who dare to enter the wood. Your fate will be your own, choose what you will. Now, I have business to attend to. Will you join me tomorrow?"

"Yes," for there was nothing more for me to say. Should I refuse his offer?

"I am not sure where you interests lie, but you may explore the castle. Betty and Sasha will answer any questions you may have."

Betty who talked too much and Sasha who wished me far away. Still, not to seem ungrateful, I nodded, and Lord Cedric strode away.

Our brief conversation left me with more questions, and although I did not know what his business was nor where he was going, I thought it might present the opportunity to snoop. After all, he gave me free rein in the castle. I assumed that reached to the grounds, although with the whispers I'd heard, I was disinclined to wander alone.

I sat in the garden and breathed in the enchanting floral scent. I had to admit, it was beautiful. Orange and blue butterflies alighted on the flowers and fluttered above the water fountain. I watched for a while, sure I had been transported to a wild land where the basic rules of life did not matter. Briefly, my thoughts flittered back to my training and the other shield-maidens. I was not popular, but I had friends who were on my side and believed in me. They would miss me and hoped I would return, but now looking back, I already knew my fate. No one returned from Whispering Vine, and I intended to find out why. But first I had to forget my strange attraction to Lord Cedric and the way he

threw me off balance, first by teasing and then by seri-
ousness.

I stood and flattened down the skirts of the dress I
was unused to wearing. Since I had plenty of time
before the mid-day meal, I set my focus back on the
castle. The garden paths were tempting but perhaps
later I could walk through them and explore. I gave a
longing glance down the cobblestone path and decided
I would return after I explored the castle.

IT WAS COLD INSIDE, and even though I wore a borrowed
pair of slippers, my gentle movement caused the dust to
resettle and echoes to bounce off the stone. I shivered as
I walked the first level, peeking into rooms from time to
time but seeing nothing more than old and disused
rooms. Some were covered in dust, others looked as
though they'd been recently used, but all hinted at
immense wealth I could not fathom.

As I walked, I wondered where everyone was. The
King's castle was full of people: the royal family who
lived there, the nobles who helped run the kingdom,
and the servants who kept order. And the army was not
far away, stationed throughout the impregnable
fortress. Yet here, in the land of exile, the castle was
forlorn and empty, as if those who would fill it with
light and happiness were chased away long ago.

I clasped my fingers together as I climbed up staircases and crept through empty halls, sometimes too
frightened to open doors. Dread settled around me as
though evil held me in its grip. When I climbed to the

third level, there was a distinct smell, an odd smell as though sulfuric vapors were trapped there. Little light drifted into those haunted halls, and my courage dropped away like a stone sinking into a pond. I swallowed hard and came to a standstill. How easy it was to believe that spirits haunted not only the castle but the forest. Something vile had happened here, I was sure of it. But would going on give me answers?

Suddenly I heard voices, but not vague whispers like I'd heard outside. Real voices.

Heart pounding in my chest, I crept down the hall toward the sounds. Dim light came from the room at the end, a wide open hall. I flattened myself against the wall and listened.

"I haven't forgotten you or your plight," a woman's voice said. It was cold and authoritative. It was obvious she was used to being obeyed.

"It is unnecessary that you leave your current posting to join us," Lord Cedric's low voice rumbled. "We can manage, as we have every year."

"I want this ended once and for all," the woman demanded. "It is not fair that you have to stay and fight, year in and year out. I will send a wave of magic and command the spirits to sleep."

"They are too strong. Last year—"

"Last year, I was new to the wildwood," the woman interrupted. "I understand it now."

"You still believe that magic alone will not defeat this," Lord Cedric growled. "It was not because of the Dark Queen that these spirits rose... You know the goddesses cursed this land."

I heard a tremor of emotion in Lord Cedric's tone,

and a horror twisted in my gut. So there were monsters in the forest, put there by the goddess? And who was Lord Cedric speaking to? Even though I knew I should not be spying, I couldn't help myself. Hardly daring to breathe, I peeked around the doorframe.

The hall was wide and empty with great windows on either side, covered in heavy drapes. Through one, I could see the dark foliage of the forest, and the leaves moved back and forth, thick and green. Daylight streamed in casting a ghostly white glow around the room. Bathed in the halo, Lord Cedric stood with his back to the entrance. His staff leaned against what looked like an altar and his hands rested on it, leaning his weight on it. His head was bowed, staring down at an object, and my breath caught.

I'd heard of the wild people who used unseemly methods to talk to the living and dead. Usually water conveyed their messages, and they could use magic to speak with someone who was not there. Those were tales I did not believe in, until now, watching Lord Cedric stand over a basin of water. Mist poured out of it but I thought I could make out a reflection in the water. The woman he spoke to? A shiver went down my spine. I began to wonder if he was who he said he was, and if I should have killed him after all.

His voice dropped, and I could no longer hear them speak, but thoughts whirled around my mind. This was why I'd been asked to assassinate Lord Cedric, because he was in cahoots with evil.

Fingers shaking, I backed away and stumbled over a vase by the door. It fell with a crash, sending shards and dust through the air. I repressed my panicked scream as I spun around.

But Lord Cedric turned at the disturbance, brushing his unruly hair back. When his purple eyes bored into mine and I saw nothing but fury written there.

7

MY INSTINCT TO FLEE FADED, and although I did not have my blade, I faced him.

He moved much faster than I expected a lame man to move and he towered above me, anger etched across his face. His scar glistened even in the low light.

"An assassin and a spy," he spat.

I swallowed my fear, balled my hands into fists and lifted my chin. Heat rose inside of me, and I knew my eyes flashed as I responded. "I am no assassin, you know this and yet you use those words against me. It was you who invited me to explore the castle. Did you hope I'd find you up here playing with dark magic? So you'd have a reason to get rid of me just like the others?"

"Do not speak of magic and darkness to me," he growled. "You know nothing of it!"

"And I know nothing about it because you won't tell me," I retorted.

"You think you deserve to know what happens here because you have come from a greater kingdom. You've stood in the King's court and seen greatness from far lands and thus think yourself far above the quaint, old ways of this land, with its beliefs and superstitions! You don't believe in the power of magic, nor spirits, nor the goddesses, and you know nothing about the enchanted wildwood. Yet you come here with your assumptions, just like the rest of them, assuming you can use the blade to make everything right when it is far, far more complicated."

When he finished, his face was only inches from me, his breath heavy with frustration. A lump came to my throat, and I swallowed hard as my fingers loosened. He was right. I'd burst into Whispering Vine with my own assumptions, but I didn't know the place, the village, the people, at all.

"Then show me," I whispered. "Let me help you. At least I can have some satisfaction before I leave."

His eyes widened and he took a deep breath, glancing away from me to gather his wits. "You surprise me, Mariel," he said gruffly, hints of anger still threading through his voice. "Never has the kingdom sent a shield-maiden before. What did they do to make you believe you could succeed here?"

I stepped back. "Don't patronize me. I am a shield-maiden. I fight. It doesn't mean that I am weak, and I don't need you looking down on me because I am a woman. Yes, I came here with assumptions, but you have been playing tricks on me since I walked in the door. You knew I was sent to spy and assassinate you, so why the tests and the traps?"

He shifted, his eyes going back to the hall where he'd performed dark magic. "There is no trust in the kingdom. There is a reason I am exiled, a reason why one guard is sent every year to kill me. It is an unending game with the kingdom: who will conquer who?"

"If they really wanted you dead, why don't they send an army? And what have you done that is so wrong?" It was brave of me to ask but I wasn't sure I wanted to know the answer.

Lord Cedric took my hand. Instead of pulling away, I let him. His was warm, almost comforting. I both desired and dreaded the contact, for it was not often that any had touched me with a friendly gesture, even hugs often turned into wrestling matches as warriors pitted their strength against each other. But this, the touch of his fingers against mine, made my pulse quicken. Suddenly it was hard to breathe. But why pull back when I had nothing to lose?

Uncertainty gave me pause. It would be easier to leave if I hated the man but the sensations stirring in my breast were not those of hate at all. I glanced down the dim hall where motes of dust danced in the gloomy lighting. I had to consider the possibility that staying could be more dangerous than leaving, but despite the dark magic and the talk of spirits, I was curious. What must it be like to be Lord Cedric, lord of a frightening castle with nothing but servants and his garden full of roses? In truth, this was a mystery I burned to unravel, to understand the lord of the castle once and for all.

His pupils darkened as they studied me.

I inhaled, the scent of smoke and sage filling my nostrils. My cheeks burned as alarm bells chimed in my head. I should run, escape this madness, but my feet would not willingly move.

His head angled above mine. "Your very presence has thrown me off kilter. I refuse to fight you nor threaten you. But I am not sure you should know the secrets of Whispering Vine."

"But you asked me to be your home's protector," I protested.

"True," he chuckled and let go of my hand. "And is a protector entitled to secrets? I think not. But come, I have something to show you."

Instead of moving, he paused, and his gaze tore down to my lips. He lifted his hand and the pads of his thumb grazed my lower lip. A tendril of longing shot through me, but he broke contact and limped down the hall.

I remained frozen in place, heart pounding in my throat. If I followed him, I would step across the realm into a place where I had no control, and with my feelings spiraling out of control, I desperately needed an anchor before I lost myself in this wild, dark castle.

He led me through the winding halls, leaning heavily on his staff. I wanted to reach out and help but he used his staff expertly to navigate the stairs—a sign of his intense upper body strength. He must have had many days and nights to practice walking around his spiraling castle.

We walked through the maze and up a curving staircase until we reached a set of carved double doors. Leaning on his staff, he used both hands to throw them open. Dust filled the air and then light, so bright it almost blinded me. I blinked, then gasped as I took in the view before me.

A gentle breeze blew as I walked out onto a balcony where brilliant sunlight warmed my skin. We were near the top of the castle, and far below me I saw the bright flowers of the rose garden, the sparkle of the water fountain, and even further, the cobblestone path winding down the mountainside. Animals grazed in the meadow, and although they were almost too far to make out clearly, I thought I saw horses.

On the slope of a hill was a vineyard thick with purple grapes. But beyond the majestic land were vague smudges, a village, and the small dots moving back and forth had to be people.

My heartbeat pulsed at the breathtaking beauty of the land, the scent of pine intertwined with flowers.

When I glanced back at Lord Cedric, he watched me, a small smile playing about his full lips. "This is my land. What do you think?"

"It is beautiful," I admitted. "But surely you do not take care of your lands alone?"

Cedric chuckled. "No, but my lands provide for the villagers and I employ many of them, as need arises. During the harvest they come here, to pick the grapes from the vineyard and make the wines that are used for trade. My horses are sold as warhorses, back to the kingdom, and the castle provides a barrier between the village and the wildwood. This is one of my favorite haunts, where I can look out and see the land is at peace."

I stilled, admiration shooting through me as he

walked over to the balcony. He belonged outside and the wind ruffled his hair as if it agreed.

"These lands are rich and fertile, and the kingdom wants to take them from me and destroy the land with armies and trade routes. I will not allow it. And what magic I do possess is enough to keep the king at bay."

Sunlight shone down on his head, and even though he stood with his back to me, I put my hand over my heart, feeling my pulse quicken. This glimpse at his life, at something he was passionate about moved me, made me realize he was human, with a soul, with things he cared about. He was more than just an exiled lord, much more than a man I was sent to kill. I swallowed hard.

He faced me. "You accuse me of dark magic, and I will admit there is truth to the rumors about Whispering Vine. But magic here is never used for evil, only for the protection of life."

Even as my heart warmed to him, the words of the ditty played through my mind. *The lord of darkness hides in his tower. Saving the land from dark monsters. . .*

8

THE NEXT MORNING, Betty woke me with a tray of breakfast and yet another elaborate dress. This one was dark green with a wide skirt. I had to admit, it was nice to wear fine clothing even though I still felt awkward. At least the country folk did not follow the styles of court and I did not have to wear a corset or hoop skirt. Still, I offered vague protests while I internally wondered what Lord Cedric would think of me.

The morning was lonely, so I went out to the gardens. But my mind was easily distracted, and every noise made me jump. Just before the midday meal, a shadow covered the patio, and Lord Cedric appeared. Today his clothes had flourishes of green which matched my dress, and he looked as dashing as ever. Heat warmed my cheeks as he walked up to me.

"Good morning, Mistress Mariel. Will you join me?"

I took his outstretched hand, but didn't miss the wicked glint in his eye as he bowed his head, giving me a view of his thick black lashes. He pressed a feather-light kiss on my hand. I felt a spark in my lower belly and forced myself to stand still.

"I'd like that," I smiled at him, relieved to find the air between us was clear. It was nice not to bicker.

He led me down a path to an adjoining building. I hadn't noticed it at first for it looked like part of the castle. It was smaller and shaped like a barn with doors standing wide open. We walked through to the other side where a hilly pasture opened up, looking out over the cliff and down into the rolling hills. I could see the track I'd followed to reach the castle, and in the distance, I saw a faint smudge.

Lord Cedric gave a sharp, shrill whistle, and a black steed galloped out of the meadow toward us. It was the largest horse I'd even seen, and my jaw dropped in surprise. Its coat was a shiny black and glistened in the light. Powerful legs moved the horse, and it trotted up to Lord Cedric, snorting as it tossed its mane.

"Mariel, this is Felix, my war horse." Lord Cedric stroked the horse's mane. "I usually ride bareback, but if you prefer a saddle there is one in the stables."

"Ride? Together?" I blurted out, and then glared down at the inappropriate dress that Betty had talked me into wearing. Forced me into wearing would be a better description.

Lord Cedric chuckled. "I would like to take you down to the village, and Felix's mate is nursing two foals. It would be wrong to take her away from her children."

I glanced around and saw a pure white horse in the meadow along with two foals, frolicking and dancing about. "Is it not late in the season for foals?"

"It is," he agreed. "But Felix and Fauna are unique war horses. They have sired many foals, and we often sell them back to the kingdom. The profit helps me retain my grounds and staff, but they are growing older and the foals are born later and later each year. Twins this year is a good omen."

"They are beautiful," I breathed. "I haven't been fortunate enough to buy my own horse, yet I've often longed for one."

"They are worthy companions."

In one swift move, he planted his staff in the ground and, using it as leverage, swung up on the horse.

I gaped, and he held out his hand to me. "Come, Mistress Mariel. Unless you're afraid."

There was an insolent question in his deep set eyes, and even though my long skirts were not made for riding, I took the dare, and gripped his hand.

My skin tingled from the contact and he pulled me up as though I weighed nothing. I'd expected to ride astride like a man behind him, but he placed me in front of him. My skirts fell mid-calf to maintain my modesty, but I sucked in a deep breath as the heat of his body pressed against me. His arm stole around my waist. I squirmed, but his hand was firm. His low voice whispered near my ear.

"Felix is a feisty horse, you will not want to fall off."

I gave in, letting him hold me, letting myself enjoy it even though my mind screamed at me to escape this folly.

Felix broke into a gallop and my hands closed around Lord Cedric's arms, my thighs squeezing the horse's back to keep my balance. I thought I heard another chuckle from Lord Cedric, but the wind streamed out behind me, whirling my short hair into my face as we bounded through the wood. Felix gathered himself and leaped over the looming gate.

A cry of pleasure burst from my throat as we galloped down the hill, and the sensation of freedom surged around me as the forest whipped past. A grin split my face and laughter burst from my throat. Lord Cedric whispered in soothing tones, calming the horse.

We slowed down into a walk, and I leaned back, chest heaving. "That was magnificent," I said, releasing my grip on Lord Cedric's arms to tuck my wild hair back into place.

This time he did laugh, a deep throated laugh. His chest expanded against my back, and I leaned back, no longer caring that I should hold myself away from him.

"I wasn't sure whether you would enjoy it or scream," he said.

"A shield-maiden does not scream with terror; she walks boldly into terror and fights."

Lord Cedric snorted. "So you do have a sense of humor."

"They don't beat it out of us," I retorted.

"Why a shield-maiden?"

I chewed my lower lip and spoke quickly. "As the daughter of a harlot, there are not many options for me. My father was an inventor for the King, but the Sisters of the Sword thought it would be better to train me."

"And your mother, what did she think?"

I frowned. "She was killed when barbarians raided the brothel. The children were spared and sent to the Sisters of the Sword. I was only five at the time, but my father would visit me, take me for a few days. We did not get along. He is a quiet man, given to thinking, not action, and others took advantage of him. Standing up for those who cannot stand up for themselves is why I wanted to fight, and becoming a warrior is the most appropriate way for those of low birth to give back to the kingdom."

"And now what? Will you go back after this?"

"I was sent here as punishment, and I cannot do as they asked. They will not have me back. I don't know what I want."

"To protect those who cannot protect themselves," Lord Cedric said.

His arm about my waist tightened, then relaxed.

"What about you?" I asked. "Why do you stay here?"

"Whispering Vine is my birthright, the castle has been in the family for generations. Even though the kingdom would like to station an army here, draw higher taxes, and force me to go to court, I will not let them. The wildwood calls. I belong here and have no reason to leave."

"But, isn't it lonely?" I spoke without thinking. "The large empty castle, the servants, your gardens and your war horses? Don't you get lonely without a companion?"

"Are you suggesting that I need a companion to be complete?"

His hand moved lower, and a tingling sensation went up my spine.

"Yes...no...I..." I stammered and trailed off, unsure what I was suggesting.

"You think it would be kind for the kingdom to send

me a wife instead of a guard? But who would stay here, in the wild lands where the spirits of the forest come alive every year? What woman would make her home in my castle? When you meet one, tell me, for I would like to meet her."

Retorts rose and died on my lips, and I turned my attention to the countryside. "I know nothing of wives. Will you tell me about Whispering Vine?"

The countryside turned to farmland as we rose and the scent of hay mixed with the sweet fragrance of nectar filled the air. Lord Cedric's rumbling voice was comforting as he answered my question.

"Whispering Vine was discovered by explorers from the kingdom. Not many adventurers traveled here, because of the wildwood. It is vast and unending and borders many villages. Those who did venture into the wood never returned. Stories and superstitions arose, but the people who lived near the wildwood knew the truth. A price must be paid for entering the forest, and those who live close to it know how to appease the Queen of the Wildwood."

I clasped my hand over my mouth to keep a sarcastic laugh from bursting out. "A queen. Of the wildwood?" My skepticism came through clearly. "Earlier you said the forest is evil, how can it be if a queen rules it? Can she not tame the wildwood?"

"The answer to your question is complicated, Mariel." He sighed. "When the King named this land as his own and called those who lived here to become his subjects, he forgot one thing. The wildwood does not acknowledge the deities of humans. Magic is its only master and each month, during a potent festival, the magic of the forest seeks to free itself. It is a threat with the potential to take over the entire world, which is why each of the bordering villages has a responsibility to help the Queen of the Wildwood keep the creatures of the forest from escaping."

A dark dread crept around me. The voices I'd discounted as nothing more than whispers in the wind could be explained if they were part of the forest.

"Go on," I begged, knots forming in my stomach.

"The Queen of the Wildwood has one task: to keep the evil of the forest from escaping and taking over the lands. The surrounding villages assist by providing the magic the queen needs to make her stronger."

"Were you speaking with her? The Queen of the Wildwood," I gasped. "The Festival of Samhain is coming. Soon."

"Yes. My village will celebrate the bountiful harvest and the coming, long dark days of winter. While the celebration proceeds, I will go to the forest and ensure no evil escapes into my land."

"Alone?" I shivered as though it were a winter day with ice and snow covering the ground. "No one helps you?"

"You are here," he replied, a warning in his tone.

My fingers shook and suddenly I wanted to dismount and run, leaving Lord Cedric to his mysterious, dark land. But I banished my fears and sat up straighter. "You and I, and the Queen of the Wildwood? Three to stand against the forest?"

"It would not be wise to have more. Ah look, here is the village."

I noted how quickly Cedric changed the subject. He

wasn't telling me something. But soon we'd go to the forest, and I'd discover his secret. In the meantime, I turned my attention to the village, and the cloud of dread receded. I'd enjoy what little time I had with him for my future was bleak and unknown.

9

INDEED, this was the village I'd expected to see when I first arrived. Rows of buildings lined a wide cobblestone road. In the center was a water fountain, so large that even twenty people standing in a circle, holding hands, would not reach all the way around it. Pink, yellow and white flower petals twirled in the breeze, rich orange pumpkins rested on each doorstep, and wreaths made of golden wheat, green leaves and red berries hung on every door.

Men, women and children filled the streets, dressed in their best. When they caught sight of Lord Cedric's horse, they shouted and threw flower petals, welcoming us to the celebration. Children chased each other down the streets, and some were bold enough to splash the waters of the fountain at each other.

My breath caught, and suddenly I felt young and carefree, almost girlish as I watched.

In the village square, couples danced to stringed

music. A bard sang of a maiden who fell in love with a cursed lord.

I twisted on the horse to catch a glimpse of Cedric's face. Shadows covered his eyes until he noticed me peering up at him, and he smiled. "What do you think?"

I glanced back at the lively square, the villagers cheering and dancing and caught the scent of something delectable. My stomach rumbled, reminding me we'd missed the mid-day meal. "I thought the celebration of Samhain was in a couple of weeks. Not today."

"True, it is. A celebration I never have the fortune to attend. So the villagers decided to begin the festival today, but the real celebration takes place on Samhain."

"They do this for you?" I stared at him, surprised.

I assumed he was unloved, as most of the lords and ladies of the land were. The kingdom bowed down to nobility because of who they were. Nobles. But no one had real love for them. At least, not enough to change the date of a celebration and hold them in high esteem as the guest of honor.

I touched his hand, allowing myself to enjoy the tingling sensation that went up my spine.

"Go," he encouraged. "Have fun. When it is time to return, I will come for you."

He was lame, I remembered with a sigh. There would be no dancing for him, and he'd left his staff at the castle, planted in the meadow as though it were a tree.

"Where will you go?"

"To feast," he smiled.

"Do you mind if I came with you?"

"If it pleases you," his voice went low, husky. His

purple eyes held mine, searching. "Because the people of the village believe in me, it assuages your fears?"

"Yes," I whispered, holding his gaze. "It does. In the kingdom, no one loves those who rule over them, but they respect them because of threats and fear. But here it is clear that you are a good man, a good lord, and the people honor you because of it."

Something flashed in his eyes, and his grip around my waist tightened. I faced forward again as a surge of emotion swept through me.

A FEAST WAS LAID out among the tables. Someone came for Felix while Lord Cedric made his way to the head of the table and sat down upon a chair covered in leaves and foliage, a throne for the king of the harvest. A little girl ran up to him, carrying a crown, and Lord Cedric leaned down to allow her to place it on his head. A cheer went up, and the child ran away, blushing.

Lord Cedric laughed and held out a hand to me, indicating I should sit at his right side. I studied the gathering as I took a seat and saw Betty gossiping with a group of women. She waved at me when I glanced in her direction, and I was thankful she'd forced me to wear the pretty dress. Once Lord Cedric sat down, the villagers flocked to the tables which lined the meadow, as though his presence were a bell, summoning them to the feast. Young and old they came, dressed in their finest. They shouted and laughed, some already drunk on wine.

Someone handed me a goblet of elderflower wine.

The sweet fragrance filled my nostrils, and I took a sip, laughing as I met Lord Cedric's eyes. He toasted me, lifted his goblet and the villagers lifted theirs and chanted.

> *Grateful for this feast*
> *Grateful for this bounty*
> *Thankful for the hands*
> *Who have prepared this bounty*
> *Thank the light*
> *Thank the sun*
> *Thank the rain*
> *Grateful for this feast*
> *Grateful for this bounty*

AND THEN THE food was served. A roasted suckling pig melted in my mouth along with smoky meat pies, rich vegetable pies and yellow roasted corn. There were cheeses, some sharp, others smoky, a scattering of nuts and bread with herbs. Every bite was rich and flavorful, all washed down with the light elderberry wine.

A dreamlike sensation hovered over me, and often I caught Lord Cedric studying me. His purple eyes sparkled, but there was something else, a deep hunger that made me long to be alone with him. Instead I lifted my goblet and raised an eyebrow at him. As if on cue, the music began.

A litany of strings filled the air, and villagers began to rise. Women in white dresses joined hands with men dressed in black. They left their tables and moved to the fountains where the music set their feet tapping. Hands clapped, and the beat thrummed through the air, pulsing a rhythm. I did not know who grabbed my hand and pulled me out of my seat, but the next thing I knew I was with the villagers, my feet tapping in tune and my skirts twirling as I danced.

The heaviness that had sat on my shoulders ever since I learned I was sentenced to Whispering Vine faded, and I danced until the stars came out and poured their blessing down upon that night. And as I whirled and watched the happiness of his people—happiness he was fighting for—I realized I might be falling in love with Lord Cedric.

10

PANTING, I sat down on the edge of the fountain to take a break. Around me, the people still danced with boundless energy. The lanterns were lit and a combination of bonfires and torches were scattered around the village. Couples stole kisses in the shadows, and my face warmed. I hadn't seen Lord Cedric in a while and wondered whether he was still at the feasting tables. I would go in search of him except my slippers were torn and my feet bruised from dancing on the cobblestones.

"You're still here?"

A question invaded my peace.

I glanced up at Sasha, the unfriendly maid.

"Oh, hello," I said, determined to be friendly despite the scowl in her face. How could someone be so unhappy during such a celebration?

Sasha perched on the other side of me and glanced around, her eyes wide, almost frantic. "I warned you to leave," she hissed.

I narrowed my eyes at her. This. Again. "Why?

Because the forest is evil?"

"I'm trying to help you," Sasha urged. "Go, before the festival of Samhain. Otherwise it will be too late, and the Lord of Darkness will come for you."

I laughed. Lord of the Darkness indeed! There was no mention of him in Lord Cedric's stories. "Are you jealous because you want Lord Cedric all to yourself?"

The words flew from my lips before I could stop them, but the scowl faded from Sasha's face, leaving surprise. "I'm not the one who's in love with him," she retorted, leaning away from me. "When the time comes, just remember, I tried to help you."

She rose and brushed her hands on her sky-blue gown. "I tried to help," she murmured again and disappeared into the crowd.

My joy evaporated as I weighed her words. The Lord of Darkness sounded frightening, and I could not ignore the fact that the guards who had come before me all disappeared. But Lord Cedric had a reasonable explanation and I had no reason to believe he lied to me. Besides, the words I'd seen in the book were made up. Weren't they?

The lord of darkness hides in his tower
Saving the land from dark monsters

No, Sasha wanted to frighten me, after all, she'd been rude and unkind since my first day. I pushed her cryptic words out of my mind. In the morning, I'd ask Betty, but for now I wanted to find Lord Cedric. A fluttering sensation beat in my breast as I stood and made my way through the crowd.

The light was low around the tables and villagers still feasted, mainly drinking goblets of wine and laughing into them. I walked to the throne where Lord Cedric had sat, but it was empty.

"Looking for me?"

I whirled, my hand going to my throat. Then I smiled.

Out of the shadows appeared Lord Cedric with Felix behind him.

"Yes," I admitted. "I am done dancing and came to spend time with you."

"As I recall it, you are forced to spend time with me because you are my protector," he moved closer, allowing the light to shine on his scarred face.

I took a deep breath and stepped toward him, the elderberry wine emboldening me. "As I recall it, I am a shield-maiden, and I choose who I spend time with. Tonight it is you."

"Then you will forgive my forwardness," he took another step toward me.

"Of course, my lord," my voice dropped as I closed the distance between us.

The scent of wine, deep and bold hung in the air, along with the distant scent of fire. But I only had eyes for Lord Cedric as I gazed up into his dark eyes. Past, present and future faded in that stolen moment, and it was only us standing among the shadows. I matched his breath and reached out, touching his hand, tracing the lines of muscle up his arms. My breath caught as his arm stole around my waist, pressing me to him.

"Mariel, you have bewitched me," he said, leaning his forehead toward mine. "You are not what I expected."

"Nor are you," I lifted my face toward his and parted my lips, desperate for his touch.

"I assume you desire to leave at the end of the month, but all I ask is for one night."

Excitement throbbed in my veins. I was here, and so was he, and there was nothing to lose. Instead of replying, I lifted my lips to his. He met them with his own. The power and potency of that kiss filled me, and I closed my eyes, desiring nothing more than to let him kiss away my lingering doubts.

Cedric broke the kiss with a groan and leaned his forehead against mine. I heard his heart pounding just as quickly as my own. The warmth of his breath against my lips hinted at more. A moan escaped my throat, and I pressed a hand against the broad expanse of his chest. Cedric's breath fanned the base of my neck before he pressed a kiss there. My skin prickled but just as suddenly he pulled away, leaving my legs wobbly, and a strange sensation of loss bloomed in my chest. I made an attempt to catch his eye, but he adverted my gaze and swept me up in his powerful arms. He practically tossed me onto Felix's back and mounted up behind me, although how he did so without his staff, I did not know.

"What's wrong?" I pled, reaching for his hand, hoping to bring him back with skin to skin contact.

"Trust me, Mariel." His voice was distant, gruff. "It is not you. There are circumstances beyond my control."

His arm tightened around my waist as he pressed a kiss against my ear. I melted back against his hard body, a sigh of relief bursting from my lungs. "But something is wrong. I sense the barrier between us."

"Time is short, Mariel, and it is not my intent to bring you unhappiness. Remember this evening, and enjoy it with me."

"But something is making you unhappy," I replied, frustration mounting. "It is because of Samhain, isn't it?"

At first he stiffened and then relaxed behind me. "Yes, Mariel, you are quite perceptive. I am often uneasy and restless before the festival. Once it is over, I will rest easy again."

"I will sit with you tonight, if you wish it and hope my presence calms you," I offered, even though there was selfishness there. I did not want to let him out of my sight.

"I would like that, Mariel," he replied.

We fell silent as Felix galloped home. When we reached the stables, Julius was waiting, a frown upon his long face. He did not spare me a glance but immediately turned his attentions to grooming Felix.

Lord Cedric took up his staff and leaned heavily on it as we made our way down the garden path back to the castle. He was silent and kept me tucked under his arm. I found it unnerving, and Sasha's bold words returned to mind. Lord of Darkness. Who was he?

"Mariel."

Lord Cedric's low whispers made me halt and I stared up at his face. He looked pale and worn. "I am weary, and although I'd like to walk you to your room, I am tired."

"You must rest," I agreed. "Let me walk you to your room, I can stay…"

He held up a hand. "I would be honored, but I have

taken up enough of your time. Sleep, my Mariel. Then brighten my day with your presence."

Confusion rode me. The feelings between us were precious and fragile as though one wrong move and they'd break, never to be discovered again. It was too soon to leave each other's presence, and I did not know how to make Lord Cedric understand. Although he was an exiled lord and I was naught but a shield-maiden. I was wrong to desire him, someone so noble and above my class, and yet it did not matter to me. Why should it matter to him?

As if responding to my inner desires, he pressed me against his chest. He smelled of the wildwood and roses. I inhaled his scent as though it were the only thing to hold me over during a long night alone. His hand strayed past my waist, squeezing my bottom. Desire washed over me as his lips hovered above mine.

"I would warn you, do not walk the halls after midnight. But you will be safe in your room."

Then his lips consumed mine. His tongue pushed into my mouth and intertwined with my own. His hand against my bottom pulled me closer to him, until I could feel his hardened muscles through his clothes. I squirmed, wanting more, but he bit my bottom lip, reproaching me for my forwardness. Then his tongue devoured mine again, and cry of pleasure burst from my lips. At some point, he let go of his staff and threaded his other hand through my hair. I dug my fingers in his hips and just when I thought I'd reach the height of my pleasure, he let go, took his staff and swept away, leaving me breathless, knees weak as I slumped against the wall.

11

FOR THE NEXT TWO WEEKS, I took the one positive senti-
ment my mother had given me and acted upon it. *It is
not possible to enjoy every moment in life, but take pleasure
when and where you can and relish it to the fullest.* Even
though those words were meant to describe the work
she did, I took them to heart and enjoyed my moments
with Lord Cedric, even though a dark knowing loomed
in the back of my mind. Soon it would be the night of
Samhain and then I would leave him. Forever.

There was no talk of my staying, and at night, I lay
awake both aroused and worried, thoughts of Lord
Cedric twisting through my mind. He was handsome
and dark, barbaric yet he made me laugh. I watched the
way he tended his garden and took care of his horses.
But I also noticed no one came to visit him, and his
staff, Betty, Sasha and Julius, were scarce during that
time. I caught glimpses of them now and again, but
nothing more.

Inevitably at some point each evening, Lord Cedric

became drawn and pale. I wondered if his leg pained him but I'd not worked up the courage to ask. He left me with the same warning each night. *Do not walk the halls after midnight.*

Then he'd kiss me long and deep as though he drank my very soul, and left me breathless, longing for more like a traveler crossing a dry desert with only a drop of water at the end of each day. It has only been a couple of weeks. I reminded myself. That was all and yet the kinship I felt toward him went much deeper. I'd touch a finger to my swollen lips and fall asleep anticipating the morning.

One morning, the air felt different. The Festival of Samhain. I bolted out of bed and saw my breakfast, steaming on the table as usual. Betty usually left a frilly dress laid out for me to wear, but today I saw my own clothes and my armor. My heart leapt into my throat. I walked over to them, noticing that both my sword and the knife Lord Cedric had taken from me were there. I ran my fingers down the blade. It had been freshly sharpened.

Anticipation twisted in my gut. Tonight was the night. The reason I had come. It was my duty to protect Lord Cedric, since I hadn't been able to kill him. And then. In the morning I'd leave. Grief stole my breath away even though I tried to shake it off. It was foolish to grieve for a man I'd known for such a little bit of time. The potential of a future with him drifted through my mind, but no. He was a lord and I was naught but a mere shield-maiden. But I did not know where I would go nor what I would do.

Dumbfounded, I tugged on my shirt and mail,

tucked my pants into my boots, and strapped the gauntlets onto my arms. I pulled my belt on and tucked my sword and knife into it but left my helmet on the table. I glanced at the table, knowing I'd need the food, but the thought of eating left my stomach feeling queasy. Leaving the breakfast untouched, I exited the room and made my way through the halls.

The castle was eerily quiet and gloomy. As were my thoughts. But I could not find Lord Cedric. The rose garden was empty, and Felix and Fauna grazed in the pasture while their foals frolicked around them. I watched them for a time before ambling aimlessly through the vineyards. Bees buzzed overhead and birds chirped as they flew back and forth, but Lord Cedric was nowhere. As I returned to the castle, I heard whispers.

Look. She's still here.

Where did you think she'd go?

She looks forlorn to me.

Pining for the lord of the castle.

Twitters twirled through the air, and I spun, searching for the voices. My fingers curled into fists and then I lashed out. "I can hear you, you know!" I shouted to the wind. "I can hear your whispers and I don't appreciate them. If you have something to say, then say it!"

There was silence and then:

Oh she's angry now.

She said she could hear us, why are you still talking?

She'll be in for a surprise tonight.

Hush. Hush.

I stormed inside, my foul mood ruining everything,

and I still couldn't find Lord Cedric. I followed the wide halls to the study, where rich sunlight poured in and hints of dried ink hung in the air. Biting my tongue, I climbed the stairs to the third floor where the bowl of divining water sat still, and then up into the towers overlooking the town. I could see all the way to the village, but my legs ached from climbing. The only place I hadn't looked were his rooms, and while I wanted to venture there, I was also embarrassed. What would he think of me if I burst in on him? I retired to my own chambers, grouchy, frustrated and very hungry. The mid-day meal awaited me and I ate in silence, unsure what my next course of action should be.

THE SHADOWS WERE GROWING LONG when a knock came on the door. I flung it open, and Lord Cedric stood on the other side. He was dressed in black from head to toe, and a broad sword hung from his waist. His dark hair flowed long about his shoulders, and his scar stood out more prominently in the low light.

"Mistress Mariel," he bowed slightly and then his eyes went to my blades. "I see you are prepared."

"Where were you?" I demanded, crossing my arms over my chest. "I looked for you everywhere!"

His purple eyes clouded over with regret. "My intent was not to distress you, Mariel. But time is of the essence now."

I glanced to my window where daylight still reigned. A lump settled in my throat. What was about to happen?

"Come," he said.

Words failed me as I followed him down the long halls. Listening to him drag his lame foot the whole way pained me, and yet I could offer no consolation.

Lord Cedric led me to the front doors of the castle, and for a moment I feared he would toss me out. But no, Felix was saddled and pawed the ground anxiously. We mounted up, but this time Cedric rode in front while I sat behind him. I wrapped my arms around his waist and pressed my face into his back, allowing his shirt to soak up my foolish tears. Something unspoken had happened between us, causing him to grow distant. Was it because I was leaving or because of what might happen tonight? I bit my lower lip and tried to staunch the flow of my silent tears.

When my tears dried, I saw we'd ridden down the hill, away from the castle. An almost invisible road led toward the forest, and Felix followed it as though he knew it by heart. There was a moment before we were plunged into the darkness of the enchanted wildwood. Thick foliage crept around trees, and orange and red flowers blossomed with a thick liquid pooling inside. The air smelled of pine, but there was another flavor, thick and hazy. Peppery. I wrinkled my nose. We trotted deeper for a while, and when I looked back, it seemed as though the trees had moved for there was no discernible path. I was unsure whether I should be afraid or not, but we pressed on as darkness consumed the forest. Eventually yellow lights began to wink in and out of view, and we came to a circular clearing.

Lord Cedric dismounted. When he reached up to help me, I ignored his hand and slid down beside him, jarring my feet against the ground. I gritted my teeth but said nothing.

"Be gone with you," Cedric patted Felix on the rump. The horse jumped and trotted away, leaving us stranded in the wildwood.

Cedric lifted his staff with both hands, and in one violent motion drove it into the ground. Then, and only then did he face me. His eyes went soft as they lingered on my face. When he reached for my hand, all of my resilience wilted. Although I could not keep the disappointment from my eyes. I lifted my gaze to his, studying the planes of his face, his scar and the way he looked at me. I melted under his gaze, and my eyes closed when he lifted my hand to his lips and kissed it. I felt that kiss through every pore of my being. It tingled up my arm and down my spine all the way to my toes.

"I'm sorry for what is to come, Mariel." His deep voice rumbled. "I could have loved you. If you wish to leave, I understand."

Puzzled, I opened my mouth to respond, but an eerie cry shattered the silence of the glade.

Lord Cedric drew his sword.

I stepped to his side and reached for mine. Twelve days without training was the longest I'd gone since I began to learn the lesson of the blade, but when my fingers wrapped around the hilt, the familiar movements came back to me. The sword scraped against the sheath as I drew it, the sound ringing out in the hushed ambience of the wildwood. Once again the familiar comfort of holding the blade enfolded me. But it wasn't just that. It was also the knowledge that I was invincible, that none could willingly hurt me when I held a blade. I would make them scream before they harmed me, and yet the ache in my heart would not go away.

"Stand firm and do not rush at them. Let them come to us," Lord Cedric warned me.

I rested my blade against my gauntlet and crouched into my battle stance. I was ready. But the creatures that lurched out of the trees weren't what I expected. They were tall as the trees, oddly skinny, and a grotesque mixture between beast and human. Twisted roots took the place of legs, forcing them to stumble as they walked. Knobby heads without eyes boggled on the tops of their tree-trunk-like body. But their bark was black, and dark moss covered their rotting bodies.

Lord Cedric clasped one hand around his staff, using it as his anchor as the beasts lurched toward him. One creature moved faster than the others and bore down upon us, waving branch-like arms. It swung as though it meant to sweep us off our feet and flatten us with its trunk.

Cedric lifted his weapon but I stepped in front of him and slashed my sword in an arc. My blade cut through the creature's arms as neatly as if they were no more than blades of grass. The tree-like creature fell with a creaking thud just as a second one took its place. I whirled my blade around and slashed through the second creature's trunk. It slid into two pieces then shattered on the forest floor. Bloodlust boiled in my belly, for even though the creatures were dark and ugly, I felt brave for killing them.

Within mere minutes, the tree creatures lay in shambles around us, nothing more than broken branches and smashed wood. Chest heaving from effort, I turned back to Lord Cedric. He stood taller than before, his legs spread, one hand still holding tightly to the staff. I blinked as I looked at it, for it seemed as though the bud on top had opened, like a flower, about to bloom.

Shaking away the potent sense of dread, I asked, "That was it?"

"No, only the first wave." He rolled his shoulders

back and swung his blade. "The waves will be swift. Stand firm. Hold your ground."

I lifted my chin. I'd already shown him I could hold my ground, but if more came, we would not last long. The creatures would overwhelm us, and he would lose ground. I swallowed a lump in my throat and once again took up my battle stance.

A deep throated cry burst from the wood, and a blur of darkness dashed toward me. Out of the corner of my eye, I saw a flash of silver. A howl went up, and the beast crashed onto the forest floor with a knife in its throat. It was no creature I knew a word for, some sort of demented human with skin black as night and eyes red as blood. My skin crawled with fear as another blur went by, almost too fast for me to see, and then they were upon us, dropping down out of tree branches and dashing out of the wood.

Stepping forward, I swung my blade, but the creatures moved past me, knocking me off my feet. I landed on my back, the wind knocked out of me, but I kept my blade in my hand and drove it straight up as a weight settled across my body. The sword cut through flesh. Shoving the beast off my stomach, I stumbled to my feet and had to pull twice in order to free my sword. It came free trailing clumps of molted flesh and blue blood.

The vile scent of sulfur filled the air. But there was no time to recover. Another beast was upon me, and another. Behind me I heard Lord Cedric roar as he fought, skewering the creatures with his sword. I whirled, driving my blade in and out, quickly losing ground. There was nothing but the beasts, their cries, their claws, their teeth, their blades, and the rot as they died, as though they were already dead beings that had come back to life.

The air stunk of death. Sweat trickled down my neck and gathered under my arms. Fear drove me on as I realized exactly what this horror was. The fight for life, the fight for the village and the fight to stop these creatures, even just one, from escaping out into the village.

The eyes of the villagers, uplifted in joy as they celebrated, flashed before me. The young and old, the women and children, they all deserved better than this. For what if these ghastly creatures broke into their homes? What then? Perhaps they knew the danger, and it was why they were thankful for Lord Cedric. For they knew what he saved them from.

I spun, trying to catch sight of him through the madness. Year after year, how could he stand this horror? We'd only just begun and already I'd had enough. Enough of the blood, the violence and the darkness that seemed as if it would overwhelm me. My fingers would not let go of the sword, and my arms shook from fatigue, but there was no rest, no stopping, only the fingers of death which reached out greedily, ready to suck life away.

A beast knocked me to my knees, and I slashed at it, slitting the back of its legs. I stumbled to my feet only to be knocked down again. This time I rose slower. A blade slammed into my gauntlet, and my teeth clattered in my skull. A battle cry came out of my lips, but it was raw and hoarse. My blade was heavy in my hands. Another beast slammed into my back. I fell, catching myself on my hands and knees.

My throat was parched, my hair hung in my face, soaked with sweat and blood. I peered up just as a roar split the air. The sound of it reverberated through me and it seemed as though everything froze. The beasts halted their attack, and even the forest seemed to hold its breath.

Light caught my eye and my mouth fell open as I saw that Cedric's staff had bloomed. Ominous purple light spread out in an arc around him. He held up both hands, his gaze fixated on the trees, and his mouth wide open in a roar.

My breath stole away as I watched his human form change. His hair grew longer, wilder, almost covering his face and body. The muscles of his arms and legs lengthened and stretched, his hands turning into the claws of a monster. Those eyes I loved to look into changed from purple into pools of endless black. His open mouth revealed a row of teeth as sharp as the edge of a knife. His clothing ripped and tore as he transformed, and horns appeared on his head, curling up like branches of the great trees.

Bile rose in my throat as I watched the man I loved shift into something horrible, evil and impossible. When his transformation was complete, I dropped to my knees. Dread crushed my heart for I knew I had come face to face with the Lord of Darkness.

My heart sunk like a stone seeking its watery grave as understanding washed over me. My stomach clenched for now Sasha's unkind whispers made sense. The Lord of the Castle was the Lord of Darkness. Surely the kingdom did not know this for a fact, and yet they still sent a guard to kill him. Or was it kill and be killed?

Once my initial shock and fear faded, a cold numbness came over me. Roars shook the forest as the Lord of Darkness fought on all fours like a wild beast. He was a barbarian after all, and the dark creatures flew as he ripped and tore, bellowing as he mowed them down like wheat during the harvest.

The creatures of the wood came on with a manic madness. They fought long and hard until the bodies piled up around us and the scent of death filled the air. And then, the onslaught decreased until there were no more. The Lord of Darkness walked away from the melee back to his staff which stood alone in the glade, unbothered. He dragged one of his legs behind him and then rose up on two feet, like a man.

I watched as he looked around, and then those orb-like black eyes settled on me. We stared at each other, breathless and I searched that monstrous face for a sign of Lord Cedric. Was he in there, somewhere, deep inside the monster? But I saw nothing, not even a faint flicker of recognition to give me hope. My hand, fisted around my sword, loosened and the blade thumped onto the forest floor. My limbs were weary with exhaustion but my heart hurt as though it had been thrashed with a hundred whips. I hadn't become a shield-maiden for this horror. My training taught me that monsters must die, but this situation was complex. There was no one to tell me what I should do. If I ran he might overtake me, and I could not be sure he was lucid inside of the monster's body. If I fought or fled, would he slay me?

Finally, the Lord of Darkness tore his eyes away from me, grunted and reached for the staff. Motes of purple light danced around him as he transformed and the flower on top of the staff closed, resuming its dormant position as a bud. His hair grew short, and his limbs changed back into those of a man. His clothes hung in tattered rags on his body. When he faced me again, he was the Lord Cedric I knew. But suddenly his eyes rolled back in his head, and he collapsed.

I was by his side in a moment and decisions ripped through my mind. I had to leave. I'd done my duty and the past month had gone by like a dream in which I was suspended from reality. But now I knew the truth about Whispering Vine. The villagers refused to face the truth and lived in blissful ignorance. The monster they should fear most had already entrapped them. He held their trust, he cared for them and protected them. Perhaps they knew. Perhaps they didn't. But it did not matter as long as they were safe and happy. And could I, a shield-maiden, sworn to protect the crown, allow such darkness to live, unquestioned, unaccountable.

Tears streaked my face and my vision blurred more than once. I pulled my knife free and held it in both hands to keep them from shaking. The pointed end would drive into his heart, but I couldn't make my arms move, couldn't take the plunge. It was a curse that the man I loved was also the Lord of Darkness. But how could a lord reign in the realm of humans if he wasn't human himself? Such darkness would ruin all. But why did it have to be me? The man I saw the most potential with. The villagers celebrated him. The rose garden grew under his care, and everything and everyone he touched loved him. Was this his curse, the gift of being loved by all when damnation happened every year on the night of Samhain?

His chest rose and fell, steadily breathing. He was still alive. But mine would be the killing blow. Even as I lifted the knife higher, I knew it would not come down. For how could I kill a man I loved, misunderstood and yet loved all the same? Now his actions made sense, the way he'd turned from me every night, as though he only deserved stolen glimpses of happiness. But I knew he deserved so much more.

"If you kill him, the wood-wrights will walk free," said a voice.

I whirled, my hair flying in my face as I caught a

glimpse of red. The knife shook in my hands, now pointed at the intruder as I stared at a woman. She looked like a human, standing a bit taller than me with brown skin, wide brown eyes and glossy black hair that tumbled free to her waist. Her hands were empty but she wore a red dress, and behind her a man stood, his naked sword glistening with blood in the low light. He kept his gaze trained on her, admiration written across his face as the woman in red strode toward me. Her presence was commanding, and even as I rose to my feet, I knew she was a kind of royalty.

"Who are you?" I breathed.

She glanced briefly at me, but then her gaze went to Lord Cedric and studied him. "I am called Yula, Queen of the Wildwood, and this is my knight, Sir Aelbrin. And you are the one who was sent to kill Lord Cedric." She spoke matter-of-factly.

"But," I paused. This was the woman Lord Cedric had spoken to the day I spied on him. "He is the Lord of Darkness. He is a monster…"

"Yes," Yula waved her hand over his body, and her brow furrowed. "I did not know he was lame."

"It pains him," I added, "If anything can be done—"

The Queen of the Wildwood stared at me. "Yes, if anything can be done. You were going to kill him?" She pointed at my blade.

My face went hot, and my fingers shook. "I cannot kill someone I love."

The Queen of the Wildwood crossed her arms. "Then don't. He is nothing compared to the monsters that inhibit the wood. I warn you, if you give your heart to him, you must understand that he will always be the

Lord of Darkness. When the wood-wrights rise, he is the one who will keep them from invading the village and slaying all who live there."

I took deep shuddering breaths as I tried to make sense of what she said. "Will more come?" I asked, emotion making my words thick.

"It is done," she said.

I dropped my blade, and it sank into the ground.

The Queen of the Wildwood turned her back on me and knelt beside Lord Cedric. I hissed as she touched his lame leg. Closing her eyes, she whispered under her breath. A flash of light came and went, like lightning.

"There," the Queen of the Wildwood stood. "Last year during the Festival of Yule, a healer came to me for help, and I took some of her magic. Now it seems that the Lord of Darkness is worthy of it. The gift of the healer is his and no longer will he be lame."

"Thank you," I gasped.

Her brown eyes regarded me. "Don't thank me. One day, the darkness will rise up stronger than before. When it does, I will call upon the Lord of Darkness for help. If you are still with him, you will come fight with us too."

She stood, her red dress fluttering out behind her as she made her way back to Sir Aelbrin. He put his blade away and took her hand, and then they faded into the wildwood.

14

IN THE WEE hours of the morning, sometime before dawn, Felix trotted into the glade. Lord Cedric was still passed out, but after struggling with his bulk and some help from Felix, we were able to mount up and rode back to the sprawling dark castle. Exhaustion washed over me, and when we arrived I let Julius take Lord Cedric while Betty bustled me upstairs and into a hot bath. For once her face was drawn and words did not tumble from her lips. While I appreciated the silence, my mind buzzed with unanswered questions while I relaxed in the bath. Betty toweled me off and I let her, too weary to protest as she helped me into a gown and practically carried me to bed.

One by one she blew out the candles and then hovered over me like a mother. "Sleep a dreamless sleep," she whispered. I detected hints of lavender in the air before I passed out.

I did not dream of monsters, nor the dark beings that came out of the wood to hunt and destroy. I did not dream of Lord Cedric nor his other form and the way he could shift and twist into a deadly beast. Instead, my sleep was dreamless, and when I woke the sun was high in the sky and cast beams of light across the room.

Clarity came to me as I opened my eyes. Soreness made me move stiffly as I stepped out of bed and hunger ate at my insides. It was time. Time to leave. Enough though I did not want to, how could I stay when the man I loved was a monster?

My bag was packed and slumped against the wall by the door, untouched since I'd entered. But my armor was gone, which made sense. It was dirty and needed a cleaning. Instead there was a dark yellow dress laid out for me, with a pattern of roses stitched around the bodice. I pulled it on, struggling for it lay lower on my chest than I expected, showing more hints of cleavage than I was comfortable with. But no matter, I was hungry, and once I found food, I'd come up with a plan and leave without disturbing the Lord of the Castle.

I opened the door and almost slammed it shut, my heart pounding in my chest like a thousand war drums beating endlessly. He sat outside my door, in a straight-back chair. Waiting. His wild hair was brushed back away from his brow, slowing off his high cheek bones and highlighting the scar. When he caught sight of me his face went pale and his lips parted, but his eyes were wide, expectant, almost, desperate.

All the air rushed out of me, and my hand dropped from the doorframe. I willed myself to remain calm as I met his gaze. It was easy to be brave in my room alone, to have thoughts of leaving for good. But even though I knew who he was, *what* he was, I wasn't running. My feet wouldn't move, and secretly, I did not want them to.

"You did not leave," he breathed, his voice thick with emotion.

"I wanted to." I could not look away from him, paralyzed by his gaze. "You did not tell me…" I trailed off.

He stood, wincing, and then walked slowly over to me. My gaze went down to his leg, no longer lame.

"She came," I went on. "The Queen of the Wildwood, and healed your leg."

A smile softened his features. "She said she would come, even though there was no need."

"I thought we would die," I burst out. "But you are him. Aren't you? The Lord of Darkness who protects the people? But how can you protect and be a monster? It goes against—"

"Against everything you know, Mariel." His hands dropped to his side and misery shone out of his eyes. "It is a burden to bear, and I, alone, will bear it. There must always be a Lord of Darkness, for this land was wrought with evil, and the goddesses cursed it. And while the Queen of the Wildwood fights against evil, she cannot do it alone. I know, all too well, that one who kills the Lord of Darkness becomes the Lord of Darkness. It is why I dwell here, apart from the people, why I have never married and why I keep a loyal staff. Unafraid and trustworthy. This is not a burden everyone can bear. But I am glad you did not leave without saying goodbye."

Goodbye. Yes. Leaving would be the right course of action, to go on, to go back and forget this dream, this waking nightmare. "But you will be alone," I protested.

"Year after year, the kingdom will send someone and you must fight the creature of the wood. It is relentless, when will it end?"

He closed the distance between us and one of his rough fingers tilted my chin up, forcing me to stare directly into his eyes. His expression softened. He tucked my hair behind my ears, and when he spoke, my whole being leaned toward him.

"Then stay. Stay here with me. Forget the past, think only of this, of us. It is not wrong to protect those you care about, and it will satisfy your longing to protect others. It is a worthy cause. You can still be my shield-maiden, and protect the village along with me. But remember this, unlike the kingdom, you would be free to come and go as you wish."

"As your mistress?" I held his gaze, for I would belong to no man as a mistress. I would not be like my mother.

His fingers brushed my cheek and his eyes smoldered. "Not as my mistress."

"As a free woman then?" My breath caught as he shook his head.

Oh goddess. I would give in if he kept touching me like this. His arm stole around my waist, pressing me against the warmth of his body.

"You are free if you want to be free, but I would have you as my wife because you are strong enough to keep your own counsel, good enough to choose your own actions, and kind, you truly care about others. During the past weeks I've seen the way you treat Betty, who talks too much, Sasha, who is frightened and often responds with anger, and even Julius who is cold and unfriendly. But you are patient and generous, and even strong enough to take up the challenge of protecting this town with me. If you would be my wife, I would cherish you, body and soul until our dying day."

I blinked away the wetness behind my eyes and rested my hands on his chest. Shivers went down my spine as I opened my mouth to respond and closed it again. My voice dropped away to a whisper. "But how can you know this is what you want? We barely know each other."

He cocked his head. "Do you not believe me? Do you not feel this way yourself? I've felt the fever in your kisses, I've seen the way your eyes watched me, haunted and disappointed when I tore myself away from you, night after night. You think with your head, not your heart, and it has served you well. Until now."

I held onto his shirt, pulling him closer. I licked my lips, but no other protests came to mind, and the ferocity of his gaze dragged me away from reason. Deep inside, I knew he would never hurt me, but he was who he was, unapologetic. It was the kingdom that was small-minded, and I'd given into their ways, trying to belong, when, in truth, aside from a few friends, no one else would miss me. I swallowed hard.

In truth, even as I fought for excuses, my mind was already made up. The words I'd spoken to the Queen of the Wildwood in the enchanted forest were true. I was in love with Lord Cedric, with his sense of humor, his ability to make light of an impossible situation and, more than anything else, the way he cared about others. Unlike the kingdom he was not after wealth or political gain, he truly cared about his land and the people who dwelled there. And he cared about me. Even as he held me, I knew he would not force me to stay. If I choose, I could walk away. Away from the man who made me feel strong and worth more than a blade. A man who listened when I spoke and truly desired for me to be happy.

"Then I am yours, Lord Cedric, body and soul."

His hand cupped my cheek as he slumped against me. "Say it again," he demanded.

"I am yours, yours alone."

A groan escaped his lips, and he pressed me against his chest, holding me close as though he would never let go. When he crushed his lips against mine I was lost, hopelessly lost.

15

"CEDRIC," I whispered as he broke the kiss.

His feathered breath whispered above my swollen lips. I leaned against him, dizzy with longing and lust.

"I still have questions." I reached up to trace the scar under this eye.

"More questions, at a time like this?" he chuckled before his gaze went serious again.

My hunger for food faded, replaced with a desperate longing for him, and him alone.

"Mariel?" he pressed when I did not immediately answer, although his gaze drifted to the open door of my borrowed room.

I threaded a finger through the buttonhole of his shirt, seeking bare flesh. "On the first evening I arrived, I heard voices. Whispers. They weren't talking to me but they were talking about me. What do you know about them?"

He pulled back suddenly, his eyes so wide I could see the white around them. "This is incredulous," he breathed. "You heard them? For so long I've been the only one who hears them speak."

My hands stilled as I bit my lower lip. Not more spirits. "Who are they?"

Lord Cedric cupped my face in his hands and studied me as though he were seeing me for the first time. "Mariel, what other secrets will you reveal? The voices you heard are the Guardians of Whispering Vine. They are the trees that line the wildwood and warn me when danger approaches, when the dark creatures awake, and when the time comes to transform."

My mouth fell open, but after last night, I could do nothing more than believe his words. "Trees have spirits?"

"Mariel, there is much for you to learn. But yes, the spirits of the trees lay dormant for years, until last year, during the Festival of Mabon. A new queen took her place in the wildwood, and the trees awoke and began to speak again. There is something in her magic that brings a glimmer of hope."

"Hope," I repeated, recalling the Queen of the Wild-wood and her knight, the spark of love between them and the warning she'd given me.

But my heart was already committed. I placed my hand on the side of Cedric's face and ran my hand over the stubble on his jaw, curious about what other secrets he'd reveal. He closed his eyes, as though my touch alone would transform him. Then a growl escaped his lips. Lifting me in his arms, his strode into the room, kicking the door shut behind him.

His mouth moved over mine. "I've waited for you Mariel, for someone like you to come, and see, and accept me for who I am instead of running, screaming into the night. It is not lost on me what your acceptance means, and what you give up to stay here, with me."

"Nothing else, no one else is more important," I managed to say, before he covered my mouth with his.

The kiss consumed me like the flames of a fire licking up my body, driving away all hesitations. I tilted my head, angling for a deeper kiss. His tongue intertwined with mine, and I went limp in his arms. When at last he placed me on my feet again, I had to hold on to him for support.

He tossed his shirt aside and slipped my dress off my shoulders. Lust boiled deep in my belly as the dress fell around my hips, leaving my breasts naked to his caress. Cool air made my nipples tighten, and he pressed his rough hand against my bare stomach, igniting sensations of desire that made my vision go fuzzy.

I trailed my hands over his hard chest, my fingers nimbly undoing his belt as he kissed me again, my cheeks, my mouth, my neck, my shoulders. His dark head bent over me, and a raw hunger came to his eyes before he took a nipple in his mouth, pulling and sucking. Wetness spread down my legs, and I threw my head back, gasping as waves of pleasure surged through me. My fingernails bit into his flesh. A cry burst out of my lips.

The fabric of my dress ripped. My eyes flew open in surprise as he tossed it aside. His dark and dangerous eyes raked down my body. Then he picked me up and tossed me on the bed. I fell with a bounce onto the gentle give of the bed, but he was on top of me in a moment. A moan escaped my lips as I opened my thighs to him, no longer caring about anything else, other than him. I raised my hips, longing to feel the length of him deep inside me.

His pupils dilated at my wanton behavior, and he traced a line up my legs to my inner thigh, his gaze holding mine as he watched me tremble and beg, arousal consuming me. This was what I wanted, what I had desired. I reached for him, traced his scars, stroked his hardness, but he took my hands and pinned them above my head. Nudging my legs wider apart he toyed with the tight buds of my nipples, rolling and teasing.

"Cedric," I moaned, arching my back, "please."

Purple eyes smoldered as he continued to tease me. "You are exquisite," he whispered.

His words, his touch made me flush and I squirmed, determined to regain some sense of control, to have him. Just when I thought I couldn't hold out any longer, he took me, drove into me. Hard. Again and again. Heat consumed me as he held me tight against his hard body, his lips on mine as he possessed me, as he took me, body and soul.

I trembled at the depth of his emotion, stunned at how easily I'd given in but how right it felt. The mysteries of the dark castle were unveiled, and I'd found a home which would allow me to be my true self. But even more than that, I'd found my man, my love, my very own lord of darkness.

HEART OF THE RAVEN

1

A SCREAM of terror died in my throat as the nightmare gave way to reality. I bolted upright, one hand pressed to my mouth while blood rushed to my ears. Beads of sweat gathered around my neck and dripped down my back. Ripping the covers off, I stumbled out of the heavy blankets and paced, my feet sinking into the padded carpet of my borrowed room in my cousin Cedric's mysterious castle. Hiding in the castle hadn't been my first choice, and with my nightmares intensifying, I knew I had to make yet another life changing decision.

With shaking fingers, I pulled on a silk robe to keep the chill away and hoped my scream hadn't woken anyone. But none disturbed my rest. I posed as a maid to hide my identity. I was a shameful maid, but visitors came to the castle only once a year. Betty, the house-keeper, did most of the work herself, occasionally giving me minor grievances for not helping more. But she understood my plight. I was a noble, not some servant. Pretending to be a maid could not change the fact I was used to others waiting on me hand and foot. Not the other way around.

I fumbled for a candle and lit it with the quick strike of flint against stone. I almost screamed when I caught my shadow in the mirror and settled down on the stool in front of it, dropping my head into my hands before studying my reflection. My father used to tell me my eyes were the color of copper and he nicknamed me his "little Jewel". But now my eyes were red-rimmed from lack of sleep and the nightmares that frayed my nerves. I was tall and willowy with an oval face and high cheekbones that accented my eyes and mouth. Wisps of my bright yellow hair tumbled out of the bun I'd twirled on top of my head. My sunlight colored hair was a sharp contrast to my dark skin. I got my darker coloring from my father and my hair from my mother. Unlike me, she was a pale beauty while I was a dark one, but just like her, I was strong-willed and stubborn to a fault. Because the women in my family were renowned for our beauty, I assumed life would be easy. I did not expect trouble to find me, nor nightmares to flood my dreams.

Watching the candle light flicker, I took a deep breath and recalled my dream. Betty said that dreams were nods to the future, and recalling them, or writing them down, could help unravel what might happen. Dreams were omens to keep one from falling into folly or to assist with making the right choice when a decision came. A question had been in the back of my mind before, but now the dream seemed to make it clear. I rubbed my thumbs across my wrists, an old habit to help calm my nerves. I closed my eyes, and I was right back in the dream.

SHADOWS SURROUNDED ME, and although I could only make out vague shapes, I knew they were the trunks of old trees. I stood in a glade, lost, alone, searching for the way out while a voice called to me, thin and whispery. Sasha. Come to me, child. Come and discover your destiny.

Shadows blurred into one unending stream of darkness. The ground below me opened, and I fell into a nameless void while the wind streamed around me and that voice shouted my name. Sasha! Not down there, not to where the Goddess sleeps.

Velvet feathers, darker than ink, swirled around me, and then came the caw of a raven as it flew after me. I opened my mouth. A scream tore out, too late. I was hurled, weightless, into darkness.

MY EYES CAME open but the darkness clogged my throat. It was within me, around me, pressing in as though it would take my life. I fought to stay in control of my panic while I watched the flame flicker, casting more shadows across the room. It was foolish to be afraid of the dark, but I needed the light. I needed the sun.

The stool tumbled to the floor as I leaped up and paced back and forth. My silk robe swept the floor with each turn. There would be no more sleep for me tonight. I had to stop the recurring nightmares; I had to find someone who could help me. As I paced in the wee hours of dawn, an idea came to me. My family was not close, and I was an only child, but Mother had spoken with disgust about her mother's mother. A woman who hadn't been born into wealth and continued to live as a common peasant. Mother Misha. She was a fortune-teller who lived in Capern. The city would take two weeks to reach by foot, faster by horse, but it was spring. The trade routes were opening back up and if the fates were with me, I could secure passage with the next traders and get answers. I sat down again to put ink to parchment and scribbled a note. My blood ran cold in my veins at the thought of leaving, but I knew it was time.

2

"SASHA! YOU'VE ARRIVED!" An excited voice shouted as I trotted up to the wagon.

I rode on the back of a white warhorse whose mane and tail I'd braided with red ribbon. I was proud of the horse my cousin had given me and named her Lotus after the white flowers that floated in the water fountains both in the village of Whispering Vine and back at my cousin's castle.

"Yes, I'm here," I replied, gently pulling on the reins to bring Lotus to a stop. "Where else would I be?"

My friend, Mari, laughed from the seat of the wagon, her black hair braided around the crown of her head. Wisps fell free, and she smiled at me as she rested a hand on her belly. She had a wide mouth and flat nose, but her eyes sparkled with mischief. She'd seen through my cold exterior at once and had become a close friend in the village. "Jorge said that at the last moment you'd change your mind and wouldn't come." She grinned.

Jorge, the tradesman, was her husband. Each spring,

when the weather cleared, he loaded up a shipment of wines from Lord Cedric's vineyard and took them to the nearby villages to trade. A small group always went with him. Since the journey was long, and I wanted to reach Capern, his wife, Mari, had agreed to come. They had been married a year and had no children yet, but her eyes sparkled with the thought of adventure. Although I could have warned her that her bottom would soon be sore from sitting on the wagon bench day after day and sleeping in the dew-soaked grass was miserable. Already, I missed the comforts of Lord Cedric's castle. But no matter, it was time I set off on my own. Comforts would come aplenty for me, I'd see that they did.

"Did you place a bet?" I asked, for Mari seemed the sort.

"Aye," she snickered, "he owes us a bottle of wine that we'll share at sundown."

Despite my misgivings, her gaiety won me over, and I gave her a thin smile.

"Tell me now." Mari's eyes went to the horse. "You're pretending to be a maid in the castle and yet you have a war horse?"

Few knew I was Lord Cedric's cousin, and I intended to keep it that way. The less they knew about me, the better. "He would not take no for an answer," I replied.

Mari paused a moment, studying me. I recognized what she saw. Although I did minor work at the castle from time to time, my hands were still smooth. I often wore gowns made of expensive silk. Today featured a sky blue dress, low cut in the front and a bright red cloak which matched the ribbons I'd woven into Lotus' mane. My yellow hair was piled on top of my head in a sophisticated bun, emphasizing my long neck. I'd even put rouge on my cheeks and lips, blending it into my light brown skin. Too much for a hard journey, but I wanted to feel comfortable. My three bundles had been bustled away into the wagon by the servant sent down from the castle to walk with me. I refused to let Lord Cedric and his lady see me off. It would only confirm my identity, something I did not want. Although, from the way Mari studied me, taking in the war horse, the bundles and the slight flaring of her nostrils, I knew I had gone too far.

Mari eyed my war horse. "Look, I know you don't want me to say this, but you need to be careful if you don't want to draw unwanted attention to yourself."

I pursed my lips together, well aware I'd overdone it. Mari was the one villager I trusted with my secret. Her compassion and curiosity finally made me give in. During one of the first festivals I spent in Whispering Vine, I drank too much wine, as was the custom, and ended up spilling my secret to Mari. She'd hooted with laughter. Being able to share boosted my spirits. Although Mari was not of high birth, I liked her. Her spirits were always light, and she often found reason to laugh.

"It's just a horse," I replied, "No different from the horses you have."

"Oh, really?" Mari rolled her eyes. "Your white mare is for nobility, but no matter, if anyone asks we're going to sell her for breeding. Actually," she held up a finger, "that's not a bad idea. If things don't go as planned in Capern, you can always sell the horse."

I wanted to scowl at her but couldn't. The horse wasn't for sale. What was the point in having possessions if one had to sell them all the time?

"Now come sit." Mari patted the wagon. "Amuse me while the men finish loading. I want to know why you decided to leave."

Once Jorge and the seven other men traveling with us finished loading the wagons, we set off. I noticed one of the dark-haired youths staring at me, lust gleaming in his eye. I winked at him and then rode ahead, wondering if we would have some fun later. There was no harm in it, stolen kisses in the dark, heavy groping over clothes, something that added a bit of fun to the journey and excitement when darkness fell. Sleeping alone in the dark made me feel uneasy, even though there was a bed wagon for the women to sleep in.

We set off at a quick pace, moving through the village while onlookers threw flowers at us, and wished us good luck. It was like a celebration, and a pang struck my heart as we left it behind. Even though Whispering Vine was overshadowed by the enchanted wildwood, it was also protected. The forest frightened me, but I'd come to accept the fact there was nowhere I could go to escape from it. It was vast, bordering a multitude of villages and unknown lands. I'd heard it reached as far as the great sea, where people live on islands, wore clothes made of grass and lived in huts made of straw and mud. I'd also heard it reached as far as the mountains, where firedrakes came down from their holes and great worms rose out of the ground to consume the tribes who dwelt there. Still, I shuddered at the looming trees for an aura of destiny hung about them. My cousin's dark magic stemmed from the wood, and I turned away, trying to ignore what gift the wildwood might have for me.

"How many trade routes have you been on?" I asked Mari as we left Whispering Vine.

"Too many to count." She beamed. "It's always the same, the excitement of packing up and leaving, the thrill of the first few days. And then it turns into a countdown until we arrive at the next village. There's constantly something to look forward to. One time, we camped in some rolling hills and built a great bonfire. A band of ruffians found us, and instead of robbing us blind, they joined us for food and song. We were so frightened." Mari giggled. "But it was all for naught."

I shivered, hoping that ruffians would stay away from us. The last thing I wanted was to run into a group of outlaws on the road, although I was aware it happened from time to time. But it wasn't the fear of what they might do to us, it was what might come out of me.

3

THE FIRST DAY was quiet with the mellow beauty of early spring. I rode Lotus until my thighs ached and that space between them was sore. When I dismounted, my feet were numb and stung the ground with a sharp reminder that I hated traveling. Even the scent of wildflowers on either side of the path, and the song of the thrush in the meadow, did nothing to lighten my mood.

The men were busy tying up the horses and feeding them when Mari grabbed my arm. "You look angry." She smiled. "Food will make you feel better."

"I can never get used to the road," I grumbled, handing my horse's lead to the young man who'd winked at me.

"It's only for a little while." Mari shrugged, sitting down on a fallen log before a bundle of firewood.

I joined her, surprised at how quickly the men worked. We sat in a circle with the wagons on the outside, the horses on the inside and then the men, weaving in and out as they finished the chore of setting up camp.

Mari lit the fire, leaning on her knees and blowing on it as she watched it catch fire. "I'm always happier out in the wild," she declared, feeding sticks into the flame to keep it burning. "I believe I'm a child of nature, born to live off the land."

"Like the Druids and gypsies," I answered, twisting my hands in my lap instead of helping.

"Not quite, they have magic, and I have none." Mari shook her head.

"I was born to live in a house, with a roof over my head, keeping out the elements," I told her. "And although I don't mind a stroll through nature, I always long to return to a bed of feathers in a room."

Mari's dark eyes laughed at me. "Aye, and every pleasant thing at your fingertips." She lowered her voice. "Tell me then, why are you doing this? Was marriage so bad?"

I reached for a twig and fed it into the fire, glad to be doing something after all. "If it were anyone else, perhaps I might have considered it." Even thoughts of his dark aura made a steady rhythm pulse under my skin. My thoughts flickered back to the day everything changed.

"LADY SASHA," Lord Brecken's tone was cold, as though he were about to scold a maid for dropping his afternoon tea.

A lump formed in my throat as he stood and disgust snaked down my back. Deep-set eyes that flashed with malice set in the middle of his perfect face. Too perfect. His hair was swept back from his forehead, giving him a severe appearance and the way his nose jutted out, sharp and slightly curved, made him look hawkish. My insides quivered at the very thought of marrying that man, belonging to him, and allowing him to touch me. My stomach twisted, and I thought I'd be sick as he crowded my personal space. The dark mystery of his aura surrounded me and my head throbbed with the need to escape from him. I cursed my slow reaction for allowing myself to be caught in the room alone with him.

"Soon you will be my wife, wealth and power will be ours."
He strode across the room toward me.

His gait was stiff, and he wore the uniform of an army commander, with his sword. That sword never left his side and my eyes were drawn to it. I'd heard bone-chilling tales of how he used it. Sometimes beating servants who displeased him with the flat blade, other times, running an animal through, for no reason at all. When he lost his temper, he was not a man to cross swords with.

I rose, my eyes darting toward the door. Escape.

"Come, have a taste with what life with me will be like,"
he said as he stood in front of me.

I swallowed my fear and raised my chin. He wasn't much taller than me, and our eyes were almost level. "My lord, we are not married and it would be inappropriate to do anything that might tarnish our reputations, before we say our vows."

His lips twisted into a hideous sneer. "Why should you wait for propriety, when you are already mine?"

Mine. I detested that word coming from his lips and he must have seen my muscles twitch when I failed to keep my expression blank. A black cloud covered his face as he sensed my imprudence. "You will soon learn I expect obedience in all things," he growled through clenched teeth. "I am a kind lord." Ha. What a lie! "And you will experience my love, as long as you obey."

My stomach twisted again, and I thought I might hurl on his boots. "My lord, I am feeling poorly from the meal. If you will excuse me, we can continue this conversation at a later time."

Eyes narrowed, he settled his hand on my throat, lightly applying pressure. My eyes went wide, and a mortified squeak came from my lips. He pressed harder and then roughly crushed his lips against mine. I was too startled to react, and nausea churned in my belly. One of his hands dipped down to pinch my bottom through my thick skirts.

Somehow I wrestled out of his grasp and pressed a fist to my mouth.

He held out his hand toward the door. "Another time then, my lady."

I fled from the room and hurled the contents of my stomach into the first bucket I could find. Then, wiping my mouth with my handkerchief, I stood, one hand on my stomach as thoughts darted through my mind. He was a monster and marrying him would condemn me to a life of misery.

After washing my mouth out, I went in search of my mother, heart pounding. She was in her study, writing letters, and gave me a sour look when I walked in. "I have to break off the engagement," I burst out. "I can't marry him."

She fixed her steely gaze on me, her mouth in a firm line that I recognized whenever we argued. "Can't? Or won't?" she demanded, massaging her temples.

I should have felt sorry for her. She'd married my father, a foreigner to the kingdom, for love. My mother had two sisters who had both passed away. One leaving a son, Lord Cedric, who was exiled to Whispering Vine, and the other who had no children. After father died, it was just her and I. Although I knew she was searching for a man to remarry and provide her with wealth and pleasure for the rest of her life. My marriage to Lord Brecken would provide her with an ideal situation and ensure her needs were met for the rest of her days. My refusal to take his hand would not be dealt with kindly. But she had to know.

"Sasha, we've been over this before and I grow weary of your selfishness. Arranged marriages are just what happens here, accept it. Lord Brecken is not a man who will be denied, but you already understand what kind of man he is. He will be kind to you, as long as you please him, and it will be good for you. We will have a home and we will not be destitute when the money runs out."

There it was, her own selfish reasoning. "I don't love him, and his very touch makes me ill," I disagreed.

Mother laughed. "Who said anything about love? Marriage isn't for love but necessity. We need a roof over our heads and I am unwilling to give up our comfortable lifestyle, and neither are you. Look at you, in your fine silks, rouge on your cheeks and every hair in place. If you don't bathe every day, you sink into a dark mood. Do you want to be like the peasants, out there toiling the fields with dirt under their fingernails? Stinking of sweat and dung? Trust me, you don't want to find out what it's like to work for everything you need, to dig food up out of the soil, to stand in a hot kitchen over a fire, hoping you won't burn a leg of meat."

I crossed my hands over my chest and glared at her. The life of a servant did not seem ideal and yet, I couldn't marry him.

"I won't marry him." I stamped my foot. "And that's final."

The sudden slap made me stumble backward, and I held my burning cheek, tears brimming over.

"You ungrateful child," she hissed. "You'll do as you're told, or else. . ."

Spinning, I dashed to my room and barricaded myself inside, tears streaming down my face at the unfairness of it all. I didn't ask to be a noblewoman, nor marry a lord. At the thought of his lips on mine, another wave of nausea burned my throat. I had to get out.

When I closed my eyes, a vision filled my sleep. A dark forest loomed, but beside it rose a castle, tall and dark, with sturdy walls, and my cousin with mysterious magic. Magic I wanted no part of and yet, I could go and be exiled with him. All I needed to do was be bold and brave enough to venture out.

When I woke, I gathered a few things and snuck out of the house to the barn. Guilt rode me, but I promised myself that I'd write to my mother as soon as I arrived in Whispering Vine. She'd be furious that I defied her, but if she wanted to continue to live her life as a noblewoman, she would figure out a way.

4

"You're quiet," Mari said as we walked down the road.

On one side of us loomed the enchanted wildwood, its thick boughs giving away no secrets. On the other side of the road was a cliff, with grass running up to the sharp sides where it dropped away into nothing.

It was the fifth day of our journey and I needed a break from riding. I was in a foul mood. My bottom was sore and other places that a lady should not mention aloud. It was my fault. Mari had warned me I'd overdo it by riding Lotus all day, too many days in a row. But I usually only listened to my own counsel and now I was paying for it.

My slippers weren't meant for the road and after a few hours my feet would be chaffed, but no matter, I had to take turns giving my bottom or my feet a rest. "I had a nightmare last night," I told her. The aura of that frightful dream made my body tense as I recalled it.

I stood in the glade of shadows while trees moved, their trunks turning into faces that watched me out of sinister eyes.

Stumbling, I fell to my knees, mouth dry as I searched for a way out. In the distance I heard the cawing of a raven, and as I listened, I sensed that instead of mocking me it was calling out in warning. I reached for something to steady myself, but my fingernails sank into soft mud, and then the ground opened beneath me, pulling me down into that endless void.

Mari lay a hand on my arm, startling me. "Why didn't you wake me?"

Shrugging, I turned away from her pitying gaze, and a flutter of wings caught my eyes. High in the sky I glimpsed a bird with wings as dark as night. It flew toward the closest tree and alighted there. The sound that came out of its mouth made dread whisper through me. *Caw. Caw. Caw.* Was it a warning?

I flashed her a smile to reassure her I was fine, although I folded my hands together and rubbed my thumbs on the inside of my wrists. "No, you need your rest." I gave her a pointed look.

Her hand dropped to her belly. "It's too early to tell, I am hopeful but. . ."

"It will not happen if I keep sharing the wagon with you," I said.

"Sasha!" Mari exclaimed. "You are too bold."

"Too honest?" I smirked.

Unable to hold back her shock, Mari dissolved into giggles. "Jorge says the next village is only a day's ride from here. Tomorrow we'll relax at an inn." She winked.

I raised an eyebrow. Peasants seemed to look forward to an inn, but from my previous journey, I'd discovered they weren't what they seemed. My frustration leaked out before I could stop myself. "An inn? With their hay mattresses, sour ale and day old soup? I just want to get to where I'm going, nothing more, nothing less."

Mari poked me. "You're just grumpy because you're spoiled. You can always go back, if you want to."

I grimaced. "Going back would be easier, but I won't. I need to stand on my own two feet, become an independent woman."

Her voice dropped to a conservative whisper. "There aren't many opportunities for women. Especially alone. Are you sure the lord was so bad?"

Rubbing the back of my neck, I frowned. My skin tingled and I couldn't shake the feeling we were being watched. But Mari spoke to my inner fears. I'd ruined my life by fleeing my arranged marriage. Who would marry an outcast noblewoman? What chances did I have? Lord Brecken was powerful enough to ensure that no one would cross him. No nobleman would take me as his wife now.

"Riders!" The shout saved me from answering the question.

Mari snatched up my hand. "Quick, get into the wagon."

"Why?" I demanded, picking up my skirts to run.

"Riders could mean many things. Outlaws, other traders, king's men, it's best not to be seen until the men call the all clear. Usually it's nothing," she gave me a light-hearted smile. "But on the road it's better to be safe."

My throat went dry, but I shook off the sixth sense that nipped at me. "Do we have to hide in the wagon? It is not unusual for women to travel?" I asked Mari as I followed her into the wagon.

A cry interrupted her reply, and then a shout. Mari frowned and motioned for me to lie down as she pulled the covering over the wagon. Goosebumps pebbled on my arms and my tongue felt thick. "What do you think it is?" I whispered, trying not to let panic take over.

Mari pressed a finger to her lips and waited.

Another shout came, and then something slammed into the side of the wagon. I couldn't help the scream that left my throat as the wagon shook. And then there was nothing but noise. The pounding of hooves on the ground, the shouts and cries of men, the frightened neigh of horses.

"Something is happening." Mari swallowed back a moan. "Oh, Jorge, I have to see."

"No." I snatched at her hand as dread gripped my heart. "Please Mari. Stay here."

Staying low, she crawled to the edge of the wagon. "Stay here," she told me.

I tried to catch her arm, but she dashed out of the wagon and crept away. Alone, in the shadows, I curled up in a ball, listening to the frightful sounds. Blade struck blade with a ringing, hollow sound. Who was out there? Bandits? It had to be. Who else would attack us? It was true that we carried valuables. Other than my war horse there was the wine and whatever else was packed in the wagon.

A moment later, the wagon doors swung open and relief surged through me. It was over. We would be fine. I uncurled myself from the fetal position and lifted my face to the light. But instead of Mari, a man's shadow blocked the light. My mouth went dry as he lunged for me. Grabbing a handful of my hair, he dragged me out of the wagon. I screamed as pain radiated across my skull and my hands went to my head to pull his fingers out of my hair. He let go, and I tumbled to the ground, rolling for a moment before catching myself. Dust covered my red gown and the gravel on the road embedded itself in my legs. I cursed and spit as I stood to my feet.

Chaos echoed around me. Knights on horses galloped in circles, their blades flashing as they cut down the men I traveled with. One of them slashed at the horses hitched to the wagon. They reared up, bucking in fear until the wagon fell over with a crash. Plumes of dust rose, and I saw my war horse, red ribbons flying, charge into the midst, rearing and kicking as though she alone were the only one who could drive back the riders.

My mouth filled with bile. I recognized their livery. A buzzing began in my skull where the man had held my hair, and my stomach clenched. Dizzy with fear, I turned, searching for somewhere to run, somewhere to hide. But the man who had yanked me so cruelly out of the wagon came up behind me. He put one arm around my waist and the other on my neck. As soon as I felt his touch, I knew who he was. Lord Brecken.

Darkness swirled around me, and blood burned in my veins. This was his revenge on my rejection and ruining what could have been. But who had told him I was on the road and where I was going? Betrayal cut through me like a knife splitting me open. I'd told no one but my cousin and my mother, feeling I owed it to her. In her maliciousness had she told Lord Brecken and tried to salvage a marriage that never could be?

"Look!" His harsh voice whispered in my ear. "Look at what you have wrought."

Peering through my blurred vision, I looked while his hand squeezed my throat. All I saw was red blood, pooling on the road, and the bodies of Jorge, his seven companions and, worst of all. Mari. Her eyes were sightless, glazed over, and her mouth still open in shock.

Lord Brecken's fingers tightened around my throat and I choked and clawed at his grip, to no avail. "This is what happens to those who displease me," he went on. "You made a mockery of me, Lady Sasha. You dared repay my kindness by running away from our marriage. It is an insult I cannot forgive. You embarrassed me in court and my enemies dared to stand against me. This is a lesson to those who displease me. You shall not survive."

A trembling came over me and a roar of anger rose within me. Instead of clawing at the hand that held me firmly, my fingers clenched into fists.

I kicked out, but he held me firm. A hoarse scream rose in my throat and my limbs flailed wildly. I would not be another collection of his to be used and abused. Fear and rage twisted in my belly, gurgled up and filled my mouth. I rasped against the pain in my throat and a cloud of darkness rolled out of my mouth.

It surged toward the men like a winged creature of death, seeking to consume. Men shouted and ran, frightened of the sudden cloud. Even Lord Brecken stiffened and a curse burst from his lips. The arm around my throat loosened and the back of his hand struck me, hard, against the side of my head. Pain exploded in my head as I dropped to the ground.

Vaguely I saw the black cloud surge into dust and, once again, arms wrapped around me. Not arms, more like wings, with feathers. As they lifted me, I sensed something within me had been caught and bottled.

Those wings closed around me, filling me with the fragrance of the forest, pine, and sandalwood with hints of patchouli. Blackness surrounded me. I fought, determined to get away, but my breath came ragged and slow until I fainted away in the arms of my captor.

5

I OPENED MY EYES. Was I dead?

Golden light floated above me and a haze of green swam as my vision cleared. I saw white buds and pink petals, and then pain came rushing in. I wasn't dead at all. My legs stung from falling on the gritty gravel ground, and my stomach was sore as though I'd vomited my insides out. My throat was raw, my lips dry, and the faint pounding behind my eyes made me feel sick. I glanced down at my dress, ripped and torn at the bottom. The swells of my chest were further darkened with dirt, and dust covered my arms. I groaned and leaned back against the smooth wood of a white tree. As I did, the attack came rushing back. Lord Brecken's threats and the arms that bore me away. Nostrils flaring, I searched the ground for a rock or branch, anything to use against my captor.

My lips parted when I saw him, and my fingers stilled. He stood a few feet away, leaning against a tree and staring off into the wood as though he did not have a care in the world. He was not Lord Brecken, nor did he wear the colors of Brecken's knights.

Disheveled black hair covered his head and swept across his forehead. From his side profile I could see the impish tilt of his wide lips and his straight nose. Thick lashes framed black eyes. I shivered as my gaze ran the length of his body. He wore a coat made of feathers, patterns with dark green and ivy black that reflected the wildwood. They glistened in the sunlight and my heart beat a pitter-patter. Folding his arms he shifted toward me.

I glimpsed his bare chest, for he wore no shirt underneath his cloak of feathers. Locks of jet black hair slipped across his face and I pushed to my feet, pointing a finger at him. "You're the man from my dreams!"

A smirk came to his lips. "It's not every day a beautiful woman faints in my arms and tells me I'm the man from her dreams."

Rude and cocky. I scowled as I attempted to shake the dust off my arms. My throat was raw from Lord Brecken's fingers and I ached for a drink of water. "Who are you?" I studied my surroundings and assumed I must be deep in the forest, for no matter which way I peered between the trees, I could see no way out. "Why did you take me?"

His coal-black eyes danced with mischief as he stepped toward me, and I noticed the way he kept his eyes on my face, as though looking anywhere else would lead to temptation. "I'm the man of your dreams, shouldn't you be ready to go anywhere with me?"

"From my dreams, not of them," I retorted and wrapped my arms across my chest.

His gaze shifted to the trees, and he bit his bottom lip as though keeping a retort from leaving his tongue. "Listen." He scratched the back of his neck. "I don't know what happened out there. I heard screams and then I saw the cloud of magic that came out of you."

The skin on his forehead pinched as he studied me.

I took a shuddering breath, feeling faint again. "You saw that?" My hand went to my stomach. Was the soreness an effect of the magic?

"I bound your magic before more could escape."

I glanced at his face. A question lay there. He guessed I had started the battle. He assumed it was my fault.

Panic raced through me. "It wasn't my fault. We were on the road and they attacked us, for no reason. They killed my friends!" I snapped, whirling away from him.

My heart pounded in my throat, and I waited for the sob to burst out of my lips, that sob that never came. Anger often overrode my grief, and it was happening again. I couldn't weep for them because I was so angry. It was my fault for making a powerful enemy. I'd underestimated Lord Brecken. And what of the magic that had burst out of me? I pressed my hands to my head and moved back and forth, taking deep breaths.

"Hey, hey, hey," the man whispered, soothing me. "I'm not blaming you. I sensed your magic and when the man attacked you, I came to assist."

I spun around to study him. "Who are you? And what do you know about magic?"

He lifted his hands. His cloak made his arms look like wings. "I am the Raven." He bowed.

Raven. A whisper hushed through me, a knowing. I knew this man, not just from my dreams, but. . .my thoughts flitted back to a moonless night. The same night I fled from home. I'd coaxed the horse to jump the fence, and the pounding of hooves startled a bird who'd been watching me. "And?" I shook my head, thoughts chasing each other through my head. I was destitute once again. Should I return to Whispering Vine or proceed to Capern? Regardless, I had to hide. Should I appeal to him for help? I'd seen him in my dreams. He was the one who warned me.

He straightened, confusion crossing his handsome face. "And. What?"

"That's your name?"

He shrugged. "Call me Raven. And you are?"

"Sasha."

Mischief glittered in his eyes again, and this time he couldn't stop his gaze from traveling the length of my body. "Lady Sasha," he echoed. "How can I be of assistance?"

My brow furrowed. "What do you mean?"

"You're a damsel in distress. I came to your aid but you have powerful magic, which, I must admit, I am attracted to."

He had the audacity to wink at me and although his words were harmless, I felt the need to slap the smile off his lips. A man offered to help me and the only thing I could think of was slapping him. I licked my lips and paced again. I needed his help.

"Let's get one thing right," I said, planting myself in front of him. "I am not a damsel in distress. I am on my way to Capern to meet a relative, and a lord who is angry with me for refusing his hand in marriage attacked me. I need to stay hidden. Will you be my guide to Capern?"

A wide grin covered his lips, showing off his straight white teeth. "A guide to Capern? I accept but," he held up two fingers, "only if we travel through the forest and you meet with the Queen of the Wildwood and recommend my services to her."

A bargain. An exchange. Something in it for me and something in it for him. Despite the fairness of such an agreement, a thrumming began in the back of my mind. My throat ached again, and I desperately wanted water. "Why the Queen of the Wildwood?" I whispered. Would speaking her name aloud summon her?

I hoped not, for I knew who she was. A powerful queen who controlled the evil that dwelt in the wildwood, the same queen who often spoke with my cousin. They had an alliance, and I wanted nothing to do with it.

"She doesn't trust me," Raven explained. A shadow crossed his face. "I have spent the last two years trying to prove to her I am not the evil monster I used to be. But she won't relent."

Evil. Monster. I took a step back. Eyes wide. "Why? What have you done?"

But I thought I already knew. Two years ago, everything had changed in the wildwood.

"I used to serve the Dark Queen. She was wicked, it was easy to cavort with her, but along came Yula, and changed everything. I only survived by flying away, and for a long time I thought she might kill me. But here I am. Still alive."

6

HESITATING, I studied him again. Okay. He had problems, but so did I. If we could assist each other at the end of this, we could part ways, both gaining what we wanted. The fact that he served the Dark Queen gave me qualms, but I couldn't worry about it right now. My mind was still reeling from what had just happened, I would worry about his dark history later, but if he gave me any cause to doubt him, I'd flee. And go where? I had no idea. I glanced down at my torn and muddied clothes. "We have to go back," I announced.

He groaned. "No, we are not going back to the scene of the crime."

"Everything I possess is back there," I protested. "My clothes, my horse, I can't travel through the wildwood like this."

He studied me more closely, taking in the cut of my gown, the scratches on my arms and legs. His eyes narrowed. "You aren't a mere peasant, traveling with a group of tradesmen, are you?"

I swallowed hard but lifted my chin in defiance, eyes flashing. "It is none of your concern."

His lips twitched. "Everything about you concerns me, Sasha. I'm the one who appears in your dreams. Our paths have led us to each other. But why?" He cocked his head and the way he studied me very much made me think of a raven.

I frowned. "Why are you wasting time? We will travel together and will have plenty of time to discuss. Now let's go, before someone else happens upon the scene."

With a sigh, he brushed his unruly hair out of his face. "Are you always this bossy?" he retorted. Without waiting for an answer, he strode off into the wildwood.

I followed as best I could, pulling my skirts up to keep them from snagging on every bramble and bush that stuck out. The foliage of the forest was thick, as though it did not desire to give anyone safe passage. I sensed it was alive, watching, listening, then reporting back to the queen. A faint hum hovered in the air, and I was relieved when I saw a patch of open forest.

Raven glanced back with a finger over his lips. He pointed, and I crept up beside him, peering over a bush to see what he saw. The wreckage of the caravan lay strew out on the road, bottles of wine were broken and smashed, bolts of silk torn in half and bundles of food and clothes strewn across the road. And then I saw what Raven saw. People dressed in dark leather moved, collecting the bolts of silk that were still intact and the wine. They were men and women, working quickly, effortlessly as though they'd practiced.

"Outlaws," I hissed. "They have no right."

I moved forward, but Raven grabbed my wrist. "You can't fight outlaws."

"They are taking what's mine," I insisted.

"Do you know what they will do to you if you go out there?" he demanded.

I gritted my teeth. But he was right. I blinked back tears as I watched them finish stacking the bodies in the wagon. They set fire to it and then slipped away, taking my war horse with them. My legs gave way. I collapsed on the ground, tucked my knees under my chin, and wrapped my arms around my legs. Burying my head on my knees, I rocked back and forth as I took deep breaths. Trying to stay strong.

Raven cleared his throat awkwardly. "Lady Sasha," he said, as though a cloud of black magic might roar out of me again.

I lifted my head, brushed tears away, and held out a hand. He pulled me to my feet. His touch was comforting, and even though we'd just met, I stepped closer, until our bodies were aligned.

His eyes widened just the slightest, as though he realized my intent, and opened his mouth to protest. Regardless, I wrapped my arms around his waist and leaned into him, resting my cheek against the feathers of his cloak. And then those great arms came around me in a gentle embrace. I heard the rhythmic thud of his heart skip a beat, and then he pulled away, shaking his head.

"Follow me." He tossed the words over his shoulder and set off into the wood.

I followed, perplexed about his reaction to me. Usually, men craved my attention, but Raven could barely bring himself to embrace me. Why was that? Did it have something to do with his dark past?

As I followed him into the wood, I found myself willing to let go of my grief to unravel the mystery of Raven.

A TERSE SILENCE rose between us as I followed him. Brambles and dense vines blocked our way, but somehow the forest seemed to open up in Raven's wake. I stumbled as quickly as I could behind him, a wave of sorrow washing over me. Why was I the only one who escaped? I should be with them. But the dark magic within me had saved my life, and while I was grateful for it, I wanted nothing to do with magic.

My throat was dry and my belly ached, but rather than complain loudly to my guide, I stumbled on bravely, tears streaking my cheeks until he spoke.

"You shouldn't want me," he stated, without turning around.

I jerked, my chin wobbling as I flashed the back of his head a furious stare. "What makes you think I desire you?" I demanded.

"Back there when we saw the outlaws." He faced me. "You wanted me to hold you."

"I was upset," I sputtered, wiping signs of tears off my already grimy face. "And seeking comfort. You are the only one here."

His somber eyes narrowed. "Yes, I am well aware. But I am dangerous. Just because I've reformed doesn't mean I'm not. . . tempted."

He drew out the last word slowly while his heated gazed flickered across my body.

For a moment I saw a flash of how dangerous he could truly be. I swallowed hard, my cheeks burning. "Okay." I had to keep my resolve. "Then why did you agree to help me?"

"It's a deal I cannot pass up, just keep your distance." With that final warning, he strode on.

7

I THOUGHT the skin would peel off the bottom of my feet by the time we stopped. My throat was so choked and dry I wasn't sure I could manage words.

"Wait here," Raven instructed, then disappeared around a tree.

I slumped to my knees and bit back a sob as the events of the day sunk in. I was alone, and even worst, destitute. The jewels I'd packed away were in my lost bundles. I'd have to live like a peasant and survive by the goodwill of others. Once I left the forest, I could send a note to Lord Cedric. He'd been against my journey from the start, and while it would be embarrassing to crawl back into his good graces, it was the only home I had left. Until I found Mother Misha in Capern. And could I trust Raven to lead me?

I remembered Mari and her laughing eyes. What would she have done in my place? Gone on, no doubt. But was I risking my life in the wildwood? Would it be better to return to the road where Lord Brecken could find me again?

That's the one thing I did not understand. Even if Lord Brecken heard about my journey, why would he come after me? He was betrothed to another. Unless it was solely because I embarrassed him. He was a lord used to getting what he wanted. And for the first time, I questioned whether my mother had been forced to suffer for my disappearance. A fluttering began in my stomach. Something was within me. The sooner I reached Capern, the better. I needed to speak to Mother Misha and understand my future.

"Lady Sasha?" Raven had returned, and his brow furrowed when he saw me kneeling on the ground. He stepped closed and held out what looked like a pouch of water. "Drink. The hot springs are near and it is safe. You can wash, then sleep."

Hot springs. At the sound of it, my entire body ached. I snatched the water out of his hand and guzzled it down, some of it spilling over my lips and dripping down my chin, much to my chagrin.

Raven had the decency to look away, although I detected the smirk on his arrogant face. His warning came back to me, but I needed him right now. As soon as I regained my strength and sense of direction, I'd be on my way.

"How far to the springs?" I asked, the water bringing vibrancy back to my veins. I wanted to stand, but my body was unwilling, unused as it was to such abuse.

The trees swayed above us, and the faint scent of water hung in the air. Raven glanced up and put a hand on a tree, his face tight with. . .irritation? "Must you always eavesdrop and share my deeds?" he muttered, raking a hand through his wavy locks.

My chest tightened, and suddenly the air felt thick. I lowered my voice. "Who do you speak to?"

"It is of no concern." His face brightened. "Come, can you walk?"

I attempted to rise to my feet and sharp shards of pain tingled up and down my legs. I grimaced and sat back, frustrated. I feared if I were too much of a nuisance he'd leave me in the wildwood, and I desperately did not want to be left alone where the unfriendly trees loomed over my head and shut out the sunlight.

Raven was by my side without waiting for an answer. He scooped me up in his arms as if I weighed nothing. Despite his earlier warning, I leaned into him, eyes closed.

When I opened my eyes, the shadows of the green wood had grown stronger and we walked between the yawning walls of a rock. They towered above us, signs and symbols carved into them. The ground beneath Raven's feet was nothing but a path of rich green moss, adding a softness to the harsh gray stones. A chill I could not shake rose within me, and then I heard the voice of water bubbling in the deep.

I gasped at the sight which came into view. It seemed as if we were in a cave and yet not in a cave. Although the rocks rose as high as the trees on either side, they were open to the sky, where sunlight created a green haze. The path of moss over rocks and boulders led right up to a pool of water, embedded in what looked like the rock wall, with a circle of stone surrounding it like an altar. The stones glistened, wet, while others shone like jewels in the light, winking at me as though we were old friends.

"No one will bother you here," Raven said. "I'm going hunting and will return shortly. But I'll call out before I come near." He placed me down on a nearby boulder. And then, as if he had a second thought, handed me the water. "Drink it sparingly, I'll return with more."

A numbness came over me at his considerateness. He'd warned me that he was a dark knight, and yet he'd done me a small kindness by bringing me to this place. "Thank you," I said, hoping to catch his eye.

But he did not look at me. With a quick nod, he was off, and I watched until his shape was nothing more than a dark smudge before rising. Nervous at being left alone, and unsure whether to trust his words that no one would sneak up and surprise me here, I tip-toed toward the pool like a thief, casting furtive glances in each direction. When a bird flew off the rock wall high above me, I stiffened. Glancing around, I picked up a few rocks and stacked them near the pool. I felt better knowing I had rocks to throw, even should a wild animal venture near. I'd heard enough stories about the wildwood.

My slippers had holes in them and were thick with dirt and bramble. I peeled them off my feet, dismayed at how useless my beautiful shoes were in the forest. Oh, how I missed Lotus. I hadn't counted on walking far. What a fool I was. My dress was filthy and ripped, and as I shrugged it off, I realized I had no way to clean it. Frowning, I spread it out on a nearby rock, hoping some magic would make it clean and comfortable for me again. And then I stepped over the edge into the hot spring.

Warmth surged around me and quickly I climbed in, pleased to find I could easily reach the bottom. The pool was as blue as a deep cerulean sky, and my fingers touched a hidden ledge. I sat back on it while the warmth enveloped my body and the waters massaged my weary skin, as though it were alive and knew exactly what my body needed.

Loosening my hair, I let it flow down until sky met sunshine, and my anxiety melted away. There in the waters it appeared everything would be alright. After all, the fates had allowed me to cross paths with the Raven. The soothing sensation of the tiny waves lulled me to sleep and for the first time in a while, I slept without nightmares.

8

WHEN I RETURNED TO CONSCIOUSNESS, it felt as though I slept on a bed of fur, and for a moment I assumed I was back at Lord Cedric's castle. A cool wind kissed my face, and I opened my eyes to starlight. I sat up with a jerk, and warm water sloshed around my body. I'd fallen asleep! In the hot spring! I whirled in the water, panic setting in when I saw a fire, orange flames licking the chilly night air and a shape sat hunched over it. The aroma of cooked meat hung in the air and my mouth watered.

"You must be awake," called Raven.

A relief I could not make sense of seeped through me at the sound of his voice. Still, I made a frantic reach for my dress, wondering if he were a true gentleman or if he'd spied on me while I slept. The thought made me go both cold and hot all at the same time.

I didn't bother replying to his statement. Sometimes it was best to stay quiet, instead of filling the silence with awkward words.

"I left clothes for you by the rock, don't worry, I won't look," he assured me with his silver tongue.

The light from the fire showed me a small bundle just near the pool. Slowly I emerged from the water, like a lady of the lake. There was a rough shirt, a tunic, and pants. No dress. Men's clothing. How could I wear such a thing? Were these. . . his? I shuddered, but when my eyes fell on my filthy dress, I gave in and dressed quickly. Soon this adventure would be over, and I'd wear dresses, wash daily, and likely never travel again.

With a sigh, I pulled my hair up on top of my head, the one style I'd learned to do myself before I fled. "Where did you find these?" I asked as I joined him in front of the fire. I had to admit, the clothes were much warmer than my dress, and I was thankful for them as the chill of night stole over the stones.

His mouth tilted up as he examined me. "The pants are on backward." He grinned.

I scowled at him. "It's dark, and these are clothes for a man. . ."

"You are welcome to your dress." He pointed.

I lifted my chin and perched on a rock near the fire, determined not to lose my temper. "No, I'd rather be clean and warm."

"Would you like to catch your own food too? Or shall I share?"

Unsure how to respond, I opened my mouth and closed it again.

"I'm only jesting, I would not let you go hungry." He handed me a stick with a leg of meat skewed on the edge of it.

I starcd, unsure how to eat it.

"Just bite into it," he said, ripping into his with his teeth.

Still, I paused, for it was unladylike, and while traveling I'd never had the opportunity to eat meat from the bone.

"There are storehouses throughout the forest for knights of the queen," Raven told me as I puzzled over my meal. "With food, clothing, and herbs. I know these woods for they are my home. If you'd rather not sleep outside, we will journey from safe house to safe house. I assume you are in a hurry to reach Capern, but first, we will meet with the Queen of the Wildwood."

I stared at him as I took a bite; the meat was tender, juicy, and almost melted in my mouth. I resisted the urge to rip off another bite, although I didn't know who I was trying to impress.

"How do I know you will keep your word?" I demanded. "After we meet with the Queen of the Wildwood?"

Leaning back, he tucked his hands behind his head. "I suppose you'll just have to trust me."

I frowned and took another bite, trying not to let him see how much he frustrated me.

The weight of his gaze penetrated my concentration. "I wonder, though, why are you in such a hurry to get to Capern? And why do you dream about me?"

I ate faster, unwilling to answer his questions. It had been a long day, and despite my earlier nap, a weariness hung over me again. We finished in silence and the stars twinkled above, casting a path across the deep blue night sky, like a finger pointing the way. I studied it for a moment, wondering if it were a sign, but there was nothing, just the warmth of the fire on my cheeks, the cool wind at my back, and Raven, unrolling two bedrolls and handing me one.

Wordlessly, I followed Raven's lead and lay down to spend my first night in the wildwood. No sooner had I propped my head up against a boulder, wondering how I could possibly sleep in such an uncomfortable environment, I heard a howl.

I bolted upright, my chest rising and falling as I heard it again, a long, drawn-out moan. A wolf? Something else?

"Sleep, Lady Sasha," Raven said, although there was nothing reassuring about his voice. "As I stated earlier, nothing will bother you here. I am the Raven, and the teeth of the forest always have to contend with me."

If his words were meant to comfort me, they did not. Instead, a shiver went through me. I lay still on my back, watching the stars twinkle while the wild animals hunted and fought deep in the wildwood. Sleep did not come easily for me that night.

9

I WOKE JUST BEFORE DAWN. The warm fire was nothing more than smoking ashes, mixed with a thick mist that hung over the pool. My fingertips grazed cool rock as I stretched, my body sore from sleeping on the stony ground. Raven lay still, and I peeked over the fire to study his face. A cloak of black feathers covered his body, and his broad fingers clenched a knife to his waist as he slept. If no one would bother us, why did he sleep with a knife?

More than just the morning chill made goose-bumps break out on my exposed skin. I studied his features. Even in sleep, his lips had an impetuous twist to them. His devilish eyes were closed and his long lashes seemed to brush his high cheekbones. His jawline was strong and his nose had an arrogant tilt to it. Closing my eyes, I took a breath to steel my nerves. He was rough, wild. Dangerous? I hadn't seen that side of him. Still, a fluttering in the pit of my stomach confirmed my attraction to him. But I couldn't be allured by him, even though I wanted him to want me. It would make the journey through the wildwood less tiresome.

Sucking the inside of my cheek, I scolded myself. I wasn't a noblewoman anymore. I'd given up that life when I rejected Lord Brecken. I couldn't tease and flirt and play coy with men, especially out in the wild with one who might take my flirting the wrong way. Nay, I could not encourage the Raven because I needed his guidance.

I washed my face in the pool, relieved to see my reflection peering back at me. My eyes were large and sad with a permanent droop to my lips. I pushed away thoughts of Mari and the unfortunate circumstance that ripped her life away. Too early, too young. I was lucky enough to be alive.

When I reached for my dress a gasp left my lips. It was clean and laid out on the rocks as though someone had washed it for me. I clasped my hand to my mouth while my eyes darted across the pool, searching, although I already knew no one was there except Raven. Then I saw it, a buzzing of wings, moving almost too fast for the eye to see, then a spark of blue light. A tiny creature landed on my dress, picked out a speck of dirt, and flew off again.

I squinted against the dawning light as I watched it disappear beyond the rock walls.

"Have the faerie been here?" Raven's quiet voice almost made me scream.

I spun around to face him, surprised at how silently he'd risen and stood behind me, a pack slung over one shoulder. "Faerie?" My face flushed as I forced my gaze away from his well-defined chest. Why did he have to leave his cloak open?

His gaze flickered up. "Aye, they've returned to the wildwood to cause mischief, but some are known for their good deeds. Apparently, they like you." He gestured to my dress.

I picked it up, relieved it was clean and smelled of sage and cedar wood. At least I'd have something to wear when we reached Capern, but for the trek through the wood, the borrowed clothes Raven had provided would do.

"Are you hungry?" he prompted when I did not respond to his earlier explanation. I shook my head, avoiding his eyes. "You're a quiet one." He then led the way out of the safety of rocks, back out to the forest.

I was sorry to see the hidden pool disappear and glanced back as the thick trees shut out the sky. We lost the gentle light of dawn to the shadows of tree and leaf.

"I have little to say," I admitted as I followed him with the distinct knowledge that talking would help keep my mind off my dire situation.

Raven snorted. "I've never met a woman who didn't have much to say."

I frowned at the insult, but he was right. "I don't like to gossip, it leads to nothing good."

"Humm. Gossip, as I understand it, is usually talking about someone else, judging or making fun of them. I'm more curious about you."

The fluttering in my belly came again, and I had to remind myself he was not interested in me personally, but merely passing the time, as was I. "There's not much to tell," I admitted.

"I'll be the judge of that. A woman alone in a forest? With strange magic?"

A lump formed in my throat. Would he understand? But it was he who sensed my magic.

"It runs in my bloodline," I admitted. "Sometimes it skips a generation. My mother doesn't have magic, but my cousin does."

"Your cousin?"

"Lord Cedric of Whispering Vine, perhaps you've heard of him?"

"Indeed." Those dark eyes assessed me. "He's your cousin and yet you ask me to guide you through the wildwood?"

I twisted my fingers together and rubbed my thumbs against my wrists. "He doesn't know what happened to me. He was against this and now. . . He was right. I never should have left. I thought it was safe."

"Safe?" He raised an eyebrow. "Then you know who attacked you?"

"Yes," my shoulders slumped. "Three years ago I was supposed to marry a lord, but he is cruel and unjust. I fled to my cousin's castle, because he has dark magic. No one will attack him. Not even the king. Since the lord announced his betrothal to another, I assumed it was safe to leave. But you saw what happened on the road. He killed my friends all because I insulted him. . ." I trailed off, an unnatural stirring in my chest. Was it hate? No. I wanted revenge.

"Sasha," he breathed. He whirled to face me and touched my wrist, towering over me as he examined my face. My heart skipped a beat at his touch, and a memory rose as he spoke. "I remember you. Outside the estate you rode upon a gray horse and galloped bravely into the night. I followed you and when the horse threw its shoe, I helped you to town. You were fierce and feisty and didn't trust me at all."

I studied his face, barely daring to breathe and I recalled that first adventure. The cry of a raven, the reminder of feathers, and the scent of the wildwood. He was the mysterious man who helped me, and I still recalled the dangerous spark in his eyes. After Lord Brecken I was loath to deal with another man. That was years ago. But now. . .

When his knuckle brushed my chin, giving him a better view of my face, I had to resist the urge to press my hands against his chest.

"You're always running away, and I'm always finding you."

"It's not you I'm running away from, just everyone else's expectations."

A muscle in his cheek jerked. "I expect nothing from you, and the wildwood has no expectations."

"I am aware." I sighed with more bitterness than I intended.

His face shifted from curious to pained as he studied me. As he opened his mouth to speak a high whistling sound came from over our heads and an arrow slammed into the tree behind us. Raven pushed me behind him and turned to face our attackers.

10

I STIFLED a cry as I hid behind Raven, crouching down while panic zinged through my veins. A familiar heat made my ears burn and suddenly the world rushed around me, spinning and flashing. I gasped for breath, fingers clawing at my throat. Raven tugged the arrow out of the tree and faced our attackers.

"Who goes there?" he demanded. "And what fight do you have with me?"

"If it isn't Master Raven," a rough voice growled.

I calmed myself down enough to peer out from behind Raven and wished I hadn't. Two creatures stood in front of him, one looked like a wolfman, who stood on two legs and yet the rest of his body was covered in gray fur, and fangs hung out of his snarling mouth. Beady black eyes flashed when they saw me and a long pink tongue came out.

The second was the one who had shot the arrow, for his bow and arrow still pointed at Raven, as though one wrong word, one wrong move, and he'd run him through without a care in the world. The tingling in my hands grew stronger and my belly rolled. The second creature was all muscle with tusks coming out of his fat lips and ashy gray skin. He wore nothing but a loincloth around his waist and a chain of bones rattled on his neck. Thick wiry hair stuck up straight off his head, only a few inches in the air. I knew, without hearing another word from him, what he was. An orc.

They were rumored to dwell in the wildwood, but I'd never seen one, and why would I? All I'd heard were tales of the wildwood that made me want to stay away, and now I regretted ever leaving Lord Cedric's castle. I stifled a scream as the orc's bold gaze lingered on my hair.

"Well, well," he spoke again in his hard voice. "It seems the Raven has company. You didn't tell us you were entertaining, nor did you invite us to share this delightful morsel you've found, and selfishly kept all to yourself."

Bile rose in my throat, but I couldn't move. I sensed Raven's shoulders go stiff, and when he spoke his voice was as cold as melted snow. "Your quarrel is with me, and me alone. My comings and goings, and who I keep company with, are none of your business."

"I think they are. Raven." The orc took another threatening step forward and raised the arrow to eye level. "Especially when you owe us."

"Listen," Raven raised his hands, palms facing out. "I haven't forgotten about our wager, I'll pay you back, but not today."

"You'll pay us back alright," the orc demanded. "And

you'll pay us back now. Or we'll be entertaining your little twat tonight."

A strangled cry came from Raven's throat, and he moved so quickly I almost missed it. His fists came up just as the arrow twanged out of the bowstring. It shattered as it sank into Raven's shoulder, but he continued as though he did not feel it. His knife came out, cutting a low arc through the air and slicing open the orc's belly.

A raw roar of hate and pain mixed with the horrid scent of dung filled the air. I scrambled back on my hands, scraping my palms on bark and brambles. The wolfman lunged, teeth bared and claws out. Raven went down hard underneath him and the two struggled. I screamed. Paws flashed in the air as Raven rolled on top of the beast and quickly slit its throat. The knife muted the beast's howl and two dead bodies lay, almost hidden, on the forest floor.

Hands shaking, face flushed, I weakly stood to my feet. I couldn't stop staring at the glazed, vacant expression on the orc's face, nor the wolf, eyes still open, one paw ready to slice through the air.

Raven faced me, his hair tousled, chest heaving, mouth open. Blood dripped from the wound in his shoulder. His knuckles were pale where they gripped the curved knife, but his eyes gave me pause. They were wild, almost black without pupils, and glared at me, soulless, dangerous.

A warning twisted in my stomach and I took a step back, my hands grasping for something to defend myself.

"Get away from me," Raven ordered, his voice rough.

"I'm in the throes of bloodlust and know not what I will do. Walk away before I take your life too."

I stumbled back another step, but something gave me pause, something stopped me from running headlong into the forest.

My nightmare flashed before my vision, the looming trees, the swirling hole, and the features of the Raven, saving me from being sucked under. I couldn't run into the wildwood and leave him in his bloodlust, searching for death. He'd saved me twice, nay, now made thrice, and although I didn't know what his past was, who he had been and what he'd done, I could guess.

I took a tentative step toward him, flinching when a warning growl rumbled from his chest. His jaw was set tight, and the knife in his hand shook. One bright drop of crimson fell to the ground, creating a pool by his feet. I slowed down my uneven breathing and took another step, holding out my hands to show him I meant no harm, although I sensed, somewhere underneath the bloodlust, he understood that. I hoped.

"You know not what you do," the words choked out of his throat.

"I do," I said, my voice shaking. My eyes were wet with unshed tears of fright as I took another step. "I know what I do. You're the Raven, and you've saved me. Many times. It's only fair that this time, I save you."

His grip on the knife loosened, but I kept my gaze fixed on his dilated pupils.

"I am Raven. An omen of death. Destruction follows in my wake, for I steal life from all who draw too near to me. You don't know enough, but if you come closer, I will teach you to fear me. It is my nature. Get back!"

The last words he uttered were sharp and sudden, and I blinked as a rush of heat came to my face. But I held his gaze, barely daring to breathe as my lips moved. "No. You had your chance yesterday on the road, again when I slept in the hot springs, and a final time last night. You could have handed me over to the wolf and the orc, but you slayed them and protected my honor. You said it before you are reformed, there is more than death within you. There is good."

The knife fell and landed with a thud in a patch of heather. I was so close to him, I could see his liquid gaze, the slow return to sanity while his fingers shook. His jaw clenched and unclenched as the battle within him took place. I stood still, aware that in one moment he could squeeze the life out of me, or refrain.

Oh Goddess. I hoped he wouldn't slay me. What if I had made a mistake? The silence stretched between us until I was conscious of nothing more than his labored breath. His eyes glistened as they returned to normal and his shoulders slumped. He collasped to his knees in front of me, hands pressed together as though I were the great Goddess who formed the wildwood.

"Why did you do that?" he murmured. "Why didn't you run? I could have killed you."

I desperately wanted to touch him, to bring him some comfort. He looked so miserable kneeling on the ground, his face ashen as he looked around and saw what he had done in his anger. An anger I did not blame him for.

"But you didn't," I studied the arch of his nose, the line of his powerful jaw. "You did not touch a hair on my head."

He stared at me in wonder, his mouth opening and closing before he formed more words. "No one believes I can change."

"No. Words mean nothing unless you have actions to prove them." The words seemed to come to me, but not on my own.

He lifted a hand, his fingers touching mine, gently, hesitantly. Tipping back his head, he studied me, and I saw, not the confident, cocky man I'd met in the forest, but a lost soul, searching for a place to belong. A lump formed in my throat and tears filled my eyes again, but this time not of fright, but of understanding. For I felt the same way, like a lost soul, searching for meaning, purpose, a place to call home. Perhaps that's why he wanted me to speak to the Queen of the Wildwood, because it was Her who could restore purpose to his life. And if that's what he wanted, nay, what he needed, who was I to stand between him and his desires?

"Your shoulder is bleeding," I said, "and it's only midday. We have to meet the Queen of the Wildwood and neither of us are presentable to stand in her court."

"Ah." The soulful look left his eyes as he stood. "Come, Lady Sasha, the day is wasting."

11

A NEW SILENCE rose between us, as though what had happened had united us somehow, someway.

Raven pulled the remains of the arrow out of his shoulder and we continued on.

Aside from being approached by those dark creatures earlier, the forest was calm, although an ominous aura hung in the air. At any moment I expected something terrible would pop out from behind a tree. But nothing else did.

It was late afternoon when we came upon a grassy knoll, and Raven paused. He pointed to the thicket up ahead, where a strange glow hovered. "We're almost to the mushroom forest where we'll rest for the night. I think you'll enjoy sleeping on a bed again." He gave me a crooked smile. "I must admit, I expected more complaints from you."

I frowned, although I found it impossible to be frustrated with him and folding my arms across my chest. "Do you think I am one of those spoiled noblewomen?"

He gave me an impish wink. "You looked like one when I found you, although now," he gestured at the borrowed clothes, "not so much."

I pressed my lips together and sighed. "The problem with being a noblewoman is people look at me and make assumptions. They assume I am proud, haughty, and spoiled, but they don't take the time to get to know me."

"Perhaps you won't let them," Raven dropped his voice and headed for the thicket.

We weaved between the woods until the trees gave way, as though they were opening a secret door to another land. I peered through and gasped. Brown and white mushrooms rose as tall as the trees, with thick stalks I could hardly wrap my arms around. It was dark in that hollow, with moss, dirt and even mold growing along the ground. But what made me gasp was the luminous way the mushrooms lit up the wood. The bottom of each mushroom head glowed purple and blue, while water droplets hovered on top, adding a rainbow effect to the thicket. Lightning bugs chased each other, and the low hush of water flowing gently over a riverbank. I pressed a hand to my heart, both awed and confused why such beauty existed in the wildwood. I'd thought it was dark, evil, and yet it held such charm as this.

When I glanced at Raven, he was studying me with an expression I could not read. "It's beautiful," I breathed, stepping closer to him. "Why did you bring me here?"

"Because you believe." He spread his hand out to indicate the wood. "Although there is darkness, and evil, there is another side. Beauty and light. Let me show you." He held out his hand and give me a playful bow.

Heat stirred within my belly, both at his words and the intoxicating pull of his presence. My gaze lingered on his mouth, and my cheeks flushed as I wondered how his lips against mine would feel. What sensations would they create within me?

I took his hand, as though he were my guide to another world, and stepped across the barrier into the mushroom forest. The ground was soft and sank beneath my feet, but Raven led me to stepping stones that curved deeper into the wood. I wanted to ask where we were going, but words would not leave my lips. I thought I caught sight of creatures with impossibly fast wings zing through the air. Faeries?

We followed the stones, hand in hand, while my heart beat faster and a flutter of arousal surged through me. I fought to keep control of my emotions. He was just a guide. Soon all this would be over. An uncomfortable trip through the wildwood, a meeting with the queen, and then the road to Capern and a return to civilization. Our lives were different, impossible. I belonged in a castle, being waited on hand and foot, while he belonged out here in the wild, killing and roaming, serving at the whim of the Queen of the Wildwood. But the lights in the glade made me believe in a dream I could never have. Where love, desire, and passion were mixed and I could discover the heights of pleasure. An intense yearning rose within me and when he opened a door, I almost stumbled into him.

My gaze was drawn upward to the pulsing light of a pale pink mushroom cap, a few feet above us. An arched door opened into the heart of the oversized mushroom and I stepped inside, into darkness.

"Wait here." Raven let go of my hand.

A moment later, soft yellow light filled the area, as though a hundred lightning bugs danced within. The mushroom house was nothing like the great, spiraling castle of my cousin, nor the grand manor house I lived in with my parents. It was a circular room, cozy, with heaps of furs lining the floor and a small, circular table in the middle at knee height.

Tangled green vines hung down from the walls of the mushroom and the scent of lavender hung in the air. It was soothing, a welcome change to the potent scent of mushrooms.

"It's warm, dry, you will be comfortable here," Raven said. "The top of the table comes up. Inside you will find food and water. Rest here."

"Thank you," I breathed, slipping out of my shoes. Never would I have dreamed the wildwood could offer such hospitality. And then I thought of Raven's earlier words. Storehouses were created throughout the wildwood, for the knights of the Dark Queen to rest from their travels. Perhaps this was such a house.

Raven stepped back, watching me carefully. I turned toward him in confusion. "What are you doing? Aren't you staying?"

"Nightfall comes and I have work to do. What happened today should not happen again."

I bit my bottom lip, assuming he meant the wolf and the orc. "Will you return?"

That smirk returned. "Of course, my lady." He bowed.

"Don't leave me alone out here," I pleaded, stepping closer to him.

"You have nothing to be afraid of," he persisted.

I swallowed hard and dropped my eyes, unsure how to tell him that the safety I felt in the wildwood was because of him. Miserably I watched him walk away, and then I was alone in the mushroom house. I turned slowly, taking in its beauty before recalling it had been a long time since I'd last eaten.

Inside the table I found dried meat and fruit along with water and what I thought might be a jug of wine. I put it aside, thinking I might share a glass with Raven when he returned. But weariness overwhelmed me. As soon as I ate, I stretched out on the soft furs, and the gentle lullabies of the crickets soothed me to sleep.

My first hint of consciousness was warmth, but I knew something else had woken me. I hung on to those blissful moments, huddled down in a bed as soft as feathers. The aches and pains of travel had faded, leaving only a comfortable soreness. I nestled down further into the furs, pleased that a single nightmare hadn't plagued my sleep. When I opened my eyes pales lights danced around me and the bulk of the Raven hunched over the table, eating strips of dried meat, and watching me.

Discomfort crept over me, but when I met his heated gaze he looked away, as though he did not wish to be caught staring. Blinking sleep out of my eyes, I sat up, pulling one of the furs snug around me. Suddenly the circular mushroom hut seemed smaller than before. Although the blankets surrounded the low-lying table, it seemed intimate, as if the Raven had stepped into my bedroom and watched me sleep.

I broke the silence. "What time is it?"

"Just after midnight," he shrugged off his cloak of feathers, leaving his chest bare. Sometime between his leaving and returning, he'd bathed, and the scent of moss and pine hovered in the air.

Scars trailed down one side of his body and I imagined more were on his back. Scars from what? Battle? Curiosity won over my desire to hold my tongue. "Where were you?"

His face went tight with distaste. "I had business to attend to. Debts to pay."

"Do debts always require bloodshed?" I leaned back, but the little sleep I'd had left me wide awake.

"Here?" A sneer came to his lips. "Yes." He ripped into another piece of dried meat, white teeth flashing.

"Who are you, truthfully?" I dared ask.

"First silence, then questions?" Mischief danced across his face, half-hidden in the low light.

"Since we are traveling together, yes, you might as well tell me. After all, it was you who seemed peeved by my silence."

"Ah." He cocked his head at me and a dangerous glimmer came his eyes. He pointed a wedge of cheese at me. "I propose a game, a question asked for each question answered."

A fluttering began in the bottom of my stomach. I lifted my chin. "What if I don't want to answer your questions?"

His lips tugged upward into an impish smile. "I'll trade you, answer for answer. When you don't want to answer any more. . ." He shrugged.

"It's not really a game then," I told him. "Just a trade. In a game there are winners and losers."

"Should we play for a prize, Lady Sasha?"

I paused. The way he spoke my name sent shivers down my spine, and I could only guess at what he might demand if he won. But what would I ask of him if I won? My gaze flickered to his lips and my cheeks flushed hot. I enjoyed a good flirtation. It kept my spirits high and gave me an odd surge of confidence, knowing I could tempt a man with not only my beauty but the wit of my tongue. Yet such thoughts seemed wrong, here. Flirtatious thoughts belonged at court, or during a dance, or teatime in the gardens of the lords and ladies of the kingdom. Here? In the wildwood? I sensed the rules were different.

Flushing, I dropped his gaze, though kept my head held high. "A trade it is."

He dipped his head. "As a lady, you should go first."

Twisting my fingers together in my lap, I considered my question. Raven was shrewd, and if I asked vague questions, he would answer with equal vagueness.

"Why did you decide to serve the Dark Queen?"

A cloud of darkness rolled over his face and he half turned away, so I would not see his irritation.

"She did not give me much of a choice. The price of disobeying Her was always too high. She knew how to look into one's soul, find out what they wanted most and use it against them. I did not always live here, in the wildwood, but after what she did to me, there's no reason to go back. Only forward." He sighed, and I immediately felt bad for asking such a deep and personal question. I opened my mouth to tell him he need not continue when he did. "It was during the days when orcs roamed, raiding and pillaging the villages outside the wildwood. We had warriors, but not enough to fight them. The priestess of our tribe made a blood sacrifice, asking for safety from the orcs. The smoke from the sacrifice summoned Her, and she came to answer our cry for help. But she told us, in exchange, she wanted five to serve as her knights. The first man she chose refused, for he did not want to leave his wife and children. She struck him down with her magic. Outraged by her actions, I rushed in to stop her, and that's when she sensed my magic. I served her ever since."

His lips were set in a grim line, and a wall of silence divided us. My heart thudded in my chest, both mortified at my question and distressed for what had happened to him. He'd had a home, a clan, perhaps even a family, another name? Questions rose and fell when his lips moved again. "Why did you run away from home? You're a beautiful noblewoman, many a woman has longed for your position and wealth. But you ran."

"You don't know what it's like," my words came out more viciously than I intended. "The peasants look up at the nobles, and they think we are lucky, blessed to have a life with power, position, and wealth. I supposed, in a way, we are." I twisted my hands together. They were soft, still, for I'd never worked a day in my life. I'd seen the chapped hands of peasants, their faces burned by the sun and the hollow misery in their eyes when they went hungry. Often the fates were not fair, but I'd run all the same. "Wealth brings its own problems, but I am an independent woman. No man owns me, and that's what Lord Brecken wanted to do. He's a cruel lord, treats his servants like cattle, carries his prize possessions around just to show them off, and discards them. He's only ten years my senior, but he's already had many women. My luck would be to become his wife and bear his children, nothing more. I saw him lose his temper more than once and he is indirectly responsible for the demise of my father. No. I would not have such a man. I'd rather be lost, destitute, then return to him."

A faint smile appeared on Raven's lips at my impassioned words.

"Does my tale amuse?" I demanded, eyes flashing.

"Is that your next question?" He retorted.

How quickly I'd forgotten our trade. Taking a deep breath to calm myself, I tried to think of another question that wasn't so personal. I didn't enjoy digging into my past, and perhaps if I asked something harmless, he would return the favor. "Do you ever think of leaving the woods and returning to a village, any village? The queen is dead, you are free now."

Raven chuckled, a deep hearty sound that almost made me jump. "Leave?" He shook his head, sending his black hair dancing. "The wildwood is my home. It is wild, varied and presents unusual challenges but, I know it like the skin on my body. It is an old familiar friend to me. And now that the new queen reigns, the wonders of the wood never cease to surprise me. Like you, for example. Why are you in such a hurry to get to Capern? What, or dare I ask, who is waiting there for you?"

I pointed my finger at him. "Two questions at once is not part of our trade. If you must know, I go to seek the advice of a lore keeper. Supposedly, my great grandmother lives in the village and reads others' fortunes. I hope she can explain my nightmares and teach me about my magic."

He stretched out in the blankets across from me, propping himself up on his elbow.

A suitable distance still separated us, but blood rushed to my ears and my heart beat so loudly I thought he could hear it. I squeezed my fingers together to quash my desire to run my hands across his broad chest.

"Sasha," he said gently. "You don't have to go to a lore keeper to learn about your magic. You can ask the Queen of the Wildwood."

A dark nudge thrummed in my chest. I avoided his eyes. I knew what the Queen of the Wildwood had done for my cousin, but I did not want her help.

"Why do you want to serve the Queen of the Wildwood?" I asked him, a foreboding sensation telling me our trade was ending.

He lay on his back facing the top of the mushroom hut. He rested a hand on his chest and tested his wounded shoulder. The bandage on it was still clean, as though his wound were quickly healing. I believed it, for many things that could not be explained happened in the wildwood. "Redemption, I suppose. I've spent my time here frustrated and angry and finally enjoying the tasks the Dark Queen gave me. I was her pet, her favorite, the one who brought death to her domain, who intimidated those who did not offer sacrifices and give her magic. But now I see clearly, as did the other knights who served her. Many defied her and died. Sir Aelbrin was going to be next, but I perceived everything was about to go wrong back then. Which is why I left and wasn't killed when magic exploded across the wild-wood. I hid for a long time, but slowly I saw the change. The queen has help, but she needs mine if she hopes to hold back the evil that penetrates this place. I want to serve her because I know nothing else. It has been my place for so long, and I don't see any other life for me here. Like I said earlier, the wildwood is my home, but I don't belong with the wolfmen, orcs, undead, nor the faerie, nor the trees, nor the tribes that war with each other. I belong in the queen's court, helping her hold back death. Ironic, it seems, for I used to be the harbinger of death..."

He trailed off, his chest rising and falling. His eyes closed and his breath became deep and heavy. I knew more, much more about this man now, and about his past and who he was. A killer. And yet, I did not want to run, panicked, into the wildwood. I wanted him to wake up and turn that dark gaze on me. I shivered and tucked my head in my arms. What did it mean? What did it say about me that I desired a man, nay, a creature so out of reach?

13

I WASN'T sure when sleep took me again, but my thoughts were filled with the words Raven spoke. Dreams rose, vivid and intense.

FLAMES FILLED the air as I stood outside a great forest, the wildwood perhaps, but I heard nothing but screams. Ash and fire filled the air as villagers ran, throwing water over the inferno that raved above them, but there was no stopping it. Families fled with what little possessions they could gather before the fire broke out. Mothers with loose hair, clutching fat babies to their chests and holding on to the hands of young boys and girls. They all ran toward the wildwood, toward me. But I didn't stop to help them, instead I raised my hands. Black feathers swirled through the air as the raven flew above me, screeching a cry from his beak. Dread filled my heart, for the darkness was coming, somewhere beyond that curling

mist of smoke, hiding from view. I both longed to see and dreaded it, and within me a wave of magic grew. Ready. Waiting. And then she appeared, walking through the fire as though it couldn't touch her. On her head was a crown of white bone, and her face was deathly pale. Black hair flowed like a river to her waist, and around her neck was a necklace of mail. A thin silk skirt clung around her legs, showing off flashes of her battle armor. Death flew from her fingers. Soulless eyes took in the misery around her and a laugh burst from her wicked lips. She pointed at the raven, and from her profile I saw the skeletal bones of her body, covered with a glamor of flesh. "I am the Goddess of Death. Come join your new queen."

A GASP WOKE ME, and I sat up, clutching at my throat as my thoughts raced. What were my dreams? A warning? For the first time, I glimpsed what power might be sleeping within me. I thought back, trying to remember a time when my power had revealed itself. Often it was only a vague hunch that grew stronger as I grew older. The fear which manifested throughout my life wasn't exactly fear, it was a deep knowing that something terrible might happen.

"Sasha?" Raven's concerned voice broke my musings.

I waved my hand in the air, as though I could brush away the remnants of the dream. "It was just a nightmare."

"About?"

I studied his face. Should I tell him? The Raven in

my dream had been him, and she had called out to him. As though he'd known she was waiting for him. "What do you know about the Goddess of Death?"

Raven's eyes went dark. He rose, snatching up his cloak of feathers. For a moment he looked like the bird, feathers outstretched, eyes glistening and sharp beak open. I swallowed hard and my heart thudded in my chest. A sensation in my stomach gave me pause. A wave of magic?

Raven strode to the door, brushing his hair off his forehead. He paused before smacking the door open.

Daylight streamed in, so bright it made me blink. I shielded my eyes against it, unable to see Raven's expression, only the hollow tone of his words. "The Goddess of Death and the Raven. There are tales about it. But the path of fate can be changed. If one tries hard enough."

My throat went dry as the meaning of his words seeped in. He knew. Oh Goddess. He knew where his fate lay. Was that why he'd reformed? To change the course of his destiny?

I WAS sorry to leave the mushroom glade in the morning, but I took a small sack with me, relieved I had food, clothes, and water with me. Raven led the way past thick pine trees clustered so close together, it was impossible to see how many there were. The sound of rushing water filled the air, at first a faint hum and then a gentle melody as we drew near.

"You will meet the Queen of the Wildwood today," Raven told me. "She is not at home, but each spring she comes to the waterfalls. You must go on alone, and I'll wait for you below the falls."

"She will not meet with you?" I asked.

Raven shrugged. "The first time we met, I bound her magic. She did not take kindly to it." Raven pointed to a narrow trail, almost impossible to see. "Follow it until you find her," he told me. "It's likely she will sense your magic and come to you before you get too far."

I nodded, glad I'd changed back into my red dress. It would not do to look like a lost, torn soul when I met the powerful Queen of the Wildwood. Mixed feelings twisted through me as I held my skirts and made my way up the path. It was easy to follow and no twigs and brambles reached out to trip or snarl me. The sound of the thunder grew louder, and soon I saw them, three tiers of waterfalls with pale blue water, shooting over a cliff to tumble far below. Droplets splashed up against smooth stones, creating a myriad of rainbows. I gasped, taking in the hidden cove of beauty.

The wildwood was not as it seemed. From the outside it appeared dark, enchanted, sure to lure one away to death. But inside, it had moments of beauty, like the mushroom forest, and now the waterfall cove. The warmth of sunlight tempted me and I kept going, taking in the yellow flowers that grew alongside the cliffs and white blossoms still in bud. It was early spring yet, but I imagined when the forest burst into bloom, it would be with a lovely grace unknown to those who never dared to traverse its twisted paths.

I saw her before she saw me. Near the second waterfall was a ledge, and she stood on it, overlooking the falls and, writing? She held a book in her hand and sat cross-legged, unaware of her long brown hair dancing in the breeze. A man stood by her side, speaking as she wrote. They looked peaceful, happy in the enchanted glade. Goosebumps rose on my arms. I was naught but an intruder, an unwanted presence.

Almost as soon as the thought crossed my mind, the woman turned her face toward me and rose. Placing a hand on the knight's arm, she spoke to him and then turned, following the path that led up, away from the waterfalls, and toward the slope I stood on.

I froze in place, waiting as the Queen of the Wildwood strode toward me. My fingers trembled as I held onto the threads of my silk red dress, and then she stood before me. Her forest green cloak sweeping the ground. "Are you looking for me?" she asked in way of greeting. Her words were neither kind nor hostile.

The darkness behind her eyes made me shiver. She was much younger than I expected, closer to my age, which gave me hope that she might be reasonable. I squared my shoulders and addressed her. "I come on behalf of the Raven."

"The Raven?" The queen's eyes flashed. "Don't make me laugh. He is banished."

Refusing to be cowed by her distaste, I went on. "Let me re-frame my words. My cousin is Lord Cedric. You know him."

"Aye. But I know him by another name. Blood does not give you any favors."

"Should it? How do you know that what runs in his blood doesn't run in mine?"

She studied me. "Tell me. Does it? Do you have his abilities?"

"No," I admitted, sensing the quiet flutter of magic in my stomach. "But I have something else. A darkness rises in me, but I don't want it. I want nothing to do with magic and power, especially magic I cannot control."

Sorrow softened her face. "I understand how you feel. It is both a blessing and a curse, even when you learn how to control it, it will always be with you. Seeking a moment to escape your watchfulness."

"Yes." Relief filled me. She knew how I felt and hope made my pulse pound. "Exactly. Will you take it from me?"

She laughed, but it was neither dismissive nor merry. "No. I can lift a curse or banish a spell, but I fear if I drained you of your essence I would kill you. It is a burden you must live with."

My brow furrowed as a protest rose on my lips. "But I know what you did for my cousin. You used the power of a healer."

"I merely lifted a curse and in doing so gained a whisper of her power. I saved it for the right time. But the only way I know how to conduct a transfer of power includes taking a life. And I will not take yours. Now tell me, why do you trust the Raven. Don't you know who he is?"

Twisting my fingers together, I rubbed my thumbs over my wrists. This meeting was about Raven, not about my magic. I took a breath to clear my mind and spoke. "I know that he used to serve the Dark Queen and carry out her evil deeds. I know he escaped your wrath and ruin, and he has proved by word and deed that he has changed. No longer is he an evil knight. He is on your side now and only wants to help you tame the wildwood."

She frowned. "Does he? I cannot forget what he did to me."

"No?" A faint anger rose within me and my words came out hard. "Even though he does not deserve your forgiveness, would it not be noble to give it to him anyway? To give him a chance to prove himself?"

"You care about this knight. Tell me, did he not abuse you? Take advantage of your beauty?"

I shook my head. "He has only helped me, and this is all he has asked in return. That I speak to you on his behalf. Nothing more. Nothing less. I see the desire in his eyes, but he has restrained himself."

The queen stepped back and paced. "And your magic? Did he not bind it?"

"Only to keep me from harming others. He found me on the road where knights killed those I traveled with. If nothing else, will you send word to my cousin, let him know of the attack and that I am alive and well?"

"That I can do. But as for the Raven, well, I will watch him. For I cannot be sure. There may come a time when I need him, and then I will call. And you, if you are near."

I watched her pace, and my dream came back to me. The words were out of my mouth before I could halt them. "Because of the rise of the old Goddess?"

Her eyes flashed. "How do you know that?"

"I know. I've seen it in dark dreams."

"A family of lore keepers keep her from rising," the

queen explained. "But I fear what will happen, should their land become compromised. She will gain power and the ultimate battle will begin. I shall call all keepers of power to my side when that day comes. Raven will have a part to play. Tell him I shall watch his deeds and determine whether he shall be a knight of the Queen of the Wildwood once more."

"I will tell him. But what of my power? I cannot control it."

"There was a time when rage was all that controlled my power. You will have to learn, and the best way to learn is to use it."

I frowned and crossed my arms. "Rage will not help me," I told her bluntly. "The problem is the visions, the nightmares, I don't want them."

The queen stood in front of me and held up her hands. "May I?"

I licked my lips and nodded, although I was unsure what she intended.

Stepping close to me, she placed her hands on either side of my head and closed her eyes, as though listening to the thoughts in my mind. Her brow creased. She dropped her hands and opened her eyes again. "You have suppressed your magic to the point it spills over. Right now the dreams run through your mind, twisting with your inner thoughts. If you can control the nightmares, you can call them to yourself, when you are ready to see them. Know this, you have to read your dreams. They are important, key, but what you see is not absolute truth. They are shadows of the future, what could happen if something stronger does not stop it."

My thoughts flickered back to my cousin, the sensation I'd felt when the shield-maiden, Mariel, had entered the castle. But my fearful vision hadn't come true, because. . . I understood. Love was the catalyst, the power stronger than evil. "The power of love can't save everyone," I told her.

She cocked her head at me and turned. I followed her gaze back to the waterfalls where the knight stood alone on the ledge, reading. The queen drew herself up to her full height. "It's your choice. If you stay in the wildwood, I can help you control your visions. But you intend to move on?"

"My destination is Capern," I told her, fingers of panic clawing up my throat at the thought of staying in the wildwood. Beautiful as it was, it varied from day to day and I was unsure if I could handle it long term.

"Capern. Where the lore keepers dwell," she confirmed.

"There is more than one?"

"I thought you knew. There was trouble a few years ago. Two lore keepers survived and live on a farm on the outskirts of Capern. You might seek their help should it prove difficult to find the one you seek in Capern."

My blood ran cold at her cryptic words. Had something happened to Mother Misha?

"The wildwood is not, exactly, safe in that direction," she said with decisive calmness. "The tribes of the trees war with each other, and I haven't decided if interfering will be for better or worse. If the Raven is who you say he is, he will protect you, unless he turns on you."

Her words grated on my nerves and I stepped back. "I will let him know your decision."

She looked over my shoulder, as though she could see Raven hiding far below the falls. "Tell him I shall be watching. But I will find him, should I change my mind."

14

RAVEN DID NOT SEEM surprised when I related the queen's decision, omitting the part about how she could help me with my visions if I stayed in the wildwood. "Thank you," Raven studied me. "You're quiet again. Where does your mind go?"

The fact that I was leaving seemed more real than it had ever been. Tearing my eyes away from the butterflies flitting about us, I took a breath when I realized how close he stood.

He lifted a hand and cupped my cheek ever so gently, brushing stray curls off my face. My heart swelled at his touch and every inch of me hummed with pleasure. I wanted to take another step, to bury myself in his warmth, feel his skin against mine, the heat of his lips consuming me. Whoever he'd once been, he wasn't anymore. I could see it, plain and clear, and after speaking with the Queen of the Wildwood, I did not understand why she wouldn't give him a chance. She had to, before the Goddess of Death rose and claimed him as her own. But perhaps even that was a fate he could escape. Only, I did not know how.

I stepped back even though it took all of my strength to do so.

Disappointment flashed across his face and was gone just as quickly.

"The queen mentioned we would have to travel through the territory where the tribes fight against each other."

A smirk came to his face. "Does it frighten you?"

"No," I lied. "But the sooner we go, the better." I turned my back on him, even though he was the one who would lead the way.

I sensed his hesitation before he spoke again. "Was it something I said, Lady Sasha? Are you angry with me?"

I pressed my lips together and took a deep breath to keep the shaking out of my voice. Clarity rushed around me. Perhaps the presence of the Queen of the Wildwood was more eye-opening than I'd wanted. My odd attraction to Raven had to be quashed before I did something I would regret. He was forbidden, dangerous, and belonged in the wildwood, while my destiny lay in Capern. I'd already let my thoughts stray too far.

"It was something the queen said? Wasn't it?" he muttered. "I get it, you fulfilled your end of the bargain, now you're waiting for me to fulfill mine."

"No," I blurted out, spinning and catching the corner of his sleeve. "No, it's not like that. I was just thinking that you're right." I stared up at him, imploring him to understand. "When you said I shouldn't try to get too close to you, to play with your affections, to flirt with you, ever so briefly. You're right, we're only together for a short amount of time and…"

I broke off, for with each word I spoke he took another step toward me, until the feathers of his cloak brushed my chest. His liquid gaze studied me while his hand rested on my hip. I couldn't help twisting my fingers through his cloak, pulling him toward me, sure he could read the desire on my face.

"See," I whispered, breaking the spell that held us. "You know I am right."

His hand trembled and just for a moment I thought he would give in to his desire, and to mine. I lifted my lips to receive his kiss of fire, only to be denied. Dropping his hand, he forced himself away, a strangled cry in his throat. Keeping his back to me, he punched one of the tree trunks, the sudden movement violent, angry.

I drew in a sharp breath to still my racing heartbeat. Why did he have to have self-control? Why couldn't he have given in to a few moments of forbidden fruit? But deep inside I knew it would have gone much further than just a kiss, and heat flamed my face as I realized what I wanted.

"You're right," he groaned, his back still to me. "Even though you and I desire the same thing."

"Yes." Never had an agreement come so easily from my lips. Was the wildwood changing me? Unraveling my guarded heart? "Don't you see?" I pleaded with him. "We are from different worlds. You belong here and I belong out there."

His silence was almost more deadly than the darkness I'd seen in his eyes when he killed the wolfman and the orc. At last he lifted his head and gave me a grim smile. "Come, Lady Sasha, we have a lengthy journey ahead."

I DID NOT HAVE a chance to change clothes again and wore my red dress through the wildwood, sorrow clenched tight around my heart. The sound of the joyful waterfall faded, and we descended further into the forest. At least, it felt like a descent. We traveled downhill through a place where spring hadn't touched the forest floor. Thin trees grew dark and stunted, with grotesque trunks. They seemed to glare at me like hideous faces and I glared right back, disappointment and frustration rising with me. Why had I come here and why had my luck failed me so badly? If I could have gone back to being fifteen, young, innocent, with dreams of becoming the wife of a lord and dwelling in a castle where every comfort was provided. Yet, here I was, my name being just that, only a name, while I walked through the wildwood with a dark knight as my guide. I understood why the Queen of the Wildwood was loath to have him back. Not only could he bind magic, but he was a killer. The Queen's Killer. It was why the Goddess of Death would want him by her side, to do what he did best. But was it possible for someone to change? I'd sensed his transformation, felt it. Then was it possible for me to change? But no matter what I considered, each choice led out of the forest to Capern.

By the time darkness crept near—the actual darkness of night and not the constant gloom of the wood— my feet ached, my stomach rumbled, and my fingers were stiff and numb. I thought I might descend into tears at any moment, stupid tears for not getting what I wanted.

"Tonight will not be as pleasant as the last," Raven broke the silence. "And we should not start a fire out here, it will only serve as a beacon of light to those who search."

Tears streaked my cheeks, but I nodded, even though he could not see, and we pressed on.

The night we passed on a mossy knoll. A shallow depression in the ground seemed more like the beginning of an underground tunnel than anything else. Raven bade me sleep while he sat above on a log, keeping watch. But I couldn't sleep. I sat on the damp, cold ground, a cloak spread below me to keep me warm, but it was nothing like fluffy clouds of fur and even when I nodded off, my sleep was broken by rustling in the thicket and far off howls. I was all too aware that we were not alone, and when the sky lightened I stood. More tired, if possible.

Raven handed me some dried meat. Our fingers touched and a hum of arousal vibrated in my stomach. I pulled the cloak over my red dress and nodded at him. "I'm ready."

He opened his mouth to speak, then apparently shut it as he changed his mind and led on through the dark forest.

Words burned my throat all day, and somewhere in those twisted paths, I lost my appetite. Raven glanced back at me from time to time, but even his looks would not break the burden of sorrow that hung heavy on me. If only I had someone I trusted to talk to, to explain my predicament. My thoughts flew back to Mari and her cheerful words and incessant giggles. If only my journey hadn't gone so wrong.

"Lady Sasha? Did you hear me?"

I almost ran into Raven, who stood at a fork in the road, peering around a tree. He put a finger to his lips and a hand on my shoulder. "We are in their land now, stay close."

I followed his gaze around the tree and saw hunters. They were both men and stripped to their waists. Their brown bodies were graceful and slender, and they wore their dark hair long. I gasped as I studied them, for at first I'd assumed their hair was black, but it was only a trick of the light. It was a rich blue as dark as night and one of them wore a feather, skillfully braided into his hair. On the ground between them was a deer they were carefully skinning.

I pulled away, pressing my hand to my mouth. I knew about such things as hunting and killing and skinning, but I'd never been so close to the bloody death. I stepped back and my foot landed on a twig. It snapped, the sound loud in the thicket's quiet. The two hunters moved silently, skillfully, one snatching up a bow and arrow, the other gripping a knife.

My eyes wide, I turned to apologize to Raven, but he wasn't beside me. To my horror, I saw him stride out from behind the tree and approach the hunters, arms spread wide.

"Greetings, Kian, and Harli. I mean you no harm."

The one with the knife took a menacing step forward. "What are you doing on our land?" he demanded.

15

RAVEN MOVED TOWARD THEM, keeping his hands raised. "I would not be here unless I had to be, and it is good you are here. Kian. I came to request safe passage through your land."

The man with the knife lowered his hand, but his eyes narrowed. "Why? We made it clear that your presence is unwelcome here."

Raven waved his fingers, and it took a moment before I realized he beckoned me forward. With trepidation beating in my heart, I stepped out from behind the tree. The hunters glanced at me and their expressions grew tighter, if possible.

Kian pushed past Raven to approach me, leaving Harli with an arrow trained on Raven's chest. I knew how quickly things could go wrong.

"I am Kian," said the hunter. "We mean you no harm. Is it true, are you a companion of the Raven? Has he wronged you in any way?"

I wanted to laugh, although I doubted he would

deem it appropriate. Why was everyone so concerned that I traveled with the Raven? I crossed my arms and took a stance. "I am Lady Sasha and Raven is guiding me to Capern. I hear the path lies through your land. With your blessing, we will continue. And Raven has done nothing wrong, especially not to me. He has treated me as the lady that I am and has conducted himself with the chivalry and grace that bequeaths a knight. Unless you have a problem with the company I keep, I suggest you mind your own business."

A snort came from Raven's lips while Kian's eyes went wide. "Of course, my lady, it is just. . ." he trailed off.

Enjoying my sensation of power, I moved closer. "Just that what? In the past, Raven served the Dark Queen. And you were afraid of him? Afraid of Her? The past is in the past. You would be wise to leave it there."

A thrill of pleasure went through me at the shocked expression on Kian and Harli's faces. With grim satisfaction at rising to my station and honoring my family name, if for nothing more than a stroll through the forest, I joined Raven. Taking one of his hands, still held high in the air, I faced Kian again. "Now? What shall it be? Shall we pass or will you send us back?"

Kian cleared his throat and lowered his knife. "We will guide you through, if we are with you, no one will question it."

"Thank you," I said.

Raven squeezed my hand and leaned closer to whisper. "Where did that come from?"

I shrugged. "I don't know why you're surprised. In the halls of my father, everyone obeyed my commands."

He studied me, then bowed. "After you, Lady Sasha."

The hunter named Kian led the way while Harli brought up the rear, his arrow still trained on us. It was disconcerting to walk with a weapon pointed at my back, or rather, knowing it was pointed at Raven's back. We continued through hidden paths of the forest, uphill and downhill, until I was thoroughly lost. Every now and then Kian would pause and ask if I needed a rest. I merely shook my head, grateful for his kindness, yet still feeling a dreaded haste to get out of the wildwood and on with my life. Every extra minute I spent there, the fates tempted me and voices whispered in my mind. *Stay. Sasha. Stay. Make the wildwood your home.* But I couldn't stay.

When evening fell, Kian came to a halt. "This is where we leave you," he pointed.

I followed his finger and saw a drop off stretched across the wildwood like a yawning mouth. I shivered. We weren't going down there, were we?

"We are grateful for your kindness," I told him.

A smile came to his lips, although his eyes remained serious. "I wish you well wherever your road takes you. If you should ever need the services of my tribe, please call upon us."

Raven placed his hand on my waist, as though he had more of a claim to me then Kian. But I wasn't stirred by Kian's kind words. I nodded, there was no need to tell him I was leaving the forest, and there would never be a need for his help. As the thought crossed my mind, something else flashed before me. A rainstorm, a knife with blood on it and bottled lightning. I peered at Kian again, studying his face.

347

"Beware," the words flowed from my mouth. "A storm is coming."

He blinked, unsure how to respond, but I did not give him a chance. I moved down the path toward the cliff, with Raven beside me.

When I looked back, the hunters had faded back into the wildwood.

"What was that about?" Raven asked, letting go of me.

"I don't know." I shrugged. "A thought came to me and so I said those words."

"Do you think it has something to do with your magic?"

"Perhaps. I've considered whether meeting with the Queen of the Wildwood awakened something within me."

"It is likely, she is sensitive to magic, to power like her own."

I frowned, I didn't want to talk about the queen. Or why Raven wanted to serve her. "Do we cross tonight?" I pointed to the canyon.

"If you dare to walk across the swinging bridge at nightfall," the wicked glint in Raven's eyes challenged me.

"You are my guide." I threw the choice back at him. "I will follow your decision."

"And what if I told you there is a safe house on the other side? A tiny hut, hidden among the trees, where you can rest?"

My muscles ached, and all I wanted to do was lie down and go to sleep. But the thought of a bed, an actual bed, gave me strength. "Then lead on," I told him.

Raven led the way to the mouth of the canyon while I peered nervously at the sky. Darkness crept across it faster than I realized, and by the time we reached the swinging bridge, the last glimmer of sunlight blazed in the orange sky. I watched it and swallowed hard. The bridge wasn't what I thought it would be. When I imagined a bridge, I thought it would be like the ones in the village of Whispering Vine, wooden bridges with railings on each side and secure boards, strong enough to hold a horse and wagon. But this bridge was made of rope, with planks of wood at the bottom. The darkening light made it difficult to see how steady it was, but Raven called it the swinging bridge, and as a gust of wind whipped up, I could see why.

The end of the canyon seemed so far away. I clasped my hands together and rubbed my thumbs over my wrists as my throat went dry. Warm bed or not, there was no way I could cross over the rope bridge, either in the dark or by daylight. I took a tentative step away from it and glanced at the trees, hoping there'd be a place to sleep. Instead, golden eyes started back at me.

A cry of fear left my lips, and I reached for Raven's arm and pointed. "What is that?"

"Wolves," he said. "Hungry wolves. There are several of them and I don't have time to build a fire to keep them away. We have to cross."

There. My fate was set. The wolves or the bridge. "Okay," I squeezed his sleeve and tried to summon as much bravery as I could muster.

When his rough hand touched mine, I startled. "I'll be with you," he said. A smile tugged at the corners of his mouth. It was a slight comfort as the light faded from the sky. "Walk ahead of me. If you fall, I will catch you."

His words almost made me laugh. "Are you sure it will hold us, I don't want to die. Here."

"Like I said," he thrust out his chest, "if you fall, I will catch you."

I squeezed my eyes shut and reached for the rope. It was old and rough against my palms, but it held. Raven kept a hand on my waist as I took my first step out above the canyon. It was probably good that it was dark, for my stomach clenched and as the bridge swung. I thought I would be sick.

The bridge gave a sickening creak at my next step and swayed, ever so gently. Below us, water rushed over stones, and I wondered if this was the river that later turned into waterfalls. If we fell, we'd be tossed in the waters, and if we survived, washed up, somewhere. But deep in the gorge it seemed impossible, and I had no doubt other terrors awaited us in the water. Heart hammering in my throat, I dared myself to take another step, attempting to trust Raven and his meaningless words. How could he catch me if I fell, for he'd fall too?

Through the haze of my fear, I heard stirrings in the underbrush. As the last light of sunset disappeared, a long, woeful howl went up. My shoulders tensed and goosebumps broke out on my flesh as the sound carried through the air. An answering howl went up.

"We have to move faster, they will chase us down," Raven said.

"I thought wolves did not attack unless provoked," I protested, my voice shaking.

"All creatures are provoked here," Raven replied.

But I couldn't move faster. When I tried to, my limbs froze in terror of moving too quickly and sending us over the edge. I inched my foot onto another wooden slat and it shattered. I screamed as I pitched forward, even though Raven's arm tightened around my waist and my hands squeezed the rope, hard enough to leave indentions on my palm.

"I can't do this," I pushed back against Raven. "Please, take us away from here, do something to the wolves but I don't want to die on this bridge out here."

"Sasha, Sasha," he said, breaking through my panic. "I have you. Now turn around and put your arms around my neck."

Hiccuping away tears, I took a deep breath, trying to twist my body without letting go of the rope. Raven's hand on my waist gave me courage. I flung my arms around his neck and buried my face in his cloak. A whooshing sound made me open my eyes. As Raven's arms encircled me I saw wings unfurl from his back, great black wings as dark as night. In one bound we were airborne and he lifted us up, flying over the canyon into the wood on the other side.

16

"YOU CAN FLY," I breathed when we landed in a glade. White moonlight shone down, allowing me to see the shades of ebony on Raven's wings. They arched out from his back and hung almost to his feet, giving him a wingspan of about twelve feet. I stared in awe and reached up to run my fingers over them.

Raven pulled back, his eyes shadowed as he folded his wings on his back. One moment they were there, the next they were gone, and only his cloak of feathers remained.

"Are you a shape shifter?" I asked, raking my mind for the lore and fables I'd heard about the creatures in the wildwood.

His jaw tightened, and he scrubbed his hand over his face. "Some call it is shifting, but I am who I am. I can stand here in human form. I can use my wings to transport myself wherever I wish. I can shift into the form of a raven, my most dangerous form, and watch whom I please. I bind magic where I see fit, and I am the bringer of death. I am all these things, and yet, you don't run."

A sudden weariness gripped me and I stumbled back. "You have given me no reason to fear you," I said.

"You see how others react to me, and yet. . ." he trailed off, likely recalling our conversation the day before. "Stay close, the hut is near."

Within no more than five minutes, Raven pushed his way through a hedge. I followed, although the bush poked at me, as though it had little fingers and laughed at me. Faintly in the distance I heard howls, and shuddered, knowing that wolves were still out there. But we'd escaped. For now.

Raven paused, pulled aside a bush, and opened a door. "You must duck," he called out, and disappeared. Blindly, I searched for the opening he'd found, my hand met by Raven's warm one. "Step down."

The air was still within and smelled of old leaves and moss with hints of pine. Raven moved about in the darkness, as smoothly as though he could see in the dark. Perhaps he could. I shuddered while I waited, and the coolness of the spring night gathered around me. But there was no wind, just the uncanny stillness.

"How do you know these safe houses will be empty?" I asked.

Raven was silent. I heard a sound like a breath of wind, and then a rosy glow appeared. But it wasn't firelight. My mouth fell open, and I stared at the wall, which was a giant, glowing, amber stone.

"There." Raven stepped back as the light grew brighter.

I sank down on the earthly floor, staring about in

wonder. The amber glow permeated the darkness, but it was gentle enough not to burn my eyes. We rested within the hollow truck of a tree, and far above me was the faint twinkle of starlight. In a corner was a ledge, or perhaps had once been a tree branch, jutting out and growing inward. It was wide and almost ran around the rim of the tree trunk. I saw a neat stack of blankets at one end, and on the other a bowl of nuts, water skins and a trunk of what I assumed were provisions beneath it. But most impressive of all was the jewel.

Raven grinned as he crossed the floor and stood in front of me in two steps. "This is yet another safe house. I've shown you the wildwood, but you've never once asked me where my home is," he whispered, his voice low and enticing.

The thrumming deep in my belly stirred, and when his fingers brushed my chin, I thought I'd melt.

Words forsook me as his arms came around my waist, pressing me against his chest. I inhaled his scent. He reminded of wild leaves and tree sap and, more than anything, freedom. The life of independence, to go where one wished, when they wished it, without bowing to the wishes of others. To shape one's future without wealth or power or position. I thought I under-stood why, when he gained his freedom, he choose the life of the wildwood instead of return to the kingdom where the villagers tilled and toiled and offered sacri-fices to save themselves from the wildwood. For a life out there was bondage for him, and a life in here was freedom. He wasn't human, not like me. Magic sang in his blood, he could shift depending on his needs, and none would ever catch him, except the Goddess of

Death. But perhaps even I could play a hand in changing his future. If I wanted to.

But reason called out to me. Although I'd met him before, the last few days in the wildwood I could not account for me being of sound mind. First the attack, and then the bargain with Raven. I'd been emotional, desperate, longing for any small comfort. But after speaking with the Queen of the Wildwood, I knew I had the chance to reconsider my position. Should I continue to Capern and search for the lore keepers? Or should I find my way back to the Queen of the Wildwood and work through my magic under her guidance? And...?

I pushed my final thought away as I studied Raven. The amber light displayed the stubble on his chin, the glint in his eyes as they darkened, turning to liquid pools that begged me to give in.

"I know what you said the other day," his voice was deep, husky with need. "I don't ask you to change your mind, but you have to know how I feel. Long have I wandered these woods, my days endless, never daring to believe that any would see me for who I am, would believe my tale of reforming. Until now. But you've changed all of that. You've given me hope. And perhaps I should not give in, but I sense your magic and know a change has come, and it affects me directly. You should know that I want you with a knowing I've never felt before. It was fate, destiny, that brought our paths together. Even should they split I won't regret this, I won't regret you. I tell you this, and yet I would ask if I may kiss you. To ease my conscience when you leave. For the taste of your lips is token enough, and it will sear the memory of you on my soul for eternity."

I traced the line of his jaw and unbidden tears came to my eyes at his words. Such beautiful words. But did he mean them? My thoughts gave me a moment of hesitation, before I lifted my hand to his cheek and pressed my lips against his.

17

HIS KISS SENT flutters tingling through the core of my being. The pressure of his hand on my waist made me dizzy with longing, for him to unravel all my secrets and see me, for who I truly was. For my life had changed since I'd thrown Lord Brecken's proposal in his face and fled. I was no longer a noblewoman, a lady of wealth, I was simply Sasha. Independent, free to go where I pleased, to live where I wished, to love whom I desired.

I drew a slow breath as he broke the kiss, yet the impression of it still hung on my lips. Heat buzzed around my face and swirled in the pit of my belly. My lips parted to speak, to explain my feelings for him, but words stuck in my throat. Try as I might, they would not come out. My eyes darted to his, and his smoldering gaze was almost my undoing. How could I speak when he looked at me that way? As though he would eat me alive if I said yes. Locks of his fine black hair hung in his face and his body shuddered with each breath he took as though he waited for me, waited for more. One word would be all it would take to stop our stolen tryst, two people who did not belong together and yet, in the wildwood, our pasts were stripped away, leaving nothing but the present.

Why should I hold back? Why should I think of the future when here and now was everything I needed?

A low and steady hiss of desire left his mouth while his hands tightened around my waist. I bit my bottom lip but couldn't stop my whispered confession. "I want you."

A pitiful truth and nowhere near as lovely as the words he'd spoken, his confession that rocked me to my soul. Instantly I raked my mind for more words. How could I tell him how I felt when it was much easier to show him?

Fingertips brushed my cheeks as he tilted my face toward his. "Are you sure?" his voice was nothing more than a heated whisper.

Hot surges of pleasure flooded my body, at his touch, at what he would do to me, and I to him. My fingers trembled as I touched his hand. "It is the one thing I am certain of."

The hunger in his eyes intensified. He brought his lips to mine in a slow, gentle kiss. The restrained passion behind it took my breath away and my knees went weak. When his tongue pressed against the seam of my lips, I opened my mouth to his, taking, consuming, all that he would give. His tongue swept into my mouth and my fingers threaded through his hair, holding on, as though we were on the bridge again, and he was the only one who could save me from falling. Now his words danced back, but the better meaning would have been: If you fall, I'll fall with you.

He claimed my lips with deep, sensual kisses, leaving my breath ragged, and my mind astonished by how tender his kisses were. Brushing the hair off my neck, he dropped one of his hands to my waist and pulled me tight against his hard body. I trailed my fingers down his back, enjoying the hard lines of ridged muscle that lay there, taunt against smooth flesh. Deepening the kiss, he steered me toward the ledge. Excitement and desire fired through me as he pressed his body against mine. Through his pants I felt his hardness and liquid danger spiked within me, to have him, to move past the passionate kiss to the dance of pleasure I so longed for.

He guided me down until I sat in the blankets and broke the kiss in one move. A cry of frustration burst from my lips. I spread my legs shamelessly, wanting to take him all.

"Sasha," he groaned. His warm tongue licked the hollow of my neck, tasting me as he undid the tie of my cloak. It fell back, leaving my shoulders bare, but I could not feel the cool of the spring night as his warmth consumed me. Desire coursed through my veins. I pushed his cloak of feathers down his shoulders until it dropped onto the earthly ground. Taking my time, I ran my fingers down the board expanse of his chest, emboldened by the raw desire in his eyes. When I reached the band of his pants, he froze.

Pulling back, he studied me, as though ensuring I

knew what I was doing, what I wanted. Eyes lidded with lust, I stubbornly met his gaze as I brushed my fingers over his length. The words I'd wanted to same came from my lips at last. "We are here, in the wildwood where I am no one. Just Sasha. And you are Raven. Perhaps our destinies are entwined, perhaps they aren't, but what we have is here, now, and I…" my lips stumbled over the words. "I don't know how to explain how I feel, or the sensations that twist through me, but you are real. Not a dream. You've treated me with kindness, like an equal, but it did not keep you from being honest with me. That I appreciate, but also sense that you deny yourself happiness because you believe you don't deserve it. And I do the same. When trouble strikes, I run, when choices are too heavy to face, I hide. But with you, I don't want to run, or hide, I want you to see me."

"I do, Sasha." Tenderly he took my hand, guiding it to his lips, where he kissed my open palm, holding my gaze all the while. My other hand he took from his pants, gently pulling me to my feet. "I see you."

My lips trembled as he angled his head, and his sensual lips devoured mine, eliciting sweet sensations that rushed through my veins. Hot kisses trailed down my neck. I quivered with arousal as he pressed his mouth against my bare shoulders. He slipped the dress down my shoulders, to my waist and off my hips until it pooled on the ground.

His eyes flickered to my face as I stood naked in the amber light. "You are my goddess," he breathed before continuing his relentless quest with kisses.

My breath hitched when he reached my swollen breasts and took them in both hands, his fingers tracing the inflamed peaks. Bending his dark head, he drew one of my aching nipples into his mouth and teased it with his tongue. A moan escaped my parted lips and my body went tight with desire. Twisting in his arms, I pushed myself against him, breathless in my desperation for more.

His fiery mouth moved to my other breast and took the nipple in his mouth, teasing with his tongue, sucking and biting. My nostrils flared as I struggled to regain control, but he wouldn't let me. One of his hands trailed down between my legs, teasing the soft skin of my inner thighs. He hesitated one excruciating moment before his feather-light touch grazed my damp slit. Molten need rippled through me and flamed my cheeks as I gripped his shoulders. But I was too far gone to want anything other than his touch, to experience him within me, feeling me, satisfying me.

"Raven," I whispered his name, guiding his lips back toward mine and reaching until I felt his hardness again. I tugged his pants down as I spread my legs, wanting him to take me right then and there.

"Let me love you," he said, pressing fevered kisses to my lips, each one slow and seductive.

My skin tingled with heightened pleasure, making every touch, every kiss, potent and pleasurable. I licked my lips, unable to catch my breath enough to speak as his fingers stroked my inner thigh again. I squirmed, ready for him to take me, but he drew out each delicious sensation, a devilish smirk on his face.

His heart thumped, loud and steady as he moved down my body, tasting, licking, until he reached my hips and knelt between my legs. Shuddering, I curled my fingers into his thick hair and my hips rocked back and forth, opening to his caress. His fingers stroked my wetness, opening me up like a flower budding. I arched my back, bucking into him. He paused and our passionate gasps filled the air. I moaned. The only sound I could make as I silently begged him to take me and make me his. His alone.

When his finger slipped inside me, my body jerked. He paused, studying my reaction through hooded eyes before easing his finger out and then in again. I moved with him, sliding back and forth, unashamed of my wanton behavior. If I surprised him, he was so lost in passion he did not react, only added another finger, moving back and forth as I spasmed and bucked underneath him. Finally, giving in to my needs, he removed his fingers, leaving me empty and wanting. Kneeing my thighs wide open, he entered me with one swift thrust. A cry of pleasure escaped my throat as an erotic tingling rode up and down my spine. I pressed my legs against his hips and pulled his head toward me.

"Take me," I demanded.

He lifted me in his arms until my bottom was on the ledge and he stood, moving in and out of me with rhythmic thrusts. My fingers dug into his shoulders and my cheek brushed against his stubble. He held me against himself and there was something undeniably sexy and fulfilling about his sharp pants as he rocked against me. A trembling tension built in every fiber of my body and our passion moved to a new level. Our tongues twisted, biting, tasting, teasing. His fingers stroked down my back, eliciting new sensations as he cupped and squeezed my bottom. I held onto his arms, bulging with hard muscles. We moved together, our lovemaking both rough and tender, desperate and blissful. I lost control as he took me to the brink of release and held me there with a long thrust. My body tingled as he took me over the edge with him into unending waves of ecstasy.

WHEN I WOKE my body hummed with need, desperate for his touch again, like a fire that could not be put out. A pleasurable soreness between my legs reminded me of our lovemaking, and I touched fingers to my lips. I sat up and my light hair trailed down my bare back, but I was alone in the hut. A whisper of worry made me move fast. Tugging on my dress and tossing the cloak around my shoulders, I went to the door and opened it.

Raven appeared on the other side as though I'd called him, and relief seeped through me. Words failed me at the sight of him, and something within me broke. Did I deserve to be happy? After the trouble I'd caused and the death I'd left in my wake, what would a life in the wildwood look like for me?

"I went to scout ahead," Raven explained. "The path is clear. By the end of today we'll reach forest's edge, and the road to Capern."

I couldn't miss the wistfulness in his eyes. Taking his

hand, I pressed it to my chest, as though to imprint him on my soul.

"Sasha." He stepped closer. The aura of his presence sent shivers up and down my spine.

I swallowed hard, keenly aware I wanted him just as badly as I'd wanted him last night. As though our lovemaking had done nothing to quench the fire within.

I could make excuses, claim I was tired, and we had to stay another day in the amber hut. But my resolve fizzled away. "Kiss me," I begged, searching his eyes.

Angling his head toward mine, he claimed my lips with such passion it took my breath away. Tears gathered at the corner of my eyes, but I brushed them away, hoping he would not see. He studied me a moment. "Come, Sasha," he said, and led me away from that enchanted hut, deep into the wildwood.

Both of us were quiet as our journey continued, through thick wood and mysterious glades. Every now and then I caught of glimpse of a tiny creature, with wings moving so quickly it was almost impossible to see. Their bright bodies glinted in the low light, and soon I saw the faerie followed us. I liked to think of them as a bit of luck for our journey.

Raven's words from the evening before rang in my ears and a new thought came to me. I still wanted to go to Capern, to find my great grandmother and ask her advice. I needed to speak to someone else and discover if the wildwood had only enchanted me. Maybe I would come to my senses when I left it. But another thought tangled through my mind, and when I tried to unravel it, I lost pieces of it. What if. . . I considered. What if the wildwood hadn't enchanted me, and I was lucid? What then?

I chewed a piece of dried meat as I considered, but when I saw streaks of sunset, and the end of the forest, my feet came to a halt.

"Here we are," Raven pointed.

Between the woods I saw wild open fields. Land as far as the eye could see, with no trees in sight. A wide dirt road curved away from the forest, leading into what looked like a town in the distance, only a blur against the light.

"It's not as far as it looks," Raven said, "If you hurry, you could reach the village of Capern before the dark."

I pressed my lips together. If I hurried. But the village was only a few miles away, five at most, and I wasn't sure if my feet would carry me that far. Although, given my travel through the wildwood, I'd walked much further on foot than I ever had in a day. Perhaps if I had a fast horse, it could take me that way. I realized my mind was flying through excuses because I wasn't ready to leave Raven. Not yet.

"And if the darkness comes first?" I asked, my fingers fidgeting with the clasp of my cloak.

"Then you will be forced to spend another night in the wildwood," he said.

I faced him. "I'd rather go during daylight, but I won't hold you to your bargain now, for you have fulfilled it."

An indescribable look crossed his face before he frowned. "I would not leave you alone in the wildwood," he protested. "Sasha. . .you don't have to—"

"But I do," I interrupted, then lifted my chin. "I have

to know if what is between us is real. I have to know what life outside the wildwood might mean. But Raven, should I return, how will I find you?"

He faced the hidden village, and I couldn't stand the look of hurt on his face. "I am where I choose to be, at all times, it is by luck that one would find me. But I sense magic. If you return to the wildwood, I have no doubt our souls would call to each other, and I'd find you."

I blinked to keep my tears at bay again, taken aback by the words he spoke. How could an evil knight of a Dark Queen have such a heart? And how could I leave him? In leaving I would deny him, and myself, and what if he was the love of my life, and I'd never find another who fulfilled me the way he did? Who took me on adventures to magnificent, beautiful places?

A weariness came over me and I sat down, pressing my back against a tree trunk. "Will you watch the sunset with me?" I asked.

"Aye, Lady Sasha," he replied.

His presence beside me was warm, comforting, and I leaned against his shoulder as he put his arm around me, pressing me against the hardness of his chest. And even as my eyelids closed, I knew, deep within my soul, what I would do.

19

HE WAS GONE when I woke, and somehow, someway, I was not surprised. A long, black feather lay on the ground, as though it had fallen from one of his enormous wings. I picked it up, holding it with both hands as I strode out of the wildwood, and toward the dusty road. Several times I peered back, wondering if he was still there, if he watched me walk away. My journey had been so quick through the wood, and yet, I knew I'd left my heart within it. Even a drink of water did not stop the dryness of my throat or the aching in my chest as I walked away, my magic tingling within my stomach.

As Raven had promised, the walk to town did not take long. Within an hour I arrived at the gates of a city that was much larger than I expected. My heart sank as I walked inside and followed the wide, cobblestone road toward the center where I could hear shouts and merriment taking place. I racked my thoughts, sure it was not time for a festival, not yet. Midsummer would be the next feast, and yet it seemed the town still celebrated.

When I rounded a corner, I saw what it was. A market like none I'd ever seen before. Buildings rose high above my head, their structures elegant and chiseled with symbols and faces of perhaps gods and goddesses of old. But in the middle was an open area with booths lining each side of the street and people calling out their wares. Horses and wagons went by, women shouted at children as they dashed through the streets or climbed on rooftops, shouting at each other in a game of chase. A wild dog trotted by, sniffing the street for scraps of food.

A sweet perfume in the air quickly overcame the scent of unwashed bodies and I followed it, moving through the crowded marketplace, searching for the booth of a fortune-teller. Surely it was fate that had led me here on this day, to find Mother Misha and ask her the truth about who I was and what my magic meant. Although a dark suspicion hung over me, that even though I fled the wildwood, somehow, someway, just as it was with my cousin, my own future was intertwined with it.

I turned, searching anxiously, and I collided with a woman. The impact almost knocked me off my feet and my arms whirled, trying to regain my balance as the woman gave a cry. Her basket tumbled onto the cobblestones, scattering a collection of brightly colored packets. My initial reaction was to turn up my nose and demand that she watch where she was going, a reaction that died on my lips as I realized two things: I no longer looked like a noble lady, and reacting in anger would not help my situation.

"I'm sorry," the woman said. She was already on her

knees, snatching up the items and thrusting them into her basket. "I'm always daydreaming and never watch where I'm going, it's my fault, are you alright?"

At her last words she looked up at me, tucking her curly hair behind her ear. She was young, around my age, with a wide, honest face, and sparkling eyes. I reached for the last packet and handed it to her. When our fingers touched, a sensation went through me and a flash of a vision began on the edges of my mind.

A storm. A field of lightning. Dark blue hair and...a knife with runes on its blade.

I stepped back, stunned. "Yes, I..." I trailed off. "Actually, do you have a moment?"

The woman raised her eyebrows as she tucked the basket under her arm. "I'm Rae." She smiled. "Are you new to town? I don't think I've seen you before."

I nodded. "I'm looking for someone."

"Oh, I can help." She beamed. "I live just outside of the village but my sister and I come here for market day, isn't it exciting," she went on, bouncing up and down on her toes. "We don't know everyone, but I've lived here my entire life. Who are you looking for?"

Her exuberance was rather contagious, and I relaxed in her presence. The way she moved and talked reminded me of Mari's light-hearted nature, and a sorrow pierced my heart. "My grandmother is a fortune-teller," I explained. "She lives here, or she did a while ago. I need to find her."

Rae wrinkled her nose, eyes darting around the booths. "A fortune-teller. Wait. Do you mean Mother Misha?"

"Yes." My fingers trembled. I was so close to discovering the truth.

"Oh." Rae's brow furrowed as she studied me. "I'm sorry," she reached out to touch my arm. "She passed this winter. I thought. . .I assumed her family knew."

Disappointment rocked me, and my shoulders slumped. "She's dead?" I confirmed, my mind reeling. All this travel. . . for nothing.

"She went peacefully," Rae squeezed my arm. "She was old, it was her time."

"Oh." I twisted my fingers together while panic raced through me. Dead? What would I do now?

"Listen, I know we are but strangers but if you're a friend of Mother Misha, you're a friend of mine. Come sit with my sister and I for a while. Once market day is over you can come to our farm and enjoy a warm meal and a place to rest before you decide what to do next."

I blinked hard, trying to keep tears from brimming over and sliding down my cheeks. How lucky I was, to lean on the kindness of strangers, something that would have been embarrassing if I were still who I once was.

"I didn't know Mother Misha had children," Rae went on. "She was quiet, and kept to herself, but I thought something had happened in her younger days, to make her come here. She always had a hunch toward the future, and I wondered about her past, but now. . ."

"Those who are unique often become outcasts in my family," I told her bluntly.

Her eyes went soft. "That must be hard. I'm sorry she passed before your arrival."

But as I followed Rae back to her booth, I wondered if it was only a twist of fate.

20

RAE'S SISTER, Maraini, was kind, warm and friendly, just like her. Although she was quieter, she made notations of everything that sold before they loaded up again and the wagon lumbered onward, further north until we left the bustling village in the dust.

We arrived at their farmland before sunset, and when I stepped off the wagon into that land, visions flashed stronger than they had before. I was reminded of the words the Queen of the Wildwood had spoken to me.

I studied the rolling meadow, the manor house with the barn just beyond it, and a garden full of new green shoots. I whirled to face the sisters, a question burning my lips. "You are the lore keepers. Aren't you?"

Rae dropped the empty basket she'd been carrying, and Maraini froze in the midst of unhooking the horse from the wagon. "How do you know that?" she asked, eyes wide, but whether with fright or astonishment, I could not tell.

Knowledge hummed within me and all the pieces of the puzzle fit. "The Queen of the Wildwood told me. . ."

The sisters exchanged glances as though they did not understand what I was talking about. "And the rise of the old Goddess." I glanced from one to the other, waving my hands as though I could make them understand. "The rise of the Goddess of Death."

Maraini's eyes were as big as saucers. She gestured to the house. "You should come in and tell us more over dinner. I'm afraid that, although we are the lore keepers, I haven't focused my studies on the old texts."

I shook my head, a deep awareness rising in me as I realized what I'd missed. I'd been foolish in my haste to leave the wildwood and learn the truth, when it had been within me all this time. Mother Misha wasn't just a fortune-teller, she caught glimpses of the future, and perhaps with her death the gift had risen stronger in me, until I couldn't ignore it. And the Queen of the Wildwood had tried to tell me that I was the one who could save Raven from the rise of the Goddess of Death, a Goddess who might appear tonight or in a few years or decades. Regardless, she was coming, and perhaps everything I'd seen wove together.

"I can't stay," I told them. "But I need a horse. A fast one."

"I'll saddle a horse for you, but why?" Rae asked. "The night comes swiftly."

I shook my head. Foolish as it was, I would ride through the dark if I had to. "I know, but I left someone behind, someone very important, and I want to find him before it is too late."

They exchanged glances again, no doubt perplexed

by what I'd just shared. "I have to warn you." I turned to Rae and studied her. "A storm is coming. And with the storm will come a change. Make sure your heart is open to it."

Rae's jaw dropped and her eyes went glassy. "You are Mother Misha's granddaughter, aren't you? Will you not stay? There is a place here for those who see the future."

"It's only a glimpse," I told her. "Destiny can change, based on your actions."

"Thank you," she said, then turned on her heel and ran toward the barn.

I did not know what she had to thank me for, but a panic rose in my heart as I thought of Raven, once again, alone in the wildwood, seeking his purpose. Would the Queen of the Wildwood relent and recall him to her services? Would my claim on his heart be enough to keep him from being torn away from me? I didn't know why I felt the need to hurry, but it thrummed within me.

Maraini took a step toward me. "Who are you, truly?" she asked.

"My name is Lady Sasha," I told her. "I used to be a noblewoman, but I have followed my heart, and that is a choice, I will never regret."

Maraini studied me, and a soft light came to her eyes as she smiled.

"You shouldn't travel after dark," Rae cautioned when she returned with the horse. It was a beautiful black stallion, and my breath caught in my throat as I stared at the magnificent creature. I'd always had a soft spot in my heart for horses and just seeing it standing tall, tossing its head and snorting made me want to ride it all the more. "Will you stay? Just for the night? It's better in daylight when the outlaws are gone."

"Outlaws hunt in daylight too," I replied. She was right, though, it would be wise to wait, but I didn't want to. I had no ties here, nothing holding me back, and perhaps the wildwood would be dangerous at night too, but I was sure he would come. If I needed him.

Rae handed me the reins. "Be safe."

Maraini raised a hand, as though in blessing, and suddenly I felt a kinship with the strange women. Lore keepers. I'd have to remember them.

"If I set your horse free, will it return?" I asked.

Rae rubbed the stallion's nose. "They always come back." A bit of sorrow clouded her eyes.

"Wait." Maraini held up a hand. "If you're intent on going tonight, at least let me grab a pack for you. Provisions for the road, food, light, water, a change of clothes."

I opened my mouth to tell her she didn't owe me anything and closed it again. Although I was above relying on the charity of strangers for my needs, I realized I had nothing left. Nothing to trade, no money to give, just the clothes on my back. I was lucky enough to have found the lore keepers on accident, and if they were giving gifts, I should gratefully accept them. Perhaps I could find a way to repay them, now I knew where they dwelt.

Maraini returned shortly and thrust a bundle toward me. "Tie it on the back and be safe. I don't want to hear a tale about a woman waylaid by strangers."

"You won't," I promised.

I raised my hand in farewell and nudged the horse to the road. We followed it until the farm was out of sight and I urged the stallion from a canter into a full gallop. The wind whipped by me, sending a thrill across my face. My hair tumbled out of its bun and spilled around my shoulders, and the bundle bounced on the saddle behind me. This was the closest thing to freedom.

Freedom. No regrets. Besides, my cousin had said I could always return. I had a home, if nothing else worked out.

I sent the horse around the village, not wanting to disturb the sleeping city. Soon we left it in the dust and the enchanted wildwood stretched before me. At the sight of it, dark and evil in the moon's light, a fear came over me. What if he was long gone and the wolves and orcs found me first?

21

Silver beams of moonlight graced my shoulders like a shroud of blessing as I swung down from the back of the horse. My fingers were numb from holding the reins so tightly, and I struggled to untie the bundle from the saddle.

"Thank you," I whispered, stroking the black horse's neck as I leaned into its warmth for strength. Memories of my war horse, Lotus, made a longing stir in my heart.

Tying the reins into a knot on the horse's back, so he wouldn't slip on them, I turned his nose toward home and slapped his rump. He set off in no hurry, trotting through the fields, headed home.

Home. I didn't know where it would be for me, but perhaps home wasn't a place, only a sensation of feeling, of belonging. Of comfort, of joy, of hope and, most importantly, of love.

Closing my eyes briefly, I thought of myself, three years ago, the headstrong young woman who'd run from home, desperate to escape, with my mother's unkind words ringing in my ears. I'd never expected to find myself at the foot of the wildwood, about to do something I'd never dreamed of before.

I walked toward it, my pulse throbbing so loudly I feared the wolves of the night would hear it and hunt me. It was foolish to come here in the dark, but I couldn't stay away. As I walked, a black shadow appeared on the edge of the wood. The shape of a person. Standing. Watching. My toes curled in my shoes and I pointed my feet toward the figure.

Inky black feathers glistened in the moonlight, beautiful, powerful. Even at a distance I made out the shape of his jaw, the straight line of his nose, and the slant of his mouth. His arms hung by his sides, as though he knew I would come and waited only for me. My breath hitched in my throat and part of me longed to dash into his arms, but the other part, the sensible part of me, held back. I didn't want an emotional reunion; I wanted to stand before him and explain why I'd returned.

But as soon as I was within arm's length, my resolve melted away.

"You couldn't stay away, could you?" he murmured, threading his fingers through my loose hair.

I closed my eyes, melting in pleasure.

"Not even for more than a night."

I placed my hand on his bare chest, enjoying the thumping of his heartbeat. The adoration in his eyes took my breath away. "I returned because my home is with you. When I stood in the glade and thought of where I feel safe, loved, and above all, free, it was with you, in the wildwood. And my magic, my nightmares, can be explained. The Queen of the Wildwood offered to help me. But I had a vision of the Goddess of Death. She rose and claimed you, because no one else had. So I am here to claim you as mine."

His calloused fingers cupped my face, and he pressed our foreheads together. I breathed in, taking in his scent of pine and wood. Oh Goddess, let this be my beautiful beginning.

"I know I'm falling in love with you," I plunged on, daring to say words I'd never dreamed I'd say to a man, not a nobleman and especially not a dark knight.

He covered my hand with his. "Then I am yours."

My heart beat slowed, and everything within me leaned into him, for it felt right, different, not what I would have chosen for myself but far, far better.

When our lips met, I was sure I heard a symphony sing, and when I pulled back, out of the corner of my eye I saw bright spots of color. The faerie danced as they played on miniature stringed instruments. My lips curved back into a smile and a weightlessness radiated through me.

Raven pressed me against his chest and captured my lips again with a slow, burning kiss. "Come," he said. "I will show you my home."

He spread his wings and bore me away.

SECRETS OF THE LORE KEEPERS

1

THE CRACK of thunder shattered the peaceful melody of birdsong. I dropped the basket of green herbs on the wooden table and dashed to the open window. Flinging back the white curtains, I stuck my head out and sniffed, inhaling a faint whiff of water and the vague, bitter spice of electricity. A jagged streak of lightning pierced the evening sky and my eyes went wide as saucers. I drew my head back inside and whirled, skirts flying.

"Maraini! Hurry! Get the lanterns, there's a storm tonight!" I hollered at my sister.

Twisting my curls in a messy bun on top of my head, I lunged for the jars, almost tripping over the chicken that fluttered in the kitchen. Curses. I'd brought her inside to mend her torn wing. She'd escaped the henhouse and run into the paws of a fox. I'd meant to take her back to the henhouse, but I had forgotten. Now stray feathers dotted the floor, along with dust and dirt tracked in during my trips to and from the barn and garden. The table was covered with baskets of herbs, clothes that needed mending, and a pile of books. I sighed and tapped my foot with impatience. The house needed a proper cleaning, but I had no time, and Maraini was too deep in her ink and paper to bother with it. Stories and numbers were all that were in her head, and had always been, even before we took over the family business.

"Maraini!" I shouted again, tossing a blanket over one shoulder and placing the basket of jars by the door.

"Calm down, Rae, I'm coming," she said in her smooth tone, as slow and deep as molasses. She appeared in the doorway, the picture of perfection while I hopped up and down, tugging on first one boot and then the other.

"Let's go!" I wrenched open the front door and snatched up the jars. "You have the lanterns?"

Maraini laughed and shook her head, black braids flying. "I have everything, except the rain slickers. We'll catch cold out there if we don't cover up."

"Ugh," I groaned, halfway out the door and in the dried mud. Dust kicked up under my feet, for the ground was almost barren from lack of water. "Who cares, it's the first rain this month and we can catch lightning! Lightning! Our luck has turned, you hear!"

I danced away, basket tucked under one arm as I twirled outside of our front step.

"Are you daft?" Maraini scolded as she pulled the door shut tight and hooked her arm through mine. She'd tossed a scarf over her head and hitched her skirts up with one hand. The lantern and two long poles were slung over her back. "Our luck has never turned bad, just because you don't have all the unique items to sell at market doesn't mean we have bad luck."

"Oh posh." I waved my finger in her face as best I could, since we walked side by side. "Just because you look at numbers all day doesn't mean you know what luck is."

Lightning lit up the sky enough for me to see the frown on my sister's brown face. "We have plenty of money, if that's what you mean."

I gave an exasperated sigh. "Life isn't all about money, what's the fun in counting coin? Experience is what it's all about, now come on. We don't know how long the storm will last. I'll race you to the meadow."

I tugged my arm free and took off running while Maraini laughed. But I heard her pounding footsteps behind me and knew she enjoyed our risky gallivants as much as I did.

Five years, Maraini and I had run the family business. I was only a year younger than her, but full of vibrant life and energy, for pouring myself into the work helped me forget what happened. When I was only twenty, and Maraini, twenty-one, our parents left to travel and take a break from the busy life they'd led. They set us up young, and while we had wealth stored away—sacks of gold hidden in a secret hole near the garden—I still recalled their parting with remorse. They left the land, and had been killed. Whether by outlaws or the dangerous creatures that dwelled in the wild-wood, we did not know.

We continued to run the family business without their guidance. For we had a reputation to keep in the nearby village, Capern, which bordered the enchanted wildwood. The wildwood was a place full of secrets, a place Maraini and I had been warned to stay away from all our lives. I was curious about it, but after what happened to our parents, the spark of curiosity and the yearning for adventure died.

Besides, we had our hands full with the farm animals, the garden, plus the wondrous remedies and potions we could create out of herbs and roots.

Once we reached the middle of the meadow, a flat area with no trees about, we stopped, pulses thumping, to push the poles into the ground. No small feat since I'd forgotten the shovel, and the ground hadn't been watered in weeks. I cursed, Maraini laughed and scolded, but finally we were ready, with the jars hooked on the end.

Maraini grabbed my hand, like we were five years old again, catching lightning with Papa for the first time. "Now stand back," she whispered, fingers squeezing tight.

I couldn't help but bounce on my toes as I watched the sky.

Maraini shook her head. "You never stand still, do you?"

"I can't!" I squeaked. "It's too exciting. We haven't had lightning in forever!"

"Three months," Maraini grumbled at my exaggeration.

"Whatever." I bumped her shoulder. "What a treat

for market day, they always sell the highest. What do you think people use them for?"

Maraini went still, too still. "Lightning is dangerous, and those who buy it often carry weapons. I assume they are dangerous people who use it for dangerous things."

"Lighten up." I giggled. "And don't say dangerous again, you've used it three times in one sentence."

Maraini frowned for half a second before breaking into a smile. She could never stay peeved with me for long.

A rumble of thunder shook the ground, and Maraini yanked me back. "The next one," she whispered, her voice shaking with excitement.

Sure enough, lightning lit up the sky and sizzled up the poles, diving into our jars.

"Now!" I shouted as soon as it dissipated.

We leaped forward as one, spots of lightning still danced in my eyes as we capped lids on the jars and replaced them. I held mine up, a smile splitting my face, as always, awed at being able to capture lightning in a jar.

Maraini shielded her face and pointed across the meadow. "Rae?" her voice was low with concern. "What's that?"

I followed her finger. In the shadows a shape lay on the ground, a shape I was sure hadn't been there before.

Without waiting for a response, I took off running toward it, for there was something odd about the way it sprawled in a helpless heap.

"Careful!" Maraini shouted.

"It's okay," I tossed back over my shoulder, holding

up the jar of lightning. "If it's a wild beast, I have this and if it's something else. . ."

Maraini caught up with me. "Don't be foolish," she cautioned. "You know that trouble comes with the storm."

It was an old superstition, but that was not why I slowed my pace. My stomach clenched and my thoughts flew back to the woman, Sasha, who'd appeared in the market months ago. She'd touched my arm, her words shadowed with an omen: *A storm is coming. And with the storm will come a change. Make sure your heart is open to it.* .

A shiver went down my spine at the memory, although there had been many storms since then. Still, it was an admonition to let go of my impulsiveness, slow down, use my head more and my mouth less. My fingers itched to return to the lightning rods as another boom of thunder rocked the meadow. The black storm clouds did nothing to further display the hump that lay in the grass, but when another burst of lightning broke across the sky, eerily lighting it up for mere seconds, I saw the hump clearly.

My hand flew to my throat, and I gasped. It was a man, or at least what looked like a man. He lay headlong on his stomach, as though he'd been crawling and his strength finally gave out. In the quick blink of an instance I saw one of his hands was curled around grass, and the other was under him, pressed against his stomach where a patch of darkness spread. Blood? I swallowed hard.

"Maraini, we have to help him!"

"But—" came Maraini's budding protest.

"I know, I know," I interrupted and stepped closer to him. "We know nothing about this stranger and he could be dangerous. But I don't think he's dead, just wounded, and with our potions we always help those with wounds and ailments. Besides, I have the lightning jar." I held it up, casting a thin light over her face.

Maraini's shoulders slumped. "I'll go for the wagon, but, Rae, be careful and stand back. If he wakes, he might not be kind."

I nodded, and she ran toward the barn. Although now the trip across the meadow back to our farm seemed so far. Despite her warning, I turned my attention back to the man and my heartbeat quickened. Sure, there were plenty of unmarried men in the village and surrounding farmlands. During market days I enjoyed flirting with them. But none had caught my eye, or made me want to leave my cozy home and have babies. Something inside me longed for more, much more, and I still wondered who or what had killed my parents. Part of me hoped it was all a big mistake, and they'd come striding through the door, laughing and smiling. Honestly, I knew better. An unsettling fear kept me at home, because my parents had left the land, and leaving the land brought about their death. Besides, it was easy to lose myself in the farm's work and bury my grief with responsibilities, no matter how haphazardly I carried them out.

Slowly, I knelt in the dry grass and placed the jar of lightning by my side. It gave off a tiny halo of light, just enough to allow me to scrutinize the man. He wore his hair long, past his shoulders, and it was a tangled mess of snarls and bramble. A slight smile came to my lips.

Often how my hair looked at the end of a busy day. Some of it had slipped over his cheek, although his arm, which had come up to grasp the grass, covered most of his face.

I frowned as I studied his clothes. Leather, well made. A long-sleeved shirt covered his arms, and over it was a leather jerkin. The arm I could see had a gauntlet on it, embedded with swirling designs. I studied them, questions rising. His pants were dark and his boots black and muddy. Studying his clothing led me to assume he was a well-to-do man. And if he was, why was he here? Wounded?

Another glint of lightning lit up the meadow. I saw a glimmer, just underneath him and swallowed hard as I stood up and backed away. A knife. He had a knife. The handle lay under him, but the blade was partly exposed. As I looked at it a deep foreboding came over me, like a black shadow of night. I twisted to face the farm, hoping Maraini was on her way with the horse and wagon.

Soft and steady drops of rain pitter-pattered down upon the carpeted grass, determined to soak it through and feed the hungry plants. I lifted my face to it, relishing the drops on my lips. My body stilled, for nature had a way of soothing my need to rush every-where and accomplish task after task as fast as possible. The shadow disappeared, taking my fear with it. I knelt again and placed my hand on the man's shoulder. He was still warm, and I felt his chest rise and fall. I wanted to turn him over, to study his face, but I recognized the need to wait for my sister.

"Hello, stranger," I whispered. "My name is Rae, and

you've stumbled across the farm which belongs to my sister, Maraini, and I. We are Lore Keepers and we will use our knowledge to heal you and send you on your way again. You have come to a house of faith and fortune; all we ask in return is for your silence."

2

ONCE MARAINI RETURNED, it took both of us to drag the man into the wagon. He was dead weight the entire time and didn't so much as grunt. By the time we finished, the rain was pouring down in blinding sheets.

"I'll lead the horse," Maraini said, while I gathered the jars and climbed into the back to ride with the man. I'd remembered to snatch his silver blade out of the grass, but something about it made me wrap it in my skirts and hide it from my sister. I didn't know why.

I tried to shield the man from the rain as we traveled the short distance back to the barn while my mind went wild with speculation. The occasional light only left me more curious about the stranger. His skin was bronze, a lighter shade than mine. His face was narrow, angular with deep-set eyes, long eyelashes, and a sharp nose. Who was he? A hunter who'd gotten lost? A warrior who lost his comrades? A noble in disguise?

Maraini could craft a story for him out of thin air. She'd write him into her storybooks where she cataloged tall tales from legends past, of great wars, runaway princesses, hidden princes, noble kings, and a spiraling, dangerous forest kept in the grasp of the goddesses. Stories I loved to listen to late at night, sitting in front of the fire when sleep became hard to come by. The man looked as though he had stepped out of those tales and come to enchant us. Or make our lives complex.

I shivered. Even though it was midsummer, the rain was cold against my skin, especially since the sun had gone down. Soon my hair was drenched through and through. My thoughts flitted back to the scolding I usually got from Mama after playing in the rain. She'd drag me indoors by my ear and give me a tongue lashing about how I'd catch my death out in the cold rain. Then she'd hang my clothes in front of the fire to dry, wrap a blanket around me and stow me by the hearth with a cup of peppermint tea. Often, Maraini came to snuggle up and whisper stories in my ear. I'd give anything for a tongue lashing now, if it meant seeing my mother's face again.

The mare needed no encouragement and trotted into the barn, blowing and stamping. Maraini hopped off the front of the wagon, unhitched her and started rubbing her down. "That's a good girl," she cooed, leading the horse back to her warm stall.

I glanced at the man in the wagon. Moving him would be a pain. Maraini returned and together, as gently as we were able, we rolled him off the wagon and dragged him into a stall filled with hay. The dampness of his clothes made the hay stick to him, and Maraini looked over at me. "Do you have the lightning jars?"

"Of course." I dashed back to the wagon to grab them and hung up the lantern which cast a soft pool of yellow over the stall.

Chewing my lower lip as I knelt on the other side of the man, who took slow breaths, his chest rising and falling. I still had his knife tucked into the pocket of my dress, and I moved gingerly to keep it from cutting me. I met Maraini's large brown eyes. "How do you want to do this?"

Her fingers twitched, and I knew what she was thinking. Somehow, even though we were caring for someone wounded, it seemed wrong to undress a man. I took a deep breath and reached for his jerkin, slowly undoing the ties. They were knotted, and I struggled while Maraini watched, one hand straying to the lightning jars, but he did not wake.

I peeled back the layer gently, pulling his shirt up from where it was tucked into his pants. My fingers brushing his bronzed skin, revealing the hard muscles of his stomach. Sure enough, there was a deep cut on his side. Fresh blood pooled out as I pulled the shirt away. Too much blood. He must be at death's door, and I did not have the expertise to heal such a wound.

"We must sew it up," Maraini murmured, stepping out of the stall.

We often had to bandage injuries for our animals and kept an emergency kit in the barn. Maraini returned with it while I took a steady breath and held out my hands for the needle. When it came to working with my hands, my rush to do everything as quickly as possible faded, leaving me with steady hands and a calmness in my spirit.

Maraini kept watch while I cleaned the wound, sewed him up and wrapped a bandage around him.

I shook my head when I finished, my fingers slick with blood. "It's not enough." His body had a pale hue to it, and his skin cooled under my touch. "He's lost too much blood to live."

I met Maraini's dark eyes and asked a silent question. We had healing potions, rare and difficult to make. Mama had mixed them on a midsummer's eve, with a warning we should use them only in the utmost need. I couldn't help but wonder if my parents would still be alive, had they taken the potions with them when they left.

But the man who lay before me was a stranger, and while he might be wicked, it was a risk I was willing to take. For life was precious, and it would be my guilt I'd live with if I did nothing when I could have saved him.

Maraini squeezed my arm and ran for the house.

I studied him as I waited, taking in the lines of his face, his tightly drawn lips and the slow rise and fall of his breathing. It was slower now. I didn't want him to die without finding out who he was, why he was on our land, and where he belonged. He likely had family who cared about him and would worry when they did not hear from him.

Maraini reappeared, holding a squat bottle in her hands. "He's too far gone to drink," she said. "And I don't know if he'll need the entire bottle or just a few sips. Regardless, you can try to force some down his throat, but we'll leave some water with it mixed inside in case he wakes."

Pressing my lips together to keep them from trembling, I stood, thankful for my sister's sound advice. I washed the blood off my hands in a nearby water bucket and dried them on a blanket. Maraini had finished mixing the water and potion and was tucking a blanket around him when I returned. She jerked her chin toward the potion as I slipped inside and propped up his head on a mound of hay. His body was cool to the touch as I hefted the dusty bottle and pressed it to his lips. Some dribbled down his chin, and I paused, unwilling to waste the life-giving elixir. I thought some passed between his lips, but the low light made it difficult to tell, and a sudden blush rose to my cheeks. My actions seemed intimate and wrong somehow.

Frowning, I twisted the lid on top of the bottle and tucked it into my pocket as I stood to leave.

Exchanging anxious glances, we shut the door of the stall and looked at each other.

"What if he dies?" I whispered.

Maraini shrugged. "We'll check on him in the morning. For now, let's leave."

I peeked over the stall at the stranger once more, a strange pulse stirring in my heart.

THAT NIGHT I tossed and turned on my feather mattress. The storm continued through midnight, and with each flash of lightning and rumble of thunder, I thought about the stranger who'd come with the storm. Curiosity pulsed in my veins and whispered enchantments through my dreams. What was his story? Where did he come from?

Before the first streaks of pint-tinted dawn touched the dusky sky, I bounced out of bed. My family's home was a large manor house, with two floors—three if one counted the cellar, but I never did. Upstairs was for sleeping. A set of stairs on the main level led up to the landing and a short hall led directly to the room at the back of the house. My parents' room. Ever since their deaths, Maraini and I had kept the door shut. I dared not venture in, my throat thick with grief, but I thought Maraini went to sit in there from time to time. Close to their room, it still smelled like Mama's lavender and Papa's tobacco.

On either side of the landing were two rooms, one was mine, and the other was Maraini's. My room looked as though a windstorm had recently blown through, clothes and shoes scattered about, with scraps of paper and crafts I was working on. Maraini's room was meticulous and neat, her bed tucked into a corner and her desk under a window. Stacks of books were piled on every surface, except the space on the desk she kept clear for ink and parchment. She kept the family records. Her window overlooked the herb and vegetable garden and the green pastures where our livestock grazed. My room faced the front of the house, over-looking the dusty road and the meadow where we caught lightning.

From memory I recalled my parent's room faced the road which led to the village of Capern. On a clear day we could see the village from the second floor of the house, nothing but a dark smudge on the horizon. Beyond it was the enchanted wildwood, less than a day's journey away. Maraini and I never ventured much further than the meadow to the north, or south to the village for market day. Mama and Papa always claimed it was best to leave family matters in the hands of family, for we were the Lore Keepers, known for our unique abilities. And because of our rare gifting, we could only trust family.

Without bothering to untangle my curls, I yanked on a plain shirt and tucked it into my knee-length skirt. The length of long skirts and dresses ended up being more of a hindrance than a help. Maraini and I had taken to wearing shorter garb and leaving our arms bare, especially in the summer. Before leaving my room, I snatched up my straw hat to protect my face from being burned by the sunlight and slipped out the door.

A rush of cool air kissed my face, and I squinted in the shadows. The stillness of the house told me Maraini wasn't up yet. I tiptoed downstairs, skipping the middle one which creaked, to where the first glimmer of dawn cast an unearthly glow across the room. Six-foot-tall windows on either side of the front door let in daylight, because Mama and Papa said a house with no secrets is full of light. *Welcome the sunlight, fill your body with joy,* was a mantra Mama often repeated. I had to agree. The first beams of daylight chased away sorrow, and I closed my eyes as hope imbued me.

Behind the staircase was a hall with access to the storage rooms inside the house and the cellar. We kept scraps of fabric and herbs for spells, plus our stores for the winter. We also had jars and recipes of strange concoctions. The tales those whispered about us were true, we were a family with one secret, not only did we know the lore of the world, we also used alchemy to transform nature to our wishes. I loved that about my family, the secrets, the inventions, and the magic. But ever since my parent's death a sad ache bloomed in my heart. An ache that lore could not heal.

Mixed feelings twisted through me as I wondered whether the strange man had lived through the night. Regardless, I filled a basket and with apples, cheese, and bread, and then, as an afterthought, tucked the odd knife into the bottom of the basket. Unbolting the front door, I snuck out onto the wide porch and trotted down the two steps. I glanced back at the house as I made my way down the dirt path, now muddy from last night's rain. It was a beautiful home and looked as though it were built for a lord or lady. Nobility usually lived in the kingdom, with grand estates groomed by servants. Lords and ladies kept a small army around them at all times, but honest, hard-working hands, not birthright built the land of my family. We were as wealthy as the lords and ladies of court, but there was a reason none dared come to steal our wealth away.

I made my way to the barn, pausing under Maraini's window to wave. If she were awake—and it was likely she was by now, peering at her books before coming downstairs—she'd see me and know where I went. With a pang, I recalled the lightning jars were still in the house. In a few days we'd need to pack the wagon with goods to sell at market. Oh well. I mentally made a list of tasks: feed the horses, milk the cows, fetch the eggs, find out where the goats had run off to—and the pigs. Curses! Why had we decided pigs were a good idea? Maraini and I had seen them in market—adorable piglets with their curly tails and upturned noses. We bought five of them. Five pigs who grew up to be the terror of the farm. Uprooting the garden. Burrowing under fences. And eating winter's harvest until we drove them off into the meadow, hoping they wouldn't return. When they were full-grown and fat, we'd hunt them down and roast them. But for now, it was the least of my concerns.

When I reached the barn, I ducked inside. My nose was met with the familiar smell of musk and hay. Holding the basket with a firm hand, I made my way to the stall, daring to hope he'd survived the night. I peeked over the stall door, and two brown eyes stared right back at me.

3

A GASP LEFT my parted lips as I met his haunted gaze. In the daylight, he appeared even more mysterious than the evening before. He sat up, wincing as he touched his wounded side. Shoulder-length hair moved with him, giving me a glimpse of pointed ears. I froze as his eyes held mine. They were dark, hungry, and examined me as though he were trying to read the thoughts whirling in my head.

Tension hung between us, but the sight of straw poking out of his hair, mixed with my deep relief that he was alive, broke my surprised silence. "Excuse my manners," I offered, words rolling easily off my tongue. "My sister and I found you in the meadow last night. You were wounded." I pointed at his bandaged side. "We dressed your wound and brought you here to heal. I brought some food, if you're hungry." I lifted the basket so he could see I meant no harm. My fingers grazed the latch on the stall door. "May I come in?"

His eyes narrowed, and he blinked in confusion before nodding.

I entered and sat the basket by his feet, and then retreated to stand against the stall door, giving me an exit should things go wrong. A flush came to my cheeks as I studied him. Awake there was a quiet elegance to him, as though he never spoke, never moved without deep intentions. I wanted to pester him with questions: Who was he? Where had he come from? How did he get the wound? What was his name?

He reached for the basket, this time keeping the wince off his face, and picked up an apple. He took a bite. Relief seemed to come over him. Perhaps he'd just been hungry. My eyes drifted to the water canteen, wondering if he'd finished the potion. My fingers itched with the need to do something, but I willed myself to stay calm.

"My name is Rae," I told him.

"Rae," he repeated.

The first words he'd spoken and my name on his tongue sounded as sweet as honey. A warm buzz went through me along with a slight fluttery sensation.

"Has anyone come here, looking for me?" He finished the apple in a series of rapid bites and reached for the bread and cheese.

I tilted my head, unable to keep the furrow off my brow. "Nay, no one comes here unless they are in need. This is a remote farmland, and during the storm yesterday, you're the only one we saw. Why? What's your name? Are you in some kind of trouble? Who knifed you?"

He paused to stare at me, as if I had the answers, and he was trying to read them.

A sudden sensation I could not explain came over me and I rubbed the back of my neck, recalling perhaps I should tend to the animals.

"Do you always ask this many questions?" His mellow voice pulled me back into the conversation.

"Do you always end up half dead in a field?" I retorted, mischief dancing around my lips. I would get answers, one way or another.

He shook his head, causing some hay to fall out, but not enough to make him look less silly. I sucked in one cheek and shifted my weight from one leg to the other, waiting on his answer.

"You must forgive me." He straightened his shoulders. "I. . ." he shifted in the hay, examining the food, the water, and the blanket. "I don't remember," he confessed, lifting a hand to touch his head.

As he moved the light caught his hair, and I saw it was a dark blue, not black like I'd thought. My heart beat fast. Who was this man with pointed ears and dark blue hair? When I returned to the house, I'd ask Maraini what she knew. She kept up with the lore of our ancestors, while I'd let my studies of old times slip, preferring to focus on the tasks at hand.

The more pressing issue was the fact that the man seemed to have lost his memory. Perhaps an object from his past would help jolt his mind, otherwise I'd need to prepare a memory potion for him.

"You were lying on a knife when we found you," I told him, wondering if the strange man knew his own name. "I put it in the bottom of the basket, in case it has any meaning for you. Perhaps it will help your memory, but if not, I will brew you some memory tea. And you don't have to worry about anyone following you here. Wards of protection keep this land safe."

His nostrils flared and his eyes bored into mine.

Aha! I had his attention. I waited for him to reach into the basket and take out the knife, but he just sat there, staring at me.

The silence stretched until it was awkward and I swung the stall door open. Even though I wanted to stay and find out more, I forced my feet away. "I have to do my morning chores, perhaps I'll return later and we can speak? Your wound is still healing, so I recommend rest for today. Oh, and you have hay in your hair."

I laughed as I scurried away, saying good morning to the horses and giving them nosebags of oats. I wondered if the stranger was picking hay out of his hair and realizing how ridiculous he looked. But his question bothered me. Why did he want to know if anyone was looking for him? Was he being hunted? I needed to confer with Maraini on what we should do with him. For all we knew, we could have a thief, outlaw, or bounty hunter in our barn. But what if he was on the run from the king and his soldiers? So many delightful thoughts twirled through my mind. By the time I was done milking the cows and gathering the eggs, I itched for an excuse to return to the barn.

※

AT MIDDAY, I found Maraini hiding under the shade of sunflowers, book in hand and a picnic basket beside her.

She glanced up when I arrived. Her curly black hair was braided back, as usual.

I plopped down beside her, the shadow of the six-foot-tall sunflowers cooling me off. "Reading again?" I grinned as I poked the lid off the basket.

She smiled and tucked the book away. "Forgot your lunch again?"

"Always." I unwrapped a sandwich and bit into it.

Maraini wiped her hands on her skirt and picked up the other sandwich.

A deep satisfaction filled me as I bit in to a rich collection of vine-ripe tomatoes, fragrant basil, and a mild, white cheese. The midsummer harvest was ready, but Maraini and I were already behind gathering the ripe vegetables from our garden. We met at midday to compare notes, but I was well aware the upkeep of our farm was spiraling out of our control. On market day we'd hire workers to harvest the garden and make repairs around the farmland.

"How's our guest?" Maraini asked around a mouthful of bread.

My eyes drifted toward the barn. "The potion worked. He's alive, and should heal quickly, but. . . there's one problem." My brow furrowed. "His memory is gone. I'm not sure he even knows his own name."

Maraini raised her eyebrows. "Gone? But how far gone is his mind? Is he like a newborn babe?"

I chewed my lower lip. "I don't think so but I did not speak long with him." My thoughts went to the blade, but for some reason, I didn't want to tell Maraini about it. "He asked if anyone had followed him here, and I told him no. But we did not sense his presence on our land. Why is that?"

"Do you mean the wards of protection? We have not conducted the ritual this year and it's time we did it again. I haven't forgotten Sasha's warning."

I finished my sandwich and brushed crumbs off my skirt. "I haven't forgotten either. I think knowing this land is protected would impress him."

"Oh, you wanted to impress him, huh?" Maraini giggled at me. Actually giggled.

I narrowed my eyes and glared at her.

"Rae, laugh, I'm only teasing!" she nudged my shoulder, then held up the book.

"*Spells & Such,*" I read out loud. "Ah, so you are brushing up on your knowledge."

Maraini's brown eyes turned somber. "Aye, and there's probably a recipe for a memory spell inside. The sooner the stranger heals, the sooner he can leave and our days can return to normal."

Leave? My curiosity deflated. Just when something interesting was happening, he'd leave and my life would return to the humdrum melody it played, leaving me with too much time to get lost in my own thoughts. I picked at the mud on the hem of my skirt.

Maraini lay out the book and pressed down the pages, reading through the table of contents. "Ah. There isn't a memory spell in here but look, here's the spell of protection."

Swirling handwriting caught my eye, and the picture of herbs. "Sage." I pointed.

"Aye, and salt." Maraini pointed to the bowl pictured on the second page. "And a chant. We are to walk the length of our land, sprinkling salt and sage and chanting. Then when it's done, and every inch is covered with salt and sage, we shall be protected."

"What if someone comes and steps over it?" I asked.

"That's what the chant is for." Maraini pointed to a tiny description. "It's an invisible barrier, and if anyone steps over it, we'll know."

"Anyone with ill will? Or anyone at all?" I prompted for clarity.

Maraini squinted down at the words. "That, I'm not sure." She put down the book, closed it, and stared out at the fields.

I followed her gaze and saw our garden, the green plants at waist height, some taller, others shorter. I saw the weeds sprouting up, choking some plants while a lazy vine twisted through them. Doing a spell of protection around our property meant we'd have to delay harvesting the garden. But everything was set. A day's delay wouldn't matter, but everything else we did meant something else would have to wait.

I stared around the land and saw it in fresh eyes. The roof on the chicken coop needed replacing, the garden needed weeding; the goats were—well, where were the goats? If they'd escaped and were eating someone else's garden, we'd never hear the end of it. We were ill-prepared for market day in two days. Picking and packing and prepping the wagon would take hours, not to mention the stranger. Overwhelm flooded me as though my head were underwater.

"I was thinking." Maraini twisted her hands together. "We need to read Mother's journals for other spells. Particularly one regarding memories."

I drew a sharp intake of breath but couldn't keep the hiss from leaving my lips. "Are you suggesting?"

"I think it's about time. She passed so much on to us, but I can't remember all of it, and you know how she liked to take notes. Everything is written down."

I pressed my lips together. "It's just a stranger we found in the meadow. . ."

Maraini shook her head. "Rae, it's not *just* the stranger. I've been thinking of this for a while, ever since Sasha. She mentioned the old goddess. . ."

A ripple of discomfort went through me. The old goddess. I pushed the swirl of dark feelings away. I didn't want to know. Maraini was still speaking.

"I know you don't listen in the marketplace, or read like I do, but there are stirrings, unrest, and odd tales that trickle down. They are tales about the wildwood, and the dangers spilling out of it. Something happened almost three years ago, and while the effects are slow, they are affecting people in surrounding villages."

Her knowledge of these things jolted me, and my mouth grew dry as I stared at my sister. Her gaze remained locked on the garden, but her eyes were unseeing.

"Tell me your plan, what should we do?" I asked, breathless.

"Gather the sage, I'll gather the salt," she repeated. "I'll spend the afternoon searching for a memory spell. If you can, find out all you can about the stranger."

4

I FOLLOWED the slight rise of a hill to a crest. The scent of herbs filled me with a floating sensation. I walked past the rosemary bushes, baskets in hand, and vines of mint creeping across the ground. I went past the dill, already flowering in the breeze and the great sage. I pulled my knife out of the basket, knelt by the bush and cut. Whispers in the wind swirled around my thoughts, but I couldn't focus. As soon as one basket was full, I abandoned my post, gathered some herbs and made my way to the barn.

It was quiet when I entered, and the horse whiskered. I hummed a tune, more to let the strange man know I was coming than to amuse myself. I walked up to the stall. "I come bringing gifts," I announced. Except, aside from a lump of hay and an empty basket, nothing was there. A lump formed in my throat and visions of monsters entered my mind.

"Rae?"

I almost screamed at the sound of my name and spun around.

He stood a few feet away, outside of the mare's stall, rubbing her nose.

"What are you doing?" I blurted out, pressing a hand to my racing heart.

His dark eyebrows rose as he eyed me, but he kept rubbing the mare's nose. To her credit, she was enjoying it. Her head was over the stall and she nudged his chest from time to time, searching for a treat. I spoiled her, usually bringing an apple or carrot to tempt her, but my mind was scattered today.

I cleared my throat, correcting my accusation. "I mean, your wound hasn't healed yet. You shouldn't exert yourself. Besides, I came to dress it." I held up the basket, wondering why my heart thumped in my chest as though I were caught doing something wrong.

"Thank you." A wry smile came to his lips, and he turned his gaze back to the horse.

I took advantage of the opportunity to study him. The smile changed his appearance, making him seem softer, friendlier, and less fearsome than the stranger we'd found face down in the mud yesterday. He was a head and shoulders taller than I and lean, as though he spent much of his time exerting himself. He'd picked all the hay out of his dark blue hair, and I could see where it went past his shoulders. His face was heart-shaped with a strong jawline, but his nose was sharp, giving him an overall elegance. Again, I ran my eyes over his clothes and couldn't shake the sensation that he was a man of means that went beyond the tailors, bakers, blacksmiths and tradesmen of Capern.

"I wanted to apologize," he said to the horse, "for being rude earlier. You see, I woke up here, and it was unexpected. But I owe you, and your sister, thanks. Is there anything I can do to repay your kindness?"

A snort escaped my mouth at his gallant words, as though I were a princess of some faraway land who'd happened upon him.

His brows rose and his hands dropped to his side as he faced me, no doubt shocked at my outburst.

"You don't have to thank us," I said, "we would have done the same for anyone. You just appeared, as though you came with the storm, and I've seen no one like you in these parts. Did your memory return? Do you know who you are?"

His eyes were a dusty shade of brown as he studied me, taking in my wild curls and farm-woman clothes. My face warmed under his gaze, but I refused to be intimidated.

A flash of confusion crossed his face as he pondered my words. Finally, he spoke. "My name is Kian."

He walked toward me, his gait measured and slow so not to irritate his wound. Up close I could see the plains of his wide face and the emotion behind his dark eyes, although he struggled to hide them. His slim hands moved back and forth, as though he could not decide what to do with them. "I am not from. . .here." He gestured to the barn and then looked hopefully at the daylight streaming in the open doors. "I dwell in the enchanted wildwood with my tribe."

A chill went up my spine as he said the words: *enchanted wildwood.* Twice in one day, news about it touched me. I flinched, but if he noticed, he said nothing.

"I'm not sure why I'm here, or what the blade means," he confessed. "I recall everything else. . ."

"Your tribe," I couldn't help the questions that dashed off my tongue. Blue hair. Pointed ears. "You aren't human, are you? At least not fully?"

He examined me again, noting our differences. "No, we are wood elves. Officially I am Prince Kian of the Tribe of Finros."

Wood elves? Prince? Tribe? It appeared he'd walked straight off the page of one of my sister's books. I gawked at him. "You're an elven prince and you're standing before me as casually as if you just told me you live in the neighboring farm! How can you stand here so calmly? Won't your family be worried about you?"

His expression was strained as he moved away from me, back to the stall. Slowly he took off his jerkin, his eyes shadowed. "I wish I knew. We were preparing for battle, but I doubt that's the reason I'm here."

"It would explain your wound." I set my basket on the bale of hay and stepped closer to him, reaching out to touch his arm. "If they believe you are missing, it's best for them to know as soon as possible. My sister and I lost our parents five years ago, and it still feels fresh."

"Oh." He paused his movements and met my eyes. "It is unfortunate. What happened to them?"

The gentle lilt to his voice broke down something inside me, and suddenly tears sprang to my eyes. I reached for the basket, searching for something to keep my hands busy. "I don't know. Their bodies were found outside of the wildwood. I always assumed the creatures of the forest had slain them."

I gestured for Kian to lie down and he did, taking off his shirt to show off his well-toned chest. I should have blushed with embarrassment, but when he tucked his arms above his head, a novel sensation swept through me.

Thoughts of my parents' deaths faded, replaced with a desire to trace my fingers from his chest down his abs. So consumed was I in my thoughts, I didn't hear his question at first.

"What did you say?" I met his eyes and realized he'd seen me admiring his body.

Quickly I cursed to myself and set to work changing the bandage.

"Did you find out who killed them? Did they have enemies?" Kian asked.

I shook my head, keeping my gaze on his wound, which was healing nicely. It might leave a scar, but he'd have to live with it, for I did not possess the magic of healing, just herbs.

"No," I admitted, shoulders sagging, wondering how he'd turned the tables and got me to talk about myself when I was most curious about him. "We had no clues and no place to start looking for them. Besides, the land needed us. It always has, always will."

A spark of recognition flickered in his eye before fading back into distant confusion. "The land," he repeated, as though those very words would bring back his memories.

We fell silent as I worked, and I recalled Maraini's desire to search Mama's journals for a memory potion.

What if there was a clue in those journals? A sign of where they were going and why? But no reason spoke to me.

The journals weren't accounts of daily life; they were more of a yearly almanac with accounts of the farm, the animals in the barn, how much they could produce and how much they were worth. There were notations of the herbs and plants in the garden, and the uses for them. There were details of the weather, and which plants flourished during the seasons. Some accounts included recipes, and those were my favorites, for Mama would take her time, drawing a plant in black and white beside the list of instructions. One recipe was the familiar tomato and basil sandwich that Maraini and I often ate. It went into the journal along with a picture of fat ripe tomatoes and large basil leaves as big as my hands.

When I was younger, I liked to sit on my mama's knee and watch her draw, her spidery handwriting creating something beautiful out of nothing. That was what spell work was like, the beauty of transformation, taking one thing and using words and our firm belief to turn it into something else.

"Where did you go?" Kian asked, wonder in his voice.

I realized that I was so preoccupied with my thoughts, I'd paused and sat, staring off at the wall behind him. Slowly, my eyes slid back to his face and lingered on his dry lips. I needed to bring him water, but I'd forgotten. "My mother kept records of everything that took place on this land. Perhaps she wrote down a potion for memories. I'll find one and craft a cure to help you recall what was lost."

I could feel Kian's eyes linger on me as I finished bandaging his wound. "There, you're all better now." I smiled at him, attempting to lighten the mood.

"Tell me," his voice was low, almost rough. "Are you and your sister witches?"

Laughter burst out of my lips before I could stop myself. I shook my head, almost crying from merriment. "Witches?" I sputtered. "What makes you think of that?"

Incredulous, he stared at me, as if he did not know what to think. He shrugged, reached for his shirt and stood. "Just now you mentioned a potion, earlier you spoke of wards of protection, and my wound, I imagine it was deep. I saw the dried blood in the hay and yet I barely feel it."

A stillness crept over me. He was right. The healing potion had worked far better than I imagined. Without it, he'd still be lying in the hay, unable to move.

"I've only seen you, and you claim you have a sister. But where is your husband? Where are the children? It is so quiet here, like you have something to hide."

A finger of fear touched my shoulder, and I stepped back to the entrance of the stall. Frowning, I replied. "I don't have a husband or children. It's just my sister and I. We take care of the farm. Alone." My eyes narrowed, a sudden fury rising in my chest. How dare he judge me! "As for hiding, what is it you think we're hiding?"

A flicker of confusion passed over his eyes, as though a haze kept him from understanding clearly. He waved his hand as though to brush it away. "I'm not sure why I spoke those words," he admitted. "It was merely an observation. Nothing more, nothing less."

Still, I didn't like the thought we were hiding something, and even though I had nothing to prove to an elven prince, I held the door of the stall open. "I need to go to the well, but your wound has healed enough for you to walk to the barn door. I'll show you what I see when I look out across the land. For land is wealth and wisdom and freedom. We have nothing to hide here, but we have things we don't want others to take from us."

"I did not mean to offend," he stammered, tying his jerkin. "It is the fact two young women living alone is unusual."

"Does no one live alone in your land?" I asked, my curiosity about him returning.

"Nay, no one dwells alone in my tribe. We live and work together, the hunters and gatherers, the shaman and warriors, the women and children. Everyone has their duty, and we all dwell in the sacred hollow, an interlocking group of caves and trees bound by the years." A smile came to his face. "Much darker than out here, where there are no trees, but we have each other and that is all we need."

I watched his face as he spoke, the way his eyes went soft and wistful and lines of sadness played around his mouth. Something within my chest ached, and I wanted to help him regain his happiness again. Even though it was none of my concern. "It sounds beautiful," I offered, unsure what to say at all.

His brows arched as though I'd surprised him. "Yes," he agreed. "It was. It still is." He said nothing more, but followed me out of the stall.

I felt rather bad for keeping him in there, as though he were an animal. I'd have to speak with Maraini about different living arrangements for our mysterious guest —an elven prince, no less. He was an interesting addition to our lives, and as I walked to the double doors of the barn, I realized that I was in no hurry for him to leave. None at all.

"This is our land," I said proudly, placing my hands on my hips.

I knew the view like the back of my hand, for I'd seen it a thousand times. This time, instead of looking, I watched his face, knowing what he would see. The meadow rose in front of us and a dirt path led to the gardens, growing great and green. Beyond them was a row of apple trees, a tiny grove of only six trees, standing in a circle, waving their broad leaves.

The sunflowers at the edge of the garden cast bright spots of color, as did the bluebells lining the path that led up toward the house, the back of it which could just be seen from the side of the barn. And then all beyond was rolling green, the pastures where the cows grazed— I'd forgotten to let the horses out—and the meadow where we collected lightning.

Fat yellow and white stripped bees hummed as they pollinated the flowers, birds sang and blue and black butterflies flew from flower to flower, casting their beauty across the land. Every morning when I woke up and looked out my window, this was what I saw, what I loved. The slope of the hill where the herbs grew, the rutted dirt path that winded toward Capern, a few hours south of us, and finally on to the enchanted wild-wood he spoke about so wistfully. It made sense that if he followed the road, he would have found us. But why? And who had wounded him so severely?

His face transformed, and his jaw worked up and down before he spoke. "This is your farm? You and your sister take care of this land, alone?"

I scratched the back of my head. Why did he keep harping on the fact that we were alone? We had each other. But I followed his gaze, knowing the roof of the chicken coop needed replacing, the garden needed weeding, and vines twisted around the apple trees. "Well," I protested. "It was easier when there were four of us, but now, we manage the best we can, which is why we can't run off on larks, chasing after tales in the wind about who or what killed our parents. The land needs us."

"You've never left, have you?" he said, returning those dark eyes to mine, as though he could read the thoughts dancing through my mind.

"Of course, we've never left," I said, frustration mounting. "Everything we need is here. Why would we leave?"

"But you could hire help. I'm sure many people in the nearby village would be willing to tend such a beautiful land. Are you afraid, then? To leave everything you know and understand seeking an adventure? You're comfortable here, aren't you? And even though you pine for those you lost, you'll never seek answers, because it would mean leaving this land. And if you leave it, you might lose it, and you can't lose anything else, so you hold on to what you have tightly."

My jaw dropped as I stared at him, and a haze of blindness passed before my eyes. For a moment, I couldn't see straight. "How dare you say such words to me, when you know nothing about me," I spat. "How about you get your own water!"

Furious, I stomped away, so angry with what he'd accused me of, I didn't know whether he called after me.

5

THE HOUSE SMELLED of applewood and sausage when I burst through the doors that evening, still fuming and wondering how Maraini found time to cook. She poked her head over a bag of salt and nodded at the baskets of sage I brought. "I was wondering when you'd appear, what's wrong?" Worry knit across her face as she studied me.

I filled her in on how Kian was an elven prince, still did not have his full memory, and finally repeated the words that had offended me. I'd expected her to utter some quiet words of rebuke toward him, but her eyes misted and she glanced away. "You should take dinner to him and apologize," she finally said.

I dropped a basket of sage, and my stomach knotted. "Me? Did you hear what he said about us?"

Maraini nodded as she pulled out three plates and filled them. "Sit, Rae. You should hear this from me. The stranger told you his name is Kian?"

I nodded as I washed up and then slumped into a chair beside a fat bag of salt.

"He read you well, perhaps he can see more in a few hours than we've been able to see in five years. I could only bring myself to go through one of Mother's journals, to find the ward of protection over the land, but right next to it was a binding spell."

My throat went dry. "What do you mean?" I squeaked.

"A binding spell is used to ensure whatever, or whoever you cast the spell over will stay in place. I think it may be helpful once we find the pigs." She giggled a little before her face turned serious again. "But what if it's been used on us?"

I stared, sure I could not eat dinner after that revelation. "Why?" I demanded. "It makes no sense. We love this land; we'd never leave it."

"I know, and it was only a strange sensation I got when I brushed my hands over the words. They changed colors and a soft film came off in my fingers, as though it had been used and then forgotten. Don't you remember the last words Mama and Papa said to us?"

I frowned and crossed my arms over my chest, dread sinking in. "No." I was sure I'd been daydreaming again the day they left, assuming I'd see them again within the year.

"They told us to stay here, where it's safe, for the land would provide everything we needed. Maybe they didn't want us chasing after them and getting into trouble."

"Oh." I scoffed. "No, no, our parents would never take our free will away from us. We can come and go as we please. After all we go to market every month to sell our goods, do we not?"

"We go straight there, and we come straight back, as though something tugs us back here every time. I want to know why, don't you? Don't you want to know why the land keeps producing, even though we can barely keep up with it? Why our wealth continues to pour in and why we stay here, year after year, waiting for something to happen to us when we could go out and make something happen ourselves?"

"Because land is wealth, I think you've read too much." I rose from the table, no longer interested in my dinner. "I think the stories from your books are weaving into reality."

Maraini stayed calm, her face showing none of the anger that covered mine. I wondered how she could stay so calm with the accusations against our parents she put forth. Anger rolled like a storm and my fingers trembled as I struggled to stay in control.

"I thought so too." She reached for a book lying on the table and opened it. A folded piece of paper fell out. "Until I saw this."

I stared at the folded parchment, old and weathered. I didn't want to touch it, didn't want to read any truth that might be in it.

"What is it?" I asked, meeting my sister's eyes.

"Read it," she leaned forward, a dead calmness in her eyes. "I think it explains everything. I need you to read it, to know what I know, so that we can make a plan. Together."

My throat went tight as I sat down, reaching for the

parchment. A heaviness sat on my chest, squeezing it as I read.

> Lore Keepers of the north
> Prevent the goddess from coming forth
> Protect the land from harm
> Lest the goddess awakes the calm
>
> Bind thine self to the land of the north
> Bind thine self lest she comes forth
> With words and deeds, sage and salt
> Keep her sealed in ancient vault
>
> A warning to those whose hearts are weak
> The strength of the goddess is real indeed
> Forsake your sacred duty for the mundane
> Standby and watch chaos rise again.

THE HOUSE WAS QUIET, too quiet. The flickering fire popped and crackled, the smell of sausage hung in the air, and even though there was no smoke, my eyes watered. I folded the piece of parchment and handed it to my sister, tears almost blurring my vision. "What is that? What does it mean?" I begged.

"Don't you understand?" She stared at me. "Everything I've read, the stories I've heard, what Mother and Father told us is true. We don't feel called to this land because it is our home. We are bound here. Our blood binds us here. We are meant to keep the old goddess from rising."

I shook my head. "No. No, no, no, that can't be. It's just an old rhyme from long ago, someone wrote it and put it in the book. That's all." I tried to think back, to make the connections my sister was making, but I'd never been one to sit and dwell in books. My fingers were antsy, I was almost moving, running, rolling from one activity to the next.

"We are wasting time talking about this," Maraini said, tucking the paper back into the book. "Rae, you'll just have to trust me. I've studied, I know this is true. I feel it, don't you feel it? We are rooted to this place, but I think something happened to our parents when they left, something to prevent them from coming back. And if we leave, there will be no one to stop her from returning."

I shook my head. Impossible! Yes, there were stories and I'd heard of magic, but not like this. It was incredulous to believe an old goddess was buried under our land, or the power of my family line was the only thing keeping her from rising. "This is stupid," I said, backing away. "Maraini, I'd have thought better of you."

"Don't." She held up a hand, a frown covering her face. "Just because you don't believe something doesn't mean it's not true. Later, after we refresh the wards of protection over our land, I'll show you the research I've done to come to this conclusion. But, Rae, it makes sense. I've never been gone from home for more than a day, sunup to sundown. We've never spent the night elsewhere, and I can't remember one time as a child when we went off together, as a family for longer than market day. Can you? Can you think of a time when we left this land on its own? Other farmers do it, I've heard gossip in the marketplace, but not us."

I chewed my bottom lip, determined not to give in to her persuasion, even though what she said was true. I tried to think back, but I couldn't recall. Our land was also uncannily abundant. Those who visited came for remedies or advice, but never to stay. My mind danced with theories and I sat down heavily, staring into the fire, searching for answers in the flickering flames. "If what you say is true, we need proof," I all but whispered, my voice hollow.

"Listen," Maraini said, "I'm sorry, I shouldn't have sprung this on you this way. I'll take dinner to Kian, but you should apologize to him, and take him some clothes to wear. I'm sure he'd like to wash up."

I nodded woodenly.

Maraini touched my shoulder. "Eat, you'll need your strength for tonight."

Then she took the plate of food and walked out the door.

Thoughts curled through my mind like smoke through a chimney, impossible to keep and impossible to pin down with truth. All my life, I'd known I was different, but I never expected something odd and evil under my feet. Part of me wanted to know more, but the reasonable part of me shut down, unable to process such an idea.

When Maraini returned, we gathered our bowls and set to the arduous task of warding our land. I moved woodenly around the property, mindlessly scattering sage and salt and chanting with Maraini under the light of the full moon. It was a beautiful night, warm and quiet, with the sound of crickets providing the music of the night. I heard the hoot of owls and saw their winged shadows cross over the meadow, pouncing on the small critters who wrongfully assumed they were safe in the long grass. I walked barefoot; the dirt warm beneath my feet yet still moist from rain.

Maraini was quiet, focused on the task at hand. At one point I stepped over the line of our property, that invisible line. I realized that there were no markers, but I had an innate sense; I knew where the land began, and where it ended. Stepping over the line felt like freedom, but the sensation was there, a sensation I'd never given much thought to. Within my very bones was a stirring, a longing for home. It had always been there, especially on market days. I enjoyed the colors, sights, and sounds of the village, bartering and selling our wares, and counting our coins until it was time to return home. I'd always attributed the longing to the relief of coming home again, but what if it were an itch to get back where I belonged, before it was too late?

It was midnight by the time we finished, exhausted yet relieved we'd completed our task. My mind strayed to rituals we conducted around the festivals that took place throughout the year, and my mother's quiet words. *May she sleep in peace for another year.*

I always thought she spoke of something else, an object, but not a sleeping goddess. Who was this goddess? Was she buried under our land?

When Maraini and I entered the house, we put our baskets down and I wrapped my arms around her. We held each other for a moment and then I let go. "I'm sorry I didn't trust you earlier."

"Don't apologize." She shook her head. "It was a shock."

"I want to find out more, I want to know if it's true."

"We'll find out together," she agreed. "But only after a night of sleep."

6

IN THE MORNING, as curious as I was about the ancient goddess, I recalled how I'd left things with Kian, the irritatingly handsome elven prince. Bouncing out of bed, I threw together a quick breakfast for him and snatched up the neatly folded clothes that Maraini had left on the table. They tumbled out of my too-quick fingers and I dumped them into the basket on top of the food. So, the clothes would be wrinkled. There was only so much I could do.

The sun was higher than I expected, the late night causing me to sleep longer than intended. The two cows were probably bellowing in discontent at not being milked first thing. And they'd probably woken up Kian, who needed his healing sleep. Guiltily, I crept into the barn and headed for his stall, blushing as I recalled we had to find another place for him. He couldn't keep sleeping in the stall like some animal. I peered over the door and saw a strange contraption hanging between two posts. It had a rope at both ends and a piece of cloth hung suspended over the hay. I narrowed my eyes, attempting to figure out what it was, until I noticed the stall was empty. Again. Where was he?

Stepping back, I peered down to the mare's stall and then walked up to it. He wasn't in there, but the mare was eating a bag of oats. Had Maraini gotten up and done my chores for me? But it wouldn't be like her. And there was no noise from the cows. I made my way to their stalls and almost tripped over pails of milk.

Kian! He must have done my morning chores. Heat flamed my cheeks as I marched out of the barn and immediately spotted him. He was by the well, stripped to his pants and splashing water over his body. It was odd to see a man bathe, and for a moment I lost my wits and stared at him, acutely aware of how beautiful his body looked in the daylight. I admired the tight muscles of his stomach, cutting to a deep v that disappeared inside his pants. His arms were muscular, and yet he had a slender grace to his movements. He truly was a wood elf. Drawn by an invisible lure, I pushed aside my unease and made my way toward him.

"Kian?" I called, so he would know I wasn't attempting to sneak up on him.

He was patting his face dry with his shirt and once again I was stung with how poor the hospitality from myself and my sister was.

"Rae," he returned the greeting, "good morn to you."

I liked how my name rolled off his lips and how he forwent the typical mannerisms of the day. It dispelled some of the tension between us. "Look," I said, in a haste to get out my apology. How could I have been angry with him? "I'm sorry for the way I reacted last night. It's not often someone comes here and shares a truth that is unbearable to hear."

He held up a hand, placed it over his heart, and bowed his head. "I am sorry as well; I don't know why I said those things. No matter the truth to them."

I sighed and smiled at him. He smiled back and a comfortable silence stretched between us, one I was unused to. "I brought you fresh clothes," I handed him the bundle, realizing how jumbled they appeared because of my flustered ways. "I can bring you soap, and you can take a proper bath if you wish."

His eyes crinkled. "Nay, this is fine." He shook out the shirt and held it up to him.

For just a moment, I was sorry as his bare skin disappeared. I twisted my fingers, at a loss for words. "How is your wound?"

Kian nodded as he dressed and I perched the basket of food by the well. "Better. Much better, thank you."

"You did my morning chores," I rebuked him quietly.

He leveled his gaze at me as he shook out his jerkin, but did not put it on. He looked rather handsome standing there, the neck of the shirt open while his pants fit tightly around his waist. "I did. Last night I heard you and your sister chanting in the moonlight. Confirms my suspicions, you are witches."

I shook my head, a smile playing around my lips. "Nay, you are mistaken, although I understand why your thoughts lean that way. Witches have magic, like the Sisters of the Light. It is true, we use spells and such, but none of our spells contain magic, they are all remedies wrought by nature. People often forgot that nature has healing properties, and if you understand how to use the right combinations, it often feels like magic. As for the chants, well, words and the intent behind them are powerful. I've always believed in the truth and power of words, but aside from knowledge, my sister and I possess none of the magic that witches do. We are Lore Keepers."

I could not miss the way his eyes lit up as I finished speaking, as though a spark of recognition reached his mind. It faded quickly, lost in a swirl of confusion as he lifted a finger.

"Yes, Lore Keepers." He touched the back of his head. "Lore Keepers," he said again, his brow furrowing. "There must be a reason I am here. It was urgent. . .but. . ." he trailed off; his eyes boring into mine as though I could bring the memories racing back with a wave of my fingers.

"Urgent?" I asked, a flutter of fear beating in my breast. It wasn't often that we received visitors, but if he meant to come here and share an omen with us, we had to know.

My eyes flickered toward the house. "Come with me." I trusted the warning in my gut. "Maraini is searching for a memory potion, perhaps we can help."

"What of the farm work?" he asked, taking a step toward me.

I smiled up at him. "I believe your memories are more important. The land can wait."

As it always did. Enchanted by his presence instead of moving hastily, I fell in step with him.

"MARAINI." I burst through the door, suddenly aware of how chaotic the inside of the house looked.

The thud of rapid footsteps sounded above us, and a moment later, Maraini came down the stairs, a stack of books in her arms. Her eyes widened at the sight of Kian in the house, but she gave him a quick smile. I'd invited a strange man into our home without thinking twice about it. How much did I truly know about Kian, Prince of the Wood Elves? "You're here about the ancient goddess, aren't you?" Maraini sighed.

I wasn't watching him, but the odd tone in Kian's voice made me study his face. "Ancient goddess?" he whispered, brow furrowed as though he were trying hard to recall what was so important.

The potency of the moment swept over me, and my fingers tingled with a sudden need to return the memories to this man before the sun went down. I had the sensation it was of the utmost importance. The words of Sasha the seer kept ringing back. *A storm is coming. And with the storm will come a change. Make sure your heart is open.*

"No," I corrected Maraini, my voice quavering at the thought of the ancient goddess.

After Sasha appeared, we'd made a half-hearted attempt to research the old texts. Some Mama kept in her room, but an even older book lay hidden in the cellar. Down there in the dark was spooky, with root vegetables that were molding away, some sprouting in the cool darkness. It was no place to keep an old text, for books needed to be taken care of, away from moisture. Yet there it was, in an old trunk, wrapped in a blanket to keep it dry. We got as far as opening the trunk before we heard a ruckus in the garden and had run out to find a crow attacking a snake while the cows bellowed in fright. After that, the land took up most of our attention. My thoughts strayed to it now and again, but I couldn't help but feel frightened. It wasn't a conversation Mama or Papa had had with us, yet, all the same, we knew.

"We need a memory potion," I finished, unease creeping up my spine. Was it just me, or had a shadow darkened the sunshine?

"Sit." Maraini gestured to the table. "Rae, get the tea. We can research together."

I went for the tea leaves and cups. Kian remained standing. While I plunked porcelain on the table, he turned, examining the room from every angle. I knew what he saw, for it only confirmed his suspicions. It looked like a house of herbs and lore, with jars of lightning perched on a bench, their power still glimmering. Baskets were stowed beside the door, most of them overflowing with herbs. Just outside the door were eggs for the market, and a portion of the midsummer harvest, yet we were still so far behind.

Maraini placed the stack of books on the table and coaxed the fire back to life. Once the kettle was over it the three of us gathered, Maraini at the head of the table and Kian and I on either side. I glanced at his shades of dark blue hair, enhanced by the firelight, and willed myself not to be distracted by his presence. The jittery nerves within me settled as Maraini passed me one of Mama's journals. "Here, this has potions in it, perhaps you'll find one."

Then she turned to our guest. "Kian, do you read?"

He pressed his lips together and shook his head. "There is no need in the wildwood," he explained.

My eyebrows shot up. How could one not know how to read? I clamped my mouth shut before the words sneaked out. Instead, I turned my attention to the book and lovingly flipped through the pages. Each one was covered with Mama's beautiful handwriting, a title, a list of ingredients, and mixing instructions. As I went through the book, the fragrance of lavender and peppermint lifted from the pages and a wave of homesickness passed over me. I thought of my words to Kian, of how we had no magic, and we weren't witches at all. Yet as I thought of my words, memories rose and fell away. Perhaps there was a kind of magic in our blood, to craft potions and catch lightning, perhaps that was why our wares were so popular in the marketplace. Puzzled and unsure, I realized I needed to discuss more with Maraini. I needed to know the truth about our past before I could make any decisions.

I flipped another page and there it was. "Aha." I held up the book. "I found it."

7

It took us the rest of the day to find the ingredients for the memory potion, and the next morning, Maraini and I mixed it while Kian worked outside, despite me trying to persuade him not to. Maraini and I stood across from each other, watching the steam from the kettle dissipate.

"Do you want to know what I found out?" Maraini's tone was low.

I didn't. But not knowing was worse. "You didn't sleep a wink, did you?" I asked, tension warring inside me. I tucked leaves of tea into separate bags to sell at the marketplace, even though I knew it wasn't likely that we would go to market. Not with what Maraini was going to share with me.

"I was right," she said, eyes drawn to the faded pages of parchment. "In days of old the order of the Lore Keepers was established to protect the wildwood from the rise of an ancient goddess."

Fear hummed through me as I listened.

"As we know, the magic is within our bloodline, but it's also within this land. For as long as it's known, Lore Keepers have dwelled here."

"I know," I breathed. "But that's what I don't understand. We are at least half a day's ride away from the enchanted wildwood. How can our bloodline prevent the rise of a goddess who desires to rule the wildwood?"

"That's the part that worries me," Maraini agreed. "I stayed up all night, searching for answers. The goddess was buried here on this land. And the binding spell that keeps us here is also for the goddess, to bind her to the ground, and prevent her from rising."

A wave of nausea rose over me, and I pressed my lips together. The fire seemed too warm for a midsummer day, and I had the sudden longing to dose it with water. "You mean buried here? Under this land?"

Maraini nodded.

"Where?" My body trembled at the thought. A great evil was here and had been here my entire life? What did that mean?

"I'm not sure, but. . .Rae. Don't you see? All of this means something. The death of our parents, I think it was because someone wants the goddess to return and claim the wildwood, and if the Lore Keepers are gone, no one stands in their way."

"But. . ." I crossed my arms around my chest as though to protect myself. "Who would want the goddess to return?"

"We both know the wildwood is dark and evil, full of monsters."

"And elves," I added, thinking of Kian.

Maraini nodded. "Yes. Good and evil in a never-ending war against each other, a war we've never been privy to. But you've heard the tales from other villages, what happened to the Sisters of the Light."

"That was years ago," I protested.

"Aye, but that was when a new queen took over the rule of the wildwood. I believe it's a cycle. A new queen rises, the wildwood fights against her, eventually she loses and another queen rises to take her place."

I swallowed hard. "And the goddess, you think someone wants to wake her up so she can vanquish the Queen of the Wildwood and rule in her place?"

"Not just the wildwood, but perhaps the kingdom. I'm not sure," Maraini sat down and rubbed her temples. "This all makes my head hurt. I wish Mama and Papa were here to explain. Deciphering text is our gifting, yet we've fallen so far from the original Lore Keepers. Yes, I read and study the text, but I've lost myself in legends and tales instead of focusing on our reason for existing."

Anger stirred in my belly. "Our existence is not solely for the purpose of protecting the wildwood from an ancient goddess."

Maraini shrugged. "I can't forget what Sasha said. She seemed. . .determined."

I thought back to that day. An odd day. And wondered what had become of her.

The brief conversation cast a hue of darkness and gloom over the room. Even the sun seemed to reflect my feelings, hiding behind a cloud. I edged toward the door, hungry to escape the clutches of fate. "Maraini." I paused, hand on the door. "If we are to prevent the goddess from rising, what is it we are supposed to do?"

"Stay here," she responded.

I slid out the door to find Kian, those words ringing in my ears. It sounded all so simple and passive. I didn't want to be chained to the land my entire life, through generations and generations, but that was what had happened, wasn't it? It was the Lore Keepers who prevented the rise of the goddess, because we had stayed here. Even though there was nowhere I wanted to go, and I had wanted nothing to change my daily life, I felt trapped, imprisoned in the land I loved. I could never leave. Is that why my parents had left? They thought they had a chance and look at what happened to them. Did it also mean that with the loss of my parents, the bloodline was weak? I raked my mind as I strode toward the garden, realizing with a pang it was already past midday. My parents had never pushed us to marry, to have children, to continue the bloodline. Why was that? It was mentioned from time to time, but after brief flirtations, nothing had come of it. There had to be more, much more to the puzzle. Likely in Mama's journals or in the book bound in the cellar. My mind twirled through thoughts, bringing them up and tossing them away like a windstorm.

Kian knelt in the garden among the squash, placing bright yellow and green vegetables into a basket with a gentle reverence. He was stripped to the waist, his dark blue hair pulled back, and he smiled at me as I walked down the row of soft earth. "What's wrong?" he stood and lifted a basket. I saw there were three others, full of the midsummer harvest, and tears sprang to my eyes.

He was beside me in a moment. His presence which should have been reassuring made me fear all the more.

He stepped closer, smelling like the vine-ripe tomatoes. The depth of his gaze and the intensity of his male presence made me long for a dream I'd never had. Would it be so wrong to have a moment with an elven prince? His station in life differed greatly from mine, but why would that matter? I stared up at him as he touched my shoulder, a gentle caress, but enough to awaken something deep inside me.

Maraini said I warmed to people too quickly. I was kind and wanted everyone to like me, and perhaps it was the same sensation I felt with Kian. He was otherworldly, but it wasn't just curiosity that pulled me toward him. It was something else. I didn't feel the need to flirt carelessly with him; I wanted to ask questions, to know who he was, to understand him and have him understand me. I wanted the promise of what he could offer, the strength of his arms around me, the taste of his lips, the warmth of his caress. Even though I belonged to the land, and he belonged to the forest. The truth of it swept over me like a crushing wave, and I realized after this moment, there was no turning back. I'd take him to the house where his lost memories would be returned, and he'd never be the Kian I knew. The man who slept in the barn and did my chores, who healed from his wound with the magic of the potion. His hand rested on my shoulder and his brown eyes searched mine. If I could freeze the moment, the before and after, I would.

I placed my hand on his forearm, wanting to secure myself to the moment, to study it from every angle and hold it in my mind. Blinking away the tears, I opened my mouth, my face warming as I forced myself not to look at his lips or wish for things which could not be. "The memory potion is ready."

He nodded, yet still held me a beat longer than necessary. While he tugged on his shirt, I bent to grab a basket. He picked up the other two and, wordlessly, we returned to the house.

Inside, the air was dense with the scent of herbs, and Maraini sat at the table once again, lips moving silently as she poured over words. A warning sang in my chest and it seemed a thick tension filled the air, a potent mix of anticipation and apprehension. What would Kian's memories reveal? It was easy to fall in love with the idea of a prince, to enjoy those legends and tales of old. But in reality, he was nothing more than a man, moving out of the shadow of a dream into the hard truth.

I poured a cup of the brew and handed it to him. Our fingers brushed and a hint of magic crackled between us, lost the moment he sat and drank down the liquid. He made a slight face at the taste of it and then sat back, closing his eyes as he waited.

I glanced at Maraini who watched him, her eyes red-rimmed from lack of sleep. A sensation of overwhelm crept over me at everything I'd learned the past few days. Weariness made my shoulders droop. I sat down and watched Kian remember.

A beam of sunlight stole over his face, showing the hint of stubble on his jaw and the length of his dark eyelashes. He was beautiful under the light and an ache began in my heart. Propping my elbows on the table, I rested my chin on my clasped hands as he sat up, and his eyes opened. I noticed the change immediately, the way his shoulders straightened and his chin lifted.

There had been a vagueness in his eyes that cleared, leaving them burning with intensity.

I felt like nothing more than a farm woman with dirt under her fingernails as his eyes bored into mine. My breath caught and twisted and my heart thudded. My fingers itched to be doing something, anything other than sitting still. I should mix potions, or make tea, or chop vegetables for the evening meal.

"You're the Lore Keepers," he said, urgency rising in his deep voice.

I nodded. I'd said as much earlier.

Maraini put down her book and watched him.

"They are coming," he burst out. "I came to warn you the teeth of the wildwood are coming for you. They will be here any moment; you have to prepare."

"Wait." Maraini's words broke the lyrical assault of his tone. "Slow down and tell us from the beginning."

"There is no time. I set out a few days ago. They might already be at your doorstep. They don't know the way, but they will sniff you out and find you. Before I left my tribe, the Queen of the Wildwood appeared to me. She claimed the visions of the seer led her to believe you are in grave danger. She would not leave the wildwood, nay, she said someone would have to go in her place, and the seer recommended me. She gave me a knife." His hand went to his side. "She spelled it with magic. We have to find the sleeping goddess and stab her with it to keep her from rising. You are the Lore Keepers; this is your land. We have to find the buried goddess before the attack begins."

My lips trembled. So, it was bad news. But who or what was coming for us? Creatures of the wildwood?

And how would we defend against them? "We don't know where she's buried," I said, forcing my lips to move.

Kian's expression softened. "I know. That's why I came to help. But as I was leaving the wildwood, I was attacked. I only made is this far on a wild horse, I recall slipping from its back and then there was nothing until I woke." His hand went to his side. "My wound was deep. I should not have lived, but I am grateful the horse led me true, it led me straight to you."

8

"Rae?" The question in Kian's voice only added to the violent mixture of emotions that coursed through me.

At his words, I'd fled to the porch where I could get away from the gloom that hung over my head. Uncertainty danced around me like white dandelion seeds, twirling in the warm summer breeze, their future uncertain. Shading my eyes against the sunlight, which had returned, I peered down the road, searching for intruders.

Kian had been with us for almost three full days, so why were we safe, hidden in the quiet land? If they had attacked him, I did not understand why they hadn't shown up that very night to attack Maraini and I.

"This land is protected," I faced him. "No one with ill will can enter."

"I hope, for your sake, that is true." Kian moved closer, his fingertips grazing my arm as he turned me to face him. "Rae, we must prepare. Regardless. But I wanted to say thank you."

I gave him a rueful smile. "You've said thanks many times. It is enough."

He shook his head. "It was your voice I heard in the storm. You were beside me, pulling me back to life with your words. I believe you about intent, about the strength and power of words, even if you don't believe you carry magic. I think you do, and it's that magic that saved me."

Words. What words had I said? "I'm glad you heard me, but I gave you a healing potion to bring you back."

"I'm sure it wasn't easy to make, but it was enough and so my thanks are with you."

I noticed he said nothing of my sister.

He leaned forward until his breath almost brushed my lips and all the rush went out of me as he kissed the corner of my mouth. It was unexpected, surprising yet pleasant. My eyes closed as I relished that kiss. When he pulled back, it was as if he'd taken all the warmth out of the air.

I touched two fingers to the corner of my mouth, where it tingled from his caress. "What was that for?" I asked, a comfortable buzzing in the center of my belly.

Instead of smiling, his eyes were shadowed and his voice husky as he spoke. "I've searched for a woman like you my entire life. What I did not realize was I'd need to leave my home, leave the wildwood to find you. Not only are you beautiful, but you are strong, resilient, and kind. Even though I've come with honorable intentions, I want to help you, to see your land saved because of you. And when this is over, I will ask for permission to court you, for I sense you have weathered many storms, and your very presence makes me wish to stay by your side. You say you don't have magic, but, Rae, you've enchanted me."

My stomach flip-flopped and for once words did not come readily to my lips. Stunned, I watched him slip away and pressed a hand to my heart as he disappeared into the barn. I played his words over in my head until guilt overrode my initial joy. How could I be happy that Kian returned my feelings for him when evil was approaching our doorstep?

Slipping back inside, I paused as Maraini lined up the lightning jars on the table. My brows furrowed. "What are you doing? And why is Kian going to the barn?"

She flicked a braid onto her back. "We have to prepare, don't we? If we are attacked there is little in the house to defend ourselves with, but I recall that Papa used to keep a bow and arrow in the barn for hunting. Kian is going to search for it and retrieve the knife."

Shivering, I crossed my arms and rubbed my shoulders. "I don't like this," I murmured. "It seems so sudden after all these years. Why now?"

Maraini sighed and sank into a chair, covering her face with her hands briefly. "Why now? Can't you guess? We are at our weakest. If Mama and Papa were here, they'd know what to do."

I rose on my tiptoes and then back down on the balls of my feet. "They'd only know what to do because they read it in a book. Where did Mama keep the annuals?"

Maraini reached for a lantern and lit it. "I think we'd better have a look at that book in the cellar."

Reluctantly, I followed her, twisting my curls around my fingers. The door to the cellar was toward the back of the house, down a hall with a set of stairs leading down. Maraini dragged open the heavy door, and I followed, my nose assaulted by the musty scent of mud and old vegetables. How long had it been since we cleaned out the cellar? I hated going down there, imagining rats and other creepy crawlers moving across the mud and digging between the stones in the wall. But the cellar was where we kept our winter stores, and even as I walked down the creaking steps, the coolness of the air swept over me.

Maraini hung the lantern at the bottom of the staircase. I paused beside her. The room was a sizeable square, running perhaps the length of the house. Stone columns were built into the cellar with shelves on either side, holding more food than Maraini and I could possibly eat in a year. Some of it was old and rotten, sprouting and growing dark vines that entwined around the stone, forcing it to crumble and surrender to new life.

With a sigh, Maraini weaved around them to the back of the cellar, to the wide trunk that had been shoved against the wall. The latch was thick with rust. Regardless, I lifted the lid without issue and pushed it back against the wall.

A smattering of moths rose, and a squeak left my lips as I waved my hands to brush them away. Kneeling, I unfolded the moth-eaten blankets and pulled out the thick, dusty tome. A shiver went through me again, as though someone other than Maraini watched me. I glanced over my shoulder, but there was nothing but blackness. Was there truly a sleeping goddess? If so, it was easy to imagine her in the cellar.

"Why is this book down here and not with the others?" I whispered, for the very aura of the place made me afraid to speak out loud.

"I always assumed so that no one would read it." Maraini shrugged and held out her hands.

I blew across it and scrubbed at the dirt with my dress before handing it to my sister. It was musty, and the edges had been nibbled on. Curses on the rats. I hoped they hadn't eaten the most important part of the book.

The pitter-patter of feet made me jump, and I spun around, eyes wide. "Let's get out of here." I moved toward the stairs. "This place gives me the creeps."

Heart thumping, I led the way out of the cellar and slammed the door shut, thankful for the warmth of sunlight.

"While you research," I announced. "I'm going to mix some ingredients for explosives."

Maraini narrowed her eyes at me. "Explosives? Are you trying to blow up the house?"

"Nay." I rubbed my hands together. "I've always wanted to try my hand at such things. Nothing big, just little balls we can hurl should intruders come this way."

"Don't you want to look at the book with me?" Maraini begged.

I saw what she was doing, trying to discourage me. I rubbed my hands together and peered over her shoulder. The book was thick, and when Maraini laid it on the table, a plume of dust rose. I backed away, waving my hand and coughing. The symbol on the front of the cover caught my eye, and I reached out a hand to touch it. Silver dust came away and the very air shivered as I touched it.

"What does this mean?" I pointed to the circle, with the stars on the outside of it and the moon within.

"I don't know," Maraini whispered, as though there was a spirit who would hear our words.

Forgetting about my desire to mix potions, I sat down as Maraini opened the book.

A faint breeze blew across the room as though the book were relieved to be open, and the tingling of silver bells hung in the air. I stared at the ink, the vibrant colors pulsing on the page as though it would come alive. A lady filled the page, with a dress as green as ivy and black hair tumbling down her slender shoulders. She was beautiful, powerful, with an oval face and piercing, sharp eyes, enchanting as though she could see us between the pages.

"Turn the page," I whispered, both desiring and fearing to touch the book.

The page was so thin it was almost translucent as Maraini turned it, and together we read, my heart thudding in my throat. It was an account of the first Lore Keepers. I knew the legend and yet, reading it once again, as though I were reading the pages of someone's diary, made my life seem real and important. And as I read, the clues and mysteries of my life came together. The way Mama tended the animals, the rituals I thought nothing of during every festival. It was our way of life, as easy as rolling out of bed and pulling on clothes.

Maraini and I read in sync, turning page after page, skipping some of the rudimentary spells, but paying close attention to the tales of how to bless each festival.

They were all various ways to keep the goddess from rising, an instructional book for the next generation of Lore Keepers. It wasn't until the light was dim and darkness crept around the house that I realized we'd spent the entire afternoon reading.

Rubbing my eyes, I pulled back and met Maraini's solemn face, my thoughts whirling as I attempted to decipher everything we'd read.

Maraini's fingers lingered on the pages before she met my eyes. "Rae, we haven't done everything we were supposed to do. We did not conduct the rituals of blessing on the eve of each festival, when magic is strongest. Do you think our lack of knowledge is why the magic that surrounds this place is weakening? Perhaps something has changed, and because we didn't know to be careful, to keep up the rituals, we've inadvertently caused a dark power to rise?"

I pressed my lips together and shook my head venomously. "No, we haven't allowed anything to happen. We didn't know, Maraini. And if we were supposed to, why didn't Mama and Papa tell us? Why was the book hidden in the cellar?"

"But they did tell us," Maraini insisted. "They taught us the rituals, and we carried them out every year of our lives without knowing why. It's just that I've been distracted and we've both been overwhelmed by the farm. It's too much for us. I don't think our parents meant to leave us with this much work for so long. They meant us to marry and have children and keep this land safe."

I crossed my arms and rose. Bound to the land. I didn't like it, but I saw no way out.

"Midsummer night comes in seven days. In the book it's called the Festival of Litha. A night to celebrate light overcoming darkness. I think that was the night the ancient goddess was overcome and buried."

I couldn't deny the sensibility of her words, nor what I'd read for myself in the book. Festival of Litha. I touched a finger to my lips. "Then Kian appeared to warn us that we will be attacked, likely near Litha. It is close. But which night will the creatures of the wild-wood try to break the magic? Are they powerful enough? And if we find the buried goddess and stab her with the spelled knife, will we save ourselves?"

Maraini shrugged. "I wish I had more answers, but I don't like the idea of hunting for a corpse."

I hugged myself tighter, my body going cold with dread. "Me either." A knot of dread twisted in my gut. "But we have to, don't we?"

"Oh." Maraini stood. "It's late. Let me prepare a meal. Go see Kian and invite him back to the house to eat. He must sleep inside too. I don't want to chance it."

Sleep inside. I smiled at the thought. Had he really said he'd like to court me?

"You like him, don't you?" Maraini interrupted my thoughts.

I weaved between baskets and books as I made my way to the door. Pausing with my hand on the latch to glance back at my sister, I couldn't help the grin that split my face. "He's the most interesting person I've ever met."

Maraini grunted, but I caught the sly smile on her face as I slipped out the door.

9

THE LAST LIGHT of sunset still hung in the sky, but shadows covered the farmland. On the porch I noticed a pile of rocks, a quiver of arrows, a sharpening tool, and a bow. Kian was preparing. But where was he?

A shadow moved beside the barn, tall and stealthy. I bent, picking up a rock and holding it in my hands. *No ill will can cross this land.* I thought to myself.

"Something is out there," Kian's voice floated to me from somewhere beyond the dusky sky.

I stiffened, fingers tightening around the rock as I watched him glide out of the shadows, his movements silent and stealthy. He could be a hunter, he could be anyone, and if he attacked, I'd be dead where I stood. Relieved to see him and distraught by the news, I dropped the rock back into the pile.

"Who?"

He joined me on the porch, sat down on the steps and picked up one of the arrows. "I did not get a good look. Perhaps nothing at all, although I think it was someone sent to watch the house. Learn your habits. That's what my tribe did in the wildwood. Before an attack we would study our enemy, attack when they were weakest or most distracted."

I sat down on the steps beside him, momentarily resting my head in my hands. "So, you're a warrior and a hunter?"

"The wildwood requires nothing less," he agreed, a wistfulness to his tone. "Many fear it. Although it is dangerous, beauty is often hidden within the wildwood, there for those who seek it. Much like you feel about your land, you love it, protect it, and would not leave it."

I considered his words. It was true that I loved my land, but part of me wished to explore, to see more. "Why did you leave?" I pressed, curious for more details. "Why just you, and not a small army?"

Kian ran his fingers over the arrowhead and stared off toward the barn. "I did not intend to come alone. After the Queen of the Wildwood came with word, I felt compelled to come here. As though this quest were meant for me. My right hand, Harli usually goes every-where with me. Originally, there were five of us who set out here, for we did not want to leave the tribe without warriors. But then we were attacked. I suppose I should send word that I've survived. I keep waiting for the falcon to find me."

His tribe. It was a reminder he had friends, family, perhaps a lover was waiting for him. I was never one to keep quiet, and I couldn't help the question that blurted from my lips. "But surely they'd want to know that you're alive and well? After all, you're their prince."

"Ah." He turned his body toward me. "Prince doesn't

mean the same thing in the wildwood as it does out here. I've heard of your king, and how the rule is passed down through the bloodline. In the wildwood, being the son of the king of the elves means that I should always look to prove myself, that I should be as strong, worthy to take my father's place when he passes from this land. While my father lives and is strong, his heirs are treated with respect. But our enemies are bloodthirsty, one day, should they choose, they will come and take over the tribe and slay the royal bloodline."

I gasped.

He shook his head. "It is what it is. Each year we fight, in winter we rest. It's how it has always been, so thus I thought the chance to vary my life would be worthwhile. Especially since it still includes what I do best. Fighting."

My hand went to my lips. "But you were half dead when we found you. . ."

"Yes." He cleared his throat. "Under the surprise attack, I alone escaped while the others retreated. I thought I could hold them off, but. . . I was wrong. You and your sister were inside a long time," he glanced toward the door as he changed the conversation. "Did you find answers?"

Despite the warmth of the summer air, my skin went cold. "Some, but not enough. The original Lore Keepers kept an account of their deeds which leads me to believe the attack will take place on midsummer's eve, or midsummer itself during the Festival of Litha. As Lore Keepers, we're supposed to conduct rituals during each festival to keep the land safe, but Maraini and I. . .well. We've been grieving and busy and. . .I didn't know."

The light faded from the sky, leaving us in complete darkness. Kian's broad hand closed around mine. A shiver of excitement danced through my veins and I moved closer to his warmth. His touch gave me a sense of comfort and security that made me forget everything. I wanted nothing more than to lean into him and savor the moment, forgetting my duty to the land. We sat, hand in hand, while the creatures of the night struck up soft melodies and lighting bugs offered flashes of light. Early evening held a sweet magic for me, even more so now that I sat with Kian.

"Tell me about the Lore Keepers," he whispered.

"It all goes back to the beginning of time," I explained. Telling him the legend was like baring my soul to him. "The ancients came out of water and mist and set the great tree in the land. The gods and goddesses were born, and each was given a world to create. But wars broke out over dominion, as they often do with those with power. The goddesses who formed this world fought, and the one who was evil was defeated and buried in the land. But the goddesses could not be everywhere at once. In their cleverness, they blessed a bloodline with magic and appointed them to keep the goddess buried. So began the blood-line of the Lore Keepers, one after the other, those who wrote legends and tales and kept the wisdom of this world. It all sounds so vast and glorious, from a tale." I spread my free arm wide. "I must admit I've known nothing else, but being a Lore Keeper isn't as glorious as it seems. I do sense it, though. The land is blessed so long as we carry out our rituals, and if you ask, Maraini and I know every legend, every tale across the known world. We just don't know where the goddess is buried, for that is a dark tale, one to induce nightmares, and I always look for joy and happy endings, not tales of evil and dark deeds."

"That is a beautiful tale," Kian agreed, his fingers tightened around mine. "But you have nothing, no clues?"

I shook my head again. "If it were up to me, I'd bury her on the edge of the land where no one would ever think to look. But it is creepy. I don't want to dig through the land, searching for a grave."

"Hmmm," Kian replied.

We sat in silence for a while, watching the moon appear from behind a cloud. It was white and bright, almost full, as though I could reach up, break a piece off and eat it. The quiet hum of the crickets soothed the eeriness of the night, so much so when an owl fluttered past, I did not react, only watched it, aware of the beauty of summer.

The door opened, shedding light across our backs. I dropped Kian's hand and turned, my face warming as I met Maraini's curious eyes. "There you two are. You'd better come inside, supper is ready." Her gaze shifted to Kian. "From now on, we expect you to sleep inside the house. It's not safe out there, if they do attack."

He nodded and stood, reaching for the arrows. "You do not mind if weapons are kept inside?"

"Not at all," Maraini agreed and held the door open.

We ate with zest, a delicious blend of roasted squash, fresh peas, and other garden greens. We had no meat since neither of us had found the time to go fishing or kill one of the many chickens that strutted across the farm as though they owned the place. I glanced at Kian to see if he noticed, but he didn't. Although I detected lines of tiredness on his face. To be expected after the work he'd done around the farm. Inwardly I kicked myself, for he was still recovering from his wound and we'd given him a memory potion.

We exchanged few words during the meal, and afterward, I found Kian a space to rest in one of the back rooms across from Papa's study. Since my parent's death, we hadn't had guests, but a back room was set up for a family in need to spend the night. I wondered why I hadn't thought of it before as I bade him goodnight.

The lights were low when I returned and Maraini went upstairs, leaving the book we'd found in the cellar lying on the table, pages open. I gulped as I glanced back at it, waiting for a word or sign of magic. But there was nothing.

Forgetting all about it, I went upstairs, tossed my dress on the bed and climbed under the covers. It was warm in the house, and I usually slept with the windows open to let in the evening breeze. I thought of Kian, one floor below me as I slept. My daydreams turned to more intimate pleasures, and it seemed I'd just snuggled down in bed when a sound woke me.

I bolted upright, tossing the covers off as I rose and crept to the window. My heart pounded as though I'd had a nightmare, and yet I recalled nothing of my dreams. I listened over the frantic racing of my pulse and there it came again. A distinct tap tap tap, as though someone was knocking on the door.

PULLING my cloak over my thin nightgown, I made for the stairs, surprised I did not bump into Maraini on the way down. What was that noise and how could she not have heard it? I crept down the stairs, my eyes going for the weapons, sitting in neat stacks by the door. The door would stop no one from entering and I knew a house's weakness was the windows. If someone wanted to enter, all they'd need to do was toss a rock through one of the windows. But perhaps the entering was meant to be quieter. As I reached the bottom of the staircase, my thoughts fled to stories. Creatures of the night often hoped to catch those who lived alone in a mistake. They'd stand outside, pretending to be someone known. But they could not come inside until they were invited, and once they were, it was mayhem. What if such a monster stood outside my door? One that enjoyed blood and death? Whoever it was, I dared not let them inside.

Tap tap tap. It came again, making me wish I'd

stayed in bed. I went for the fireplace, my hand fumbling over flint as I heard the creak of the door. A squeak left my lips as a dark shape moved up the hall and then, "Rae?"

"Kian!" I gasped, dropping the flint. "You gave me a fright."

"What are you doing down here?" he asked, the indistinctness of his form coming closer.

"Don't you hear it?" I pointed toward the door, even though he couldn't see my hand.

Tap. Tap. Tap.

I struck a match against flint, and his face glowed in the darkness. I tossed it into the fireplace and blew on the wood. It caught slowly while Kian picked up a bow and strung an arrow inside. "I'm going out to see what it is," he told me. "I'll return but don't open the door until you hear my voice."

"Please don't," I begged, my imagination going wild at the very idea.

"Rae," his tone was gentle, "I live in the enchanted wildwood, there's not much that frightens me."

Without another word, he slipped out the door, and the tapping ceased.

I bolted the door behind him and waited for what seemed like an eternity, pacing back and forth, all the while wondering what had become of him. While I waited, my eyes were drawn repeatedly to the book on the table. I returned to it and flipped through, admiring the colorful illustrations on the pages.

Words caught my eyes, and I stared at them. Mulling them over.

The location of the buried goddess shall never be written, for should our enemies return to wake her, they will rend the truth from the lips of the Lore Keepers. But deep inside, we know the truth, and if we follow our hearts, one already knows where to look. For sometimes the most secret truths hide in plain sight.

It was the last four words that caught my eye: *hide in plain sight.*

I flipped back a few pages to the layout of the land set forth by the original Lore Keepers. It was much the same. The house, the barn, the chicken coop, and other buildings that had been added throughout the years, but a dark terror sat inside me as I stared at the illustration. The four things that were still in the same place were the garden, the barn, the house and the small orchard. Which meant the grave could be in any of those locations.

I wished for daylight, for I had to go walk the land and be sure of myself. The house had been rebuilt since then, and so had the barn. We tilled the garden each year in preparation for the planting season. If there was anything buried there, we'd know, wouldn't we? And the orchard. I'd always looked above when I went, climbing trees or swinging up a ladder. It must be the most likely place.

Excitement thudded through my veins and I dashed to the foot of the staircase, book in hand. Maraini would want to know the news as soon as possible and would likely forgive me for waking her up in the middle of the night. Although the moment I set foot on the bottom stair, my reason came back to me. She'd spent the previous night awake and needed her sleep. We both did, for what was to come. And if the tapping hadn't woken her up, it only meant she needed to sleep. Indecision gave me pause. I wanted to share my revelation with her, but there was also Kian. The first man I'd felt a strong attraction to, likely because he was a handsome elf. I saw no reason I shouldn't share my findings with him, since he'd proven himself nothing but trustworthy.

Speaking of, where was he?

No sooner had the thought left my mind, there came a light knock on the door, followed by. "Rae? It's me."

A wave of relief washed over me and, leaving Maraini to sleep in peace, I unbolted the door and opened it. "What was it?" I asked.

"Nothing to worry about." Kian's eyes were alight with relief and the soft halo of flickering fire cast light on his elegant features.

My heart quaked as I examined his pointed ears, the fall of his blue hair and the crooked smile he offered me. I hugged the book to myself. "Oh?"

"It was falcon," he told me, resting the bow against the wall and replacing the quiver. "He found me at last and came to deliver a message from the wildwood. I sent one back with him. My tribe is secure, but they expect retaliation soon. They asked that I stay where I am until they can send an escort to guard me home."

Home. The words rang in my head as though someone had struck a gong. Of course. He had a home to return to. His presence in my land was naught but a mere blip in time, an anomaly that would be fixed as soon as we found the goddess and used the spelled knife to put her to rest. Disappointment edged around my eyes and I returned to the table, suddenly wanting nothing more than a cup of lavender and peppermint tea. Clarity. That's what I needed, and to stop being so impulsive.

"Good," I told him, turning away. "Now they know you're safe."

"Nothing else stirs tonight," Kian went on, "but I can't shake the feeling that someone or something is watching."

"Do you believe we are in danger?" I rested the book on the table and put the kettle over the fire.

"Not tonight. Like you said earlier, midsummer's eve or midsummer itself should be the night you should expect unwanted visitors." His eyes fell to my movements. "Are you staying up?"

"I can't sleep right now," I admitted. "I'm making tea to soothe my dreams and then I'll attempt to sleep." Taking a seat at the table, I brushed my fingers over the book.

"If you'll have me, I'll join you," he offered. A tingle went through my body at his words. "It is odd sleeping indoors; we have caves and all but it's much different from what I am used to. I keep waking. If the tea will help. . ."

"It will." I beckoned him closer, then paused as he sat across from me. "To be honest. I think I might know where the goddess is buried."

A sharp hiss left his mouth, and he leaned over the table, searching my eyes. "Where?"

The question was fraught with worry, panic and a hint of relief. I studied him, considering if I should reveal what the book said to him. Even though I found him attractive and easy to converse with, the secrets of the book belonged to the Lore Keepers. By all rights,

Maraini should be the second to know. But Kian had come to assist us, not just for selfish reasons, because he understood the perilousness of the situation. If we allowed the ancient goddess to rise, she might set her sights on more than just the enchanted wildwood. And the enchanted wildwood sat at the core of the world itself. It was vast and immeasurable, and many king-doms and races dwelled near to its border. In fact, the farthest anyone could go from the wildwood would be a two-week journey. Then they'd reach the edge of the world. Nay, if a dark queen took over the wildwood, stole the magic, and used it for her own purposes, life as we knew it would cease to exist. I needed all the help I could get.

I told him what I'd discovered about the four loca-tions. Opening the book and showing him the original layout of the land. He studied it, his lips moving as though he were speaking to himself.

I tapped my foot on the floor. "Well? What do you think?"

He smiled; his eyes warm. "I think you're on to something. Where will you look first?"

I glanced over at the windows, still dark with the hush of the midnight hour. "I'd like to start in the orchard. The trees are old, perhaps old as time. It makes sense that something would be hidden beneath the roots. Once daylight comes we can search."

"A wise assumption," Kian agreed.

His fingers brushed mine. I studied him, taking in the curve of his mouth, his hard body beneath the loose shirt he'd hastily thrown on.

"What are you thinking?" he asked, his voice dropping lower.

The kettle went off, steam pouring out of it. I rose, breaking the moment to pour us each a cup of tea. When I returned to the table, the fragrance of lavender and peppermint wafting over us, I realized it all felt natural. Normal. Kian at my table and myself, in my nightgown, enjoying a cup of tea.

It was inappropriate and yet I did not feel concerned, only a slight trust, and a yearning for something deeper. When all this was over, he'd return to the wildwood. Maraini and I would continue as we always did, working the land, going to market, and crafting up new creations. Market day. I'd forgotten all about it in the chaos. We'd miss it.

"I was thinking how everything has changed, and yet it hasn't," I told Kian. "After we find the ancient goddess, we'll go on, as we always have."

"Is that a bad thing?" He took a sip and hastily set the scalding hot brew down.

I stuck my tongue against my cheek to keep from laughing before blowing over my tea. "Not bad, it's just, I want more." I shrugged.

"More?"

"Yes. Now I know the truth, questions I've had about my life come up again and again. It's not that I'm not happy here. In fact, quite the opposite. I love this land, the comfort of it, the routine. But. I've never left, never gone to see what's beyond. I understand why and wonder, didn't any of the Lore Keepers want to leave? Or were they blessed with contentment and satisfaction?"

"Your parents left, did they not?"

"Yes, but they didn't get far before. . ." I trailed off, unable to speak of death.

"Have you considered that once we kill the ancient goddess, once and for all, you'll be free?"

Free? I stared at him, hackles rising. I was no prisoner. This land did not bind us! How could he speak of freedom? Before the angry words left my mouth, the scent of tea calmed my senses. I took a breath and considered his words again. "No, I must admit, I never thought of it that way. I suppose this could be a blessing, the turning point."

I wondered what it meant then, for the bloodline of Lore Keepers. Would we fade into legend if there was no longer a goddess to keep buried?

11

THE TEA DID its work in calming my mind, but only for a few hours. Before dawn I was up and tapped on Maraini's door, bursting to tell her what I'd discovered. We chatted briefly while she dressed and braided her hair, calm, sensible, and neat. As always. I'd taken care to dress in clean clothes that smelled like a blend of herbs, but my curls hung wild and free.

"Well?" I bounced up and down on the pads of my feet, waiting for Maraini's response. "Should we go to the orchard now?"

She nodded. "We should. Were you up late last night? With Kian?"

Oh, my sister. She knew all. I opened the door. "Did you hear us?"

Maraini winked. "I thought of coming downstairs, then thought better."

I closed the door again and filled Maraini in. She was such a wonderful sister. She listened without judgement and then added. "But he plans to return to wildwood?"

"He does, after this is over," I said, explaining about the falcon.

"I'm sorry," Maraini said. "He would fit in well here."

Excitement faded away, left with a longing for what could be. "He's the only man that's caught my eye," I agreed. "But what about you? What do you want? Kian said when we slay the goddess, we'll be free. . ."

Maraini paused, her finger straying across her desk. "I am happy here. I don't think there's anything more I want. One day, yes, a husband and babies. I'll go to market day for that." She smiled a secret smile as she glanced at me. "I must admit, I've had a correspondence with the blacksmith's apprentice. Young Henri. Nothing more than mere exchanges, but I think it might be something. When he's done with his apprenticeship it could be good to have a blacksmith around here. The farm is too much for us to handle alone."

"What?" I demanded. "How come you kept it a secret?"

"Oh, Rae, I never want you to feel as though this place isn't your home. Our home. Because it is. But now that Kian is here, well, if I were you, I'd enjoy every moment, and perhaps he will return."

Return. I hadn't thought of that. But, regardless, a bright future would not happen for us if we did not find the buried goddess. "You're the best sister ever," I gave her an impulsive hug. "But come on, the light has come and we have a goddess to find."

Together we made our way downstairs into the

kitchen where Kian sat, helping himself to some bread and cheese.

"I hope you don't mind," he began when he saw us.

Maraini nudged me with her elbow, and I fought to keep from giggling. "No, eat," I said. "We'll go to the orchard when you're done."

Even though I wanted the nasty nonsense with the goddess over with, I did not relish the thought of digging through the orchard. I waved away Maraini's suggestion to eat. My stomach twisted in knots as we gathered supplies and marched to the orchard. My thoughts briefly flew to the cows, but they could wait while we dug. The golden sky was still alight with the fresh glory of sunrise, the bright blades of grass wet with drops of dew, and blue and yellow flowers glistened as they held their buds up, soaking in the light.

The trees waved about us, thick trunks, wide branches all sloping upward. I stood under the breezy boughs and found it hard to believe anything evil could hide in such a place. Kian rested a shovel against a tree and we walked around the grove. I studied the knobby trunks and branches heavy with tiny green apples. It was beautiful, home, with nothing dark surrounding it. I'd thought I would have a feeling, a trepidation deep in my gut when we reached the place where the goddess was buried. But there was nothing.

"This isn't right," I announced, scratching my head, one hand on my hip. From the time I was young, I knew to trust my inner sensations. I knew when to trust people, when to wager they were telling a lie, and here, there was nothing. "The air is pure; the trees don't play host to death."

Kian placed a hand against a trunk and closed his eyes, as though listening to the spirit of the trees. "Nay, there is a lightness here I cannot explain."

Maraini, who'd brought the book along, flipped to the page with the diagram of the original layout of the land. "I don't think it's the orchard either. During the rituals, it was never a place we blessed."

I cocked my head at her. "But the barn was, and the garden. . ."

"And the house," she said, glancing back at it.

I shivered. No way there was a monster buried under the house. "But it's new," I protested. "Papa had it built for Mama. We should go to the garden."

Maraini gave me a doleful look, as though she knew I was procrastinating. But really, why would the buried goddess be under the house? It made no sense to me.

Without giving her time to respond, I spun and headed toward the garden.

"Rae," Maraini called after me.

"I'll go milk the cows," Kian offered, as though he could taste the tension in the air.

"It's not the house." I shook my head as Maraini and I reached the garden. "The house is home, it's warm, comforting, and full of good memories."

"Think about it," Maraini protested as we walked the edges of the garden. "The house can be rebuilt over and over again, but where's the one place we hate going? The one place that wouldn't be rebuilt because it's underground already?"

My shoulders sagged as I walked the warm earth. The scent of fresh fruits and vegetables hung in the air, bliss, perfection, and nothing of darkness and evil.

"The place where we found the book, as though it is a marker. That has to be the reason it's down there, instead of with the other accounts of the land. Because it's a sign, telling us where to go, where to look. Don't you see, Rae?"

"We've been down there a thousand times," I protested. "There are just rows and rows of shelves, dust, dirt, and moldy food we should toss."

"We never stay long enough to look at anything, we just run in and out as fast as we can. It's because the place has an aura about it," Maraini mused. "What if there's a labyrinth, a tunnel underneath, and all we need to do is find it?"

Frowning, I eyed the garden. There was no way anything was buried under it, aside from potatoes and carrots. It made sense that the buried goddess would be where no one would bother her, and no wild animals would dig her up. Still, I didn't want to go into the cellar. It gave me chills. "What about the barn?" I asked half-heartedly.

"No, the more I think about it I'm sure it's the house." She glanced toward it. "We are Lore Keepers. We always hold our secrets close. Look, it's probably best we do this in daylight. I'll get the lanterns while you find Kian, we'll want him with us."

She set off toward the house without another word while I shivered in the sunlight. It was a beautiful, warm summer day, and my heart was filled with nothing but dread. Spinning on one heel, I made my way to the barn where the warm sounds of happy animals could not make the thudding in my heart cease. We were truly going to find the buried goddess, and the legend would morph into truth.

I found Kian standing on the road, shielding his eyes as he studied it. I fell in step beside him and looked, noticing the distinct cloud of dust whipping up. "Do you have visitors?" he asked.

"Not today," I said. "Market day is tomorrow and if we are missed, those who have needs will come here, seeking a remedy or advice."

"Advice?" He raised an eyebrow.

"We might be young, but we are still Lore Keepers. We know the history of the world and that knowledge gives us insight."

"The seer always spoke highly of you," Kian remarked, his hand touching the small of my back.

"The seer?" I wrinkled my nose.

"Sasha, I believe her name is."

I froze. "You spoke with her? Then she is alive?"

"Did you think she was in trouble?"

I shook my head, relieved. "No, I just hoped she'd find what she was looking for, and it seems she has."

Kian pointed down the road. "And I believe those creatures have too. If you aren't having visitors, then perhaps a small troop is headed our way. Mounted riders, since they are kicking up dust."

"To the house," I said.

We set off at a run, but before we reached it, Kian grabbed my hand. "We need to board up the windows. I found supplies in the barn. . ."

"I'll help," I breathed, and ran after him.

We still had time, I thought to myself as I ran. Hopefully, the dust on the road was nothing. Not an army come to find the goddess and raise her to life. Still, dread filled my heart as we carried boards to the porch.

I burst inside, calling for Maraini and telling her about what might come.

"We are prepared," she said fiercely.

12

THE DOOR banged shut behind me with a finality. Dread seeped around, only lessoning when Kian caught my arm. He pulled me so close my cheek brushed the rise and fall of his chest. "Here." He thrust the handle of a knife into my hands. "I'll board up the windows and hold them off, should they come near. But go! Find the buried goddess, stab her, and we will be free of this madness."

I gulped. My fingers closed around the hilt as I studied the intensity behind his eyes, well aware what the rise of the goddess meant not only for Maraini and I, but also for the inhabitants of the enchanted wild-wood. Despite the direness of the situation, I was drawn to Kian and wanted a way to comfort and encourage us both. I brought a hand up to caress his cheek, wondering if he could sense the depths of my emotions in that touch.

"Go," he insisted, even though he held me firmly, as though he, too, relished our connection.

"What's all this?" Maraini appeared, her eyes going from the weapons to the boards for the windows.

Recalling the urgency of our situation, I stumbled back, breaking the embrace. As I did, a sharp twinge went through me. A warning. I felt it deep in my gut. Something with ill will had crossed the boundary line. "They are coming," I squeaked out.

Maraini sucked in a deep breath and pressed a hand to her belly. "I felt it too," she breathed, striding across the room to the window. "Those with ill will have entered our land but. . .it's too early!"

"All the same, they come," Kian's level voice calmed the frantic air of panic which was quickly invading the peaceful house.

Maraini's eyes went to the knife in my hand and understanding dawned on her face. "We do this together," she said, hands on her hips.

My eyes went wide. It wasn't often that Maraini made demands, but this was one of those times.

"From what we know, the goddess is dark, dangerous. Kian, you volunteered to come help us, to fight with us. We stay together on this. I'm not losing anyone today!"

Kian drew himself to his full height and crossed his arms over his chest. "Go," he said, gently but firmly. "Staying together will only cause delays."

"He's right," I grabbed Maraini's arm and dragged her toward the cellar, dread creeping up my spine. Not that I was in a hurry to find what was hidden in the cellar, quite the opposite. But the time for procrastination was over. We needed to do this. It was our task. Our duty.

Maraini came willingly, stopping to snatch a basket of supplies off the table.

I stole one last glance at Kian as he bent and lifted a board. The light shifted as he blocked it and a lump settled in my throat. There was no time for regrets, my path lay before me.

I opened the door to the cellar and Maraini reached into the basket. "Here. I have two lanterns but keep flint handy. I also brought sage sticks."

My fingers closed around the flint and I tucked it into my pocket as Maraini lit a lantern. A rush of fear rose like a haze around me, and for a moment all I saw was smoke. "Are we really going to do this?" I asked, wanting an excuse, a reason to escape.

Behind me, I heard banging as Kian nailed the boards up. The faint roll of thunder made the walls of the house shudder. A storm was coming, just like the seer promised.

Maraini clasped my hand, lending me her strength. "The sooner we do this, the better."

A numbness came over me and I nodded as we crept down into the musty gloom. I looked at the cellar with fresh eyes, searching for a clue, anything that would lead to the discovery of. . .what? A tomb? I shuddered at the very thought of old bones below us.

We crossed the dirt floor, weaving between the thick shelves as a cry came from above. Heart racing, I whirled toward the stairs, thinking of Kian. Alone. A boom shook the house, followed by the shattering of glass. I screamed. They were here. Were they inside?

"I don't like leaving him behind," I protested, half-heartedly following Maraini toward the trunk which rested against the wall.

"Neither do I." Maraini paused and ran her fingers over the wall. "But it was his choice."

A raw shout came, followed by a roar of pain. My feet were on the steps before I could help myself. I dashed out of the cellar, ignoring Maraini's shouts behind me. I'd found myself an elven prince, and I wasn't about to let him die.

Chaos met my eyes as I hurried down the hall and lunged for the jars of herbs. My fingers fell on the lightning jars. Snatching one in each hand, I moved toward the front room, forcing myself to slow down as I saw creatures. There was a mass of them, tall and wiry with skin as dark as night. Nightmarish eyes took over most of their faces, leaving little room for a tiny nose and snarling mouth with jagged teeth. My bravado disappeared, and a cry of fear left my lips as those horrid beasts tore toward me. I flung the lightning jar.

It flipped through the air and shattered among the creatures. I ducked as flashes of light sparked across the house. Amid screams and howls, I smelled the rancid scent of burning flesh. Uncovering my face, I looked and saw smoking remains and body parts tossed across the floor. My stomach heaved.

"Rae?" Kian moved between the torn bodies, dancing on his tiptoes until he was at my side, bow in hand, three arrows left. He caught me about the waist as my bones went limp and turned me away from the destruction. "Don't look," he said. "You were just in time." He steered me down the hall as I fought to regain my limbs. "More will come but. . .how did you do that?"

"Lightning." I swallowed my trembling reaction and forced myself to speak. "When the storm comes, we collect it. It's what we were doing when we found you."

"Witches," Kian whispered in awe.

"What were those creatures?" I shivered.

Kian shook his head. "It's best we not talk about it. They are dark beings from the wildwood. The queen must be distracted, they should not have been allowed to escape."

Everything was unraveling around me, and my determination came rushing back. We reached the cellar and by the time we moved down the stairs, pulling the door shut behind us, Maraini stood under an arch. She waved. "I found a hidden door behind the chest."

My eyes went wide as I walked up to it. Maraini had climbed on top of the chest and found a door. It rose five feet from the floor, a narrow opening into darkness. A knowing thrummed deep inside me. This was the path. This was the way, buried underneath us all this time. But something about it gave me some relief, knowing the bones were not in the house. No, they were in a tunnel.

"I'll go first," Maraini offered. "I expect nothing living to be down here."

Still, I shuddered, thinking of worms and spiders and all kinds of slithering bugs that like to live below the ground.

We moved into the gloom while Maraini's light cast a halo on the walls. At first, we had to duck, hunched together as we moved. But as we went closer in, the air dry and musty, the walls opened up. That's when I noticed they weren't made from mud. My fingers trailed over the rough shape of stones and that's when I knew someone had created this tunnel for a reason.

The walls sloped down, and with each step I was aware of the ground above me, pressing down as we wound in deeper and deeper. My breath came short and fast as I thought of the ceiling caving in, leaving us trapped in the dark, underground. There'd be no way we could dig our way out and no one would come for us, other than the dark creatures.

I heard Maraini and Kian breathing as we walked, keeping a steady pace for what seemed like an inordinate amount of time. Then Maraini gasped, and we came to a stand-still.

13

THE PASSAGEWAY WIDENED so we could stand three in a row. I drew alongside Maraini while Kian was so close, I felt his breath on my neck. The air surrounding us had a certain tang to it, ancient and dead, but not rotten. The pool of light showed a circular room, with a raised dais in the middle. And on that dais was a tomb. My fingers tightened on the knife and I wondered, what was I supposed to do? Open the casket and stab the goddess? What if she were naught but bones? Would she need to be alive? Awake?

"This is it," Maraini whispered.

I tried to swallow, but my throat was dry. "What do we do?" I whispered.

Kian must think we were pathetic for all-knowing Lore Keepers.

"We have to open it." Maraini gestured to the casket.

I took a step, fighting the instinct to turn on my heel and flee back through the dark halls, back to our cozy home which darkness had desecrated. Was Kian right?

Would more come and find us in the tunnels? Trouble ahead and trouble behind, I could not get away from darkness. But forward was our only path, our only hope.

"Keep the knife ready," Kian suggested as he slid an arrow into his bow and crept toward the dais.

Swallowing my fear, I moved behind him and Maraini slipped her hand in mine, squeezing it.

Together, we crept over the rough stone floor, ancient and aged with runes carved into it, caught by the light.

Runes had once been the study of Lore Keepers, but eventually the desire to learn faded away. Since when had we picked what we knew? If Maraini and I had kept to the old ways and studied runes, we'd be able to read what was left for us. I could only guess they were a set of instructions or wards of protection to keep the goddess at rest. From the way Maraini's brow puckered and her eyes glanced at the runes, I knew she was thinking the same thing. We had not been as vigilant as we should have been.

The steps were large blocks of stone, leading up to the sacred casket. Intangible evil wafted from it, some-thing I could not see, but I sensed the aura of something that went deeper than death and rot. *Power*, I thought. *Magic*.

Wordlessly, we stopped at the top. Maraini was the first to reach out, pressing her hand over the latches that held the casket shut. I thought they might have been locked, but there was nothing, just a latch. Maraini undid it and I lifted the knife. Nothing in my past had prepared me for this moment.

"Together," she whispered.

I pressed my hand against the cool stone and we pushed as hard as we could.

The lid to the casket creaked open slowly until it stood upright. Instinctively, I backed away.

At first it appeared nothing happened. The casket was deeper than I expected. I'd have to move closer and lean over to see what was inside.

Common sense held me in its grip, for there was no rhyme or reason that would entice me to lean over and find myself caught in the grasp of an ancient goddess. She was supposed to be dead, sleeping, but that could not stop her, could it? Goddesses were ancient, immortal, nothing like humans, mortals. I did not know what to expect or what to do. Shifting my weight from one foot to the next, I gathered the nerve to approach the casket just as a cloud of black smoke rose out of it.

I screamed and stumbled back, holding my hands in front of my face to protect myself.

The smoke curled, blotting out the light. I heard the shatter of glass. Had Maraini dropped the lantern? And we were cast into a pitiless darkness.

I pressed my arms against my side and hunched over, trying to make myself small while a numbness came over me. The knife felt heavy in my sweaty hands, and I was afraid I'd drop it as a wind rustled around me. Wind. Where was it coming from?

A dense cloud covered me, both heavy and bitter, and twisted around my body, pouring into my throat and strangling the air within me. I coughed, one hand clutching my throat, and then I heard a scream. Gagging against the bitter taste in my mouth, I turned toward the wail. "Maraini?" I tried to shout, but my words were stuffed back into my mouth by the dense cloud of gloom.

Squeezing my eyes shut, I opened them again, but there was nothing but darkness, until I could not tell whether my eyes were opened or closed. Something fluttered in front of me. Clothing? The material was smooth, silky, but I hesitated, unwilling to strike out when I could hit either Kian or my sister. A grunt came from my left and I spun toward it: *Kian?*

My lips trembled and tears pressed against my eyes as I backed away. Placing my feet carefully to keep from falling. Every muscle within my body screamed for me to run, flee, escape evil that permeated the cavern. We shouldn't have come here or opened the casket. I was sure we would die.

Lore Keepers weren't meant to face battle or evil. We were meant to sit inside, reading our books, writing, crafting, healing, and helping. Not this madness. But there was no escape. It was this or the creatures that invaded our house. My stomach rolled at the thought of them, and I wished I'd had the forethought to bring a jar of lightning with me. My shaking fingers struck my pocket, and I recalled there was flint. Light.

I squeezed it, the unevenness of the stone grounding me, somehow. I lifted the blade and struck it against the rock.

Sparks flew up, the gentle yellow light piercing the darkness, driving away evil. I heard a hiss and saw something thick and snake-like slither away from me. I had nothing to light it with, unless I found the broken end of the lantern, and it seemed impossible in the darkness. That foul hiss came nearer, and then something backhanded me.

The breath left my body, and I fell backward, arms spread out to catch my fall. I landed on the stone with a thud and dropped both the flint and the knife. Agony raced up my back, and for mere moments I couldn't move, only gasped for breath. Unless I was mistaken, what was in the casket was very much alive and angry.

A sob burst from my throat as I stretched my fingers, finding the flint again. I wiggled my arm, knowing I needed to get up, figure out a plan, make a move. My hand touched something long and branch-like. The sage stick Maraini had brought! Moving stealthily, I struck the flint against the stone, causing the sparks to rise again. This time they caught on the branches of the sage stick, which flared up. I held it up like a torch, even though it smoked, the smell of sage fighting against the darkness. The embers on the tips of the sage branch did not provide enough light to see, but I held it up as I rose to my knees, sweeping it back and forth.

The air in front of me cleared and the choking black cloud gave way. Another hiss broke the silence and then a light flared up.

I turned in the light's direction and saw Maraini holding up a torch. Blood streamed from her head, matting her dark hair. The rest of her face was hidden in shadows, yet she sat, holding the light, waiting for me. A premonition stirred in my belly and I turned toward Kian, who was below, as though he'd fallen off the dais. His bow was broken, but he picked up an arrow, pointing it at something beyond me.

Turning, I looked beyond the casket, still open, although the smoke rolling out of it was repelled by the sage stick. Around the casket was the monstrous body of a snake, head reared back, yellow eyes gleaming as it hissed. A forked tongue came out and yet instead of pouncing, the snake delayed, writhing and hissing as though something held it back. My gaze went to the sage. Was it possible?

"Rae?" Maraini cried, her voice thin with pain. "The knife!"

I lunged for it just as a white hand appeared at the edge of the casket. The creature inside sat up and turned gleaming eyes on me. I took a step back, lost my balance, and tumbled off the dais.

14

WAVES OF PAIN flared up as I landed hard on my already bruised body. Distantly I heard both Maraini and Kian calling my name, but nothing but moans escaped my lips. I could not tear my eyes away from the goddess who sprang from the casket, moving slowly, gingerly, as though she could not believe her freedom. We were the ones who'd freed her. The fact hurt like an arrow that sank between my breasts. We were the ones who'd opened the casket and soon she'd be free. Already the torchlight seemed dim, and I saw the glint of the knife above me on the dais. Another moan left my lips and as I rolled to my side, and saw a flurry of movement.

Kian dashed past me, arrows in both hands as he moved toward the goddess. He took the steps two at a time as she rose. Coming to a terrifying height she seemed to swell and grow as she stood, her head almost reaching the domed ceiling. Black eyes glared and her mouth came open as she waved, nostrils flaring at the scent of sage.

Sage and salt. I recalled the way Maraini and I had walked the land, blessing it, protecting it. Was it the key to keeping the goddess buried? She seemed to have an aversion to it. Grasping the sage stick, I crawled up the stairs while Kian struck at the goddess. He was magnificent to watch, arms whirling as he pointed the arrows toward her, evading her arms. But he'd forgotten about the snake.

"Kian!" I screamed just as the creature lunged.

The next few moments happened in a blur. I moved up the stairs faster than I thought was possible, my bruised limbs screaming in pain as I threw my flint at the snake. It bounced harmlessly off its head, but it was enough. Glowing yellow eyes met mine, and I waved the sage as the snake hissed, but did not come closer. I snatched up the knife with my free hand while the goddess struck Kian. He fell. She laughed, wicked lips twisted in mirth. And then she turned her hideous eyes on me.

I heard a voice inside my head, speaking and yet not speaking. Words danced around me, and a grim tone rang out.

I am the goddess of death. Come to me, servants of evil. I summon snake and raven, orc and wood wright. Come, aid my escape.

No. The silent scream wailed inside me. I glanced at Kian; he lay face down, unconscious, much the way I'd found him in the meadow. Tears stung my eyes, but pity for my plight, and fear for my family was replaced with one burning sensation. Rage.

I was happy; I had everything. A beautiful farm, a loving sister and the potential of an elven prince. And now the goddess of death would come to take it all away. I'd already lost my parents, and I wasn't ready to let anything else change. The fear faded away into an icy determination. I aimed the knife toward the goddess and ran. The snake slithered closer, but I danced away. The goddess lunged, and I moved out of her reach, waving the sage in front of me as I moved. I needed a plan; the branch was losing its effectiveness, and I'd never get close enough to stab the goddess.

Out of the corner of my eye, I saw movement. The torchlight grew brighter, and I knew, even before I turned around, I knew my sister was coming to distract the goddess so I could stab her. We were the Lore Keepers, and this was our duty, our task. To keep the goddess of death from rising. I recalled her words before we touched the casket. What we did. We did together.

Blood of Lore Keepers. That voice hummed in my mind. *Set me free. Creatures of death. Come to me.*

The ground shook, and I lost my footing. The goddess, seeming to assume I meant nothing to her, threw back her head and held out her hands. A hum overcame the room, low deep tones as though calling, calling creatures out of bone and shadow, dark and root. Come forth to help her.

Terror constricted my heart, and words pulsed in my mind. My numb lips moved as the words burst out. Mama's words came to me like a balm of peace, and I uttered them. As I did, the swirl of magic did not seem as dark, the bright red blood splashing on the stones did not seem as gruesome. The knife trembled in my hands but not from fright. Nay it was something else, something within me that had lain sleeping, waiting, resting, until it was time. Now it rose within me like a wave of water, and my mouth came open as words flew from my lips. I recalled I'd said it once before: *There is no power in words, there is only the intent.* And I realized what intent was. Perhaps intent and magic were one and the same, for the command that came out of my mouth was like one of dominant power.

Goddess of Death, I bind you to this place. You cannot rise nor rule the wildwood. The world is not yours; your powers are weak, you will never rise again. Your demons cannot help you, your creatures aren't coming, you will never rule another day.

The words poured out of me, but I still didn't know if I could stab her. I'd killed harmless animals before. They made my heart turn over as I blessed them, thanked them for their sacrifice and gave what I did not need back to the ground. But this? She was dark and evil and would ruin everything. I pushed past the doubt just as Maraini hurled a sage stick at the goddess.

A raw scream filled the air as the goddess hissed and spun toward Maraini. She lifted her hand, and I saw the snake move. I pivoted and thrust the knife into her side, and everything went black.

A white glow in the distance caught my eyes. I lay on my stomach, my curls in my face. On one side of me I saw Kian's prone body, and on the other was Maraini, blood dripping down her head. A sob rose in my throat. Were they alive?

But there was that light, and as it came closer, I realized it was a woman. She glided to the goddess who was transfixed as though she'd been paralyzed, and touched her, binding her with a black ribbon. When she was done she placed her hands on either side of the goddess's head and closed her eyes. Power poured from her, and as I watched, the white light disappeared, replaced with something else dark and sinister. I smelled the acrid tang of it, watched it flow out of the goddess into the woman.

When she was done, she collapsed, and what had once been the ancient goddess was nothing more than bones which fell into the casket. The woman seemed to regain her strength, for she rose and closed the casket, latching it again. And then her eyes turned on mine. They were luminous and dark at the same time, as though she'd drunk more than her share. She opened her mouth and words came out. "I am the Queen of the Wildwood and you have saved many lives here. As the seer said, there is hidden power within you. Use it well, for one day I may need your help, and I shall call upon you again."

Then she turned, the shadow of darkness flickering around her, and faded into shadow and story.

15

THE ANCIENT GODDESS WAS DEFEATED. Often, my mind returned to the moment as the days and weeks passed. Was it possible that we had defeated her? Or had the power of the Queen of the Wildwood been enough to destroy her for eternity? The moment changed me and I took to writing. Writing down what I had seen and the questions that remained. Who was the goddess? Was she truly the goddess of death? Or a lesser goddess? Would we ever know the truth of it? It seemed the Queen of the Wildwood had come and drawn the power of the goddess into herself, and it was that knowledge that frightened me the most.

Kian and Maraini hadn't seen what happened, but I knew what my eyes had seen, and it concerned me. Eventually, if one took so much darkness and evil into themselves, they became the very darkness they sought to rid the world from. I'd seen the shadows in the queen's eyes, and I worried about her. Who was she? What was she becoming by taking over the evil in the wildwood? Would she be able to hold it back, or would she morph and shift, becoming one of those evil creatures, despite her best intentions?

But anxieties of the future and what truly had happened did not consume all of my thoughts. Maraini took to bed for a few days to heal from her wounds and Kian, nothing but bruised from the encounter, stayed.

He stayed while we cleaned the house, taking away the dead bodies. No matter how many times I cleaned the house with a blend of cloves, lemons, cinnamon, eucalyptus and rosemary, I still shuddered, imagining those fouls creatures returning once again.

Kian stayed through the midsummer harvest, assisting with the trip to market and making repairs around the farm until I began to see how woefully we'd fallen. The work was too much for two women, and I appreciated his help. But more than that, I appreciated his calm presence. He knew what to do, and did it without question, and it was powerful for my scattered ways. It was a combination of both him, and writing that helped ease my soul, put away the grief from my parent's death, and calm down, once and for all.

It wasn't until I tasted the first tang of autumn in the air that I recalled Kian had a family, a place where he belonged, and yet he stayed. I let myself out that morning and made my way to the meadow, where Kian let the horses run, wild and free. I walked across the long grasses, a basket of bread and cheese tucked under my arm, but my hair, loose and free as usual. Some things had changed, but others would remain the same.

"Rae." He lifted a hand in greeting.

I smiled. He stood, arms crossed, feet apart, watching the horses gallop, enjoying their freedom.

"You forgot breakfast again," I told him, holding up the basket.

He raised an eyebrow and gave me a playful smirk. "Perhaps I simply wanted you to bring it to me," he teased.

I handed him the basket. "Well, you have your wish then."

"Rae," his voice dipped lower. "There's something else I've been meaning to tell you."

My heart clenched and just for a moment I squeezed my eyes shut. I had everything. Wealth, friendship, and love. I didn't want any part of it to be taken away.

When I opened my eyes again, he was beside me, one arm stealing around my waist to tug me closer to him. I wrapped my arms around him, pressing my face against his chest until I could feel the rapid pulse of his heartbeat. I already knew it wasn't going to be good news.

"I have to leave soon," he murmured. "Falcon returned and they are coming to escort me home."

He pulled back, one finger coming under my chin to lift my mouth to his. His thumb stroked my cheek.

"Will you go with them?" I attempted to keep the begging out of my eyes. Why would he leave this place, this paradise?

He pulled me close but looked away. I knew what he would see, his eyes taking in the house, the barn, the garden, the orchard. I held him tight, wishing the moment would last longer.

"It is my duty to go with them," he admitted, shoulders sagging. "My place is with my tribe in the wild-wood. I am a warrior, a prince, it would be wrong to leave them."

I wanted to ask: *What about us?* But I didn't. Threading my fingers through the ties of his jerkin, I whispered. "Stay."

"I must admit, my heart begs me to stay." His deep brown eyes met mine. "For I have found the land of the Lore Keepers more enchanting and mysterious than the wildwood itself."

"Stay," I said again, relishing the hum of desire between us.

His words touched every ache, every longing in my soul. I recalled the words of the seer. Then, I thought I understood them. Now, I wondered if her warning was not about the storm, but about Kian himself, with the reminder that I should keep my heart open to change, to love, to possibilities beyond my imagination. The power of the Lore Keepers was real, I'd felt that, but the power of love was potent, strange. Even though it had been two months almost to the day since Kian had arrived in my life, he'd changed it in every way for the better.

He gestured with one arm, keeping the other tightly around me. "This land is nothing but goodness, where the air is pure and untainted with war. I would have you stay here, home, where it is safe. But now that you are free and no longer need to guard the land, will you come with me? Just to see the wildwood, to meet my tribe. And then we shall return?"

Leaving. There it was, the thought I'd had in passing. We were free to come and go as we pleased now, no

SECRETS OF THE LORE KEEPERS

longer bound to the land and yet, the fear of what had happened to my parents was still there. I lifted my chin and faced him. "With you, I would go anywhere. You have my trust and my heart."

His eyes changed, his face struggling to grasp the concept, going from surprise to disbelief and then he kissed me. His lips were like flames of fire and a wave of heat surged through me, spreading from my face to tingle in my toes. I opened my mouth to his caress and he took me, holding me firmly against his hard body, his kisses deep, insistent, intense.

Before, his kisses were sweet and charming, gentle, and polite. But this kiss was rough, passionate, and stole my breath away. His fingers traced a line up my back but before he pulled away, I already knew what I wanted. My fingers fumbled at the ties of his jerkin. Sensing my need, he assisted, tossing it to the ground, his shirt and pants following shortly afterward.

"Wouldn't you be more comfortable in the house?" he asked, taking a step back from me and glancing toward the manor.

A laugh escaped my lips as I shook my head. "Surely you know, I am a daughter of the land, this is home, much more than a structure. Besides, it makes more sense, does it not, to make love in the place where we first met?"

"It does," he confirmed, his finger caressing my jaw, followed by kisses that trailed down my neck.

Sensations fired through me and I closed my eyes, letting a moan escape my lips as I enjoyed his touch. I traced the lines of his toned muscles and the faint scar left from his wound. He watched me, eyes lidded and we took turns until he captured my mouth with his again.

Untying my apron, I tossed it away and pivoted my body toward him, a silent invitation, for I could tell he wanted me as much as I wanted him. We'd been nothing but polite around each other, with a few stolen kisses, but I yearned for more. Never had a man besought me in such a way, and I thought I understood all the things I'd thought were silly before. The space between my legs ached with longing. I wanted him to fill me, to make me whole in a way no one else but him could.

His fingers undid the buttons on my dress, revealing flashes of skin as he bared my body. My breath hitched as he tugged it down around my waist, then further still until I stood naked in the glade. He went to his knees, kissed my belly and continued down, his tongue prodding into my secret place. Moisture gathered and my fingers tangled in his hair as I let out a low moan a satisfaction. But it wasn't enough, I wanted more. He held my hips steady as I bucked beneath his heated touch, then drew me down into the grass.

It waved above us, hiding us from view of the house. Aflame with need I straddled his naked body, enjoying the feel of a man beneath me. Kian's eyes took on a worshipful look and he stroked my body, his fingers tracing a line from my breasts down to my belly.

"You are beautiful indeed," he murmured, pressing me closer.

I leaned forward to kiss him, my erect nipples grazing his bare chest, sending shivers of delight up and down my spine. Each touch was more ecstatic than the last, each kiss more potent, purer. He held my hips with his broad hands and I moved above him, enticing, encouraging him to give me more.

Between panted breaths he pulled me closer until we were skin to skin, every muscle, every line of our bodies matched up evenly.

"Take me," I whispered, wondering what he was waiting for.

Our heart beat in rhythm as we moved together, at first hard and fast, passionate thrusts, an outlet for the weeks of waiting. I cried out more than once as passion overwhelmed me, matched by Kian's grunts. And again, we made love, slower, making it last, drawing out each moment. Kian's strong arms held me close to him, as though he dared not let go. When I lifted my lips, his met mine every time.

When at last we were spent, exhausted, we lay together in the meadow, and the warmth of the sun blessed us. I rested my head on Kian's chest and listened to him catch his rapid breath.

"Rae," he breathed at last.

I lifted my head and smiled at him, a glint of wickedness in my eyes. "Say you'll stay?" I asked.

He brushed my hair back from my shoulders and planted a kiss just above my heart. "My heart is yours. I'll stay as long as you'll have me."

Forever, I thought, just as a slight wind blew the grass around me. I lifted my face and smelt the air, inhaling a faint whiff of water and the vague, bitter spice of electricity. "Kian," I whispered. "I believe a storm is coming."

BRIDE OF THE KING

1

"WHAT DID you bring to trade dearie?" The old crone whispered as I slipped under the shade of her tent.

The summer sun was much hotter than I'd first thought, and my neck was damp with sweat under my chestnut hair. Every muscle in my body was sore and ached. A bruise bloomed on my shoulder from where my step-mother had pushed me last night. She was stronger than expected, and when I struck my shoulder against the fireplace mantle and fell to my knees, she'd landed a vicious kick.

Now, I knelt in the cool mud and clasped my trembling hands together. I took a deep breath, for what I would ask would break the deathbed promise I made to my father. *Never use magic.* He'd told me. *No matter how bad it gets. The cost is not worth it.*

"I was hoping I could pay on credit," I said.

The woman waved her hand, shaking the loose skin that hung off her wrinkled arm. "I can't live on your word alone. It's payment or nothing."

I'd been afraid she'd say that. Although we were alone in the stifling tent, I glanced around before pulling a coin out of my pocket. I'd wanted to save it to buy something nice for myself, but this was more important. Besides, if the magic worked, soon I'd want for nothing. I'd never spend nights lying on a bed of prickly hay, sobbing into my threadbare skirts, hunger gnawing my stomach while my body ached with bruises. I would not have to endure the sharp tongue of my step-mother and the mocking laughter of my step-sisters. No longer would I endure the shame and humiliation of being pinched and slapped when they were angry at their lot in life and took it out on me.

"Ah," the crone all but snatched the silver from my fingers and stuck it between her gums.

I looked away. The idea was to check to ensure the coin was of value by biting down on it, but the woman had almost no teeth left. Her eyes were a milky white, an indicator of her lack of vision, and she had more wrinkles on her face than a chicken had on its neck.

"Now, give me your hand. What is your question?"

I held out my hand. It was red, chapped, and my throat dry with dust. But I was lucky to be left alone. My step-sisters had gone to visit a relative, and my step-mother was out for the day. I'd left my chores undone and snuck out. Four years I'd been unhappy. No more. I needed to change my future and control my destiny. "I wish to know the magic to summon the river goddess. I wish to leave my step-mother's control, change my fortune, and find happiness."

Dread coursed through me as I waited for her to respond. I'd said the words. I wanted to use magic. I waited for lightning to strike me dead, or a storm of black clouds to cover the sky.

The crone snorted, jolting me. I pressed a hand to my racing heart, ignoring the twinge of pain from my bruised shoulder. "Magic," she murmured, more to herself than to me. "Fortune. Control. Happiness. You must be Nesrin, the half-breed, hasty to use magic. But as you wish it, the three wishes you seek shall be found. To make the winds of fate move, you must offer a sacrifice. Go to the river and make your wishes. If the river goddess grants them, you must give her whatever she demands."

My face burned under her use of the word 'half-breed'. My father was human, my mother, an elf, and so I became known as the half-breed. The term stung as though I'd been slapped, but I bit my bottom lip to keep my retort inside. "I already gave you my last coin."

"A river goddess has no use for coin," the crone shook her head, hints of mirth causing her wrinkled cheeks to sag even more. "Ask, and it shall be given. Remember to begin with the phrase: I summon thee, river goddess. Now go. Good luck, Mistress Nesrin."

An entire silver coin for that brief conversation? Gritting my teeth, I stumbled out of the tent, back into the warm summer sun, and followed the road. It was winding and dusty, the heat causing it to flake up. A row of shops perched in a semi-circle, creating the market-place of Gebeth, the village I lived in. A road led out toward the kingdom, and on one side were green pastures and open meadows for farming. On the other were trees. But no one built on the other side of the road. It was mere superstition, but among the trees you could lose yourself in the enchanted wildwood, a place where monsters bred and sacrifices were offered for the protection of the village.

Gebeth was once a proud village, one that enjoyed frequent visits from the king. But those days had passed, the wealth of the village disappeared, and the land turned to dust. The wealthy moved away, and those who could not afford to leave stayed to work the land. Part of me longed to leave, but I did not know where I'd go, or what I'd do. My past had many pleasant memories. I'd lived in a fine house with my father, a tradesman. I had love and wealth, everything except a mother. And so Father went to court where he met a fine lady and married her. She brought two daughters, who were close to my age. I'd hoped we'd be friends, but my hopes were in vain. And then, four years ago, when I was only sixteen, my father fell ill and died. The brunt of the weight of the family fell to my step-mother.

By then, Gebeth was dying and the money my father left behind was not enough to keep her fed and happy. And then there were the debts. She'd taken my share of the inheritance and spent it, claiming that if I wanted to be part of the family, I should help. I did my best, but with the way she spent money on the latest fashions, expensive cloth, rich food and decadent wines, there could not be much left. The debtors came around almost every week, and when they left my step-mother's temper was fierce. It would not be long before something terrible happened. I had to do something before I became a beggar, and with my thread-bare clothes, dirt-smudged face and unbrushed hair, I probably looked like one.

BRIDE OF THE KING

But magic, forbidden, impossible magic would save me. And so I made my way through the grove to the river. It shimmered, running along the edge of the enchanted wildwood, with wide banks open to sunlight.

Warm loam beneath my feet, I stripped off my shoes, lamenting the holes in them, and tossed my ragged gown over my head. I'd patched the dress so many times over the past two years, it no longer resembled the simple yellow dress I'd sown. Back then, I was still figuring out how to use my hands to sew, farm, and fetch, and I hadn't been as thin as I was now.

I removed my undergarments and tossed them over a bush. My eyes darted down the riverbank, but it was a lonely river and I did not expect anyone to appear during midday. Most families were busy preparing for the celebration of the first harvest, Lammas, which was two weeks away. I should be too.

My thoughts went to my little garden. I doubted it would produce much. While I enjoyed growing herbs and creating remedies, vegetables wouldn't thrive under my thumb. A shiver ran up my spine at the thought of what my step-mother would do to me, should she come home early and find me missing. My fingers touched my cheek. If last night had not been enough, this morning I'd earned a slap for burning breakfast. My light brown skin hid the mark, but it was still tender to the touch.

Recalling the old crone's words, I walked into the water, naked as the day I was born. A sort of freedom enticed me deeper into the waters, where I did not have to worry about my ill-fitting, scratchy clothes, or the heat of the summer day. The water eased the ache in my muscles like a healing balm. I lay on my back, loose hair drifting in the water, my dusky nipples pointing toward the sunlight, like an offering. Closing my eyes, I kicked and swam on my back, pretending I was a river goddess with the power to grant three wishes.

The warning tone in my father's words made me hesitant to summon the river goddess. I needed to sink into nature and spend some time with my thoughts, without fear. But perhaps instead of thinking, I should act before I lost my nerve.

Grief had wrapped me tight for years after the death of my father and the descent of my family from wealth to poverty. Instead of wearing pretty dresses and teasing the maids, I'd become the maid, cooking, cleaning, and trying my best to run my father's establishment while my step-mother and sisters pretended they were still nobility. My step-mother was a beauty, but her daughters were plain, and despite their desires, no good at finding husbands.

I dreamed of days when I'd no longer be forced to work. Perhaps a handsome prince would sweep me away. Instead of working for every bite I took, I could pour my energy into the one thing that mattered: continuing my father's work in alchemy. When he passed, his herbs and potions were sold to pay debts, but I'd snatched his book of notes and kept it tucked under my pillow. When I had time at night, I'd pore over those words, and hope that one day, I could start again. My fingers seeking herbs, finding colors, crushing them and mixing potions. I loved creating. It was like magic, taking something and transforming it into something else entirely. We had potions of healing, of energy, to keep one from feeling sick or fatigued, to relieve old pains and other ailments. But my father had dreams of going beyond rudimentary healing potions, he believed he could create a potion to make the village strong enough to fight against the creatures that crept out of the wood after dark. Those whispered secrets he shared both frightened and encouraged me.

During the festival of Lammas, we offered a blood sacrifice to the Queen of the Wildwood. She used to keep us safe from the dark creatures in the wood, but four years ago, everything changed. Rumor had it that a new queen ruled the wood. At first the attacks ceased, but the stories continued. A child found mauled by a beast, a young virgin, stolen in the night. But since there were no large attacks, the king's soldiers withdrew to the kingdom, taking our luck and livelihood with them. Gebeth had suffered ever since. There was no one to stand up to the wildwood, and the monsters that haunted us, never showing their faces, only coming in the night, and stealing.

A ripple in the water pulled me out of my thoughts. A fish? A frog? Unfortunately, I'd left my nets at home. If I hadn't, I might catch one for supper. Standing to my feet, I scrubbed my body clean, using a mixture of soap and herbs. The herbs I used to create a perfume, with lavender and wild rose. The smell made me think of my mother, who died when I was young. Her name was Rose, and hints of the smell gave me foggy memories. Being pressed against my mother's chest while gentle fingers stroked my back. The memory was so strong and poignant; it reminded me of a time when I was loved and cared for.

I'd be dirty again soon from the work that lay in front of me, and time was passing. It was now or never. Once I was clean, I felt much better. My body was only slightly sore and a well of determination rose in me. Clasping my hands together, I spoke the chant.

"I summon thee, river goddess. To grant my wishes, three. I wish for fortune to befall me. I wish to never see my step-mother and step-sisters again. I wish to find love and happiness. I have brought thee herbs of rose, to bless thy waters. Please heed my words and grant my wishes. In exchange, I will be indebted to your whims."

A flash of blue rippled in the water. A dark shape swam near me and rose, emerging from the waters without a splash. Green eyes, wide and round, glared at me out of a marshy face, covered in blue scales and webbing. I ceased swimming as she watched me, unblinkingly. "Who summons the river goddess?" she demanded, her voice as sweet and clear as crystal.

"Nesrin of Gebeth. I have three wishes," I explained, my words so soft it was a wonder she heard them.

"You call upon the magic of my waters, but I give no wishes to mortals. Now get thee gone, before my waters take you."

"Please," I begged. I hadn't considered the fact that she'd turn me down. "I'll do whatever you ask."

Her mouth twisted. "Anything? You are aware the magic will cost you. Not today, but in the future?"

"Yes. I am aware," I told her, daring to hope she'd grant my wish.

She barred wicked sharp fangs. "But why? Why should I use my magic on you, when you have nothing to give me, mortal?"

A wave rose and surged toward me. I swam away from it as my throat tightened. "Please," I begged.

Had the old crone lied to me? The river goddess seemed to think I was a joke.

"Begone, mortal, with your silly wishes." The river goddess splashed me again, a laugh in the wave as it swept over me.

Water spun me around as though I were naught but a leaf caught in a vortex.

"Have mercy," I begged, frustration and disappointment making my chest expand until I thought I would burst.

Another merciless wave sent me spinning. The water lifted me and slammed me down on the river bank. A wave of mud followed, along with the titters from the river goddess. She dived, and the waters were clear again while I lay in the mud, sobs shaking my shoulders.

It had been a fool's errand after all. Three wishes. What was I thinking? Wiping mud off my face, I grabbed my dress and made my way home.

2

"Nesrin!" my name was bellowed as though I were misbehaving.

I startled and stood, making my way out of the garden, which lay to the side of the house. Had my step-mother returned already? I'd assumed she'd be gone all day, giving me time to complete my chores before she returned. My stomach twisted and dread filled me as I ran, barefoot, wringing the water out of my dress as I went. In my haste to escape from the river, I'd left my shoes behind. My dress had only half dried, and the skirts were still wet. Instead of smelling like rose and lavender, I smelled like bog water and mud. It was likely that another slap and the name-calling of 'half-breed' awaited me in the house. So much for wishes.

"Nesrin, come here right this instance!" my step-mother shouted.

I pushed my dust-covered feet faster and came to a halt as my step-mother swept out of the house. She laid eyes on me and a smirk of displeasure covered her plump lips.

"I'm sorry," I murmured as I walked up the path to the house. "I did not expect you back so soon."

My step-mother's eyes narrowed, and she glared at me over her aristocratic nose. She was all curves, dark eyes, pale skin, and wore the latest fashion, a tightly corseted dress that swept the ground, with a ruffle I'd die for. Beautiful as she was, she was always out of breath with a nasty temper. She was going lame and carried an elegant stick to hide it, but I knew the pain in her feet gave her a reason to be cruel, and she'd used the dreaded stick on me more than once.

Peering down her nose at me, she frowned at my wet dress and bare feet. "I came to collect you but seeing as you can't be trusted to dress, or even make yourself presentable, you must go as you are. But I won't have a mud-girl ride in the carriage with me. Go sit with the driver."

She pointed at the bench of the carriage where the driver sat in his dark livery. A gasp escaped my lips, for it was rare that she allowed me to leave the farm, much less ride in the carriage. I didn't care what the day would bring, the wind had blown favorably in my direction. Perhaps the river goddess had granted my wishes. My cheeks glowing—and un-slapped—I swung up beside the driver, well aware my face was still smudged with dirt and my hair was tangled.

I twisted my fingers together, anxious about where the carriage was taking us as we traveled away from town and down a winding road. I watched out of wide eyes, taking in the beauty of the meadows. Yellow stalks of wheat waving in the breeze. Blue butterflies decorated the fields with color, and dark green trees waved on one side of us. The eyes of the wildwood were always watching, always waiting.

The air felt good against my hot skin, even though the mud from the river cracked and dried, making me itch. It came off in crumbles, but I noticed my skin underneath was smooth. Even my chapped hands had softened under the mud. Still, my face went warm as I thought of how I'd been tricked that morning. I wondered if the old crone would tell the story of the foolish girl who believed a river goddess could grant wishes.

The carriage turned off the main road and down a rutted path toward the trees. My brow furrowed. Where were we going? No one lived near the trees except for Rovers. They dwelt in tribes and came and went as they pleased, sometimes thieving from the nearby farms. My throat closed as the driver pulled the reins, halting the horses. What business did we have with Rovers?

White and yellow tents fluttered in the breeze and goats with bells around their necks moved in and out of view, munching on grass as they watched the ongoings. Woman in bright skirts hurried here and there while children were whisked away, out of sight. It was only midday, but I sensed the buzz of excitement in the air as the driver swung down and held open the carriage door for my step-mother.

She alighted and glanced around, her mouth set in a firm line and her eyes giving away nothing. Her sharp gaze darted to me. "Get down, half-breed," she ordered.

She never failed to find insults for me. Hate pinched my heart, but I climbed down, watching my feet to avoid splashing my step-mother's skirts with mud. As I did, a group of five men walked toward the wagon. The one who led the way looked like the sun god himself, with short golden hair, a trim beard and deep-set eyes that seemed to change color depending on the fall of the light. His chiseled jaw gave away nothing, and his face was set, as though he were used to being obeyed. His features had an air of familiarity, and I drew in a sharp breath as I recalled an afternoon I spent in the forest one spring, and a golden-haired man who was kind to me.

The men behind him were darker in complexion, with ruddy cheeks and hair as black as a raven's feathers. My heart dropped as I stared, and I knew I only had a second or more. Something bad was about to happen and I should flee, but indecision overrode my common sense.

The golden man studied me, taking in my disheveled hair, still damp even though the wind had done it's best to dry my waves. My yellow dress was bleached by sunlight, my face still smudged by mud as were my legs and feet. I put my hands behind my back and dropped my head, staring at the ground while tears of embarrassment pricked my eyes. I wanted to hide, but before I could run away, the man spoke.

"This is her?"

"As agreed," my step-mother responded stiffly.

Agreed? My eyes flew to my step-mother who stood apart, not looking at me.

The golden man tilted his head, and one of his men

produced a sack which jingled. Coin? He handed it to my step-mother who took it, weighing it in both hands, eyes gleaming with greed. "The price is fair," she said, then turned back to the carriage.

Shock froze my movements, and it took a moment for me to realize what had happened. She'd just sold me? To the golden man? Eyes wide, I faced her, and my lips trembled as I spit the words. "How could you?"

Lifting her chin, she stared, not at my eyes, but at my body. "You are a burden on the family no more." She lifted the bag of coins. "Your debt is fulfilled."

Tears burned my eyes. My shoulders slumped as I watched the driver shut the carriage and swing up on top. With a crack of the whip, he started the horses. I flinched, as though I'd been struck myself while dread filled my heart. She'd sold me to the outlaws, those heartless wanderers who spoke to spirits and communed with nature. I'd gone from one life of slavery to the next, except I didn't know these people, or what they would ask of me. I barely recognized the wretched cry of distress that tore from my lips and I spun, searching the trees for a place to hide. Sold! Like an animal! I could almost hear the mocking laugher of the river goddess, and it struck me like a blow to the face. One of my wishes had come true in the most devastating way.

"Lady Nesrin," the golden man towered above me, his presence making me feel insignificant. I barely registered that he called me a lady. "I am Zander, King of the Rovers," he explained. "Come, you must prepare. Our wedding ceremony will take place before sunset."

His strong fingers slid around my wrist, and I

noticed his face did not twist in disgust as mud crumbled off my arm. But I couldn't stop staring at him. Did he just say wedding ceremony? It was worse, much worse than I could have imagined. Not only had I been sold to the Rovers, but I was expected to marry their king. Nothing made sense. I tugged my hand out of his grasp as spots danced before my eyes. Lightheadedness made me stumble. I took a step, wavered in place, then fainted.

3

THE SPLASH of water brought me back. I hoped I'd only fallen asleep in the river, and the old crone, the mean river goddess, and being sold to the king were only a dream. I opened my eyes, and the fluttering of a yellow tent made my heart clench. This was no dream. I looked down as a squeak of dismay left my lips. Someone had taken my clothes and left me in a washtub. It was not unlike the ones at my father's house, a wide tub, just long enough for one to sit upright and wash. My brown hair trailed in the water, barely long enough to hide my breasts. I lifted my hands to cover my nipples and glanced around. I smelled herbs, a blend of rose and mint, and then the tent flapped open. A woman bustled in carrying a bucket and smiled when she saw I was awake. Her white hair was pulled back in a bun, she wasn't much taller than myself with a smooth face and sharp, black eyes.

"I thought you'd come around." She lifted the bucket

with surprising strength, and warm water flooded the tub. "A hot bath is good for the soul."

"Who are you?" I asked, my voice still trembling with uncertainty and fear.

"Oh posh." She waved a hand and, unasked, reached for a brush. "I'm Naomi. The king asked me to help prepare you for the ceremony, as a personal favor."

A groan left my lips as I remembered.

Naomi's eyes narrowed. "He's a good man. Any woman would be lucky to marry him," she snapped. "He had his choice of women but he was forced to choose you."

"Forced?" I raised an eyebrow. He didn't look like a man who was ever forced, but still, it did not sit well with me that I'd been sold to pay off debts. What was in it for the king? Usually it was the woman's family who paid her dowry for a marriage.

Naomi pressed her lips together and shook her head, although I noticed the hint of fear in her eyes. "Sit up so I can scrub you," she said.

"I can clean myself," I offered as the heat flushed my cheeks.

Naomi hummed. "You took a mud bath earlier, as if you wished to prepare, did you truly not know?"

I shook my head. "If my step-mother had told me, I'd have run away," I admitted.

"Don't try that here," Naomi cautioned as she rubbed soap into my hair. "The trackers will bring you back within days. Besides, it's not safe out there."

Out there. I assumed she meant how close we were to the wildwood.

I toyed with escape for I did not desire to marry a

man I did not know, or care about. He was pleasant to look at, at least, but it meant nothing. He could have a cruel, careless heart, and I was but a virgin. No man had laid hands on me, not even to kiss me. To have my wedding night forced upon me, with no time to prepare my mind or body, made terror rise in me. Would an opportunity to escape present itself? And even if it did, where would I go?

Naomi gave a sharp hiss as I sat up, and I realized she could see the bruise covering my shoulder. "Who did this to you?" She said, her fingers touching the bruise with such gentleness it did not hurt.

"I fell," I protested, the lie slipping from my lips so quickly I did not have time to think.

She scrubbed my back, applying slight pressure to the bruised areas. When she spoke again, there was a venom in her voice that both surprised and frightened me. "No one touches you like this, no one lifts a finger to you. Never again," she all but growled.

I opened my mouth, but her words made me close it again.

"Don't protest. I've seen bruises like these before, lie all you want, but I know where they really come from. No wonder that evil woman was so quick to get rid of you."

The woman's reaction and the way she stood up for me brought tears to my eyes. After Father died, I should have stood up to my step-mother, but I was used to being passive and obedient. But now? I resolved to be brave as Naomi helped me dry off. Wrapped in a towel, I sat on a stool and studied the tent while she brushed my hair dry.

Those who lived in tents were looked down upon, but it was surprisingly pleasant, either that, or I felt much better after the bath and the kindness of a stranger. Across from me was a mirror and a trunk. Aside from it and the wash tub, the tent was sparse and bare. My thoughts went to Zander, the king. I was sure I'd seen him before, even though I did not have a name.

Naomi finished my hair and opened the trunk, lifting out a beautiful white gown that took my breath away. I stood and allowed her to dress me, sighing as she wrapped my body in the softest silk. The material was cool against my warm skin and when Naomi led me to the mirror I gasped.

A fairy princess stared back at me. A braid crowned my head while my hair hung in waves down my back, almost cascading to my waist. There was a shine to my hair I'd never been able to capture during my rushed days. Naomi added a spray of purple flowers to crown the back. But the dress! I'd transformed into a graceful lady. The top of the gown left my shoulders bare and dipped at the bosom, offering a fleeting glimpse of soft flesh. It formed to my waist and then flared at the hips. The white hue of the dress faded into silver toward the bottom. Naomi stood behind me, pulling the laces tight.

"There," she said, face beaming. "We weren't sure of the size, so I added extra laces, just in case."

I turned, marveling at the bottom of the dress. It swept the ground and when I moved the skirts swished around me. Naomi handed me a bouquet of wild irises. "Now, you're ready," she proclaimed, smiling at me. Did I detect tears in her eyes?

I lifted my chin as I eyed myself in the mirror. What

witchery was this? For the first time since my step-mother had disappeared, a spark of hope rose in me. Perhaps this wasn't as bad as I thought it would be. For once I felt young and beautiful, proud to be myself. I determined to be honest with Zander, desperate to believe he could be a reasonable man.

"It is time," Naomi said. Taking my hand, she led me to the entrance of the tent.

When she opened the flap, it was much later than I expected. The soft glow of sunset cast a pink glow over the glade, and I saw white silk laid out on the ground, a path for my slippered feet to follow. A gentle music hung in the air, so sweet it made my throat ache. I squeezed Naomi's hand and turned to her. "Thank you," I whispered.

A smile lit her face, making her look young again. "My pleasure, my lady," she said. "Now go, follow the path."

I did, feeling like a faerie spirit. Flower petals moved beneath my feet, red and white and pink, while I noticed tree stumps on either side, with flickering candles and crowns woven out of flowers. As I walked, head high and shoulders back, the music became louder. My feet moved toward it, and I wanted to go, wanted to see what I would find at the end. For this seemed no haven of the outlaws, but a magical place. And I wondered if the river goddess had honored my request and granted my wishes.

Pine trees waved their evergreen branches above my head, as though they swayed in tune with the enchanting music. I imagined I saw spirits dancing, their white shapes almost invisible as they floated around me. Were my mother and father there in spirit? Watching me? A gentle comfort touched my heart at the memory of them, and although my fear did not quite disappear, a beat of anticipation pulsed in my heart.

Zander. I was sure I'd met him before. Early in the spring, after a trying day with my step-mother and step-sisters, I'd fled to the forest. The one place no one would follow me, for fear of the wildwood. The shades of evergreen comforted me. I walked, collecting herbs, and there he was, stepping out of the shadows, a cascade of light around him. He told me not to cry, for all sorrows were only for a moment, and the sun should shine again. Then he tucked a flower behind my pointed ear and asked if I were a wood elf come to bewitch him. He made me laugh; I recalled that much, but what a coincidence if it were him.

The white path led up to a clearing, where the Rovers stood in a half circle, watching me. Men, women, and children, dressed in bright colors, all smiling and swaying to the music. I stumbled with embarrassment, so many eyes were watching me I wanted to run and hide. I could have, but I didn't. Instead, I thought about every step forward, to the end where Zander, their golden king, stood, dressed in royal blue, waiting for me.

As I neared, I dared to glance at his face and saw the light in his gray eyes. He winked and his lips curled back in an encouraging smile. Despite my awkward situation, my lips parted and heat crept around my neck. I dropped my gaze to the purple flowers, heart racing as I took one step after the other, wondering why I did not flee into the darkening wood.

The music died away into a silver breeze when I reached his side. I dared not look as he took my hand and brushed his lips against my knuckles. "Lady Nesrin," he murmured.

My breath caught. I blinked at the flowers while my pulse throbbed. My hand felt clammy in his, but if he noticed, he said nothing, only held it firmly as we faced the priest. I dared peek at Zander, surprised he had a broad grin on his face. My entire body went hot, and I dropped my eyes back to the flowers. It was him! The man from the forest who'd placed a flower in my hair. Could this be real? Were the fates playing some kind of joke on me?

The ceremony passed in a blur. The sunset hovered as we spoke our vows, then faded into the night sky. A sliver of moonlight hovered as we turned, our hands wrapped in a ribbon to symbolize our union. Claps and cheers erupted, but I barely heard as I watched golden lights wink in and out of view. The scent of roses caught in the wind.

"Let us celebrate, Lady Nesrin, my queen," Zander said, and led me to the banquet table.

Wordlessly, I followed him, conscious of how the Rovers stared and cheered. A whisper of fate went through me. He'd called me his queen. Did my stepmother know, by selling me to the Rovers, she sold me into life as royalty?

I glanced at Zander as he led me to the table. "You did well," he murmured.

"Why me?" I whispered as he pulled out a chair for me. I settled into it while he moved to the head of the table.

He squeezed my hand and shook his head. "I'll tell you later."

The celebration began and there was no time for conversation. Food and wine poured aplenty, but it washed over me with a blur. My heart pounded in my ears and although I ate heartily, grateful for a full meal, I couldn't help but worry about my wedding night.

4

AFTER AN EVENING of feasting and dancing, Zander took my hand in his and led me away from the merriment. Starlight lit the way out of the glade, and lightning bugs offered glimmers of light to guide us. The Rovers continued to celebrate, but as we walked through the wood, the music dimmed and the sound of festivity faded.

Regret made me glance back, surprised to discover I'd enjoyed myself. The wonder and newness of the celebration distracted me from what was to come. I'd eaten with relish—it was the first meal I'd had all day—and it was a relief to be well-fed without the worry of being shouted at, or slapped.

The trees were silent watchers, standing like stoic gatekeepers with only the faint breeze to rustle their leaves. It was much cooler beneath the boughs and I detected the rich scent of loam. Here would be an ideal place to search for rare herbs if the opportunity arose, especially since this was my home now. I took a deep breath and glanced at Zander. All I could see was the back of his golden head as he strode ahead, almost dragging me behind him. My feet were exhausted from dancing and a zing of worry went down my spine. What would he do with me tonight? What did I *want* him to do with me?

"Zander?" I whispered his name into the hush, daring to disturb the sleeping nymphs among the trees.

He slowed, tilting his head as he came to a stop. A sliver of moonlight slid through the trees, allowing me a glimpse of his set jaw, and raised eyebrows. His eyes were hidden, unreadable in the velvet darkness. When he spoke, concern edged his tone. "My lady, you look weary."

I pressed my lips together and reached up to brush loose hair off my shoulder. Whether or not I wanted it, my life had changed unexpectedly. I had to stop being shy and passive. Like I'd done earlier that day, I had to take control of my destiny, even though my stomach twisted in knots. If this was my life now, I had to know what to expect and why he'd bought me. "It has been a trying day," I told him.

Stepping closer, until I was forced to look up at him, he twirled a strand of my hair around his fingertips. His actions were intimate, but his words sent a thrill of dread through me. "A celebration of marriage should be a happy time." His face twisted into a frown.

Displeasure?

I dropped my eyes and my heart thudded while I struggled to find words. "It's not that I'm ungrateful, but this day. . .this celebration has been unexpected."

I couldn't find the words to say marriage, and my

pulse quickened as he froze. Deep inside, I fought with myself. I wanted him to like me, needed him to smile at me again and assuage my doubts. But I wouldn't be dragged to his bed unwillingly, without knowing why I was here, why he was forced to choose me. I had to ask in a way that avoided his anger, because my step-mother reacted with violence when I questioned her. I stilled myself as his fingers left my hair and slid up the slope of my bare shoulder, guiding my chin up to meet his gaze. This time I saw a flash of irritation behind his eyes and couldn't help the shiver of fear that went through me. I blinked hard to keep tears from welling up, determined not to anger him further. If I pleased him tonight, perhaps he would be gentle with me.

"Unexpected?" His brows knitted together like storm clouds. "She did not tell you? Is that why you fainted?"

My eyes widened, but speech forsook me. I shook my head instead.

"That explains," he growled, letting go of me to rake his hand through his hair. "She never breathed a word to you? Did she? I thought something was off, I should have trusted my intuition but I thought. . ."

My stomach clenched. This had been a *plan*? I needed his confirmation. "My step-mother?"

"Yes." He waved his hand, frustration evident in his jerky movements.

My stomach clenched further as I waited for him to explain. Would this have happened if I hadn't summoned the river goddess? Was this incident the result of magic? Or the normal course of my life. I desperately wanted to know, and right now Zander was the only one who could give me answers. Except he didn't. He stood, hands by his sides, gazing off into the darkness.

Although his face was shadowed, my heart gave a little at his stillness. He'd thought I was aware of the marriage and looked forward to this day. Instead, we both stood in the wood, confused. Bitterness toward my step-mother rose like ash in my mouth. She'd been privy to my marriage to Zander and might have allowed us to get to know each other before our wedding day. Instead, she'd kept me hidden. When had she known? Had the last few weeks of abuse been her one last revenge?

"Why me?" I blurted out, trying and failing to understand. Naomi's word: *forced*, floated to the center of my thoughts. "She has other daughters."

Zander angled his body toward me and held out his hand. "Because you know the lore of herbs and potions. You are your father's daughter, are you not?"

My heart leaped at his words. "You want me to create potions? Using herbs?"

His fingers closed around mine, and we resumed our walk. "Yes. I need the lore of nature on my side to help keep away my enemies. You can help."

Ah. So it was nothing more than a trade. Another question hung on my lips. I held it back, then took a deep breath, reminded of my new mantra. No more passiveness. No more giving in without a fight. "And what do I get out of it?"

Zander's hand tightened in mine. Was he insulted by my question? "I am aware of what your step-mother did to you after your father passed. No longer will you endure her unkindness, and I am sorry I could not return sooner."

My heart skipped a beat. "Did you know my father?"

He nodded. "I was one of his customers, but my tribe travels frequently, we are Rovers. I was away for a few years when he passed, and I returned to make a deal with your step-mother. You seemed unhappy when I met you in the forest this spring. I'm not sure if you remember but—"

"Of course I remember," I interrupted. Thoughts of fleeing drifted away. He was a friend of my father's and he returned to free me from my step-mother's control. To save me. Perhaps living with him and the Rovers wouldn't be so bad. If I could get through the night, he'd give me my heart's desire. To study the lore of herbs and take up the work my father did. My fingers itched, longing to begin straight away, and the knot of tension within melted away.

Zander led me to a circle of tents, the very ones I'd seen flapping in the breeze when I first arrived. He lifted a hand to wave. Men slipped out of the shadows, armed to the teeth. One of them waved back before sliding away as smoothly as the shadows. A shiver went through me. Was this real? I was queen of the Rovers now. It made sense we would be guarded at all times. I swallowed hard as Zander held open the tent flap for me, and we were inside.

I gasped. In my ignorance, I assumed all tents were mere flaps of cloth over the ground, to give one privacy and some shade from the sun. But this tent was unlike the one I'd bathed and dressed in. Furs carpeted the ground, white silk hung down in banners from the pole in the middle. On one side were trunks, overflowing with fine cloth and jewelry. On the other was a table with two chairs, a jug, and cups upon it. Toward the back of the tent was a bed, raised up so that the top of it reached my knees. It was wide enough for three or four to sleep upon and covered with bright red blankets and plump pillows. My mouth went dry at the sight of that bed, noting the sheer curtains that were pulled back from it, ready to give one privacy, if need be.

My eyes darted back to the trunks, the mirror, and a table that sat beside them, and realized those were for me. This was my home now. A light hung from the middle of the tent, encased in crystals that spread the soft light throughout the tent. I glanced toward it and couldn't help but let my gaze flicker back to the opening. But there was no escape, even if I wanted. I had no doubt my husband was much stronger than me, and guards surrounded us.

"This is ours," Zander spread his hand, stating the obvious. "But you will have a covered wagon, just as luxurious, when we travel. I'm not sure what you will need for potions, but tomorrow we can discuss. For now, sleep."

Sleep. I had to speak up before he took my silence as acceptance. I twisted my fingers together, unsure how to tell him what I wanted, and what I *didn't* want. Turning me to face the bed, he touched the small of my back where the laces were tied. He pulled a string, and the tight fit of the gown loosened. My breath hitched as though he'd pulled it tighter. When he tugged again, I pressed a hand to my chest to keep the dress from sliding off and whirled to face him. "Zander." I held out my hand as I stumbled away, unable to look at him. Heat flamed my cheeks as I whispered, "I've never been with a man."

Closing the space between us, he peeled one of my hands away from the sagging dress and kissed it. His feather-light breath sent shivers through me, a mix of arousal and fear. I wanted to be embraced, loved, cared for, but Zander was an utter stranger. I did not understand how to care for him, nor what kind of man he might be. King of the Rovers and yet, perhaps something more? I'd heard of marriages where hearts warmed toward each other, and in giving myself to him, I'd be showing him I was willing to take a step. I'd made three wishes, and one after the other they were coming true. Perhaps this was my fresh beginning.

"You need not feel shame, I will be gentle with you," he promised. "But not tonight."

I gasped. "But. . ."

"But what?"

"Tonight is. . ." I trailed off while emotions warred within me. Part of me was relieved it would not be tonight, but I couldn't help the slight pinch of disappointment. I'd imagined, time and again, what it would be like to experience the throes of passion, for I'd heard tales that made my cheeks warm and my ears tingle. Arranged marriages were common, but I wished for love. Was it wrong to desire such a thing?

Zander slid his arms around my waist, pulling me against his warmth. When his lips pressed against my ear, my heart raced. "Trust me when I say, I will take you. I will make you writhe with desire. I'll make you hot and wet until you long for me, and me alone. You'll taste pleasure like you've tasted nothing before, and your cries of pleasure will be loud enough to wake the dead."

My face flamed with heat, and a warm and achy feeling crept over me. My limbs trembled as he stroked my bare skin and weaved his fingers through the laces of the dress, loosening them further. I clung to my dress, unsure if I was ready to be naked in front of him. Sensing my hesitation, he gently threaded his fingers through my hair and angled his head toward mine. His gaze flickered to my lips. "Should I make you wait?" he asked, a dark shadow passing over his face. Gone was the kindness, replaced by desire and dominance, and yet he restrained himself. "Or shall I give you a glimpse of pleasure to come?"

I could scarcely draw a breath. Who was I to deny the kiss of a king who looked like the sun god himself? Arousal stirred in my belly but I held myself still, very still, sure if I moved I'd break the spell. "Please," I murmured.

When his lips brushed mine, a tingling sensation went from my toes all the way to my fingertips. My head lolled to the side, and a sigh escaped my parted lips. It was both heady and delicious, and I felt as though his kiss awoke something inside of me. A deep carnal lust with a poignant desire for me. He tasted like sweet fruit and dark wine. Just as suddenly the kiss faded. I opened my eyes, and the room seemed to spin and dance.

Speech forsook my tongue, and my fingers trembled. Was this how it was supposed to be?

Zander released me and stepped back, his chest

rising and falling. Raising my open palm to his lips, he kissed it. "I look forward to getting to know you. Nesrin."

It was the third time he'd said my name, but this time it burned on his lips, along with the faint glow of the kiss, as though something had changed. I wanted another kiss, but he pivoted away. "Change. Sleep, and we shall see what daylight brings."

5

I EXPECTED to lie awake that night, but the events of the day had worn me out. As soon as I climbed into the bed, it swallowed me whole. I lay in a sweet sleep until a soft light and the scent of wild roses made me open my eyes. I stiffened, then recalled I no longer slept in the stifling attic on a lumpy mattress of prickly hay. I was wed to the king of the Rovers. Turning, I hoped to glimpse him, recalling the faint echo of his heated kiss. He hadn't returned by the time I'd changed into a soft white nightgown and lain down. My sleep had been so undisturbed, I was unsure if he'd slept on the other side of the bed at all. Sitting up, I folded my hands in my lap as I determined what to do. Zander—I assumed—controlled my destiny now, and uncertainty lay before me.

The tent flap opened, sending a breeze of warm air into the tent. Zander walked in, dressed in simple clothing. Gray pants, leather boots, and a plain blue shirt. The colors looked rich and only complimented his sandy blond hair and gray eyes. He smiled. "My lady, did you sleep well?"

I returned the smile. "I can't recall the last time I slept so well."

"Good. While you dress, I will find some breakfast." He ducked out again before I could say another word.

The trunk overflowed with dresses, and I couldn't believe all the beautiful clothing was my own. I slid into a pale yellow dress the color of daffodils blooming in the spring, and brushed my hair, leaving it loose as I waited for Zander. He returned promptly, a tray in hand, and set it down on the table. My eyebrows lifted as he sat in one chair and gestured for me to sit at the other. I knew nothing of the ways of Rovers, yet I found it disconcerting that he served me. Weren't kings and queens supposed to have servants to do their bidding?

"You don't have to wait on me," I said as I sat across from him.

He looked relaxed in the daylight, as though he did not have a care in the world. The formality of our marriage had faded away, and he looked more like the young man I'd met in the forest, and less like an intimidating king. I thought of the kiss we'd shared the evening before and hoped there would be more to come.

"I do," he said, taking a plate off the tray and filling it with bread, smoked meat, and fruit. "People assume being a king means I sit and wait for others to serve me. But that's not what it means at all, and if a king assumes such a position of privilege, he is mistaken. Being king means I serve the interests of my people, I protect them, provide for them, and do whatever I can to ensure their happiness. As my queen, I shall do the same for you."

I stared as his words sunk in. What a view he had of his duty as a king. "It sounds like servitude," I said, thinking of the way my step-mother had treated me.

Propping his elbows on the table, he tore apart a piece of meat and chewed it thoughtfully. "It is. And it isn't. Everyone here is well-treated, we are, mostly, equals, and if one has a complaint, it is brought before me and how to handle it discussed among the elders and voted on. But as king, I lead, as long as it is in the best interest of those who follow me. Say, for example, I choose to relocate the camp to the foothills of the fire-drake mountains. It would be foolhardy, since winter is coming, and the elders would veto that choice. Unless I gave a compelling reason, for example, the caves there are warm and stay dry. We would be protected from the winter snows. Then a vote would take place and we would go."

I considered his words as I took a bite of fruit. The sweet juices burst in my mouth. "It sounds like it takes a long time to decide anything, and the people choose."

"Indeed, but I am well respected for making good choices for the Rovers. Besides, if anyone dislikes the direction I take my people, they are free to leave. However, leaving is not without its perils."

"What perils?" I tilted my head and studied his relaxed attitude. He mentioned leaving. Would I be able to leave, should I choose?

"The enchanted wildwood is nearby, and we usually make camp close to it. It's rare, but sometimes the creatures of the wildwood attack. To wander alone is to make yourself vulnerable to the spirts."

I shivered and focused on my breakfast, wondering if he was warning me against running. "Why live so close to danger?"

"Land near the wildwood is free, and we are seldom welcome in the kingdom or the outer lands which are often the hold of nobles. Since there isn't a place for us, we take what we can get. Personally, I don't mind. The wildwood has its own kind of enchantment." He leaned forward and his voice softened. "When I first met you, you were in the wood, and I thought. . ." His gaze flickered to my pointed ears.

A flush crept up my neck. "What did you think?"

His hand crossed the small space between us, and his fingers rested on my wrist. "I thought you might be a wood nymph come to bless mere mortals with your magic."

I would have laughed if he hadn't said the forbidden word: *magic*. My thoughts went to the river goddess, and a lump swelled in my throat. Three wishes. Two had already come true. What price would she demand? Would I be able to pay it?

He pulled away. "You look upset."

"No," I snapped, taking a breath to calm myself. "It's just. . ." I fished for an answer that would satisfy him. "My father always spoke out against using magic and the consequences of it."

"I see." He cleared his throat.

I doubted he saw at all, and a tension hung between us, ruined by my worry.

"What will we do today?" I asked, changing the subject.

"It is up to you. I am at your disposal today." He placed a hand on his heart and bowed his head.

"Me?" Surprise took me again. "But this is your kingdom."

He stroked his jaw, then rose. "I will show it to you, if it pleases you, my lady."

"Call me Nesrin," I replied, standing.

He reached across the table and plucked an iris from a bouquet. He tucked it behind my ear before taking my hand in his. "Nesrin."

Zander held my hand as we walked throughout the camp. It was pleasant, a beautiful summer day with the trees providing ample shade from the heat. We strode among the wildflowers, moving away from the circle of colorful tents. The Rovers waved as we passed and continued to work, singing in low tunes, a jaunty melody that was carried to my ears by the breeze. I saw Naomi, sitting at a loom, weaving while children gathered around her, listening while she told them stories. People were everywhere, swaying to their own music and working in their own unique ways. Some chopped word, others carved, some played music, others danced, and I could see no rhythm or reason to it.

But Zander pulled me away from the camp and led me deeper into the grove, toward the glade where our wedding ceremony had taken place.

"What are your days like?" I asked.

"What do you mean?" He regarded me, the lines around his mouth turning up. "As in, what do I do all day?"

"When you aren't serving the people." I smiled, recalling his earlier words.

"It varies. When we aren't traveling there's hunting, fighting, negotiations, in time, you'll see. But I don't wish to bore you with the nuances of my daily routine."

"Is it not why I'm here? To help you?"

"Aye, but only in part. I would have you enjoy your days, not drown yourself in duty. But you carry on your father's work?"

I pressed my lips together. "I wanted to, but. . ." my thoughts went to my father's death and the burden of grief that sat heavy on my heart. His decline was slow. I'd known it was coming, and so did he. And yet, it still hurt knowing I wouldn't be able to sit with him in his workshop, crushing herbs while he mixed them. Talking of leaves and their properties and mixing them together. And sometimes, when I was brave enough, I'd ask about my mother and he'd tell me the tale of how he met her. A human and an elf. The impossible made possible.

Zander squeezed my hand. "I want to show you something."

Thankful for the change in conversation, we moved on to where mushrooms and wildflowers grew around the trees. We walked until we came to a glade where a circle of trees stood. Just beyond was the yawning, dark beginnings of the enchanted wildwood. A thrill went through me, the dreaded, forbidden place, where it was said that evil walked and crept out to steal those who were unaware away. Again, I wondered why the Rovers were so bold to camp so close to such a place. It seemed as if they were forcing the hand of the wildwood and inviting the creatures to attack them.

"Does it frighten you?" His voice was low, reverent.

"A bit." I shuddered. "You know the tales."

"Aye, that's why you are here," he admitted. "I do not mean it to frighten you, but Rovers have enemies too. There are those who seek to take over, to frighten us away. Before your father passed, he was working on something. I was rather hoping you'd take up where he left off, for you too have the gift."

I thought I knew what he was talking about, and I didn't think I had it in me. "What do you mean?" I glanced again at the wildwood and swallowed hard. "What is it you want me to do? You keep mentioning I have the gift, but my father worked on many things before he passed. I was only his assistant." My thoughts went back to the book I'd kept tucked under my pillow. I wondered if it was still there, and if I'd have a chance to return to my father's house and retrieve it. Some potions I knew by heart, but others, I'd need his words to familiarize myself with the steps.

Zander took a long breath and crossed his arms over his chest. "I wanted you to enjoy today, but I must be honest with you. We have enemies. I say this, not to frighten you but to help you understand our need. There is another tribe which hunts us, hoping to take over our land. They still believe in the old ways, of blood sacrifices to the wildwood. They are much larger and it is only a matter of time until they catch up with us, again. Which why we move frequently. We just want to be free, to dwell in nature, to come and go as we please, but the festival of Lammas draws near, and they usually come eight times a year, during the festivals, to take my people and sacrifice them to the wildwood. They claim it prevents the evil from escaping, but those days are past. A new queen dwells in the wildwood and protects those outside of it with her magic. I want my people to be happy."

It was as though he'd opened his heart to me and I saw his hidden desire, his need to provide peace and happiness for his people. It was why he was a king, why he served. It was his duty, and yet he believed in it wholeheartedly. My heart went out to him and I felt the threads of kinship, even as he asked for my help. Now the words of Naomi made sense. Was he forced to choose me because I was the only one who could help him, help his tribe? Suddenly I wanted to do everything in my power for him, even though a slight inkling told me what he would ask of me would be next to impossible. Unless, once again, I used forbidden magic. But the consequences, I didn't even know if I'd reap the consequences of what I'd sown. Had it only been yesterday at the river?

"I've heard tale of a man so strong he could hold off the creatures of the wildwood. I spoke to your father of this, and he said it might be possible to create a strength potion. It would last only a few hours, but it would be long enough to vanquish the tribe that haunts us. I'd hoped we'd lost their trail, but scouts reported seeing them a few weeks away. If they are coming, it will be for Lammas. I need your help. I asked, but your step-mother clarified your duties were too much to spare you. We made a deal, but now I know you were unaware of it, I will release you from your vow. I hope you'll stay, but if you do this, if you create the strength potion, you are free to go. I will not hunt you down. I will not make you stay if it goes against your heart's desire."

6

ZANDER'S WORDS stayed with me. I should have been angry with his actions, the way he'd chosen me and almost forced me to grant his wish. But I'd been so lowly, beat down and sad for so long, I did not have it in me to be angry with him. His apology, laced with words of need, was acceptable, and my mind was drawn again and again to the key fact that he was my husband.

Why? That was part of the deal I did not understand. Did my step-mother have something to do with it? I did not need to be his wife to create a potion, yet he'd married me in front of all the Rovers.

Zander woke me in the same manner the next morning, a light step at the tent entrance, and then the promise of breakfast while I dressed. I selected a pale blue dress. Was this real? I felt as though I'd passed into a dream, to another world where my worries melted away. I even pushed the niggling sensation that all wasn't well away.

Zander returned with a tray of food, a question in

his gray eyes. I sat across from him and took a breath, recalling his words from yesterday. Free to leave if I completed our bargain. "What would you like to do today, Nesrin?" he asked.

My cheeks curved up into a smile, I could get used to this. Instead of shouting I was served a meal and asked what I wanted to do. It felt good, as though a token of power had been passed to me, and he'd do anything, everything in his power to make me happy. To ensure I stayed. And if it was because of what I could give, then I would.

"I need to gather herbs," I explained. "Roots, mainly, they grow in the thick shade of woods, I thought I saw a likely spot yesterday."

"In the enchanted wildwood?" He raised an eyebrow but the way his lips curled up told me he was teasing.

"No." I bit into a hunk of bread. "Not there, plenty of herbs and roots grow outside its boundaries, although I assume the herbs within likely carry properties I am unsure how to use. And. . ." I trailed off, wondering if I should tell him about the book I needed to retrieve from my father's house. I had no desire to break the spell of happiness that had been cast upon me and return to that house, see my step-mother, and be reminded of what had happened there. Since I was only beginning to get to know Zander, I didn't want him to see the house, to see my old room and the cloud of shame that hung over that place.

His warm hand on mine jerked me out of my thoughts. "What is it, my lady?"

"Nothing." I tugged my thoughts back to the present.

"It's just, you spent the day with me yesterday. I don't want to take up all of your time."

Placing his hand on his heart, he leaned forward, his tone soft. "It is by choice, Nesrin. I am king here. I choose how to spend my days, and if it is with you, my lovely new wife, then so be it. Never worry about taking up my time, if an urgent need arises, my men will tell me. Right now, my duty is to you. I want you to feel welcome, comfortable here. Besides, I've admired you from afar, now I'd like to admire you right next me."

My fingers squeezed his hand as tears sprung to my eyes. The way he spoke chased away my remaining worries. He was real and honest and true, and sitting before me. I didn't want to wait until the river goddess summoned me with a dire consequence. No, I wanted to enjoy my life, no matter how long or short time might be. The time of waiting, and hanging back, and staying quiet, and letting things happen to me was over.

"Zander?"

"Yes?"

"Thank you," I whispered. "You don't know what those words mean to me, so thank you."

Lifting my hand to his lips, he kissed it. "Let's go see Naomi, she will have whatever is needed for herb gathering."

Hand in hand we strode through the camp which swayed with its own rhythm. Once again, I was surprised at how happy, and peaceful it seemed. "It is always like this?"

"More or less." Zander shrugged. "The people are content, happy for now and looking forward to the first harvest. Afterward, we'll move to another village where we can sell our wares or trade for supplies we need for the impending winter. Then we'll travel south, where the winters are less harsh and return here again when the spring comes."

I'd never traveled, and the thought of it sounded both intimidating and exciting. "Do you like it? Always traveling, with no place to call home?"

"Home," he mused. "What is home to you?"

I shrugged. "The house that I live in."

"But a house is only wood and stone. It is a structure, and one can be built anywhere. For me, the world is my home and while I enjoy living under open skies, it is the people that truly make a home, and home is wherever my people are happy. That is what home is to me, and so no, I don't mind traveling. In fact, I look forward to it. What upsets me the most is those who hunt down my people, who make us feel as though this is not our home. I hope to change all of that. To make us untouchable."

His words sent an ache through my heart, and I thought I detected an edge of sadness in his tone. A sadness that reminded me I did not know all about my golden king. But before I could ask more, we reached Naomi's tent and turned to the task of gathering herbs.

ON THE SEVENTH MORNING, Zander awoke me with a light kiss on my cheek. I'd grown used to his familiar caress although he did not attempt to take me. Yet his bright eyes glazed over, darkened sometimes when he looked at me. I understood he waited for my word, and yet his patience might be wearing. I wondered how long he would keep his distance. Seven days and I already longed for his embrace, looked forward to his kisses and what words he'd use to tease me.

"Nesrin," he whispered, his voice husky with sleep.

My eyelids fluttered, and I smiled at him, reaching over to take his hand in mine. I liked the weight of it, the feel of his warm body in the bed next to mine. The moment was so pure, so far from what my life had been a week ago, that I wanted nothing more than to stay in his arms, in his bed.

I turned my face toward his, words thick in my throat. I did not know him well, but everything he'd said and done in the short time we'd been married, made me determined to stay. If he wished it.

"Did you mean it?" I asked. "When you said I can leave, if I want to?"

His eyes darkened, and he pulled away. I watched him frown as he struggled to control himself. And then, "Aye. I am a man of my word. If you wish it. . ."

"I don't," I faltered, the confession burning on my lips.

"You don't," he confirmed, drawing me into his arms.

So far, I'd stayed burrowed on one side of the bed, hiding under the covers in my thin, sleeveless nightgown. The nights were warm, but I liked to sleep under the blankets and hoped my presence did not disturb Zander. Each morning and evening I dressed behind a screen, and Zander let me have my privacy. But now, one arm tucked over my body, he hovered over me, using his free hand to smooth my wild hair back from my face and cup my cheek. He smiled, but his eyes were dark as he lowered his face over mine, his gaze flickering to my lips. Dully I thought of morning breath and wild, unbrushed hair, but Zander did not seem to care. "Your words give me hope," he admitted. "Hope that you will not change your mind.

"Not likely," I murmured, wrapping my fingers around the hard muscle of his upper arm. "I am your wife, and now I have a purpose. Besides, I have nowhere else to go."

Moving his thumb up and down, circling the swell of my cheek, he leaned closer. I took a shaky breath, my heart thrumming widely. I wondered if he could hear it, if he knew how much his presence aroused me. "You never have to be shy with me, Nesrin. If your desire to stay is because of me, I would accept it. I did not need much convincing to marry you. When we met in the woods, I had hope. But now you are my wife, and you have choosen to be my wife, does it mean I can kiss you anytime I'd like to?" He leaned closer.

"Anytime," I repeated, glad I was lying down because my knees felt weak. A hint of hot heat made me want to squeeze my legs together.

When his lips met mine, they were gentle and sweet, sending trills of excitement up and down my spine. I clung to him as he parted my lips with his tongue. It was probing as he swept into my mouth, deepening the kiss. I'd experienced nothing like it. My body arched up, pressing against his and something hard pressed against my belly. My breath caught as I realized what it was, but instead of nervous fear, I only felt anticipation.

I closed my eyes just to feel, to delight in the pleasures he pulled from my body. His hand pressed against my side, near the curve of my breasts, and his groan of delight made me all the more excited. Encouraged that he wanted me.

But the sound of his name made me stiffen. "Zander!"

One of his men stood outside the tent, calling out, his voice low, urgent. "Zander!"

Zander broke the kiss and lifted his head, eyes alert. A low groan of disappointment escaped from his lips and he kissed me again before whispering in my ear. "I will have you, my queen, naked in my bed when I return."

7

AFTER ZANDER'S HASTY EXIT, I lay in bed a while longer, catching my breath before rising. With him out of the way, I knew I needed to do two things. One was to return to the river and see if the goddess would speak with me again. The second was to somehow, someway, sneak back to my father's home. I refused to think of it as now belonging to my step-mother, but I needed my father's notes if I were to craft a potion that would give the Rovers extraordinary strength. Thus far, I'd gathered roots and herbs, all with properties of strength, and I made my way to the tent where they were stored. I wasn't ready to crush and boil them yet, for although I had ideas of my own, I needed my father's notes first.

Naomi was waiting for me when I slipped inside, her white hair pulled back in a bun at the nape of her neck. "Lady Nesrin," she greeted me.

She pointed to a plate of food. Perching on the edge of a chair, I wolfed down the food while Naomi moved around the tent, organizing jars and baskets, even though they were in order already.

"Naomi?" I asked between bites. "I have a question."

"Ask," she encouraged.

I warmed to her. "I need to return to my father's house. There's something there of great importance that I left behind. Zander is busy today and I'm not sure who else to ask. Do I need to seek permission to leave these lands?"

Naomi's face went pale, and she twisted her hands together. "Leave? My lady, it is not wise without the king's permission. . ." she trailed off, hands on her hips.

"Yes," I lowered my voice. "He told me about the tribes that attack from time to time. I am aware of the danger but, no one knows who I am, and it is perfectly safe in Gebeth."

Naomi frowned. "You are precious to the king, I will not have you leave on my watch. When he returns, it will be safe." Moving closer, she placed a hand on my arm and gently squeezed. "He is happy with you, don't give him reason to grieve. Again."

There was no one else in the tent, but still, I lowered my voice. "Again? Did something happen?"

Naomi's bottom lip trembled, and her eyes filled with tears. She turned her back to me and there were some moments before she spoke. "Aye, during the last attack they stole his family. He never intended to be king, at least not this young, and he's determined they won't have more." She spun back around, taking my hands, a desperation on her face. "You will help him, won't you?"

Thoughts tumbled and twisted in my head. His

family? Did it mean he'd been married before? And I'd never asked where his parents were, or if he had siblings. Embarrassment rose. What must he think of me? I'd been so concerned about myself I hadn't asked him, hadn't pried deeper.

"His family?" I repeated, woodenly.

Naomi stared off. "I'm not sure I should tell you this." Her voice caught. "I don't intend to frighten you."

I lifted my chin. "I am not frightened," I assured her.

"They came one night, weaving through the celebration like the shadows of trees. They always take the women first, and this time was no different. They stole Zander's mother, Lilith, and his sister, Lavender, and left us stumbling in the wood, fighting off warriors with their tricks. Their magic. By the time we fought through, it was too late."

A strangled cry came from her throat, and even though I didn't know her, the empathy in me rose. I threw my arms around her, squeezing her tight, reminded of when my father passed. The overwhelming sorrow had been too much, had threatened to bury me with the numb sense of hopelessness. Why go on, when life would never be the same? Was there hope in the face of death? Would the tears ever dry? And then I understood why Zander had done what he had done. Right or wrong, I understood his pain, his need. I blurted the words out, "I'll do whatever it takes to help, but I need my father's notes."

Naomi squeezed me back. "It shall be done."

Later that afternoon, pulse pounding, I rode out with Naomi and two of the warriors. The feel of a wild horse beneath me reminded me of days when my father taught me how to ride. I'd gallop across the fields, shrieking with laughter, my hair flying out wildly behind me. The way the wind blew made me feel light as a feather, as though I could fly away, like the birds that migrate during the winter, flying away to warmer places. Whenever I rode a horse, it made me feel alive.

The Rovers weren't as far from the village as I expected. All too soon, our quick ride ended, much faster than a carriage ride, and we pulled up in front of the house. It was just the same, hard to believe I'd left it only seven days ago. I thought about what I'd say to my step-mother, and my mouth went dry. Slowly, I dismounted, and Naomi rested a hand on my shoulder. The bruises had faded under her care and yet haunted memories hung around that house. Both good and bad. Together we walked up to the door, and I swallowed hard at the thought of seeing my step-mother's deceptive face again. But when we reached the door, it stood ajar.

I swallowed hard, and raised my hand to knock, but Naomi pushed it further open. Immediately I saw an empty room, and the silence was deafening. They were gone. My thoughts returned to the pouch of money Zander had handed my step-mother. She must have used it to return to the kingdom, to leave the backward village of Gebeth where hopes and dreams died. A sense of relief passed over me, and even though the house held ghosts of the past, vague memories, I walked through it, waving Naomi away.

She must have sensed that I needed time, and let me trail up the staircase alone, back to the attic. It was just as hot and stuffy as I had left it, the room just the same.

I looked at my poor belongings, an echo of the fear I'd once had slipping away. There was something pure about coming back to an empty house, as though everything that had happened had been erased and given a fresh start.

The thought made me want to leave and return to my new life. And so I dug under the mattress until I found my father's notes, and hurried away, leaving everything else behind. I was no longer Nesrin of Gebeth. I was Nesrin, Queen of the Rovers, who would create a potion to protect my people. I was ready; I was strong.

But as I left the house and traveled back to the rover camp, I couldn't help but glance toward the path that led to the river. Perhaps my fate should be left to the unknown. Perhaps if I ignored the river goddess, she'd forget the three wishes she'd granted me and let me live out my days in happiness. Perhaps there would be no consequences for my actions. And so I pushed the dark thought that something terrible might happen aside and choose to live out my days in happiness. For my fortune had changed and my three wishes, if not true already, were well on their way of coming true.

8

THREE DAYS LATER, he still hadn't returned. A scout came to tell us of the delay, and yet my heart twisted as the camp waited for the return of the king. I poured myself into my work, a welcome distraction, and by the end of the third day, I completed a potion. An experiment. I drank it down, hoping to feel a tingling sensation, a sign that I'd gained additional strength. But there was only the heady warmth of drinking a potion, nothing else. I'd worked side by side with my father to know the first option was rarely the final version, but I had little time left to tinker with it before the need for it arose.

Naomi drew a hot bath for me. I relaxed my muscles in the warm water, but I couldn't help running the potion over in my mind, trying to determine what I could improve. A weariness sank over me as I thought of it. Time was ticking, and although I should not, under any circumstance, use magic again, what if I did, just this once? But no one could know. I'd have to sneak away under the pretense of gathering herbs and make my way back to the river. Decision made, I climbed out of the bath and I went to my tent to rest.

I AWOKE in the half light, to his arm curled around my waist, his breath against my neck. "Zander," I whispered, a sense of relief sweeping over me, surprising me with the strength of it.

I liked that he'd returned and held me so close, giving me a sense of security.

"I'm sorry I was gone so long," he lamented. "I did not intend to leave you so soon."

Blinking my drowsiness away, I tilted my head toward his. "All is well, I had my work."

"Still," he said, his fingers inching my nightgown up around my hips. "I feel I neglected you."

"You are here now," I breathed.

He placed his hand on the flat of my bare stomach, his voice turning deeper. "All the same, I missed you."

Missed me? My breath went ragged. "I missed you too," I dared to say back as my heart raced.

"Is that so?" He swept my nightgown up, and I allowed him to lift it over my head, exposing my body to him for the first time.

Every nerve in my body tingled, waiting for him to touch me. His hand came up, lazily playing with my breasts, squeezing gently as he traced slow circles around my nipples. My heart beat quickened, but I lay still, unwilling to break the spell with more words. Every stroke ignited something within. It felt good, better than I expected. His fingers were gentle and brought out the part of me that lay trapped. Desire. Pleasure. My nipples hardened under his touch and my breath came faster.

Heat flared between my thighs and a wetness pooled there. My face flushed with heat, glad for the cover of night to hide my arousal, although my nipples betrayed me. He moved to my other breast, those lazy circles driving me wild. An ache built between my legs and with each touch it grew stronger. That want. That desperate need. Desire. This was what others experienced, wasn't it? This was what I had been missing and oh, it was delightful. How had I not known? How had I missed out on this my entire life? Sheltered away from the intensity of what could be.

When he took one of my nipples between two fingers and squeezed, I couldn't help the pant of pleasure that burst from my lips, my mouth open, breath hissing out, moaning as he awoke everything that had been buried deep. The need for love, for pleasure, to be held, to be wanted. It was so beautiful, so powerful, I almost missed it when he trapped one of my legs between his, opening my most secret place to him.

My breath hitched and a gasp burst from my lips. He held my erect nipple with on hand, continuing to squeeze the tender skin, and then his mouth was against my ear. Wet lips nipped at my earlobe, and his honeyed whisper came. "If you ask me to stop, I will."

"Don't stop," I begged and drew in a deep breath, fighting for control as his other hand slid down my belly in slow strokes, touching, tip-toping around my belly button, sending shivers across my skin. Could he feel how hot I was for him, how much I needed him?

"Let go of your inhibitions, just experience it," he encouraged.

His fingers moved lower, just about the soft hairs. He palmed my quivering folds and kissed my lips, teeth biting, lips sucking. I opened my mouth, gasping as he eased one finger down into my wetness. My entire body shuddered from the touch. He pulled back, his finger-tips grazing my heated core, then opening my folds his finger dove inside, exploring, touching, sending shivers of desire up and down my spine. All the while, his other hand played with my nipple, squeezing, releasing, tracing circles, and then squeezing again. He held my body in suspended delight and my cries of pleasure became louder, faster as he played with me.

When he slipped one finger inside, all the way to the knuckle, my entire body arched up toward him. My hips bucked on their own accord. The control I held over my body had slipped away completely into his hands. My skin felt hot, flushed under his touch, and when he pulled out and slipped his finger back inside, sawing back and forth, my hips moved, forcing me onto him. I struggled for my trapped leg to help me move, but he held me firm. When I tried again, his hand came back and slapped my wetness. A sharp gasp from my lips. A slap! But it wasn't painful at all. Instead, pleasure shot through every nerve of my body and a shrill scream of pleasure came from my lips.

This time he added two fingers, spreading me, pushing me open, readying me for him. He pulled out again and played with my hard nub, rubbing my wetness over it. My chest heaved, and I thought I'd spring off the bed. Deep shudders wracked my body, and I moved against him, wanting, nay, needing more. It wasn't enough! And even as I thought it, I felt a deep stirring in the pit of my belly. Something was building, growing, and a frenzy came over me, a panic. I struggled wildly in his arms, ragged gasps bursting from my lips. What was this? These sensations, these feelings? Was this what making love was? This purity, this rapture? I thought I'd explode, erupt. I'd never felt such sensations, such pleasure, and with each move he seemed to wind me tighter, move me to another level.

He licked my earlobe, pinched my nipple, and kissed me breathless. I pulsated around him, another scream leaving my lips. I thought he added a third finger, but I couldn't be sure. I was skewered on him, panting, heedless of anything and everything but the way he drove me wild.

And then he moved, spreading my legs wider and pushing his hardness against me. I reached up, my fingers digging into his shoulders as he covered my mouth with his and slipped inside. I cried out and everything exploded. White hot stars danced around me and the very tent spun as he moved inside me. His body was slick with sweat, but my legs were weak, trembling under him. I cried out again and again as I spasmed around him, faintly aware of his strangled grunts and bliss surrounded me. I wanted more.

9

"I'M SORRY ABOUT YOUR FAMILY," I whispered in the half light, when I could breathe again. I lifted a hand to touch him, my fingers brushing the stubble on his jaw.

Instead of responding with words, his arms tightened around me. I felt the uptick of his heartbeat as though I'd touched a fragile part of his heart and fresh blood spilled. He was still for a long moment, and I'd almost drifted to sleep when his words came again. "I'm sorry. It was selfish of me to drag you into this feud. I'm sorry."

I was too sleepy to think about his words or even respond. I drifted off to a pleasurable sleep.

The sun was up when I woke next, and I felt a slight ache down there. Zander still lay beside me, his chest rising and falling as he slept. Sometime in the night we'd shifted positions, and he no longer held me. I sat up slowly, hoping I wouldn't wake him. My thoughts drifted back to his last words. He was sorry. Which implied he'd done something wrong. A sensation of uneasiness passed over me as I slipped out of bed to wash up, for there was blood between my thighs.

My face heated each time I thought of what had happened last night. It had been more, much more than the tales I'd heard. I wondered if there would be blood next time. As I washed, I touched my lower belly, but other than a slight tenderness, there was nothing else to remind me of what had taken place. So that was what everyone talked about, the hidden whispers, the secret pleasures. A smile came to my lips, and I quickly hid it behind my hands. Peeking over the screen, I studied Zander on the bed. His blond hair was tousled, one arm flung over his head. He looked so peaceful. I couldn't hold back the smile, and I thought I might be falling in love with my husband.

This time, I'd be the one to bring us breakfast. I slipped out of the tent to find Naomi, humming as I moved between the tents. I sniffed the air, surprised I didn't smell the scent of cooking. And it was quiet. Far too quiet. Where were the children? My feet slowed to a stop, and I looked at the colorful tents flapping in the breeze. What if? But I wasn't able to finish the thought when a rough male voice called, "There she is!"

I spun and saw two men running toward me. They were big, stocky brutes of men with thick corded muscles and enormous noses. They looked alike. Twins? With knives in hand and black scarves around their necks. A scream escaped my throat. "Zander," I shouted, realizing I was too far away from his tent to warn him. "Zander!"

And then I took off running, toward the wood and down the track where I got married. Where had the thieves come from? Had they snuck up in the night? My breath came thick and fast, the first sign of panic. I forced it down, forced it away as tears threatened to ruin my concentration. I hadn't need to run before, but I was small and swift, my elvish blood allowing me to maneuver quickly through the trees. If only my heavy breathing wouldn't give me away. I scrambled down a slight rise, almost tearing my slippers as I ran among bushes and brambles.

Behind me, I heard a curse. They were coming. They were coming fast! Tears filled my eyes as I pushed my burning feet onward. What had they done with Zander? What had they done with the Rovers? Had they snuck up in the dead of night and slaughtered them all? Or held them as prisoners? And why did they want me? What had I done?

I rounded a curve and dashed behind some trees, working hard to curb loud breaths. The two men came closer, and between the thick foliage I saw their knives glinting in the light. Pressing both hands to my mouth to keep from crying out, I watched as they slowed, eyes on the ground, searching for my tracks. Were they trackers? Hunters? If so, I'd done a poor job at hiding. Keeping as silent as I could, I moved, continuing downhill through the trees. I wasn't in the wildwood, but I could see the enchanted forest looming on one side and I was close, too close to its heavy boughs and dark fumes. Glancing at it gave me pause and then came a shout. "There she is!"

I pushed myself onward, my feet kicking up dust as I fled. Why had I slowed down? Why had I stopped? They were far too close and, slim and fast as I was, they were catching up. I could taste blood in my throat as I pushed myself on, legs pumping, arms swinging. The trees thinned, giving way to the strength of sunlight. A light breeze blew past me, but sweat dripped down my neck and made my dress cling to my body. A sob burst out of my mouth as fingers snatched at my dress and missed.

They were going to take me. What would they do with me? It was that fear that gave me one last surge of speed. Ahead of me I saw the winding river that flowed from Gebeth into the enchanted wildwood. I'd never considered whether what was in the wildwood came out, using the river, but a sudden chill came over me as I ran toward it.

The waters moved as I fled toward them, the gentle hum of the river turning into something else, something dangerous. The roar of a wave came and a cyclone of water rose, spinning, terrifying, as silver droplets sprayed the air. My fleet feet came to a pause, and I stood in the tall grass, eyes wide as I stared. The wall of water fell with a splash, sending mud and water overflowing onto the bank. And there she was.

Fear churned in my belly and bile rose in my throat, even though I hadn't had a bite to eat—or drink. The creature that rose out of the waters was none other than the river goddess herself, scales glistening in the light, her mud-colored face gleaming as she laid eyes on me. My heart beat a rhythm in my ears. All the breath left my body as I stared at her malicious face, and my father's words came back to me. *Never use magic. No matter how bad it gets. The cost is not worth it.*

"Nesrin of Gebeth," she quipped, a coldness worse than death in her tone. "You've returned to my waters.

A timely return, for I have need of you. It's time to pay for your wishes."

My throat went tight. She hadn't forgotten. But one glance at her round eyes told me I could not hope for favors. I opened my mouth to respond and found that I was trembling all over. The shaking overcame me from head to toe because I knew I'd meddled with a darkness I did not understand.

"It's time for you to pay the toll," the river goddess went on. "It's time for you to die."

Die. The world jolted me and protests rose on my lips. What had I done to deserve death? A ragged cry tore from my lips and I spun, but the men were on either side, eyes glittering as they approached me. I turned back to the river goddess, clasping my hands in front of me as I sank to my knees. "Please. Not death. Anything else, but not death."

She wrinkled her nose and narrowed her eyes before pointing a finger at me. "You were the one who came to my waters. You begged me for three wishes. Wishes which I granted, in exchange. Are you saying you don't want to keep up your end of the bargain? You don't want to make an exchange?"

"Yes, no," I cried, misery engulfing me as I realized I was trapped. Bitterness laced my words. "What is the point in granting me three wishes if you're going to take away my life? In doing so, you nullify the wishes."

The river goddess had the audacity to laugh. Head thrown back, droplets of water shimmering off her glistening scales. Her laugh was rough, laced with something deeper. Something that forced an undercurrent of fear to swim through me.

"It's magic," the river goddess snapped, her expression changing from mirth to annoyance. "You'll pay the price, whether you like it or not. You were the one who did not name the terms, who asked for three foolish wishes. One only has so long until payment is due. When you entered my waters, I felt it, I knew there was something different about you, and the time, the time is almost right. Take her away," she snarled to the men. "Prepare for the ritual."

I opened my mouth to respond, to protest. The men on either side of me grabbed my arms. A scream tore out of my throat, but one man pressed a cloth against my face. It smelled like mist and fog, with a sharp acid tang. I took a breath, recognizing the scent. It was a herb to make one pass out, generally used if someone were in pain from an injury, it was a way to give them some peace while their wounds were treated. Knowing it was being used on me made me terrified, and even as a wave of blackness passed over me, I fought for consciousness. My eyelids fluttered, heavy with the need to close. I lost control of my limbs. As I went limp, I was vaguely aware of the two men lowering me to the ground. A sob escaped my lips. My last conscious thought was: *I don't want to die.*

10

A POUNDING headache woke me from my unwanted slumber. My head rested against something damp, cold, and hard. A stone? My eyelids fluttered as I tried to make sense of where I was. I lifted a hand to my head, and it all came crashing back. My beautiful night with Zander, waking in the peaceful tent only to be chased down by the men, and captured by the river goddess. It was all my fault, wasn't it? If I hadn't used magic, none of this would have happened. I couldn't be sure, but Zander had chosen me long ago, perhaps my fate would have changed, without the use of magic. I sank down into the darkness, wishing again for the herb to put me out of my misery, let me forget. Hot tears streamed down my cheeks, as I lay still, trying to let my headache evaporate so I could figure out what to do. But it wouldn't go away.

Finally, the stuffiness of the place where I was being held and the prickliness of the hay made me sit up. It was dark out. From what I could tell, I sat in a barn, with the scent of animal musk around me. In fact, I could hear a beast chewing, the sound oddly comforting in the darkness. I lifted my hands and touched my head, surprised I was free to move. But when I stood, there was a tug at my ankle. I'd been tied by my foot to the stall and could only move in a small circle. Sitting down again, I felt for the rope in the darkness, and my fingers happened on a knot. It was tight, but I worked at it. If I could free myself and escape, I wouldn't have to die.

My thoughts raced back to the rover camp. What had happened? Was Zander still alive? Lammas was almost here. Had they taken Zander? Would they sacrifice him? Although Naomi said it was only the women whom they sacrificed to the wildwood. I'd heard tales of those bloody sacrifices and wondered what it meant for me. Why did the river goddess want me, especially, to die? It wasn't because of the deal, or lack of deal, I'd made with her. Her words made me shiver, for it felt as though she'd chosen me, because I was Nesrin, just as Zander had chosen me.

One of my nails bent and broke, sending a sharp pain up my arm. A curse escaped my lips, but I redoubled my efforts. I had to escape. I wouldn't let them sacrifice me. Again I thought of Zander's face, the anguish behind his voice when he spoke of his family. I was going the same way they were, wasn't I? It wasn't fair.

I worked on the knot until my nails broke and my fingers bled. It didn't budge. My head swam, but at least the headache lessened as the light grew. I didn't notice it at first, but there it was, a gray light bringing a whisper of a breeze. I listened as I worked, even though it was useless, it felt good for my hands to be doing something.

The sound of a door swinging open made me lift my head and a beam of sunlight filled the room. They came with the light, walking out of the mist with their long black robes flapping in the breeze. Every part of their skin was covered, from the gloves on their hands to the masks on their faces. The only feature displayed were their eyes, some hard and cruel, others softer, almost gentle. Men and women. Was this the tribe Zander had spoken of? Who were they? Outlaws? Those who followed the old ways, making blood sacrifices for protection? I assumed that's what I was, for I could make no other headway. I was to be a Lammas sacrifice to the wildwood. That's why I had to die. They would get protection, and as for the river goddess, well, I wasn't sure what she would gain. She had her reasonings, and it did not matter, it only mattered that I hadn't escaped in the night.

I stumbled to rise on numb feet, moving back toward the wall as a sniffling cry left my lips. Cold sweat dripped down my back and my heart raced. They wouldn't. They couldn't! But words hung in my throat and unable to scream, unable to beg them to let me live, I only gave a brief struggle as they surrounded me. They tied my arms behind my back and pulled a hood over my face. I stumbled as I was led out, I thought, but the hood over my face was thick and allowed me to only see varying shades of light. I was told to climb up into what felt like a wagon and sit again on yet another bed of prickly hay. I was beginning to hate the feel of hay itself.

An itch rose in my nose and I sneezed. A horse whinnied, and the wagon set off with a jolt.

I was bumped and jolted the entire way until it felt like my teeth had come loose and rolled around in my jaw. I had no idea how long it had been, but my head was pounding and my eyes smarted with tears when the wagon stopped. They hauled me down and led me somewhere stuffy and too warm. I waited, arms still tied, knees drawn up, waiting for death.

At some point, I must have fallen asleep, for I recalled dreaming of my mother. Which was odd. Her face was one I hardly saw in dreams, for I could barely recall what she looked like. She stood in a field, dotted with majestic trees which seemed to reach the ancient blue sky and graze the fluffy white clouds that drifted lazily through it. Laughing, mother spun around, her chestnut colored hair flying in the breeze. Cupping her hands, she smiled at me.

Why are you smiling? I asked.

Because of the magic. She winked. *It is within you.*

Frowning, I replied. *No, it isn't. If that were true, I wouldn't be where I am now.*

She shook her head, a smile still playing around her lips. *Oh, sweetheart, you are where you are because of it.*

WHEN THEY CAME for me it was late. I smelled the smoke from a fire and heard chanting as they removed my hood and led me out. There were two on either side, women, I thought, because of their slim forms even the robes could not hide. Leaving my arms tied behind my back, they grasped my elbows and led me out into the twilight. I swallowed hard, my throat dry from lack of water, but my stomach churned, too nervous to recall I hadn't eaten in almost a day. At least, that was how long I thought it had been.

They led me down a path between the weaving trees, where fairy lights brightened the way. I couldn't help but think of my wedding for it was a similar procession. But instead of walking freely, with flowers in my hair and hands, I was led unwillingly down the path toward the flickering bonfire where the assembly was gathered.

The darkness made it difficult to see how many there were, dressed in black, chanting and weaving between the shadows as we approached. In the background I saw a thick forest, it had to be the enchanted wildwood, and beneath the scent of fire I smelled bog water. River water. I shifted my gaze to the right, and sure enough, we'd come to a place where the riverbank curved away, leading further into the thick wood.

The river goddess must have come to watch. But why?

Numbly I allowed myself to be led up past the fire, sparks hissing, to an altar crafted out of stones. It was higher than my waist, and I realized what their intention was as the rope binding my arms was cut. I cried out as my arms came back to life, pinpricks of pain shooting up and down them. But my captors paid no heed, only chanted in low voices as they lifted me up onto the stones. Four of them bound me in place, lifting my arms above my head and securing the rope to my ankles. I was laid out as a sacrifice to the wildwood. As they retreated, the surrealness of my situation melted away, replaced with hard, cold, fear.

For all my life, I'd let experiences happen to me. I'd let my father teach me how to craft potions, I'd let my step-mother abuse me, and I'd let grief overcome my desires and needs. But it was Zander who'd showed me. Despite taking me as his own, he was willing to give me anything, everything I wanted. It was he who was concerned about my happiness, even though he wanted to protect his people. And now, before I could find out what kind of life I could have with him, or save his people, I'd been laid out to die. Just because I wished. Nay. It wasn't my three wishes that summoned the death bell. It was the river goddess.

Above the chanting I could almost hear her laughing, and hate rose thick in my gut, swelling, growing, building. A buzzing began in the back of my mind and my fingers tightened into fists, despite my bounds. What right did the river goddess have to determine who lived and who died? What right did she have to take away my happiness? Deserved or not, I would take it. It was time to stop being passive and letting things happen to me. It was time to take control. Why hadn't I fought earlier?

A shadow rose beside me. A man with a curved knife raised in his gloved hand. I opened my mouth and screamed.

11

THE ROAR that flooded my ears sounded like a wave of rushing water. I arched my back and strained about my bounds with all my might as a rush of energy filled me. Vaguely I heard shouting as though it came from far away. "Now! Do it now!"

The figure holding the knife glided closer and, holding the blade with both fists, hovered it over my heart. I thrashed as he lifted the blade high and a flash of light split my vision. I yanked hard on my bonds as fury twisted through me and a wave of rage I did not recognize in myself. This man did not know me at all, and yet he would take my life as a blood sacrifice. Hatred made my screams taste like ash in my mouth, and there came a ripping sound as something tore free. It took me a moment to realize it was the rope that held me, shredding.

But it was too late. The knife descended, aimed toward my heart. Quick as a flash, as though it were not myself making the movement, I brought my fist up and punched the man's wrists. He gave a cry of surprise. Taking advantage of his disconcertion, I brought my knee up and kicked out. My heel slammed into his belly and he dropped the knife with a groan. I snatched it up in my hands and rolled to a crouch in one fluid motion.

My screaming had stopped. The chanting died away and a sea of shadows stared at me, frozen in horror. It was then that I noticed the glow around my hands and felt something surge within, something deep and powerful. Something strong. I swallowed and pressed one hand to my belly, but it was still there. I raked my mind for an explanation. I'd taken a drought of the strength potion a couple of days ago—was it possible that it worked? Dizzy with the thought, I stood to my feet and leaped off the altar.

I'd forgotten about the river, but I quickly remembered as the waters churned and the river goddess surged toward the bank, arms reaching for me. She was only a dozen feet away and would have to leave the river to reach me, yet still I recoiled, stumbling as I backed away.

"Your debt is not fulfilled," she roared. "You owe me your life, your magic, it is the price you must pay."

Magic? She thought I had magic? But the thought died away as the people chanted and moved closer to reclaim me. Even the man whose task it was to kill me had recovered and stood to his feet, lurching toward me as he held his stomach with one hand.

I whirled, searching for an escape, for help. The enchanted wildwood rose behind me, fearsome and dark. If I went inside, would I escape? Or be entwined in more magic? My momentary indecision vanished as a bolt of what looked like black lightning streaked out of the wildwood.

"Enough!" roared a woman's voice.

The bolt came again, but this time I saw it land in the waters, as though a ball of power had been thrown. Darkness surged out of it like rope and wrapped around the river goddess. She screamed as the darkness took her, swallowing her whole. She continued to wail as magic dragged her down and the waters swallowed her. I watched, unblinking, as she disappeared, and it felt as though a weight was removed from my shoulders. I turned to face the wildwood and gripped the blade tighter.

A woman walked out of the wood, one arm outstretched, her forest green cloak billowing out and her dark hair flying. Her eyes flashed as she took in the gathering, and something twisted on her face. Behind her were two men, one wearing a cloak of feathers with raven black hair. His fists were clenched while the other held a sword, a green cloak over his shoulder and light dancing in his waves of ruffled hair.

I'd heard the tale of the Queen of the Wildwood and her knights, those who helped her contain the enchantments of the wood. Was it possible they were here because of me?

"Haven't you had enough?" the woman shouted, her voice laced with anger. "Enough bloodshed? Enough battle? Enough death? Why do you come here on this eve, determined to ruin it all? If you ever do this again, I will bring ruin upon you. Free your prisoners and leave before I unleash my anger on you."

Another ball of light came from her fingers, this

time she hurled it into the fire. It exploded, knocking those closest to it on their backs, while wood and fire twirled through the air. Screams and shouts came and then running as the crowd disbursed. Gray smoke covered their flight, but still I heard the thunder of horse hooves and people crying out as they fled in terror for their lives.

My lips curved upward, and for the first time in my life I felt strong, invincible. Until the Queen of the Wildwood turned, and her eyes fell on mine. My hand came open, and the knife dropped to the ground as she examined me. "You are free to go," she said, an edge to her tone. "The river goddess will make demands from you no more."

I pressed my lips together and cleared my throat. "I asked her for help," the confession came out, as though it had been burning inside me, waiting for me to tell someone. "I asked her to grant three wishes, and I promised to pay the price."

The Queen of the Wildwood frowned. "Then you were tricked. The river goddess had no right to make a deal with you, when she only wanted your magic."

Now it was my turn to frown. "I have no magic," I protested.

"I saw you escape from your bounds, an impossible feat. Without magic."

I wanted to tell her it was the potion I'd taken, but the words died on my lips as another consideration rose. If I were tricked— "What of my wishes?"

"What of them?" the Queen of the Wildwood shrugged. "Wishes are as real as you want them to be. If you found what you were looking for, perhaps it had no

BRIDE OF THE KING

bearing on what happened between you and the river goddess."

I thought of Zander and swallowed hard. What would I do now? But just as the thought left my mind, I heard my name. "Nesrin?"

Turning away from the Queen of the Wildwood and her knights, I saw a man limping toward me, his hair mused, his face bloody. "Zander?" I cried, and suddenly tears blurred my vision.

I ran toward him, forgetting about what had happened, so relieved to see him again. He'd been roughed up, but still he caught me with one arm and pressed me against his body. "I thought. . ." he murmured.

"I didn't know they captured you. What of the other Rovers? What happened? I thought they were after me, I ran to keep you safe."

"I heard you call my name in a dream." He kissed my forehead, his lips were dry and chapped, but I needed that kiss, and hung on to the thought of it as though it were a token. "They snuck into the camp that night, only because we had a traitor in our midst. But Nesrin." He pulled back and searched my eyes. "I am sorry for putting you in danger, for stealing you away from your life for this."

He thought it was all his fault. And I didn't know what to think. Were wishes true? Did I truly have a deal with the river goddess? But I couldn't let him take all the blame. "I used the magic of the river goddess," I admitted. "And she wanted my death in exchange. I wanted more than a life with my step-mother, more than the life of a servant."

"Nesrin." He stroked my cheek with his thumb. "And what do you want now?"

Him. I thought. But instead of saying those words, I took his hand in mine, clenching it. "I want to stop being afraid, I want to speak up, I want to be heard, and more than anything, I want to start over. With you."

"Nesrin," he breathed, and this time it sounded like a prayer.

Tears welled up in my eyes, just at the way he said my name, the way he stood there, holding me, forgiving all. I lay my head on his chest while he pressed me close, leaning his head against mine.

"I'd like to start over," he whispered. "I'd like that very much."

12

THE SCENT of wild herbs woke me. Instinctively I
reached out to ensure Zander was still beside me.
Weeks had passed since the incident and our rough
beginning. After Lammas, we returned to the rover
camp and rebuilt what had been left in shatters. Others
had been taken prisoner, mainly the warriors, and they
returned with nothing more than bruises and a story to
tell of how the Queen of the Wildwood saved our lives.

   She'd faded back into the forest with her knights
before I had a chance to ask her what my magic was or
how to use it. I still wondered whether the river
goddess had granted my wishes, or if it were an unfortunate coincidence. Regardless, as the time passed, I
found I had everything I wanted. My fate had changed, I
no longer lived under the control of my step-mother,
and I had wealth and love and friendship. My hand
went to my belly, and a smile pinched my cheeks. And
perhaps something more.

   As for magic, well, I decided mixing potions was

enough for me. I'd listen to my father's words, for the consequences of magic were not worth it, even though sometimes when the wind blew and I smelled the scent of water, I wondered.

Zander leaned over, cupping my face, and kissed me, long and deep. The sort of kiss I'd never grow tired of. I looked up at his gray eyes, clearing as sleep left them, turning to something more heated. A shiver of arousal went through me and I pulled him closer. There was no need for magic when I had love.

ACKNOWLEDGMENTS

A special thanks goes out to readers far and wide who enjoy these kinds of stories and send kind words and notes. I'm always happy to hear from fans. I truly hope you enjoyed this tale and are looking forward to the many fantastical stories to come.

Don't miss this exclusive short story.

He's an immortal fae knight, she's a cursed warrior. To save their people from annihilation, they must go where the living have never gone before.

Every few years, the swarm comes, a terrifying pestilence that consumes the living. One sting from the deadly creatures brings not death but something much worse. . .

Every few years, Rainer, a fae knight sworn to protect the mountains, prepares his people to lose everything.

No one knows why the swarm comes, and no one can stop it.

Except for her.

Zelma is a warrior, sent to find the legendary firedrakes in the mountain. Instead, she's attacked by the swarm and left to die.

When she awakens in the hall of the fae knight, she's determined to continue her quest.

However, the sting has changed her, and new, frightening abilities awaken.

Afraid of becoming the target of the fae knight's wrath, she fights to control her magic as they travel into the heart of the mountains.

Will Rainer and Zelma save their people? Or will her magic kill them first?

Of Fae and Flame **is a complete, stand-alone short story set in the Nomadian universe.**

Only available at: https://angelajford.com/product/of-fae-and-flames/

A complete five-book epic fantasy adventure series featuring an enchantress, a wizard, and a sarcastic dragon.

Night of the Dark Fae Trilogy (romantic epic fantasy)

A complete epic fantasy trilogy featuring a strong heroine, dark fae, orcs, goblins, dragons, antiheroes, magic, and romance.

Tales of the Enchanted Wildwood (fairy tale romance)

Adult fairy tales blending fantasy action-adventure with steamy

romance. Each short story can be read as a stand-alone and features a different couple.

Tower Knights (fantasy romance)

Gothic-inspired adult steamy fantasy romance. Each novel can be read as a stand-alone and features a different couple.

Gods & Goddesses of Labraid (epic fantasy)

A warrior princess with a dire future embarks on a perilous quest to regain her fallen kingdom.

Lore of Nomadia Trilogy (epic fantasy romance)

The story of an alluring nymph, a curious librarian, a renowned hunter, and a mad sorceress as they seek to save—or destroy—the empire of Nomadia.

Visit angelajford.com for autographed books, exclusive book swag and book boxes.

ABOUT THE AUTHOR

 Angela J. Ford is a best-selling author who writes epic fantasy and steamy fantasy romance with vivid worlds, gray characters, and endings you just can't guess. She has written and published over twenty books.

She enjoys traveling, hiking, and playing World of Warcraft with her husband. First and foremost, Angela is a reader and can often be found with her nose in a book.

Aside from writing, she enjoys the challenge of working with marketing technology and builds websites for authors.

If you happen to be in Nashville, you'll most likely find her enjoying a white chocolate mocha and daydreaming about her next book.

facebook.com/angelajfordauthor
twitter.com/aford21
instagram.com/aford21
amazon.com/Angela-J-Ford/e/B0052U9PZO
bookbub.com/authors/angela-j-ford

Made in the USA
Coppell, TX
17 March 2022

75143985R00353